SARDANA RENAISSANCE

Book III

Ray Harwood

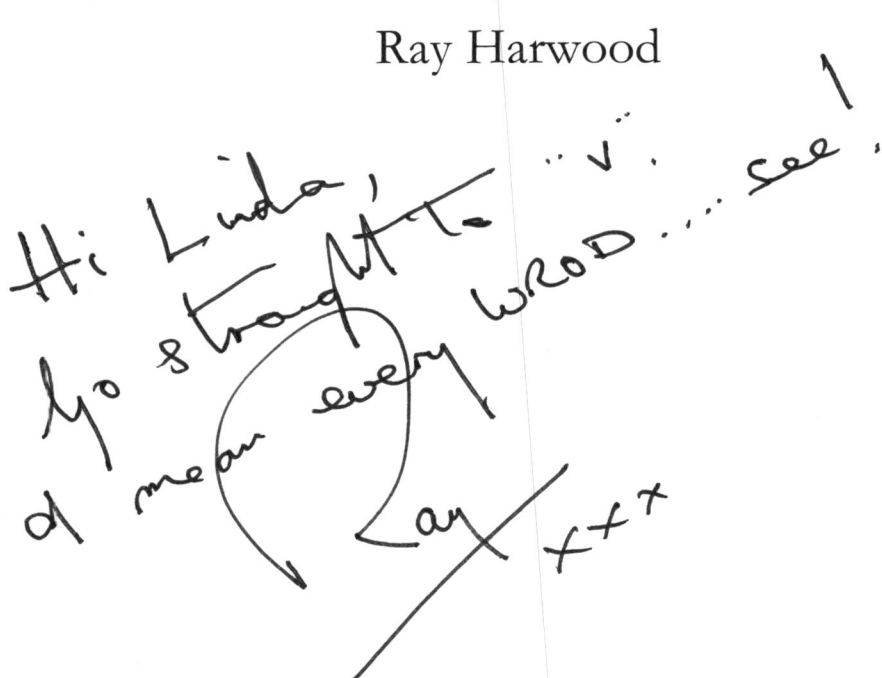

Copyright © 2015 Ray Harwood

The moral right of the author has been asserted.

Apart from any fair dealing for the purposes of research or private study, or criticism or review, as permitted under the Copyright, Designs and Patents Act 1988, this publication may only be reproduced, stored or transmitted, in any form or by any means, with the prior permission in writing of the publishers, or in the case of reprographic reproduction in accordance with the terms of licences issued by the Copyright Licensing Agency. Enquiries concerning reproduction outside those terms should be sent to the publishers.

This is a work of fiction. Names, characters, businesses, places, events and incidents are either the products of the author's imagination or used in a fictitious manner. Any resemblance to actual persons, living or dead, or actual events is purely coincidental.

Matador
9 Priory Business Park,
Wistow Road, Kibworth Beauchamp,
Leicestershire. LE8 0RX
Tel: 0116 279 2299
Email: books@troubador.co.uk
Web: www.troubador.co.uk/matador
Twitter: @matadorbooks

ISBN 978 1785891 519

British Library Cataloguing in Publication Data.
A catalogue record for this book is available from the British Library.

Printed and bound in the UK by TJ International, Padstow, Cornwall

Matador is an imprint of Troubador Publishing Ltd

Followed by others in the series:

Letters to Peter

…and the Sun did Blush

To follow:

Sardana Shadows

Also by the same author:

Last Sardana

Sardana Encore

Blokes, Jokes and Forty Stags

*Cover Design: Jacqueline Abromeit
at www.goodcoverdesign.co.uk*

The Sardana: Links In The Chain

If you have already been party to a Sardana chain, most probably on holiday on the Costa Brava, or equally if that experience is yet to come, I hope you find that you do not partake in just one sequence of the dance, set to the traditional music played by a Cobla band.

It is, for most people, addictive and therefore likely that you will keep going back for more until your legs grow weary and you need to resuscitate yourself to avoid dehydration, which is surely a mark of true enjoyment of the experience.

I would be kidding myself if I believed that those who have assisted in the compilation of *Sardana Renaissance* and its two predecessors (in the knowledge that there are going to be other sequels beyond the trilogy) have been fired by the same enjoyable enthusiasm as those who experience the fun and fervour of the Catalan dance.

However, I am delighted to say that my own Sardana circle is still supported by my wife Dean, Alison Clarke and Kristina Tang, and the places where I have been happiest writing remain pretty well the same. I thank my own trilogy of contributors, and our hosts in places where I enjoy the Sardanas… my way.

The one person who joined the chain late, which one can do in any circumstance, providing there is no break in the rhythm, is my much appreciated supportive editor and critic, Linda Lloyd. Her suggestions have been most constructive.

Likewise, Jacqueline Abromeit's interpretations of the storyline into a separate art form on the cover is hugely complementary to what we set out to achieve.

How very pleasant to have such constructive support all the way round.

Introduction

In some it would have been called rehabilitation, but in the case of Peter Martinez, he interpreted his close brush with death and subsequent recovery as a new dawn. On the one hand, quite by accident, he was introduced to the Olympic movement, and particularly the need to encourage amputees to be treated as 'abled' people, as opposed to the common connotation of the reverse.

On the other hand, in his mind, he went through a short phase during which he was overzealous in seeking a replacement for Anna, the previous stabilising influence in his life. Infatuation became a ruling factor for a while in his relationships, where, without fully recognising the symptoms, lust rather than love was his agenda.

At the time of his recuperation, Sylvia Pez entered Peter's focus and provided the balanced support he needed, upon which to start rebuilding a new phase of his life, following his teenage traumas and his experiences in later years.

The Martinez family tradition had never been to look or go backwards, and Peter epitomised that philosophy. It seemed his tracts would be unstoppable… although others might try and ensure that was not to be.

Chapter 1

The main females in Peter's life were variously experiencing different Mondays.

Gina normally got through her working day with little trouble. She usually finished by four, which gave her time to get home and talk to the girls about their day at school and to prepare the family meal. A shower usually restored her. But on this particular Monday evening, she was struggling and really hoped it didn't show.

The family had been pleased to see her on her return from the medical conference. They all thought her being included in such an important event was a sort of promotion for her. To an extent she too hoped it was, and not just a welcome opportunity for her to have a lustful time with Benito Alvor.

She thought she'd probably sobbed all the way back to Palafrugell from Barcelona. First she had said it was the music Benito had selected on his tape in the car. Then it was because he squeezed her hand. Then, when their eyes had met in the rear-view mirror, and finally when he pulled off the road into a farm track and said, "Just one final hug," that had really set her off. And then again when they got to the hospital car park, and the reality hit that their nights together had come to an end.

The greeting she received back home made her feel inwardly soiled. She had cheated on them all... but then, looking at Marcel, he had cheated on her too – by not having lifted her to the peak of satisfaction in 20 years, which Benito had done in just 48 hours.

She'd made up tales to tell about how busy she'd been and whom she had met, and how Benito Alvor was tied up a lot of the time with people he knew and preparing to deliver his paper. She told them how pleased she had been to have been referred to in his delivery as, "A most important part of my team."

"Wow, Mum!" her older daughter had spurted out. "You're famous!"

It was the girls who said Gina looked tired.

"Well, there was the travelling and nobody got any time to rest."

As she said that, her stomach positively heaved. She thought momentarily she might be sick as she had a vision of Benito above her, his head held high and proud as his surgeon's body operated upon hers. He was sweaty, unlike his coolness in the clinical surroundings of the theatre.

She held back her recent memories, changing her vision to the table they had all just sat around having supper, which she, noticeably, hadn't eaten.

"They laid on a huge afternoon buffet and insisted we all ate. We'd had breakfast too."

She went to the bathroom. Usually she locked the door anyway: both her daughters were used to just charging in, always presuming the room was free. Fortunately they had a separate toilet, which each in the family unit seemed to respect for the privacy it deserved.

She stripped off, looking at each part of her body as it was exposed in front of the mirror. She'd expected to be bruised and scratched, bearing the scars of what each time started out as lovemaking, but which so often finished in frenzied animal activity, during which either one of them was likely to suffer permanent damage. Surprisingly, Gina had come through apparently unscathed, certainly insofar as Marcel was likely to discern in the lights-out conditions of their bedroom.

Oh God, she thought. Would the two-day break have a stimulating effect on him, encouraging him to ask how she felt about making each other feel good? If only he knew. He had never made her feel good… so she'd say she was just too tired. Tomorrow, perhaps.

She washed thoroughly and put on a long nightdress. She hoped she would sleep. In fact she felt she hadn't slept at all. She had a recurring bad dream all that night that she would be confronted by Benito the next day, aloof, nonplussed, spent and uninterested.

Having reached one of her normal parking spot choices in the hospital car park, her legs turned to jelly as she switched off the ignition and checked the rear-view mirror just to see if she looked "put together". She was startled by a tap on the passenger door window, which made her jump.

It was him, bent over looking in, tapping like a bird on a cold day seeking the comfort of a warm home. She leant across and unlocked the passenger door. He didn't, thank God, look aloof or uninterested.

"I wanted to say hi before we met inside."

She was so pleased, she blurted it out instinctively. "Oh Ben, I do so love you! I'm so sorry about that. We said it wouldn't happen."

"Well it has," he said comfortingly, "so we'll have to see how that gets sorted."

"It doesn't," she said firmly. "We said no one gets hurt except us. It's our sin. Our bad luck, but ours is not to screw up the dreams and ideals of others."

Suddenly she was the strong one. Hitting his firm thigh with her clenched right fist, she said, "Come on, we've work to do, maybe lives to save. Get out of my car, you wicked surgeon."

So, as it happened, the ice was broken and work mode began.

Jan, too, was dreading her first day back. It would be the first day she wouldn't have seen Peter in a while and she would miss that.

He was her extreme man. The first time they'd met, he was in control: strong, a touch unapproachable but kind. When she had arrived in Spain, that kindness was the first emotion to show through, but there'd been an overwhelming weakness about him. Not that he had, to any degree, shown a lack of resolve; he was simply the owner of a body in transit between being smashed to bits and recreated, which had seemingly taken him back in time. He was forcing himself to be humorous. He hadn't previously been flirty and perhaps it was the anaesthetic to blame, but he apparently thought quite a lot about sex.

Jan felt she had been a leading player in that rebuilding process thus far. Her seeing eye-to-eye with Maria was a good thing. At least if Peter had decided to resist the proper course of treatment, he'd have to face the wrath of his mother and she supposed she would be off the hook for actual blame. She might even receive a bonus of appreciation from Maria if she influenced Peter's decision positively.

It was a bit like one of Peter's dreaded situations with an advising accountant or other parasitical consultant who always worked on two-way options. On the one hand, Jan and he had a deep friendship built over the first 15 minutes of their first meeting, which potentially would last on a professional and long-term basis. There had been an instant trust and respect. Now, on the other hand, as it were, she felt that had moved on to a more spiritual relationship, which also might last for a lifetime. Love, beyond that showered upon her by her protective mother in particular, had never really entered her life before. With Richard, it had really just been friends. They hadn't enough in common to build beyond that, and when her career became more important than his, any underlying affection between them was hit by some great tidal wave, and prospects of a longer term association had crashed into a muddy debris.

Part of her was scared. Most Monday mornings, she would wake up to the excitement of another week. The interviews and articles would be lined up by her agent, out of which he would rob 30 per cent. But she would be the one left with any accolades brought about by her skill with a pen, and the remaining 70 per cent (subject to tax, she always reminded herself).

Yet this Monday everything seemed dull around her. It was probably sleeping, in the purely literal sense, with Peter and then the emotion of leaving him in the care of others, particularly the tall blonde bitch. That emotional upset and the flight home had probably caused her to go 'off games', as she put it, referring back to those boarding school days, when it was instilled in the girls not to discuss their cycles like a female factory worker, but to keep it dignified, not an open reason to sulk or feel sorry for themselves. But it was accepted they'd go off games. With most of her contemporaries, it was the matron who had guided them into puberty, not distant mothers, who received the occasional note home ("by the way, I'm 'off games'"), which, as their daughters grew older and more fertile, the mothers were always delighted to read.

Damn it, she had thought, but was relieved that the early event, according to a cross in her diary, had not occurred 48 hours before in Girasol.

Girasol, she reflected. What a lovely, calm and happy place. How on earth could it have been there that Peter nearly lost everything? They said if it wasn't for the fact the police were able to call in the new helicopter addition to the hospital service, there was a strong chance Peter would have bled to death. Still, he hadn't. Now she was confused by their relationship. She was nonetheless up to her neck in this new scenario.

The sound of the phone bell ringing snapped her out of her daydreams. *Martin*. It'd be Martin, the great vulture making out he'd missed her, artificially saying he loved her and then getting to the reason for the call. The 30 per cents.

"Darling. It's lovely to hear your voice knowing you're in England, probably with no clothes on and praying that I might suddenly arrive and sweep you back into bed."

"Piss off, Martin. I'm retaining water, sad to be home and you and me in bed hasn't been, and never will be, an agenda item between us."

"So you're not pleased to hear my dulcet tones?"

"In one, darling – no!"

"OK, so let's stick to business. You've pissed Mr William off."

"Why?"

"You haven't reported what he wanted to hear."

"Tough bloody luck! He ought to know Jan Roberts is the truth reporter. If he wants muck and slush, go find another."

"Well yes, darling, but couldn't there have been just some hesitation as to whether all the anaesthetics and stuff had damaged the rational, resolving elements of Peter's brain?"

"But it bloody hadn't," she said emphatically.

"Anyway," Martin informed her, "he's got Paul Williams to do a feature for In House, the group magazine. They all had to face up to the fact that Peter Martinez might not overcome his various handicaps to continue what he'd started in such a potentially exciting way."

Shit! Jan thought hard. "Martin, that's all wrong. It's just not true. I spoke to Peter last night and, subject to him getting a phone installed, and I don't doubt he will, he'll network all the important Executives, and the non-Executives, saying he's up and working and the hiccup in his life is behind him."

"OK. So where do you think your future livelihood lies at BCG? Main man, William or under-pressure Peter?"

"Peter's not under pressure. He carries huge support. He's the new inspiration to the group, without a doubt," she said thoughtfully. "It's with Peter."

"So you've sodding well slept with him. Eh?"

"Sod off, Martin. No, I bloody haven't and incidentally, you'd best be careful – there are plenty of good agents in the world. I'll ring you."

She slammed the phone down. She was furious but inwardly worried. The phone rang.

It's bloody Martin to creep back into my good books, she thought. Let it bloody ring. It cut into answerphone mode. She'd listen to his juvenile pleadings to get back into her books, let alone the chance of them being her good ones. He must have realised he'd touched a raw edge.

"Hi darling," the voice announced, "you're out and about early."

Sod it, it's Peter, she screeched as she lunged for the phone.

"Hi! It's me, you lovely man. You certainly know when a girl needs picking up."

"Thought you were going to be out already. I'm pleased you're not. What's up? I can tell you're upset."

"Oh, Peter. It's nothing. Now how are you, how did you sleep, did you kick that bitch of an Australian girl out of bed, what's your programme… ?"

"Hey! The question. You haven't answered it. What's up?"

"Peter. It's trivia."

"I don't believe you. Jan, tell me!"

"It's sodding William."

"You mean the article going into In House."

"How do you know?"

"I rang new girl Val yesterday afternoon to secretly get a whole list of phone numbers for my calls today, and she told me. They'd tried to get her to say her conversations with me were muddled. But, of course, she wouldn't play ball. Don't worry about it. I'll have the bastard stuffed and in a case by Wednesday. You'll see."

"How do you plan that?" They were now understanding each other at their best.

"I'm speaking to Jim Bowen at the FT, Steve Jones at The Times and Rebecca David at The Independent. I'm going to leak that I'm increasing my share stake on the basis of the new thrust I'm planning down here to widen our net in Europe, to replace the Sudan deal where, quietly, of course, I'll leak it's gone wrong due to the fact the payments weren't bonded and the cash is now held up since the change of power in that volatile region. I see Europe as contributing great stability. Oh, by the way, I've got a feeling in my bones that's right. I've just got to find some openings… but by Christ, I will."

"Peter! You're marvellous. When I was purely your interviewer, I couldn't afford to drop my defences. I did like you, though. Now I love you so much."

"Oh, by the way. She's not Australian. She's a Bok."

"That, my dear Peter, makes no difference whatsoever. You'll see, baby," she said in a heavy American accent. She was now cheerful again.

"Tell you what. I'll get those guys I'm contacting to give you a call, if you don't mind, and they can ask you how I really am. Say you've been in close contact with me for a while and you ought to know."

"Beautiful, I'll say. How's the phone connection coming along?"

"That's one reason why I rang. It's on."

"On? That was quick."

"They've got a sort of paranoia about the impression I'm a VIP or something, so they put a guy in here at the crack of dawn, apparently."

He gave her the number and arranged for them to speak later. Jan knew it would be more about business than his need for her, but c'est la vie. She blew a kiss down the mouthpiece and he reciprocated. The lines went dead.

She needed a shower. She felt grubby. She'd covered up her disappointment when, in response to her saying she loved him, he'd reverted to the blonde bitch being a 'Bok'.

The phone rang again. Without question, she knew who it would be and, ruling out the answerphone as a defence, she picked up the receiver.

It was Martin, as she had predicted.

"Who the hell have you been speaking to for so long?" he blurted down the line.

"A new agent."

He was silent for a moment, then: "Listen, about our little outburst. Sorry I hit a raw spot… none of my business, I suppose. So let's get back to why I rang earlier…"

"Why's that? Do you think you've still got the job?"

"Let me tell you what the best agent in the world has got lined up for you."

"Give me an option."

"Dinner."

Martin didn't usually do dinner if he was doing the inviting.

"Christ," she said. "What, out of your 25 per cent?"

"Bitch. You wouldn't drop my fee to 25, would you?"

"Darling, I already have!" She'd been wanting to do that for ages. Her fees to clients had escalated on the strength of her success ratings, so he was up on the take anyway.

"Are you really serious?" he implored.

"Yup, and if you whinge any more, I'm close to 20 per cent and take it or leave it."

"Twenty-five. I'll write to you about it. Dinner's on him."

"Who?"

"William."

"I'm not having bloody dinner at his expense. He's a shit. He's all but burying Peter Martinez."

"OK, OK. We know about that but he needs you, and I've told him that. He must see it, otherwise he would have just laughed it off. He wants your advice as to whether he can get to see Peter and sort out where they're going. He's prepared to ditch Paul Williams who, as the script now goes, conned him into believing his version of Peter without actually going out to see for himself. That, of course, was principally because William wouldn't agree to pay his fare as part of the retainer. You know Paul, a bottle of Scotch and a cheap pen and you can mould any story any which way you want.

"Come on, dinner on William should be fun. He's suggested the Connaught, so he's obviously keen to get you back on board."

"I'll let you know later about that," Jan said, knowing she ought to check it out with Peter. "What's the rest of the agenda, before we revert to the 20 per cent discussion?"

Maria was having a flat Monday too. She'd been very sad to have to wave her little Pedro off one more time in her life. It seemed full always of au revoirs.

To an extent, the timing of his departure with Jan was most opportune. It had been less than 12 hours since he'd left, at one in the morning on the Saturday, that José's father had rung. José and Maria were fast asleep. José was the first to be awakened by the phone ringing in the hallway. He had recognised his father's voice instantly, and the panic it reeked out.

"Your mother."

"Yes, Papa?"

"She's ill."

"How ill?"

"Waiting for an ambulance."

"What's wrong?"

"I'd say a stroke. Can't feel one side. She's confused. Didn't know me at first. I'd say pretty serious."

"Where will they take her?"

"I'd think Llanfranc."

"Ring me when they arrive and confirm. I'll meet you there."

Within 15 minutes, his father had confirmed the two single words. "Llanfranc, stroke…"

"Don't worry, Papa. It'll be alright. I'll see you there."

Overnight, his mother had been stable but delirious, so José had stayed on. He'd phoned Maria and explained and she had fully understood.

She'd just about been accepted now by José's parents. For a time, she'd been the wicked woman stealing their son, and grandson, from the rightful clutches of their dearly departed daughter-in-law. They were from simple Catholic stock, which preached just that little further than the openly declared vows. Marriage to them went beyond 'in sickness and in health, till death do us part', leaving the bereaved party to co-exist with their late spouse until death captured them as well. No way would their God have allowed another life of happiness, otherwise the murder rate would have escalated.

So Maria, and particularly as she should have been honouring her deceased husband too, was at first an intruder in her parents-in-law's eyes. But gradually they had softened. She was now accepted, because they could see the happiness she had created for their only son.

Maria and José ordinarily survived adequately with one car, which José had used in the middle of the night to get to see his mother and support his father. Maria had borrowed Marco's car to visit yet another hospital, so soon, again to see someone in need of serious attention.

The mood was grey as José stood up from the chair she found him slumped in, outside the room where his mother was receiving treatment. They clinched each other, as they did ordinarily and naturally. They'd seen enough trauma together now over the years.

"How is it, my poor darling?"

"Not good. It seems she had a stroke and then, when she got here, she had another. She doesn't recognise my father or me. Which is upsetting. She's on medication but the doctor says not to be too hopeful. Twenty-four hours should tell us more."

So it had. His mother had passed into a coma, from which she never resurfaced.

So Monday morning was blue for Maria. She wasn't sure if Peter would really need to know. Yes, he had to know but he needn't be bothered by it.

It was José Jnr who was the problem. Tough, competitive, pro-golfer that he was, he didn't take kindly to the fact that the second most important lady in his life had passed on. His grandmother had taken over where his mother was forced to leave off. The fact that his father had not been able to reach him in Valderama, where he was competing in a regional competition, made him feel worse.

Although José Snr had said there was nothing Jnr could have done, in José Jnr's view, one would never know. It was about joining in family prayer for his grandmother's safe conduct into the next world, which might have helped.

Maria was surprised and gladdened by how sorry Peter appeared to be about the news when he phoned her as one of the string of important calls he had made that Monday morning. He was still her nice boy.

Maria let Marco and Virginia know about José's mother. They both went a little quiet and said to give their condolences to José, but they were sure they would see him later to reiterate those personally.

Maria had resolved the night before that she would contact Petra and Alex and update them again on their father's progress, as she had been doing.

Sometimes she found it easier to talk with Petra. They had developed more of a friendship than a grandmother-grand-daughter one when Petra, particularly, spent her school summer holidays in Spain after her mother's tragic accident.

Alex was a different kettle of fish. He would be off entertaining himself with children of clients staying in the hotel, or by going to the local football pitch to see if he could get included in an informal game, which more often than not he did.

Maria and Petra cooked experimentally together, which a girl of 12 needed to do. They found reasons to shop, and it was her grandmother Petra had turned to when she discovered that she was catching up with some of her contemporaries at boarding school as they returned on the first day of term, proudly displaying the new shape of their bodies in underwear they had bought with their mothers during the school holidays.

Maria could do no wrong in Petra's eyes, except that she was inclined to forget the time difference between Spain and Argentina. When the opportunity arose for Maria to phone her grand-daughter, it was usually at a time when she had a break for coffee at her desk, and she would phone on impulse.

There was nothing new about this Monday morning when the phone rang on the bedside table let into the headboard of Petra's king-sized bed, which she shared with her Argentinian husband all those miles and time zones away.

Petra didn't have to guess who was calling at four in the morning. She always tried to be gentle, though, with her grandmother, who was, after all, not just five hours ahead but many years older too.

"Hi, Maria." Maria had always wanted to have a contemporary relationship with her grandchildren. She said it made her feel younger.

"I know the way you've said that, darling. I've got the time zone the wrong way round again."

"It doesn't matter, providing you're going to give me good news of Papa. I'm happy whatever the time is."

"Well, yes darling. At least I think it's good news. Peter has shipped himself… well, to be precise, we've all told him he can't yet go back to the UK, so he's given in and reluctantly accepted a really good rehab opportunity in a specialist unit in Barcelona. It's got the reputation of being a bit of a boot camp but they apparently get excellent results. He went in yesterday. Have you heard the name of Jan, darling?"

"I don't think so…" Petra got out of bed, taking the portable handset with her so she could continue to take the call in the living area, so as not to disturb her husband. He'd already stirred and had given a grumpy grunt when he realised it was Maria again.

The deal between him and Petra was not uncommon in households with a hardworking husband and non-working wife, in that it was important for the money earner to be refreshed. As was the case with Petra, she would be able to nap during the day if the need arose.

Petra caught up on all the news about this new lady, Jan. If Maria had accepted her, that was good enough for Petra. After all, she had grown up seeing a devastated and lonely father in the immediate years after her mother's death. Particularly as a teenager, she hadn't wanted to appear disloyal to her mother, but she could see that her pining father was not a happy person and, although she wouldn't have wanted her mother to know it, she sometimes prayed that a really nice gentle lady would come along and make him happy again. The caveat was that she should in no way be as beautiful as Anna and would not expect Petra to love her. Accept, yes, but love, no, she had reasoned.

Petra had many of her father's genes within her. As she grew older after Anna's death, she paid more attention to family detail and came to realise that Peter had lost his own father at a similar age. So, with her deep rich Mediterranean hair, and a fair share of Peter's height, and certainly his intelligence and personality, which helped her to converse easily with people, combined with her mother's classic stature and ability to appreciate art and cultural things, Petra was bound to have star quality.

Grandmother and grand-daughter exchanged general news. Maria was always interested in the progress of her great-grandchildren too, and found the tales of them growing up reminiscent of some of the antics Peter got up to at a similar age.

Now she looked at her watch. "Goodness me, darling. I must go, and I mustn't stop you from what you're doing. We'll speak again soon when I get an update on whether Peter will actually be prepared to stay in this apparently wonderful hospital."

Stop me from doing what I was doing, Petra smiled to herself after they'd hung up. She was sure at 4.30am she would now have trouble getting back to sleep, so she headed into the kitchen and made some tea.

The sun was not far off coming up and she could tell that the air on the terrace was warm. So she took her tea and a ginger nut biscuit out onto the patio beside their pool.

"So Dad's OK again," she said, looking up at the brightening sky. "There you go, Mama. I know it's not very fair of me being pleased that Papa isn't going to die, because it means you won't be getting together again yet. But I'm certain you'll forgive him and be proud that he's got a lot more yet to achieve on this planet for the good and protection of the family, Alex, the children, Maria, Marco, Virginia and everybody else he seems to come into contact with."

"I still so miss you, of course, but I hope you can see that we're alright, though still dreadfully upset about your accident."

Petra found herself staring into the blackness of the water in the pool. The underwater lights were now off, as the sensor read that the ambient light was now enough to swim by – if anyone did want to swim at five on a Monday morning.

In the surface reflection of the water, she imagined she could see Peter with an arm over each of her own and Alex's shoulders, standing with her sobbing maternal grandparents and Anna's sister, Auntie Alicia, who had tried to take over Anna's role by being a surrogate mother. Petra had inwardly resisted that and, had it not been that she knew her mother would have wanted that relationship to develop, she would have shunned all the approaches and encouragement her aunt showed to her when she alternated school holidays between Spain and Argentina.

Peter had sat Petra and Alex down on the night of the burial and mapped out a survival plan for the three of them without Anna.

"We've always got to behave," he had said. "We always have to make out we're happy, even when the three of us know that we're not. We must all continue to do beautiful things and enjoy anything with quality about it.

"You, Petra, have got to train and train and train again to reach the star quality Mama saw in you. You can do that. You have an inherited classical form and, with my determination bred into you, one day you'll dance solo in the Argentine National Ballet. You'll receive huge bunches of beautiful flowers, which Anna will be able to see and smell from wherever she's watching, I promise you.

"You, Alex… well, Anna won't be too pleased so I don't want you to go too far, but you must try to be the best footballer in each of the years while you're at school, but then not aspire to international or national level. Mama would hate that. Then you're to marry a classically beautiful wife, as your mother would have chosen with you, and produce children of your own for her to look down upon and enjoy."

The three of them cried and then laughed, because they all agreed Anna would have laughed with them.

For a number of years after Anna's death, they'd made their own tripartite pilgrimage to her final resting place. It was a tradition that each year they would carry one white Arum lily and lay it on the white marble grave, beneath which she was laid.

Petra had come to terms with the reality that, as her brother Alex's life moved on and his responsibilities within the UK and Europe became greater, and her father had reached the pinnacle of success to date, it had become, sadly, more difficult and less practical for them all to meet up at Anna's grave as they once had.

She still went, by herself usually, as husband Eduardo hadn't known her mother, although he had gone along to hold her hand on a couple of occasions. It saddened her that neither of Anna's parents was able to visit the cemetery now.

Petra contemplated the disappointments of being split from her father and brother, and to a point her Uncle Max, Anna's twin brother, and his wife and family, and definitely Grandmama Maria, while gazing into the pool water, which was now lightening up as the day dawned.

If she asked Eduardo if she could take a week out from her family responsibilities and fly across to see her father, she was sure he would readily agree. But he had been so busy himself, she felt it would hardly be fair to burden him with the responsibility of the kids.

It seemed, anyway, that Peter was on the mend.

She turned as she heard the patio door open and then oh so gently close, and was surprised to see the little figure of young Max, who was four, walking sleepily towards her.

She held her hand out and his slid into it and she pulled him to her with an all-embracing hug.

"... And little man. What are you doing up at this time?"

"I was having that nasty dream again about all the rabbits who attacked the little white one and I came into your room and you weren't there and I thought I saw you out here, so I've come to find you."

What would he have done if she had been in Europe? she thought. No, she couldn't leave the family, she decided.

With that, the patio door opened again. This time it wasn't closed with such care and Anna, two years older than Max, and known for being an over-active child, made her presence felt. She pushed Max away enough for her to get into the morning hug with her mother and brother.

"... And so young lady, what brings you out of bed so early?"

"I woke up and could see you by the pool from my bedroom window. Why were *you* up so early?"

"That naughty Grandmama Maria made her mistake again and phoned me in the middle of our sleeping time. So I got up and made a cup of tea and I've been sitting here thinking."

"What have you been thinking?"

"Oh! Nothing really, darling, this and that."

"When you say that it usually means you're thinking about Grandpapa Peter."

"I suppose I was, actually. That was very clever of you to work out. He's on the mend, darling, so Maria says."

"How did he hurt his leg?"

"I think he fell over."

"Are you sure he wasn't shot?"

That took Petra back a bit. How would little Anna think that?

"What makes you think that?"

"Will I get ticked off if I say?"

"Of course not, darling."

"Well I heard you speaking to Uncle Max about it. But I thought I wasn't meant to know."

"Well I didn't want to worry you about it. But he *was* shot and Daddy and I didn't think you needed to know."

Little Max was very wide-eyed.

"Is he dead then?"

"No, darling, I've said he's getting better."

"But I thought when you got shot you were dead. That's what happens when Daddy goes hunting, isn't it?"

"Well... yes. But you see he's dealing with little animals and some birds, which we then eat. So they have to be dead, and they're small. To kill a big strong man like Grandpapa would take more than one accidental bullet, and that's what I'm sure it was. It was a mistake, probably somebody like Daddy out on a day's hunting and a bullet came down and hit him. But he's OK."

She hated lying to the children but they didn't need to know about there being cruel people in the world. It was bad enough little Max's white rabbit always seemingly being attacked by the others. Perhaps she ought to enquire if Max was being bullied at school, and saw himself as the white rabbit always under attack.

Both children went into thought, which was temporarily the generator of silence.

"Mama?"

"Yes, dear?" It was Anna, about to make one of her profound statements.

"When can we see Grandpapa Peter? I don't remember what he looks like."

Max chipped in. "Will I be allowed to see him too?"

"Of course to your question, Max, and to yours, Anna. Uncle Max is coming out in a few weeks' time and I'll write a letter to Grandpapa and tell him we're all missing him and if he doesn't come to see us, we'll jolly well go over there to see him."

"Oh, we don't want to do that, Mama." Young Max was profound in that opinion.

"Why on earth not?"

"Because it means going in an aeroplane."

"So? What's wrong with that?"

"They get shot at and crash out of the sky."

"Don't be silly, they don't."

"They do. On television I saw some men in the army and they were fighting at each other from a plane and the bad men fired at the good ones and they did crash and the plane caught fire."

"Oh, silly Max! That was only a film. It doesn't happen to real people. But we'll see. I'll promise to write and see what we can arrange, and it will be lovely."

"We could go by boat," Anna said.

"No. They sink."

"Max. You're watching too much TV. Not all boats sink."

"The one where they were all dancing sank."

"Bless you, little fellow. That was a film too. It wouldn't happen if Mummy and Daddy were with you. Especially if we were going to see Grandpapa. God would look after us."

"Oh, I see."

"Anyway, you children have to go to school. I have to get Daddy ready for his hard day. So run along. It's been lovely chatting with you. Max, you've got to forget about white rabbits always being in fights and planes and boats being dangerous. OK?"

"Yes, Mama."

Petra sent Eduardo and the children off in their various Monday morning directions, showered, dressed and then assessed getting to grips with their lovely house, which bore all the marks of a weekend occupation by the whole family, as well as invited friends of the children who came to play and share the odd meal and a Saturday night barbecue with them. Petra, as a rule, loathed Mondays. Friday evenings were full of prospects for a relaxing weekend with lots of family activity. Monday mornings were something of a hangover.

Tania on her Monday morning woke with a certain bitterness inside her. She was frustrated at not really knowing whether this new woman, who'd come out from England, challenged Peter's potential need to turn to herself for favours, was a serious one or not. While Peter was off the agenda and abroad, where Tania had no knowledge of what he was up to, he didn't concern her. But on home territory she was protective. He and Jan had left, but she had no idea where they were going. There had been no mention. For all she knew, they'd opened up his Girasol house for a week or so, but as quickly as they had arrived one of the gardeners said he'd seen them leave.

So he was gone again, a troubled, injured Peter, for which she would have to claim a large slice of responsibility. He really should have stayed away those weeks before, but she had not been fully aware of the danger that lurked in the trees on the hillside. Not only for Peter but for anyone who stumbled into the pathway of the cousins' plans.

The Coca Cola salesman always called early on a Monday morning. He lived locally and Tania's was his first port of call, to top up the hotel's needs and to have his first morning espresso. He was Alano Carlos, father of a boy and a girl and another now due, on his wife's reckoning, a week or two away. He was a good-looking man, and would talk to Tania about his Sunday games of football, and unload the personal intimacies of his relationship with his wife onto her. Some Mondays it would be all about her demands for new clothes for the children, and how she felt they needed a new cot for this coming child. Those were the days that Tania worked out he had not had his weekend oats.

On others, he would tell how they had been to the village on the Saturday with friends and he would take her through the venue and the number of jugs of sangria they had consumed. On such occasions, his wife was obviously unable either to hold back her own sexual drive towards personal gratification, or was too inebriated to resist his.

This particular Monday, Tania knew she needed something. Some*one* even. She usually felt like that when she'd seen Peter, and lost him again. She doubted she'd have to lead Mr Coca Cola on. She knew he was fascinated by her firm gypsy rear, and particularly on the days when she wore a soft-fronted bra, which allowed very little to an onlooker's imagination as to the goodies within. Not that she had a major plan for those days, as such; her choice of underwear was a rotational thing, by way of habit. Of course, if there was a fiesta or special party, she'd wear suitably chosen gear 'just in case', she always used to playfully think.

With Peter in mind, she was still grumpy and as she walked from the kitchen area into the bar adjoining the reception area carrying a tray of freshly dish-washered glasses, she was startled by Alano's presence.

"Buenos dias, Señorita Tania," he said with a smile, noticing the effect the shock of his presence had had on her breasts. She too noticed the tingle that momentarily ran through her body. She had never quite realised it before but, particularly in the half light of the early morning, he had features very similar to Peter's. Their height was not too different. Their bodies were equally well looked after and honed. Alano had got a new liveried Coca Cola T-shirt and fawn lightweight trousers. His black shoes were always clean on his first call of the day.

"Hi, Alano Carlos. You frightened me. I hadn't seen your van."

It was a good system. He carried around a full stock and was therefore able to replenish all but the major supermarkets' demands instantly.

"Do you need anything?" he asked.

Suddenly it was *Yes, don't bother with Coke or Sprite, even Fanta. Let's go straight to what I need. I need sex, not for long. Not all-day sex. I need to be screwed, just to spite Peter Martinez. He comes in here. Plays with my emotions and then leaves like the wind in the trees at the last thrust of a storm, before the calm.* Those were her thoughts. Did she dare? He would be bound to say yes, his wife being in the state she was in, he'd be too male to say no.

"We've got a promotion on Fanta."

The word promotion took her mind off servicing her body and back to the needs of the bar.

"Promotion. What's it this time? Free stickers for the kids again?"

"No. It's something new. For each tray you stock, we throw in a can of Fanta lemon which is a new line."

"Big deal," she said, a little sarcastically, "you'll have to do better than that."

He wished he could say head office would throw him into the equation for an hour or so if she bought, say, ten things. If he could do his own bargains, she could have him on a one-tray order only.

"OK. Five trays gets you six cans of lemon."

"Five trays gets me a tray."

"Señorita Tania. They'd kill me. Five trays gets you ten and I'll probably have to make up the sale out of my commission."

She put the tray of glasses she realised she was still holding onto the bar and took the three paces that separated them to be nearly close enough for their bodies to meet... she lifted her right hand playfully and pinched his youthful left cheek.

"Now. We wouldn't want you losing your commission at the moment. How far off is your third kid?"

"Oh! I hope it's today. You should hear my wife going on..." He continued but she didn't listen.

"Carry on. I'll check my stock." Deliberately, she leant into the depths of the freezer cabinet, which she knew would lift the back of her short black skirt and outline her rear. She could see his transfixed stare reflected in the mirror clock advertising Torres wines.

She lifted herself out of the depths slowly and with most effect.

"Alano. Do you understand electrics?"

His brain had taken him miles away. "Sorry," he said. "Electrics. Why?"

"I've a problem in Mr Martinez's house and I can't get hold of the electrician and Mr Martinez will be back later and scold me if I haven't got it fixed. At times I so wish I was a man and knew about such things."

"Don't ever think of giving up your gender." He actually tried to reassure her sincerely.

"What, my sex for yours? Oh, I'd jump at the chance."

Christ! She was a temptress. Was she inviting him? Shit, he couldn't tell.

"I mean gender for yours," she clarified, and smiled. "So are you any good at electrics?"

"Basic ones, yes. Let me have a look and I'll tell you."

"Do you know his house?"

"It's at the end of the finger, isn't it? It's the best one in the complex, they say. There was loads of gossip about how well it would sell when he got shot up. But presumably he's OK if he was here."

"He seems fine. Drop the five trays and, OK, let's say eight Fanta lemons and take your van up there and I'll meet you outside."

He affirmed and went out to sort the goods from the van.

Tania took her bike from the rear shed, still the treasured one Mr Peter had bought her, and took the short cut across the hotel's composite grounds, getting to the house before the van arrived.

She went straight to the fuseboard and took out the individual fuse marked 'upper floor BRs'. She bit through the five-amp wire, risking the teeth she'd cherished for so long. It severed easily. She replaced it in its rightful spot, flicked her hands through her hair, splashed a little cologne behind her ears from the downstairs visitors' bathroom and opened the front door just as Alano Carlos arrived.

"So do you know where the problem is?"

"On the upper floor," she said, "I think he said the lights don't work."

"Did he say about the power?"

"Oh, Alano! Don't get too technical," she said with a helpless girlie giggle, "come and have a look for yourself."

Without a thought, she took his hand and, as though it was the way any electrician would be led to a problem, he took it and was lured to the upper floor.

"Try lights and power in here. If you like," she said, entering Peter's bedroom.

She positioned herself between the bed and the doorway so that he saw both together. He made no attempt to switch on the light. The power failure played no part in his thinking.

Gypsy body, bed… Christ, he thought.

She knew. She lowered her gaze purposely to his belt line, or just below, in fact. It was his turn to feel uncomfortable. Still with a fixed gaze into his lower region, she said, "Don't you think one of us ought to try the light?"

He seemed to come out of his trance. He moved past her to the door. Flicked the switch. No lights.

"Does the bedside lamp work?" he asked.

"I don't know," she said, allowing him to brush her hip as he went towards the bedside table.

He located the torpedo switch on the cable. There was a metallic click. The light didn't come on.

He turned round, now barely a metre from her.

"Fuse," he said.

"So what?" she said.

"So what?"

"Spark," she said. "Yes. Spark. You to me." Her arm went onto his shoulder.

"Oh Christ!" he said, as her free hand undid the buckle of his belt and deftly unzipped his fly.

"Didn't you see it?" she whispered.

"What?"

"The spark."

He was unable to answer. She was pulling him towards her body. She slipped her skirt down and then stepped back and took off her blouse. He undid the buttons on his shirt.

"It's as well they hadn't made the bed, that would have been a waste," she said gently but with a practical air as she moved across and onto the bed, taking his hand and the appendage being his body with her.

"Christ!" It was her turn to blaspheme.

The bed reeked of Peter. The pillows bore the indent of his strong male head. There was the odd black hair left to remind her of where he had lain just hours before. The fact it was now a full day did not remove the warmth his body had left with which to caress her anxious body.

Alano Carlos, Coca Cola salesman with a van and a lousy deal on Fanta, no longer existed. Her Peter Martinez, lover, all male and victim of abuse from all the remainder of her family, had started to gently make love to her and was now screwing her to a frenzied climax.

The rest was history, and the fact that Alano Carlos mended the fuse was irrelevant, save that he had the energy left to do it. An additional result was that he smiled all the way through the rest of the day.

Chapter 2

Maria's call to Alex was at least at a more civilised hour, since for him there was just an hour's difference. She had only recently been using the telephone to him in London as a means of communication. Now, in order to speed up the delivery of information, she was somewhat reluctantly using landlines through the various linking networks between Spain and the UK.

What she didn't realise was the difference when she got through to Alex's office, as compared with when she phoned Peter. She had got used to Peter's various receptionists, who always seemed to instantly recognise her and would nurse her through the waiting and 'putting you through' process. Once she understood what that meant, she was relaxed, but it was one of those very difficult English ways of putting something, if not a meaningless one.

She didn't have to do too much 'hanging around', which she now knew had nothing to do with her first attempts at translation: something to do with capital punishment or art galleries.

"Hello darling," she said with some relief once she was connected.

"Grandmama, how are you?"

She liked talking to her only grandson because he reminded her very much of Peter. Oh, how proud Paco would have been, she used to tell herself. Poor Paco, she also often thought. He had missed out on so much.

Alex was an absolute asset to the Martinez family tree. He was, in fact, potentially the end of the line. Paco had produced just the one son, and Peter was seemingly better at producing daughters. But Alex was his offspring and so her call was to the next in line, upon whose shoulders her own surname's existence into the future would rest.

"Darling, I know you're bound to be busy but it's just to let you know what I said was recommended to happen, has actually happened…"

Alex was the quick-thinker, somewhat impatient, whereas Petra was more than happy to let Maria drag her news out. He was the one who would try to end the call as quickly as would be respectable, without being rude.

"I'm never too busy to speak to my favourite grandmama. But I am a bit stretched," was almost his stock reply.

"But you've only got one grandmother. So what's it to me if I am favourite?"

"Grandmama, if I had 20, you'd still be favourite. Anyway, what's news of Father?" As he said that, his heart sank.

"Father." He'd wished years ago that he and his father had a more modern relationship, such as he had seen with the chaps he mixed with at university. In almost all cases, when his friends introduced him to their fathers, they would do so by saying, "This is John," or, "This is Michael." It was the norm for his mates, once they had started shaving, to become more matey with their dads, and on Christian-name terms.

Alex always, always, *always* had enormous respect for the fact that, despite the loss of their mother, Peter had held the family unit together in material terms. Alex was never without somebody around to watch him play cricket, which was his number one sport. It might have been Uncle Max or, at worst, the chauffeur of the day would be told to turn up and report to Peter how Alex had performed.

When school broke up, if Peter was abroad, the network behind him would ensure that a car was there to run Alex to either Heathrow, if he was going to be farmed out to Argentina for the school holidays, or Gatwick, if it was Grandmama Maria's turn.

Alex fully appreciated that supporting his and Petra's education could not be achieved if Peter had a nine-to-five job and an understanding boss. He was the boss and nine-to-five would not have achieved the results shareholders demanded.

Peter shared his four weeks of holiday with either his daughter or Alex, and sometimes those lovely family occasions, when the three of them had time together – except, of course, that Petra used to say that what Alex and Peter wanted to do, the wind surfing, skiing, sailing or even watching a test match, was either all too physical or boring, as compared with her apparently one and only interest, her ballet.

So sometimes Alex and Peter would leave Lords to meet up with Petra and, in Alex's case, pretend to love their way through a ballet at the Opera House or Sadler's Wells. Even then, Alex made a bit of a sport out of it by scanning the chorus lines of cygnets to choose the girl he would one day, when he could afford a car like Peter's, whisk into his bed via a short diversion into a late night brasserie for some pasta.

During one of those rare but relaxed times, Alex had joked about whether his father ever planned to re-marry. Peter had been pretty negative about that; it would only be another mouth to feed, he said, and someone to try and devote time to, and share things with, so he was not looking very hard.

But there was another aspect to Alex's relationship with Peter, which he struggled with.

He accepted it was brilliant that your one remaining parent let it be known in sufficiently strong terms that he loved you enough for your absent parent as well. There was never a shortage in that regard, which really comforted Alex.

The problem was, however, that most people thought it would please Alex to know they thought that he was beginning to become a chip off the old block.

Alex loved his father dearly, and he had been brought up very much on the basis of the close but all-too-brief relationship Peter had had with his own father. By living in each other's pockets when Paco was not at sea, Peter had learnt the basics in life, such as to how to hunt, shoot and fish. Therefore Peter's principal education had been conducted away from the inevitable church school in the village of Rosas, and it was when he was thrown into the university of life that his natural talents really came out.

The first time, having moved to Calella, Peter had touched a football, he had known just how to handle it with his feet, both by instinct and from what Paco had taught him.

The same thing happened with Alex when, on his third birthday, Peter bought him a football and said now he could teach him how to kick it. He was only three, but Alex was pretty sure he knew what to do.

The same with a tennis racket… and a squash one. But the cricket bat was different. Peter had never used one, although he was taken with the sport on a spectator basis. He'd even got himself nominated through Max to the MCC, with a view to using his membership for entertaining business clients.

Alex, though, saw participating in cricket as an important part of his own life. As soon as he had touched a cricket bat, and smelt the distinctive fragrance of linseed oil and leather, he felt at home with that sport. He especially wanted to achieve something without using bits and pieces of chips off the old block, attributes not inherited through his father's genes, and that suited his ambitious, inbuilt desire to be his own person. What he failed to appreciate at an earlier age was that, in taking that stance, he was, in fact, clearly cloning himself, as ambition and independence were two of the greatest assets in Peter's gene bank, inevitably to be passed on to a subsequent generation.

When it came to advanced study, Alex accepted that he'd have a natural ability in written and spoken Spanish. But whereas Peter had leaned towards creative studies, Alex intentionally headed towards a different space in academia.

Yet without knowing it, all the time he was formulating these ideas in his younger life, Alex was always following his father's example.

Alex took up history and geography, which he saw as academic subjects, and he also took a serious look at the sciences. By pursuing these, he avoided the creative subjects like the plague. He actually tried to not be able to draw a straight line, so as not to be constantly told he was, "So like your father." He then realised that by not being able to draw creatively, as in producing something nice to look at, or to live in or sit upon, his drawing became a bit free and not easy to understand – until his art master at prep school told the entire class to walk away as far as they all could from Alex's painting, and unanimously declared it to be a masterpiece of modern art. That helped to make his mind up and he gave all forms of art, design and technology a miss, deciding to carry on, as he effectively was, to see what fresh talents he could develop and pass into the Martinez bloodstream.

He thought his father was oblivious to all this, but in fact Peter realised how creative Alex was in trying to pitch himself into pastures new, rather than the hereditary outlets Peter had been allowed to develop for himself.

Now Maria reported, "Your father, my dearest grandson, has accepted all the advice that's been given and he's taken himself off to Barcelona and a specialist medical unit at the Hospital De Mar, where they have excellent facilities for rebuilding damaged muscle tissue, and the like."

"Good God, I never thought he'd take that option up! He must have been severely damaged and have a lot of making good to be done."

"He did, and has, darling. But listen, you mustn't fret." As Maria said that, she coloured up a picture of her grandson's concern and loneliness. "Listen, Alex, you mustn't worry or be concerned, I know you are... why can't you find yourself a lovely wife who'd be able to help you to share things in difficult times?"

"Because, Grandmama, I was born into the wrong religion and, as I'm basically lazy about taking the route you'd like me to take, I'm not really looking for such a permanent arrangement. But if Father had rebelled against your Catholicism and taken the Muslim route, for example, I'd be sitting back having all number of beautiful girls being paraded in front of me to choose from."

"Sometimes, my boy, you're worse than your father. That's exactly the thing he would have been likely to say at your age. You have so many things in common."

"Grandmama, what you tend to forget is that I had a mother too, whose genes also got into me. So please leave me to my own devices. I'm quite happy to worry and resolve things by myself."

"Just like Peter does, my dear."

That was just too much for Alex to hear. "Hold on, Grandmama, please."

She heard him speaking to a colleague on another line, "What? For me? In connection with what? OK. Give me 20 seconds to say goodbye to the caller currently on my line."

There was a pause.

"Grandmama. I've got an important business call on the line, I've got to go. I'm sorry. Adiós."

"Don't worry, darling. Your father does that all the time. Adiós... and remember what I've said."

"I couldn't forget, you wicked, lovely lady."

Alex had cheated on his grandmother. There had been no incoming call. He continued with his very busy day in the media industry, into which he had directed himself when he came down from university with his BA (Hons) in English, plus a diploma in Communications.

That was his own idea. On the diploma course, he'd learnt the importance of confidentiality, how to receive information and how to release just enough to whet the odd appetite, while holding the whole story back until the propitious moment.

Such was the skill he applied to the case of Anne Marie.

Alex had been deeply ensconced in sport at school, and Peter wanted to encourage his participation in cricket. He suggested that extra coaching would improve this or that, or that Alex should join a particular club to extend his experience during the school holidays – all of which paid off eventually.

So when Alex got to university, he found he could play a game of cricket and score more runs and was not intimidated by the Sunday evening phone call home, when Peter, to be fair, was so interested in the blow-by-blow account and actual delivery of every ball detail that it seemed a permanent inquisition, but without Alex's actual batting prowess having been watched by his father sitting on the boundary.

Alex had played in his penultimate game for his college, after which he and his team members were due to quickly change, sit and take tea with the opposition, then repair to the local pub, where they would see the evening out with the assistance of a number of beers. There were occasionally female camp followers, but Alex was never too interested.

Alex had always thought that his father, after the death of his mother, to whom he was enormously attached, probably had lots of female acquaintances who were allowed out from a number of cupboards during term time, then stowed away during the holidays so that Peter would not be fettered in his desire, and need, to concentrate on his children.

Alex and Petra had talked about that, and he had listened to his elder sister's advice, which was that if you don't know about it then you can't get upset about it.

"But what about our beautiful mother? Shouldn't we be thinking about her?" Alex had once said.

"Yes, if you like, protectively, but there are two things about that. Firstly, you don't know if there is an afterlife. So secondly, you don't know what Mama might be getting up to. So you mustn't discriminate against Papa until you actually know the facts, or otherwise. If you're that interested, ask him."

It seemed good advice but Alex had decided he would bide his time and wait for the right young lady to come into Peter's vision, when he was sure they would be included.

The tea, after the penultimate game of the season, was held in the clubhouse at the opponent's college ground.

The building was of great architectural interest, going back the pre-Victorian times. There was a raised verandah, through which access to the locker and changing rooms had been built. The effect to Alex as he approached reminded him, in reverse, of the tunnel at Wembley on FA Cup Final day, from whose inner darkness the participating teams emerged into the bright daylight, amid the rousing cheers of the supporters as the team made its way to the pitch. His walk in was from lightness to total shade and shadow.

As he checked the scoreboard, he was really chuffed to see his score of 107 against him as batsman number three. He'd had a glorious innings and his final boundary for four runs was enough to give him his fifth century of the season, and the team the three runs they needed in the last over of the day to beat their arch rivals.

The remainder of his team and supporters were standing on the left of the verandah, clapping vigorously at the innings he had carved out for himself, as the team had now gained the extra points needed to be certain, with one game left to play, of winning the University College Challenge Cup – Cricket.

Alex held his bat high in acknowledgement.

The other team, which would no doubt have filled the right-hand side of the verandah as he approached, was virtually empty, as they had been fielding.

There was an elderly man poring over the score record book, sitting at an old college desk that had obviously been bequeathed for the purpose by a previous undergraduate owner, probably after he'd moved on to become a High Court Judge or Captain of Industry.

Suddenly a vision stepped out from what had been a shadowed area of the deck.

The cameras, which in fact were his own eyes and not those on a film set, rolled. But they did the job of indelibly imprinting the vision on that celluloid film we all have in our brains, to record a memory never to be forgotten.

She was blonde, and wore sunglasses of a size which hinted that behind were clear, probably blue eyes. Maybe, he thought quickly, green. She was tanned, but perhaps that was exaggerated by the fact that she was wearing a white jacket with black piping down the lapels. He was sure that he could tell through the slats on the rails to the verandah that she was wearing a tight black skirt; beyond that, to be as tall as she appeared to be, she must have been wearing fairly high heels.

As if to bring herself into full view of the camera crew, and ultimately the viewers, she stepped further forward, looking down on him from above as he reached the tunnel opening. She mouthed, "Well done," as she smiled and clapped excitedly.

Alex kept walking after failing to hold back his own beaming smile of appreciation, accompanied by a polite nod. His batsman partner clomped into the visitors' changing room behind him. He threw his bat a few yards' distance ahead and it fell into his kit bag. Turning to Alex, he indicated that they should bear-hug.

"Well done, mate. Well done. We'll know what to do next year."

"What's that, Jim? Sorry. What do we have to do next year?"

"Go on. Be honest. You should bring your girlfriend with you again. Obviously it encourages you to show off, you bad macho man."

"Jim, I don't have a girlfriend."

"Then who was the excited young lady who'll be in dreadful trouble with the other college if she's not with you, and should be supporting the other side? Because before I came in to bat, we were looking over at her and she clapped every one of your boundaries, every run, in fact. We all worked out she was your secret."

"Jim. I've never seen her before in my life."

"So you noticed her."

"Piss off, mate."

"Tetchy, aren't we? If you're not careful I won't get you an introduction over tea."

"How would you do that anyway?"

"I was at Westminster with Josh Sayer, the Captain of Budes, he'll surely know who she is, since she was on their verandah. Look, mate, despite you being a bit uptight about having your leg pulled, I'll still do it."

"Well, up to you. But look, if she wants to come out from behind those shades to be introduced to me of her own accord, OK. But suggest I want to meet her, and you won't be needing to wear a box next season, and you'll get back into the college choir as a treble."

"Would I want that, mate?"

Alex had showered and donned the obligatory grey flannels and blazer but had not put on a tie, which after the game was optional, though before it essential.

He felt a tap on his shoulder, as the coach finished his round-up address to the team and his praise for Alex's innings.

Alex hesitated and turned to see Jim Havers with a broad grin on his face.

"Alex, I'd like you to meet Anne Marie."

She had wedged her sunglasses on to the top of her head. She oozed a most beautiful fragrance. Her eyes were blue and there was a hint of a green circle around the pupils which made them all the more piercing. Yet they were also soft and sincere.

She held her hand forward and he took it. Alex clung to each of her first words to him, which seemed to be some kind of an explanation.

"I don't know too much about cricket, you see, I've always had to watch my brother play and it's always seemed so boring." She hesitated and turned to Jim. "You did say Alex, didn't you?"

"Yes. Sorry… Alex Martinez."

"I thought you must be Mediterranean or South American. Alex… but what I was going to say was that you gave me a new watching experience. Are you an artist?"

"Not knowingly," he replied.

"Well you positively stroked the shots you played. Everything I've had to watch before has all been so clumsy. You played as though you had music playing through your brain."

"Strange you should say it, because that's something I *have* got. As far as I'm aware, I've inherited it. It's something I hadn't consciously worked out but I do try to have a favourite piece of music in my mind. Rhythm and stroke play in cricket, and golf, is probably a very essential ingredient to run-making and hole-putting."

"Do you dance?" Anne Marie enquired.

"I was forced into lessons."

"Would you and Jim come to our May Ball? The men in our college are mainly reading Theology or Politics and my best friend and I had decided not to go. Josh Sayer said you're fun, Jim, and I'm sure you'd get on with Sam. Samantha James. Do come. Will you both come? Say yes. Please."

"I'm on," Jim said. "Are you, Alex?"

"I'd be very delighted. Incidentally, I'm fun too."

"Oh, I knew that. Your smile is a giveaway. You try to keep it all to yourself."

Alex smiled to himself. If only his grandmother knew that Anne Marie and he had been an item now for almost two years.

OK, they might be currently going through a bad patch, but he was sure that their great affection for each other would get them through that.

Then he thought again. He had a feeling his grandmother was right. He did have someone to share his worries with, so perhaps he should commit more.

That created a spur-of-the moment reaction as he had looked at his watch. Anne Marie worked ten minutes' away. He'd surprise her and call her to see if she'd have lunch.

"Lunch? No, Alex. Not for me. I'm too busy."

"Then a quick drink."

"I'm not drinking."

"Then how the hell can I get to propose to you in the next 30 minutes?"

His question met with silence.

"Who the fuck told you?" she said eventually.

Anne Marie rarely swore and never the 'f' word. So what the hell was all this about?

"Told me. Told me what?"

"OK. So you've guessed why I'm humpy."

"Anne Marie, darling. I've told you I want to ask you to marry me. What's all this inquisition about?"

"You only want to marry me to do the decent thing. You know I'm pregnant. No, you bugger, not *I'm* pregnant. *We* are *both* pregnant!"

Alex was stunned. "I didn't know!"

She was now silent. Then: "So you just wanted to marry me?"

"Well yes. I did. But now I want to even more. It's very exciting."

"What about your father, and my parents? Don't you think they'll feel let down thinking we're *having* to get married?"

"Not at all. My father's quite contemporary, and I'd imagine yours would be too. Can I see you in, say, 15 minutes?"

"Yes. Of course."

"Right. I'll be outside your office."

"I love you, Alex."

"I love you too. See you then."

"… Oh… Alex. Don't go."

"I'm still here."

"Could we eat? I'm starving. I'm eating for two, you see."

"Of course. Go and get ready."

Maria had never met Coco. She had, of course, heard all about her newly discovered grand-daughter from Peter. She had the advantage, too, of being grandmother to both Alex and Petra. She felt it her duty to Anna, although in truth she had never really related to her, to tie the family unit together as indeed Paco would have done if he'd lived and had the social ability to do so. Also, Maria felt herself fortunate to have inherited the social graces to play that central pivotal role. The few years she'd spent on the arm of Carlos during his mayoral stint had clearly helped her in that regard.

She wouldn't have wanted any of the others within the trio of grandchildren to know, but the letters she sent out to each of them were identical, other than the salutation.

There was no chance of Coco learning that anyway because her half-brother and sister didn't even know of her existence. But unbeknown to Maria, Alex and Petra had worked out that the letters were identical, and phoned each other to compare notes. It did not matter to either of them. It just showed their favourite grandmother to be bright, practical and nonetheless loving through her economies of communication.

"Your father is now doing really well. The operations seem well behind him and the reports from Señor Alvor are very encouraging. He can do little more but has recommended intensive physio treatment in Barcelona.

Whether we can get Peter to continue to see the sense of that is in the lap of the Gods. So if you do have a moment, offer up a little prayer that he doesn't change his mind and does what will be good for him."

With one prayer being generated from South America, another from England, to where Alex had now returned – both of which would have been made to the God Maria herself prayed to – and a third from Malaysia – to, Maria presumed, the different God Coco confided in – Peter would be well protected and was bound to pull through with all that spiritual help, and move forward on the correct route to normality.

In one of their late night 'getting to know each other' sessions, Coco had told Peter how perplexed she was about having his blood but a different God. They'd eventually come to the conclusion, influenced no doubt by a bottle of Peter's favourite Montrachet, that it didn't matter a jot as long as they both tried to lead good, honest lives, doing no harm to anybody.

"How would you feel, though, if harm had been done to you by somebody first? Wouldn't it be fair for you to get just a little bit even?" Coco had postulated.

Little then did she know Peter was to be tested in that direction. Now, as she prayed for him, she asked Allah to permit him just a little bit of justice should the opportunity present itself… but to please restore his strength to enable him to do it.

So Maria had networked the current news about Peter's move to rehab in Barcelona. She didn't include the sad news about José's mother. It didn't seem relevant and would not necessarily mean anything to Coco.

"Now before you are on the phone saying should you come across I'd say no. Your father is going to be there for a while and if you appear on the scene, he will probably skip and do a runner in order to spend time with you in Barcelona on a classical tour of Gaudi monstrosities.

He doesn't want to be there anyway, so the slightest excuse and he would give the course up and I think regret it for the rest of his life.

Drop him a line with all your news, that would be better. It's the Hospital de Mar, Barcelona, España. He'd love to hear from you. That's enough from me for now. Look after yourself. Do not hesitate to contact me for news. I'll update you anyway when I have seen progress for myself."

Chapter 3

Peter lay contemplating, having had another good night's sleep, to prepare him for the days of purgatory he'd been badgered into by Jan and his mother.

Every morning, however, he felt he'd benefited from the previous day's physio. He still had no idea they'd singled him out as likely not to stay the course, and he had certainly not got wise to the fact that his bait was the plant, nor that his challenge with Pablito, although very real, was a put-up job.

He wasn't sure whether it was today the lad would get his limb. If it was, there would doubtless be a lot of 'friggin' noise about it, so he'd soon know. Cas would know. She usually called in on Peter as she came on duty at seven. So he had to be up, shaved and presentable by that time.

It was amazing how he had always reacted to a female presence from beginnings that had been in many ways so male orientated, as his father tried to teach him the ways of the world from the distinctly masculine side of the hunting, shooting and fishing fence. But it was surely a compliment to the closeness that had developed between mother and son that he usually upped his game when there was a female pair of legs on the scene.

Cas confirmed it was 'L for limb' day and agreed it was unlikely to be an uneventful one.

"How do you reckon I'm doing for the contest? Am I on schedule?"

"You men do make me laugh. What's it matter who wins? Isn't there something written somewhere about it being the taking part that counts?"

"Shit!" Peter announced, astounded. "You can friggin' talk! OK, so today on the treadmill you slow me down a bit so that I get to pat your bum and I'll remind you of what you've said."

Cas laughed. "No, come on, Chief." Chief had become her nickname for him after they'd got round to talking through how Peter had made the money he had clearly made, and what his role in life was, given normal circumstances.

"CEO," she'd repeated. "What's a CEO?"

He appreciated that somebody outside would be unlikely to know. First time round, he'd said it stood for 'Sexual Education Organiser'.

"Really?" she said with interest. "So 'C' as in Sexual. Go on, pull the other one." He already had. "I don't believe you."

"OK. I was kidding. I'm a Creative Employment Organiser."

"What's one of them do?"

"We create employment."

"What sort of employment?"

"Well, take road-sweeping."

"Road-sweeping?"

"Yes. Why do you think we need road-sweepers?"

"To clear up the mess."

"That's right. So where do you think the mess comes from? It doesn't just happen. So in countries where they're short of jobs, we ship in mess and have lorries that distribute it around the roads and then all hell breaks out and it needs sweeping up. So we train the road-sweepers."

"Really," she said. Then, "You are now definitely pulling my leg. I'm not at all interested now in what a CEO is. I was trying to be interested but you've spoilt it."

That same evening, just before she went off duty and for her wind-down in the pool, she had popped her head round his door, in fact as he was on the phone. She'd looked disappointed. He held his hand up, beckoning her over as he mouthed, "Sorry," and indicating that she should not leave. She got that message and hovered.

At the appropriate moment, he said to the caller, "Can you just hold on for a second. One of the physios needs to say something to me before going off duty." He put his hand over the mouthpiece. "Hi!" he said. "Sorry," pointing to the phone, "have a good swim."

"Thanks." She came over to him from the door, leant over and pecked his forehead.

"What's that for?" he whispered in surprise.

"Oh, I now know I'm healing a craver."

"A craver?" he whispered back indignantly.

"Yes, a CEO. That's what I'm told a guy with a craving for emotional obsession is."

She left him this time with his bad leg pulled.

"Sorry about that," he said into the mouthpiece, uncomfortably, after Cas had gone. "So what was the deal from Mr William?"

He was on to Jan the day after she'd had dinner with her agent and the Chairman.

"Well clearly he's been talked round by all the guys you spoke to, and I suspect Vera too. The city has reacted to the leaks that you're buying and not least that it shows you're up and well. So it was talk of your revival and how could William look into that. As a starting point, he cancelled the release of In House and wanted me to do a quick positive review on the basis that I'd been seeing you in Spain."

"So what did you say?"

"Well, I might be in trouble. But I had this feeling in the pit of my stomach that you wouldn't want that. So I said I wasn't ethically free to do it because when I was in Spain, I was ostensibly working with you and it could be seen that writing a complimentary article about your health, et cetera, was to further my own ends in the involvement I'd had in the hospital deal."

There was silence from Peter.

"Shit, did I get that wrong?" Jan asked, with a degree of trepidation.

"No, you got it absolutely right. Go back to him through Martin, I'd suggest... well, you might as well drop him in it as well... and say you've had a word with me and I'd prefer you don't do it on account of the other thing we're working up in Europe."

"Peter, I can't lie. You know that. There isn't another thing we're working up, so I can't say that."

"There is. It's just that I haven't told you about it yet."

"You're spoofing. There's not."

"I bet there will be, though. Be a love, play him my way. He'll be beside himself wanting to know."

"There's another thing. He wants to fly out to see you for himself."

"Well, he can certainly do that. But I've told him I'm officially on leave so it can be at the end of the month. So there you are. One positive and one negative for him to get his teeth into."

"He'll do that for sure! Anyway, that's enough of the business chat. Tell me about your body. I'd prefer to hear all about that."

Peter gave her a blow-by-blow account of the fitness ritual he was being put through and didn't underplay the pain. She found the tales of his 'friggin' young friend really quite amusing and said it was probably a good thing to have someone to compete against, in their own ways. She then plucked up courage.

"And the Bok? What's news on her?"

"She's fine. Bloody cruel. Gives me a hell of a pasting all day long."

"... And so she should. Hate her for it, for me, if you would. I can't bear the thought of her having your companionship, let alone you gawping at her all day long."

"I don't. It's a professional thing. She's a hard South African bitch, and that's the way she'll keep it."

"So are you saying that's not the way you would?"

"Now come on, don't let's get silly about it. It stays a professional relationship. You'll see for yourself when you come out. Any ideas when that might be?"

There was no positive reaction to that.

"Come on, you're keeping me in suspense. I'm missing you."

That was what it took to cheer Jan up.

"Is that true? Isn't the Bok keeping you occupied?"

"Look, Jan. Let's get this right out of the way. I thought she was a dyed, dumb blonde at first but now I can tell you there's some sincere depth of conversation in her. But principally she's a bloody good motivator, and, as that's what you all say I need, I'm going along with it. The days are hectic physically, but I can assure you the nights are longer. So! Happy now? Any news on when you can get out?"

"Could be the weekend after next. I'll try. I've got loads to catch up on. I'll really try. Sorry if I've been edgy."

"No, you haven't. It's hard being apart."

"We'll speak tomorrow. Missing you. There's a kiss coming your way." She pursed her lips and sent the embrace down the wires. He returned it.

The lines went dead. *Wow, that certainly was a bit edgy,* he thought. He supposed he hadn't been too kind to Cas behind her back. The vision of her athletic South African back came into his mind. That was a different story. It led down to the nicest bottom he'd been invited to follow for a long while. Memories of Marcia's, on that first athletic chase, sprang to mind.

It was the next morning that Cas had started the 'Chief' bit, and it had stuck. On that same day, Professor Han had come to review his progress with him.

"Cas tells me you're like a veritable greyhound after a hare. We don't want you overdoing it, you know… and remember, Pablito is well under half your age and has the mentality of a mule. He'll get his limb, and whatever the tournament is between you, I have to advise he'll win. That's not just an assessment of your capabilities. It's his. I didn't know him, of course, before his accident but from his physical condition, whether he knew it or not, he would have been destined to become quite an athlete if, perchance, he'd got himself into the right hands. Now there's every chance he will. Since he's accepted the principle of training in anticipation of the new leg, he's leapt ahead of schedule. Nature is sometimes kind and his is a classic case. His thigh development has been amazing, which tells us it was there to be developed."

Peter interrupted what was obviously going to become a Han lecture, though a lecture in the most pleasant way. In his own soft way, Professor Han was inspirational, with the ability to draw a positive scenario out of what was bound to be seen by many as a pretty negative one. That was his job, and it was his favourite technique to use the success of one patient to raise the game of the next one, and to see that passed further into a chain. He had established this conveyor belt of success, which had achieved him his reputation as a master in his own field.

"You said something just now. It was something like if Pablito had got himself into the right hands he could have been quite an athlete, and then that there's now every chance he could still do that. Surely a kid with half a leg is never going to do that?"

"Peter, I like you and I like your spirit, but you're in the mould of so many fit people, fit *complete* people, even. You've got a down on 'handicap'."

Peter was quick to react. "Not me. Not so. Actually if you really knew me, you'd know that not to be the case. Educate me. Try not to talk in riddles. Spell out what you mean. Give me a chance to understand."

"Sorry. I thought you'd know about these things. At one stage, the handicapped were left to remain that way, handicapped for life. Now there's technology and teaching. It's not too new, you'll know the tale of the Englishman, Douglas Bader, who lost both legs in the war. So, OK, the development of artificial limbs in his case allowed him to walk. His competition was against himself in order to convince the RAF to allow him to fly. But in his case, if he crashed a Spitfire, the next result was permanent damage to himself, probably terminal damage that is, and a cost to the British taxpayer.

"Put a young man in a wheelchair today and if somebody recognises his talent and ambition, then the best thing that can happen is for him to get out there with another fellow, or even a bit of female bait to chase after, and he'll get control first and speed next. In a wheelchair, you can still fire a bow or a rifle, throw darts, wheel yourself through marathons. Even given a new limb, one can be trained. Given six, seven, eight naturally in the same handicapped state, you can arrange a race, just like at kindergarten when they stick a spoon in your mouth and put an egg on the end of it and you're told to run like hell without dropping it to show off to your mother and father, and all the other parents.

"That needn't change. Get those eight equally equipped and one or two may well become physically more developed and more successful than the others. But you should have a really determined race on your hands. Get yourself sponsors and you've got the prospect of competitive games. Spread the idea through neighbouring nations and then around the world and you've potentially got an Olympian event. Surely you've seen the recently developing paraplegic events catching the imagination of the media?

"But back to the point. If ever I've seen the right raw material at the age of 13, and with a temperament to be built upon – providing we can find a retired sergeant major to crack his current unacceptable form – Pablito is it. He could be on a rostrum at the Barcelona Paraplegic Games in five years' time."

"Barcelona?"

"Yes. You see, Peter, and I say this in spirited fun, you possibly celebrated Spain winning the appointment for the XXV Olympiad and automatically fixed your mind on lithe Russian girls doing runs, jumps, somersaults and work on parallel bars, or honed Caribbean bodies throwing themselves down a track to make them the fastest humans on earth. Well, handicapped athletes now get the same forum, though not yet at the one event for practical and logistical reasons. Yes, we've won the right to stage the Paraplegic Olympics right here. Using exactly the same facilities as the two-legged humans with whom we've been placed on this same great planet we've called Earth, as a stepping stone towards whichever heaven, or final sanctuary, you believe in. There, at whichever one, I doubt if your God or my Maker will be at the door, turning away girls or boys, or grown men and women who arrive with their artificial limb tucked under their arm."

Han looked at his watch. "Good God, as you say, I've spent far too long on my hobby horse."

"Professor. May we speak again about this?"

"Sure. Providing I haven't offended you by my comment that you're like so many of the others."

"Not at all."

It was shades of Jaimé all over again. The deaf mute with talent bordering on supernatural genius that needed outing. How fortunate he had been in helping to develop that. With Jaimé now a mature successful artist, they still shared each other's company when they could. They were, in the strictest sense, the closest of friends.

Young Rottweiler Pablito was a different prospect.

"Friggin'!" had become a joke word among that current intake of patients. Only two were older than Peter. Both had had internal replacements, knees or hips, which had gone wrong during the normal operational process and now needed intensive rehab, at the expense of a couple of unfortunate surgeons' insurance companies. There was a handful of industrial injuries being patched with replacement bits and pieces. Others had been born with deformities and were now getting their promised rectification. And then there were the amputees. Most of them were hoping just for a real, ordinary existence. Young tiger man was not.

So it was the day of the limb. All was confirmed. Peter suggested at breakfast they all ought to be issued with friggin' ear plugs, or better still, to be allowed out for the day. Professor Han himself was there in anticipation of the first fitting. As it transpired, Peter's treatment was in the adjoining room. Cas seemed nervous.

"What's wrong, chick?" Peter mused. He was always worried about telling a female she seemed below par because there was a one in 28 chance of him being absolutely right. So he qualified his statement by saying, "You seem anxious."

"That's kind of you to notice, Chief. Unfortunately I've been here before. The kid will expect to get up and run. He'll think the limb is going to be his new key to life and it's just not going to be like that. He's got hours, weeks and years to get near to what he'll judge to be normality."

"He's got five years. That's OK."

"Five?"

"The Olympics."

"Oh! Professor Han's been talking to you, eh?"

"He's been educating me. I'd say I trust the Professor totally. He's my boss anyway but I think he'll have a disappointment. The lad won't make it.

He may do physically but he'll get disqualified all the way through because he's perhaps got a bigger behavioural problem than he has a disability one."

"Do you really think that's true?"

"I'm sorry to say – yes."

"Mark was a bit like that. He was wild and hot-headed when I first met him."

"What was the attraction then?"

"You do friggin' pry, don't you?"

"OK. I'm sorry. I don't need to know. People just fascinate me. Anyway, you brought the conversation up."

"It was because he was so unbelievably wild, I think I thought I could change him. Tame him. I'd rate I was being pretty successful until he found power. It seems in your case, you can control it and it may just be because you've got wealth to go with it. If you've got power and second-hand junk that you've made go fast… you break your neck. I'm scared Pablito will do the same."

"First we'll get him knocked into an acceptable human state of mind… and then get him sponsored. How about that?"

"Do you really mean that? You really do, don't you, Chief? Christ! Who the friggin' hell are you? One of the new disciples?"

Peter went into silent thought for a while, then: "Do you know anything about Pablito's family?"

"No. The father doesn't seem to feature. We've seen his mother once. Doesn't seem to worry too much. Comes from the south of Spain, apparently. Has a long journey."

"I'd guess he's never had a paternal influence. That was his first handicap, if he didn't have the right mother as well. Well, believe or not, I'd expect him to be untameable."

It was as though a battle had begun. It was almost where Peter came in.

The poor physio seconded to the lad, together with Juan, was still trying to be in charge. Cas and Peter could hear the clanking of the crutches used by their patient marching outside, towards their adjacent room. Then it sounded like a mixture of breaking glass and crashing steel all at once, as first one crutch was thrown into the corridor, then the other.

"Won't be needing these friggin' sticks!" Pablito shouted, as the second one hit the deck.

Peter lifted himself onto his elbows. Cas looked anxiously up into his face from her activity of giving a heavy deep massage to his right thigh. They both smiled – more in amazement than amusement as they realised the lad had thrown the sticks out of his playpen.

She broke the ice by letting out a girlish giggle. "Shit!"

"Double shit."

"Han won't cope."

"Reckon he will," Peter replied.

"We'll friggin' see."

They both laughed again. Peter went back down onto his back.

They heard the calm voice of Professor Han. It still had the hint of the Orient about it.

"So this, young man, is at least one of the days you've been looking forward to."

"Who says? I suppose you do."

Han tried to be firm. "Yes I do," he replied.

"You're wrong. But I'll tell you one thing… the day I got crocked wasn't one of the days I was looking forward to either."

"Well, let me put it this way. I hope this will be a good turning point in what I think you'll go on to achieve."

"Can we cut the sweet talk," the boy dictated. "Let's get the limb out of the wrapper and slap it on me and I'll give it a try."

"You'll have to be patient. It's a slow process."

From the other side of the wall, they could tell from the silence that great preparations were underway. Peter had learnt the artificial components had been manufactured in Germany and that Han had them specially shipped down, obviously made to measure. They had sent a technician down to take some measurements and check out the anatomy onto which it was to fit.

The silence was broken. The talk was loud and wild.

"Look at the friggin' colour of that! It's nothing like my other one! It looks as though it's been made for one of those geeks I was in hospital with. You know… what are they… all white-pink, no hair and that… it's a joke… it's the wrong friggin' order… trust the friggin' Krauts!"

Han was clearly annoyed. "Now listen here, young man…"

He didn't. "No, you listen to me, you old Chink, it'll have to be changed."

Peter raised himself from the treatment couch again but this time high enough to reach Cas's right shoulder. Exerting some of the power developed from his tennis, he began firmly but gently pushing her away. She pulled back, not quite understanding his expectations. He slid his backside down the couch and eased himself up onto both legs, far more proficiently than would have been the case back in Palafrugell or Girasol with Jan. He walked unaided now, after Cas's bullying.

"Where are you going?" she said in utter amazement. "You know the rules. I have to accompany you. Where are you going?"

"You can come and watch if you like. I'm always talking about slapping arse, you can feel for yourself what it's like."

He walked firmly to the open door of his own treatment room. Upright. He turned to the left and covered the few paces to the closed door of the adjoining room really very quickly. His hand went to the handle and, with one firm twist, he had opened it.

There were five medics around the boy on the low, flat fitting table. He had not had time to consider how sterile the surroundings had been made.

They all looked round in utter surprise to see Peter and his entourage of one bewildered looking Cas both come charging in. The boy was surprised too and lifted himself into a semi-sitting position.

"What the frig are you doing here? Come to see the wrong-coloured limb, I suppose."

"Not at all," Peter said. "I've come to see the biggest arse in Spain and give it the lesson of a lifetime."

With that, he grabbed Pablito by the shoulders and twisted them heavily. Probably because the lad didn't have a full leg to resist the momentous force, he rolled over. As he did, Peter pushed the boy's head down onto the pillowed surface.

"That will muffle the friggin' screams," he announced to all around.

With one deft blow from his open-palmed right hand across the lad's exposed backside, Peter hit target.

"That's for being a spoilt brat."

He landed a second blow on approximately the same spot. "That's for every Kraut who had a part in the manufacture of the limb."

Then again. "That's from everybody from the Orient," and again: "and every palomino, and each of the dedicated nursing staff and, if you're counting…"

Peter wasn't quite sure if he had asphyxiated the poor kid. Certainly he'd stifled the screams.

"… The fifth one is from me, for being on the same planet as you. The sixth is the one either your father or mother should have given you years ago… and the seventh… is for luck. Seven is an extremely lucky number and by Christ, are you going to friggin' well need all the bloody luck you can get!"

Peter removed the boy's head from the pillow and calmly stood back as the boy turned to look up at Peter in amazement.

"Let me apologise to all the sane ones amongst you for this little outburst." Then, turning and looking down into Pablito's open but astonished face: "Your apologies will be welcomed. Heaven help you when we get that little competition of ours over and then, if by then you can actually sit down, we'll still friggin' get to the football… and here's a very good idea. Let's, none of us, use that word in this hospital ever again."

He left centre stage, leaving a stunned audience behind him – a silence that was suddenly shattered when Pablito's two crutches, which an orderly had stood against the wall, landed back in the middle of the fitting room.

"I'll guess you'll be needing these if you've got any sense," was Peter's parting shot having propelled the sticks back into the treatment room.

He returned to his personal couch, followed closely by Cas. He automatically lay back down, looking up at the ceiling. Cas had closed the door and appeared to be holding it shut by the pressure of both hands behind her back.

"Well!" He broke the silence.

"Well!" she replied.

"Well!" he said again, to release the pressure.

"Well! Where were we? I was doing your thigh, I believe."

"Yes, and then your bottom button was undone, not done up as it now appears to have been in nervous reaction to a display by Peter Martinez, CEO, slapping butt."

"Christ! And don't you know how!"

Silence reigned from the adjoining room.

Peter was led away to do his floor work. It appeared only the six other witnesses to the outburst knew about what had happened. Elsewhere in the hospital, it was business as usual. Peter was then back to his quarters for his break time.

Cas said the phone was to be out of bounds till the evening. Being that strung up was not good for him. He had to relax.

"Tell you what. Hop in here," he said, as he lay on the bed. "Show me how to…" patting the narrow part of the mattress alongside him, "… How to relax, that is!"

"You know my view. Fiancées come first in my book, Peter, and it sounds like a really dumb blonde girlie thing to say, but what you did was fantastic."

"I'm actually sorry about it. But what do they say, you have to be cruel to be kind. Who knows, we might have just changed the lad's life."

"We? How come 'we'? It seemed from where I was standing it was a one-man show."

"Oh, come on! You were a great audience. You all seemed so stunned."

"Rest. We've got a heavy workout this afternoon. That guy's going to be after your blood when you compete."

After their lunch break, Peter reported to Cas as usual. Her forecast was then proved perfectly correct. It was heavy. It seemed to Peter that his Bok had moved up a gear. Maybe it was that she realised Pablito would now be on an extra charge in their head-to-head, if and when it arrived.

Peter was actually quite pleased with his own progress. He was loads stronger and didn't have to be reminded about not swinging from the hip, as was the original problem. In terms of being match fit, being the realist he was, he would not have put himself beyond 70 to 75 per cent.

Bloody gypsy, he often thought to himself. But, as he was beginning to see, there were plenty of people in a worse state than he was.

He was back in his room following the afternoon and subsequent evening meal, resting and thinking of ringing Jan, when there came a knock on the door. Whoever it was was bound to have the right, in any event, just to walk in.

It was Cas, showered after her day's activity, into which she had injected a special and considerable physical and mental effort, it seemed. She had obviously washed her hair in the process, as it was now hanging softly around her shoulders, unrestrained by bunches or ribbon. She had changed out of her linen coat into one of her clingy tracksuits, which Peter saw as having three-quarter length cycle pants, though Cas always said they were not.

During the afternoon, Cas had seemed quieter than usual, as if deep in thought, beyond the mechanics of her pre-planned exercise routine. The afternoon rushed by. They had finished at about five as normal, and Peter asked if Cas was going to swim.

"Length after length after length," she replied.

He wasn't quite sure how to interpret the response. There was a tinge of sarcasm in it, yet also a hint of greater depth.

"Cas. We've got to know each other pretty well, eh?"

"Hang on. I recognise this tack. You're about to pry."

"No, I'm not, I promise you. Maybe about to observe. Do you think we've got to know each other pretty well?"

"Sure, Chief. I'd say pretty well."

"You're quiet."

"Not specially."

"Well, you are. But that aside, why the sarcastic response about swimming?"

She looked disappointed. "Hell! Did I make it sound like that?"

"A little."

"Oh, I'm sorry. It wasn't like that at all. It was meant to sound confessional."

"Confessional?"

"You see, you don't know me that well. I'll help you a little along that route. I'm not good nowadays at being emotional… showing my feelings… when I do, I either get more hurt or have my mother on the phone day after day, week after week, asking if I'm alright.

"Behind my 'confessional' was the fact that I was deeply moved by your strength, and the depth of your feelings, in the fracas with Pablito. I took some of the beating you gave him for myself, to punish me for some of my own selfishness and self-promotion. I think everybody there wanted to share the experience of being put under control, into perspective – we've all got a need for that but rarely does an influence come into our lives to beat some sense into us. Well, in my case," she continued, "my father tried to instill some sense into me when I was in the early days of going out with Mark.

"I was young, but not as young as Pablito, and… well, you know how it is… you don't want to know… don't want to listen… can't see the fault lines. So I took no notice. Of course, Daddy was right. If I'd listened… I'm not going to say Mark wouldn't have killed himself one way or the other anyway, because he was a natural show-off. But if I'd taken the advice, I wouldn't have lost such a big part of me, and in doing that also lost my ability to do emotions like all the other girls. So, thinking about you beating Pablito, I was praying that he'd take the advice you gave him with your firm hand. It would be so sad if he missed out on the opportunity you've tried to give him."

"To give him?" Peter questioned. "All I did was to slap arse."

"Slap arse! Call it what you like. I can tell you, though, if somebody had knocked sense into me like you did to him, I would have ditched Mark. My father was so right."

"Tell me, is there anything you need beating out of your system now that you're all grown up?"

Cas withdrew immediately. She took a deep breath and held back her intuitive answer. A little wry smile crossed the corners of her mouth.

"Now, you bastard, that's when you friggin' pry."

Peter burst into laughter. "Come on, let it out. What do you need a beating for?"

"Right. Pry you have, you sod. I'll tell you. That beating made me horny. I go swimming, and I swim length after length until I exhaust it out of me so that none of you male scavengers get to score."

She strutted to where he was resting and pecked him on the cheek. "Seriously, you were so brilliant today. I hope Pablito loves you for it."

She stood back quickly, flicked her hair back into place and headed for the door. With her hand on the handle, she turned back.

"If you really want to know the deeper, meaner side of me, what I was also thinking was that I really hope you and Jan bust your engagement, at least while I can reach you. Call me bitch if you want."

She opened the door to leave.

"Cas," Peter said, in a loud, stern voice, "come back!"

She hesitated. This time maybe she should react to the advice.

"Yes, Chief?" she said, as she re-entered the doorway, framing herself between the cream-painted architraves.

"Jan and I aren't actually engaged, though I've never contradicted your impression. Maybe I used the word fiancée to give a bit of respectability to my target."

"You truly are a bastard, you know. Wait until I tell you I'm horny, probably nothing more than hormonal, in fact, and then tell me you're actually free. Well, if you cheated from the start, how am I to know you're not just saying what you've said to try and score. So! I'm still off swimming. I shall do four extra lengths when I know I've burnt off my raunchiness… oh, and on my way down, I'll tell Juan about your availability."

She left, the door resounding shut behind her. She felt sick in the pit of her stomach.

Before Peter had fully recovered from the outburst, there was another gentle knock at the door.

Professor Han entered. Peter wondered if it was international visiting night.

"Peter!" Han said in a gracious manner.

"Professor."

"What do I say?"

"That I shouldn't have interfered."

"Not at all. I might say we are all, and I mean all, delighted that you did. Unfortunately, I shall have to do a report based upon an intra-patient incident. Shall we say, I'll describe it as a discussion, which I'm bound to say got out of hand. Pablito, of course, is unlikely to file a different version. No. I just wanted to say your intervention and handling of the situation was perfect. We are all indebted to you. I came simply to shake your hand and to thank you profusely."

He became more Oriental as his thanks grew in gratitude, to put no finer point on it.

There seemed to follow a string of visitors, all with similar themes. Both physios, the registrar and one of the other medics attending to the 'first fit of the limb'. Juan made an appearance. Fortunately it seemed Cas had not carried out her threat, or promise (Peter wasn't sure which), as there was no hint of an invitation in either what Juan said or his body language.

Peter hoped he had had the last of the visits. He ought to ring Jan.

He had hesitated before dialling her number. He had a twinge of guilt about wanting to let Cas know their status. Well, she did rather keep throwing Jan's existence into his face. They weren't engaged, that was a fact. They'd had a two-day relationship, at the time of the interview. Sure, they got on. It was just as well they did, otherwise the whole tone of the article may have been different, though he'd hope not if Jan was the professional she undoubtedly was.

Then, he supposed, she arrived on the scene at the right time to take over his life for a while. Of course there was a spark. Jan was the only person in the world outside his medical carers to be around – excluding his mother, of course. On balance again, they had come together more over a business subject than by way of that total infatuation Peter had always interpreted as love, until he had met Anna.

He'd had a short-term obsession with Marcia, and with Honey a true passion, cut sadly short. He'd, of course, had longer infatuations in the learning curve of his adolescence. Tania was a purely physical thing.

But Jan was not like any of those. To get her into bed was a fight, and one he was beginning to think had been overplayed, although there was talk of him winning that challenge as soon as he reached Jan's requirement of peak condition for the act.

OK, he thought. There was Girasol, where Jan had told him that she loved him. But what judge of that could she be when she had only previously had time for an involvement with this Richard fellow, who seemed a bit of a wimp anyway.

His thoughts had taken him away from his intended objective. The unused phone was still in his hand.

He replaced the receiver without dialling, enabling his thoughts to continue unfettered. How much was he being influenced by a flirty young nurse with South African origins and what appeared to be a wonderful body, however much her white physio's coat and untailored trousers might disguise the fact? His architectural feel for dimension enabled him to visualise what lay within the three dimensions God had created for the human eye to read. Yet there were other dimensions he had always been sure could not be seen by the eye, but just sensed – the deeper, invisible components of emotion and the like.

OK, he admitted to himself, Cas was an intervention but Jan was behaving differently now that she was back in her natural habitat. She was more matter-of-fact, less interested in his progress, and clearly not prioritising the trip out to see him. In a nutshell, she'd become slightly boring as she appeared to want to finish their calls once she knew Peter was making progress and had returned her words of affection, however automatically.

He must call. He retrieved the receiver and dialled in the 0044 code to return him to the UK. If only it was as easy to get back as just that, he thought, as he went into automatic mode on the remaining numbers.

He had learnt how to anticipate the receptiveness or otherwise of Jan's mood by the number of rings before she answered the call. Two meant she would be in busy mode, needing to get on, deadlines to meet, jobs to be done. Into six or seven and she'd be in relaxed mode, having settled herself down into her comfy chair, or occasionally decided to take herself off to bed early.

It took about one-and-a-half rings for her to answer this time. Then it was a hurried, "Hi!"; not particularly personalised for Peter, but for anyone who might call. He would usually get another softer, "Hi," and then be allowed to open the conversation with a, "… so how are you… how are you doing… gosh you sound as though you're missing me…" or the occasional, "tell me I've caught you stepping out of the bath with no clothes on…"

He certainly got the opening. "Hi."

He responded. "Hi. So guess. It's me."

"What kept you?"

That was a new one. He wasn't aware that he was part of a timetable or had to check in at certain times. So his only and obvious response was, rather unoriginally, to repeat what she'd said, though maybe hers was an octave or two higher.

"What kept me?"

"You're late calling."

"Late calling?"

"Peter, my sweet. I can't see the point of a call when you just repeat what I say. OK, I know what it'll be. The Bok took you out for a therapeutic walk in the park and it got dark and you lost your way and finished up back at her place to get a map."

"Jan! What the hell are you on today? You've obviously got a very sore head and a bitter jealousy of someone who's actually getting me fit to come back to the UK, certainly not back to her flat… which it happens doesn't exist because she kips in the nursing quarters at the hospital."

"Listen. I'm not on anything. I need to go out. I didn't want to disappoint you and not be here. I've tried to phone you but there's always been someone in your room so they won't put calls through… and yes, I don't trust the Bok. Remember it's my job to read eyes and judge trust, and to extract things from people's brains… where they exist."

"Jan, that's a horrendous thing to say."

"What?"

"Oh come on! It's you who's judged Cas through your own eyes and whatever's going on in your own brain."

"No, darling. That's paranoia interpreting what I didn't say… look, enough of this unpleasantness. I was worried because you phoned later than usual, concerned that there was a reason for that. You've had more visits than normal, which made me think there must be something wrong. After all, the girl told me one visit was from the Professor, then the registrar. It seems all sorts of physios have been looking at you… and the Bok's gone missing. So those are my concerns.

"Oh, and by the way, you're quick to say how this Cas girl is getting you ready for the UK meat market. Who got you to Barcelona in the first place? I haven't heard a word of thanks yet for that… but then I'm not looking for praise."

"Look, things are fine. I had a fight with an in-patient, which seems to have been appreciated. Almost everybody called by to say so."

There was a short silence between them.

"Look Peter, I really must go."

"Yes, I think that's a good idea."

"What do you mean by that?"

"Jan… I think we're washed up."

Her voice softened. There was a note of shock in it.

"Washed up as in finished?"

He had no idea what caused him to burst forth with the news.

"Jan, I'm happy to talk it through when you're in a different frame of mind. Things haven't been the same at a distance… and they should be. We'll talk another day. Maybe it would be better face to face, when you come out. Any idea when that might be?"

"You've got a fucking cheek! Come out there to be told to my face I've done my job. I've rehabbed you, got together your game plan with William, saved your share price and possibly the job… no, sunshine, I won't be coming out there to be buried and to cry like one of those little piggies all the way home. I'm too upset. Now I'm gently putting the phone down, not slamming it. Goodbye."

She'd gone. Peter too replaced the handset.

He spoke to the wall opposite. "What a friggin' day!"

He got up from the bedside chair and climbed onto the bed. Clasping his hands behind his head, he stared upwards at the ceiling and contemplated his recent discussions, particularly with Jan. He supposed it was for the best, before they got too embroiled. He'd had to accept the death of Anna parting them, but he had hoped never to have a relationship that might end in divorce, like so many of his unhappy contemporaries.

His many thoughts blurred and merged into abstraction as he dozed to recuperate from the traumas of the day. He later worked out that at one point, probably a couple of hours into his nap, he had a dim awareness of somebody being present in the room. Whether the click of a door catch or a sudden draught had jolted his brain out of sleep mode, he opened one eye and then the other. They took a while to focus. In the interim he thought he was dreaming. He had seen eyes like that before. Eyes of hate. Eyes that said he was about to suffer pain. The piercing eyes controlling a Romany brain, which only knew the one code: to inflict damage.

The eyes pulled back from his face, exposing a youthful skin and a not unpleasant nose, then a soft mouth. As if in a slow motion panning shot in the hands of an expert film director, the whole then became clear. It moved away quickly enough to allow Peter to lift his shoulders off the bed and sit bolt upright, out of his troubled dream.

"Christ! Pablito!" he shouted. "You scared the living daylights out of me!"

Suddenly the hurt in the eyes changed to a smile. The face that had been peering at his was still young but friendly.

"I couldn't tell if you were asleep," the youngster confessed.

"Asleep? Don't you usually shut your eyes when you sleep? Or did you think I was dead?"

"Dead, Mr Peter? Why would you be dead? I wasn't going to disturb you. I was going to come back later."

Peter confidently swung both legs over the side of the bed. He couldn't have done that when he first entered the rehab unit.

"Well, now that you've woken me from my nightmare, I'm sure you didn't come into my room just to stare closely at all the pores in my skin."

"I did knock. They told me to knock."

"Who told you to knock?"

"Juan and Kristina."

"So you knocked and presumably I said come in. So what's it all about?"

"I came to tell you I'd got a sore bottom."

Peter laughed. "Look old son, I could have told you that. So what about your sore arse?"

The boy looked down at the floor. "You're not going to friggin' laugh and make fun of me, are you?"

There was a sense of despair in the way he asked for Peter to treat him seriously.

"Pab! Of course not. If you've come in here, broken down my door to get in and then nearly given me a heart attack because you've got something to say, then of course, I won't laugh off whatever it is you're going to tell me, providing you're not just here to state the obvious."

"I came to say thank you."

Peter was taken aback. Momentarily he rechecked his promise not to make fun of what the boy was saying and not to retort that Pablito didn't need to thank him for beating his arse, as he might have done.

"Thank you, for what?" seemed the right answer.

"Thank you for the beating."

That made Peter smile. "Now you can't seriously expect me to believe that. Come on! Thank you for what?"

"Thank you for teaching me the lesson of my life, just in time."

"What's the lesson of your life?"

"That I've been acting like a spoiled brat."

Pablito lowered his head and established a fixed gaze at the floor. As in all the hospital rooms, it was a type of linoleum. Peter observed a droplet of water land alongside Pablito's shoe. Then another. The boy was crying. Peter put an arm around the lad's shoulder and turned him to sit on the edge of the bed, then pulled his upper torso into his own chest. They were silent for a minute or two as the boy sobbed.

"You see…" Pablito said, sniffing back the tears. Peter produced a handkerchief.

"Here. Have a good blow."

Pablito did as Peter suggested.

"You see… this limb means a lot to me and I was disappointed. I can see that now. But, do you know, there are kids in Africa who lose legs and arms and bits and pieces, and they have to live without any help. A lot of the time, the thing is just chopped off and some witch doctor puts a couple of stitches in to hold back the skin and the kid just has to make the most of it. They don't even have a shoe for the good leg that they've still got, either."

He had obviously been given a talking to. By whoever it was didn't matter, but the principle had sunk in.

"Is that so?" Peter said intently. "But that doesn't affect you. You don't live in Africa. So what's the point in you knowing about that?"

Pablito looked surprised. "Look, I had no right to act like I did. As I said, you've taught me that I'm part of a much bigger world than just one containing me. I think I must have always known that but because of my brothers and sisters, I hadn't realised it."

"What do you mean 'because of my brothers and sisters'? What difference does that make?"

"Well, it's my mum."

"What about your mum?"

"She had seven kids."

"And what number were you?"

"The seventh."

"So how did that affect you?"

"Well, she never hugged me like you just did. She'd had enough of hugging all the others, and she said when I came along, she was tired of hugging. So I had to compete for attention, and I imagine in doing that my world became smaller and I just focused on myself. So when I had my accident, in my mind I became the only one in the world without a limb. But I've seen now how wrong that's been and, although I've got a really sore bum, I've got you to thank for it."

"Who's told you this?"

"What do you mean?"

"Who told you to come and thank me?"

"No one. Just me. I asked Juan if he thought it would be alright. He said provided I knocked he thought you wouldn't mind."

"Stand up, Pab."

He stood up, wiping his face with the back of his hand.

"Walk to the window."

Pablito looked at Peter, trying to work out the catch. He didn't think there was one. Dressed in jeans and supported by the two crutches he had previously tried to jettison, he walked steadily towards the curtains Peter had drawn once the sun had gone down at the end of his afternoon workout and that other confrontation with the Bok. "So if I said from where I am, I can't tell the colour of your limb, what would you say?"

"Of course you can't. I can see that now but I hadn't worked out that my jeans would cover it. I was only focused on my world. The one where I get attention when I wear shorts."

"Shorts? You're losing me. When are you intending to get attention by wearing shorts?"

"I'm going to be a Para champion."

"Really! In what?"

"Probably four hundreds."

"Four hundreds?"

"Metres. You know. Four hundred metres."

"That seems a tough target."

46

"Not to me, it doesn't."

"Do you realise how tough that's going to be?"

"Yup."

"Are you planning to do it for yourself alone?"

"That's it really."

"What? For you alone?"

"No. I've got to be good on my own. I've got to focus on winning for myself. But then, you see, I'll have the relay and then we'll do it together."

"Good thinking, Pab. That's the fourth best news of the day."

Peter could see how Pablito was concerned about being the centre of focus. Once he heard that was only the fourth best piece of news, he needed to know about the others. A bit, Peter supposed, like having the six brothers and sisters.

"The first and probably best news of the day was seeing your backside and nobody restraining me from beating it, and how that had the desired effect. Then there's your acknowledgment that there are others in a worse position than you, and that sharing and teamwork have an equal role to play alongside solo efforts.

"Look, we'll talk more tomorrow. I'm sure you need to get back to your quarters. You've had a hard day, an emotional one."

"That's only two," Pablito said.

"Two?"

"Two of the bits of best news. What was the third?"

It was his conversation with Jan, Peter supposed.

"Never you mind, young man. You appear to have learnt enough for one long day. Off you go. I appreciate your thank you."

Pablito approached Peter, who had remained on the bed.

"Could I ask a favour?"

"Of course!"

"I don't mean like Juan, you understand."

"Pablito, you'll have to make allowance for the fact that there've been many things about you I haven't understood. But a lot is now coming clear. But when you talk in riddles, I'm lost."

"I mean not like queers."

"Pablito!" Peter exploded with a laugh. "What the friggin' hell do you mean?"

"We don't use that word here anymore either. It's the favour I wanted to ask. Could I have just one more hug, like you did before? But it's not because I'm queer or anything like that. I want kids, you see. Just two or three. Anyone can get a hug from Juan. No, I mean a man to man hug like you gave me before. I promise I don't need to cry again."

"Come here, dear young man. Of course, we can have a hug."

They clenched each other firmly. As they broke away, Peter said, "Another thing. I'm sorry I hurt you so much. I lost it."

"It actually really does hurt."

With that, and a smile, Pablito was gone.

Peter was alone. In every sense. He sat back in his bedside chair, looked at his watch. Eight o'clock. He'd missed supper. He'd still got his workout tracksuit on and he hadn't showered. His whole routine, in fact his whole day, had been wrecked.

All at once, he realised what had been bothering him – the way Pablito, through his paddy, reminded him of himself, and the fiasco of trying to get his trousers on. The offending trouser leg had been his limb. He should have got his own arse beaten.

Peter stripped and went into the shower cubicle just off his private room. The cool water invigorated his body. He towelled down and slipped into a sweatshirt and shorts, then headed for the refectory.

One of the staff was doing a final clear-up.

"Suppose you don't have anything left?" Peter said hopefully.

"You too, Sir? What's going on today? You're all missing meals."

"Who else?"

"Miss Cas."

"Cas? How's she missed out?"

"Oh, according to her, she got carried away in the pool. Lost count of the lengths, so she said. Didn't realise the time."

Peter smiled. "Is that so! Did you find her anything?"

"A bowl of pasta."

"Any of that left?"

"I could heat you a bowl."

"That would do fine. Oh, by the way, did the Professor speak to the staff to leave a bottle of wine out?"

Until that point, Peter had no idea whether the hospital had wine hidden away anyway.

"Nobody mentioned it to me. But I did hear you're a bit of a hero. You're the flavour of the year, they're saying. So it doesn't surprise me if that's what the Professor said. But nobody told me."

"Do you have the key?"

"Well, yes."

"Then you stick the pasta on. I'll watch that and you be a good girl and open up the vault and pass me out a bottle of red wine… oh, and a corkscrew."

"Good girl!" she giggled. "I like that. I'm probably old enough to be your mother! You'll have to sign for it."

"Of course… and by the way, mum's the word. You know what I mean, not a word to the others."

"Go on, you're just making something out of me saying about my age."

Off she went, out of sight, happy in her work.

Peter hadn't had an alcoholic drink since lunch with his mother and Marco and Virginia. With Jan, of course. He'd ring his mother after he'd eaten in the solitude of his own room, on account of not wanting anybody to see the wine.

The pasta was good and he felt refuelled. He'd just poured a third glass of wine when there was a knock at the door. It would be the lady for the dirties, he expected.

"Sure! Come in."

"You're sounding more like a doctor with a busy surgery now you're the hero of the place."

"Cas! I thought you were the lady to collect the dirties."

"Who says I'm not?" she said, throwing her head back in relaxed laughter. Then: "Christ! What the hell's this? Some wine fiesta? Where the shit did you get the wine? This is a hospital, not a club."

"Now hear this, young lady. First, I don't see myself as ever running a doctor's surgery. Next, I robbed... well... more cheated my way to the bottle of wine. Thirdly, I've had a bit of a day. Fourthly, what brings the Bok to the private client quarters after hours? Oh... and finally, it's good to see you. I need a bit of sanity."

"Well, let's start again. I'll go outside, with the dirties, I'll knock, and you say out loud 'God, I hope it's Cas to introduce some sanity into my life, come in!' Then I'll enter and we can start again," she giggled.

"OK, go on. This whole place is getting a little serious. Out you go then. Try me with the fresh grand entrance."

The Bok collected the dish and tray and pretended to put the half-full wine bottle on it.

"Hey!" he shouted.

"Sorry, Chief." She took the bottle and topped up his glass, then lifted it to her lips and swigged a couple of large gulps. "Santé. Now I won't split if I get to share it." She then disappeared, as per her pre-scripted second visit.

Peter found it all light and amusing. There was a knock at the door.

"God, I hope it's Cas..." Then, as had so often been the case in his life, he ad-libbed. "... And that swimming the lengths didn't produce the required result."

He opened the door. Cas was motionless.

"Bastard," she said.

"Beautiful Bok," he replied, and held out a hand.

She hesitated, then took it and followed him into the room. He closed the door. Led her to the edge of the bed.

"Listen. I've phoned Jan. That's finished."

"You've got a bloody cheek! What's it to do with you whether, as you put it, it did or didn't produce the required result?"

"Everything! You're still horny. Me too. OK."

Cas smiled. "And if I said the swim had worked? That would leave you horny and me satisfied."

"Cas, sweetheart, if the swim had worked, a) you wouldn't have eaten pasta to satisfy you, and b) you wouldn't have come knocking at my door and c) you would have kept your underclothes on under the physio coat, which you really have no need to be wearing at nine at night."

Her mouth dropped open in astonishment.

"Here, you'll need this," he said, offering her the glass. She emptied it, and then accepted his outstretched hand, inviting her to his bed.

"The door," she murmured.

"What about the door?"

"I'll lock it."

"Fine! Sorry, I'm not that good at understanding we might command an audience."

"Oh, chief, you should be so lucky! This one is for me. Not anyone else."

Her athletic body entwined with his. She whispered, "Watch your knee. Or your back," then all but raped him.

Afterwards, they lay together in initial silence.

"Thank you," she said at last, "thank you so much. Thank you for letting me show you what I needed. I'll explain another time. Now's not the moment to get emotional. Peter, you really are a lovely man in every sense. I need you to know that was for me. Not for you. You don't need that sort of thing. I'm sure you can command it any time you want. So thank you. Thank you for Pablito too. Thank you for getting your knee shot to pieces. Thank you for coming to Barcelona."

She lifted herself off the bed. Peter was still speechless and on his back. She leant over him and kissed him softly on his lips.

"One favour," she said.

"Sure," he said, confidently.

"Could you lie on your stomach?"

He didn't question why. He was used to her commands.

The sudden pain was enormous. She had set fire to his backside with the palm of her right hand.

"Thanks, bastard!" she said, as she bent and kissed his raging wound. "See you in the morning, my beautiful patient."

There was a click as she unlocked the door and a clunk as it closed behind her.

Peter smiled. As he blew out breath, he advised the non-responsive ceiling, "That has been one hell of a day!"

Chapter 4

Peter did not remember actually going to sleep and at first wondered why he was on top of his duvet in his underpants. As soon as he attempted his first move of the day, the aches of his body locked in and his memory jerked into action. The Bok, he remembered. Then each of her visits came back to him. He smiled a smile of contentment, a little less so as he realised how every muscle in his body was reacting to what had clearly been an over-strenuous workout in response to her demands.

He swung his feet over the edge of the bed. Would his knee take the strain? he wondered. It did, and he made his way gingerly to the luxury of his modest en-suite. The reflection in the mirror was not one he was particularly pleased with. It was unusual for his wavy Mediterranean hair to be dishevelled, but it was. He rarely did not shave and today was to be no exception. The shower revived him and his body loosened up in response to the heat of the water and the use of the soap. He felt and looked better.

After donning a tracksuit, he made his way to the communal breakfast area. That was normally where the patients first met up with their carers for the day. There were only a couple of patients in the refectory and not a white coat in sight, let alone the one which hid Cas's athletic body from the viewing public.

"Where's everybody?" Peter enquired of one of the kitchen staff.

"It's Saturday, dear. Don't you remember? They're all off at weekends and some of the patients are on a weekend out. Aren't you due for one of those yet?"

Peter momentarily felt cheated. He'd not see Cas, it seemed, in order to recap on the previous night's activity. Although he'd only spent a couple of weekends at the Hospital De Mar, he did hate them. The place was like a morgue. He chose his breakfast from the buffet – cereal, toast, scrambled eggs and coffee – and carried his tray to an empty table.

One of the swing doors opened and the Professor entered in his usual brisk way. He was never seen to move slowly. He went straight to the servery and asked for a black coffee. As he collected it, he turned to survey the refectory, deciding where he would sit. Not recognising any member of staff, he reacted to Peter's gaze. He smiled and made his way across.

"Don't get up," he commanded, "I don't want to disturb your breakfast. How are you?"

"Good. Thank you, Professor. Actually, very good. What brings you in on a weekend? Don't you usually take well-earned time off?"

"Usually," he replied. "I got a call to the boy, though."

"Oh! Nothing serious, I hope." Peter remembered Pablito had seemed fine when he'd left him the night before.

"No. I hope not. Just a minor setback. He's going to be hard to control. Once he got his limb, he had strict instructions to rest. But it appears he's tried to do all sorts of things to test it out. He must have walked a long way, climbed stairs and got up to all sorts of antics. In overdoing it he's already worn a sore of some proportions and panicked when he woke and found blood on the bedclothes."

"How much of a setback is it for him?"

"Oh, to a normal teenager, minor, but to him, he reckons we've set him back months in his training programme. Someone has told him about us being five years away from the Paralympics and the lad already has his name on a medal. I'll leave you to discern the colour he's got in mind."

"So what's the treatment?"

"Patience and rest."

"Will he obey?"

"I've told him he has to."

"Would it help if I had a word?"

"Well, it would do no harm. Peter, I have to say again you've been very generous with your help already. Please don't overdo it."

"I won't. Be sure of that."

The Professor had drunk his coffee. He stood up and held his hand out towards Peter. "Have a good weekend. Are you here?"

Peter looked puzzled. "Here?"

"Yes. Aren't you on a weekend out like some of the others?"

"I haven't been told."

"Oh, I expect it's Cas's way of keeping you here because it's her weekend on."

"Go on! I thought she would be off."

"I think I'm right. But anyway, I'll check who's on duty and sign you out on a weekend pass if you want."

The Professor had almost reached the door when he turned back.

"Look, can I just say something?" he said in a serious tone.

Christ, Peter thought. *He knows I screwed a member of staff. I bet that gets me thrown out.* But there was no way he could say to the main man that he couldn't speak out.

"Of course you can," Peter eventually answered.

"Well, it's a question really. You see, I don't know how tied up you are. I know you work principally from the UK but as you originate from these parts, I'd imagine you get back to see the family you've talked about quite often. So you may be able to help. You seemed very interested in what I said about paraplegic activity. If you would like to find out more, we've got a reception here on Wednesday evening. It's actually for the Paraplegic Federation d'Espanole, the PFE, and all the bigwigs are coming here. There'll be a short formal meeting so they can update us on their plans for 1992 which, of course, is a huge event for us all. Then they'll host a reception for interested parties. A number of sponsors will be represented. I'd say you'd find it interesting. If young Pablito behaves himself, I'll invite him along as an example of likely material for special mention and attention. Who knows, you might just keep him in order.

"What do you say? Would you like to come along?"

"Coming along on Wednesday would be a pleasure but I don't understand the questions about how busy I am and whether I get back out to Spain…"

"Well, I suppose it's a pipe-dream really but as you see, and it's my own personal view only, most of the people on the organising committees are… well, a little, as I think you say, 'fuddy duddy', do-gooders, getting exposure because their wealth and position demand that for them. You have an obvious dynamic, go-ahead unselfish quality about you — how that showed only yesterday! I think the whole paraplegic world could benefit from the enthusiasm and reality I think you could show. The current committee are bound, and I shouldn't really say this, to put themselves forward for supply contracts, either for themselves or their companies. There are some lucrative orders to be placed. Equipment, construction, TV rights. You name it, the Olympics have it, or more correctly need it."

"But surely the main Olympic committee deals with that?"

"Not at all. We have high representation on the combined panel. Remember, we use the facilities for the same length of time as the abled guys do. We just don't get the level of attention the young ladies in Lycra do, with their well-honed bodies. A few of our chaps are not the prettiest sight.

"However, prior to the '92 Olympics it is 'mooted', as I think you would say, that the various paraplegic organisations will be brought together as the International Paralympic Committee, the IPC. Then there will be real clout. Moreover, we'll be real people just like you to have firm beliefs and strong voices. That will surely lead to professionalism in the disabled sport."

"Do you really believe that?" Peter enquired earnestly.

"I wish not to. But I'm a realist, I think a little like yourself. But visualise Mark Spitz on an advert for, say, Adidas sports shoes alongside Pablito. Spitz would at least use the pair to maximum design effect. Poor old Pab would, in truth, only do justice to one, in advertisers' eyes."

"That's pretty dreadful. Surely we ought to be finding the right commodity for the likes of Pablito, promoting and pushing him forward in true competition with somebody who has both their legs. Like raising money for the kids in Africa, for example."

"Peter! Precisely! That's why I really do believe you could help. What do you say? Would you just come along? See how it fits with you?"

"It will cost you a weekend pass."

"That's done."

The doors swung open. Cas paused in the doorway as she quickly scanned the dining room. She spotted Peter and turned away.

"Miss Cas!" Peter shouted out for all to hear. She had turned and was about to leave. Peter shouted again. "Miss Cas… the Professor and I need your help."

Cas could now hardly run away from a command that came not just from the chief but the real boss too. She turned slowly and advanced to where Peter was sitting and Professor Han was standing. Han eased the situation, which now had the rapt attention of the six or eight patients who had come to receive their first meal of the day.

"Good morning, Cas."

"Morning, Professor."

Peter stood up. "God, you look good, Miss Cas. You forecast the swim would revive you."

"… And that alone did," she replied with one of her gentle sunny smiles.

"Listen, we need your help." Peter took over in a businesslike way. "Professor Han has kindly asked me if I would consider an involvement with paraplegics and it all hinges on a reception on Wednesday evening."

"Yes, I know that's coming up," she replied, just so as not to let him control the conversation totally. He looked good this morning too. "You've got your spark back, I have to say. You were very flat when I went off duty last night. I said a good night's sleep would do you good."

Peter now smiled. *Touché*, he thought.

"Well, I'd like to go but I'd be embarrassed to turn up in a tracksuit or shorts and T-shirt, and that's all I've got here. The Professor has given me a weekend pass and I'm suggesting that I'll drive up to my place at Girasol to pick up a suit. But he can't advise me to drive, so he wondered if you would run me up there?"

Professor Han made his excuses, saying, "Look, you two work it out. I must get on."

Initially Cas was stunned. He'd spoken about Girasol during one or two of the treatments. It was both his special place and the catalyst for his current problems.

"Isn't your fiancée available?" she said, by way of throwing down a gauntlet.

"I told you last night that I'd phoned Jan and that we're finished. Wedding plans are off. Doesn't want to be burdened with a semi-cripple, so she says."

"You say you told me that last night? Do you mean after I'd taken what I'd needed and I assumed you were just trying to remove some sort of guilt you were going through about cheating on your wife to be?"

"As for you being a semi-cripple. You're not…" she said in an over-quick reaction which she wished she could withdraw. "… And about driving you up to your place. I can't."

"Can't or won't?" Peter challenged.

"Can't. I'm on duty for one, and I've a date tonight."

"Han had already promised he could spare you from, say, 3pm, there won't be any rotas after that… would that get you back in time for your date?"

"I'll have to make a call," she said, feeling boxed in.

"Han also said he can see my point. That I'll want to be at my best for Wednesday."

"I've seen you apparently at your best… in shorts… with Pablito yesterday. You don't need a suit."

Peter knew she was playing with him.

"No, before it seemed you were more concerned with getting cross with me about how I'd suggested your swim hadn't worked."

"Oh dear! OK, I have to confess you'd turned me on so much I probably lost concentration for anything other than my selfish needs."

Her mood had changed, quite why even she couldn't work out. If she had been given just one final wish, she supposed high on her menu would be time out with Peter on a one-to-one. Inwardly, though, her defence mechanism towards him had showed in her reaction to his fiancée's 'half crippled' assessment. She was feeling exposed by that sort of feeling, and how she had given herself to him the previous night, so she made out she had used his body for her own selfish and much-needed gratification. Although it was what she wanted, the professional involvement made her feel cornered.

"Now listen here…" Their eyes met. "I've made it quite clear last night was for me and me alone… I don't know what your devious plan is… but if you're trying to make more out of an annual event than was meant by it… you'll have to go and get yourself a different sort of tart… So what's your big game? You must have dozens of people you could call on to drive you up the coast."

"No big game. You made it perfectly clear that you had a perfectly normal physical need for relief." He was speaking in a hushed confidential tone, just one-to-one. His tone, unlike hers, was soft.

"If I'm expected to be lustful for a quick repeat of what was nothing more than a very pleasant but emotionless rape, then you should have another thought coming… that's if you'll forgive the bad choice of words."

At that, Peter beamed out one of his great broad smiles. He knew she'd react. He loved it when she was roused.

"You really are a clever bastard. OK, I tell you it wasn't like you say… rape… but I won't expect you to understand that." A tear appeared first in her left eye and then the right. He pulled out a handkerchief and handed it to her.

"Now listen," he said in a continuing gentle tone, "then don't ever say to me again, or to anyone, come to that, that any such act is just for you. You took what you think you needed to take but, maybe unknowingly, you gave too. At least for me, you did. You gave more than clearly you're ever going to know about. Now is it a 'yes' to doing the driving? And a full mutual understanding? That's the only deal."

"Yes." She continued to blot her eyes.

"… And the dummy date… on your working weekend… ?"

"Peter, all I ask is, please don't get emotional. If that's a promise, I'll ditch the date… he's a bit too weak for me anyway." She forced a smile. "And I'll give you the drive of your life."

"Coffee?" Peter offered.

"Spring water, please."

He went up to the counter and picked up a bottle of Evian and a clean glass. When he returned, she had pulled herself together.

"We haven't got a car."

"We'll get one. Maybe just a Hertz but that'll do."

In the broken minutes alone, Cas had already assessed the relatively small wardrobe she had in her hospital digs. There was the odd little number she'd worn on her couple of previous mid-week dates. She also had that mini-skirt, which would make a change from hospital physio coats and trousers, or tracksuits. She'd want to get back that evening anyway. So she'd drive in the skirt and throw in a couple of other bits and pieces. This man was a threat to her life, so she'd avoid the inevitable invite to an overnight stay.

The Professor arrived back on cue. "All fixed?"

It was Cas who replied. "Yes, seems that way but we've agreed it's on my terms."

Peter was now self-disciplined in his quest to achieve physical recovery, so he worked out on the gymnastic equipment as he ordinarily would. He exercised until midday. Cas had briefly looked in on him to see how he was doing. She had been calm and relaxed, quite smiley, hiding her inward excitement at the prospect of having Peter to herself, at least for a few hours.

After Peter considered he had done sufficient exercise and muscle redevelopment, he found his way to Pablito's ward. The youngster was lying on his bed without the limb fitted.

"Bad luck," Peter announced.

"I think I overdid it," Pablito said honestly. "Rubbed the skin away. Tell you what, my bum wasn't as painful as my stump is now."

"How long will it take to heal?" Peter enquired.

"The Professor says two days. But I'll have it on again by tomorrow."

"Be sensible," Peter advised.

"If I wasn't being sensible, I'd have it back on now, but you see I could get an infection."

"Pab! Who tells you these things that you seem to accept and believe in, even though usually you don't listen to advice? The story you told me about African kids. What you've just said about infection. A week or so back you would have scoffed at such information."

"Guess what! I'll be able to have kids, or have I already told you that?"

"Yes, you have actually. Limited to two or three. So you said."

"Yes, but that doesn't mean you only get to do sex twice or three times. You can do it as often as you and your partner want to."

"Is that a fact?"

"Yup. You see, you can wear a rubber. Listen, are you winding me up? You know all these things, don't you?"

"Yes, of course, but I didn't know them at your age."

"Really?"

"So who's been educating you?"

"Oh, my friend. The nurse. Not Juan. The African one."

"Pab, let me give you a bit of guidance. You should say 'the South African one'…"

"What's the difference?"

"Well, it's just customary to refer to Africans by the country in Africa where they live. Otherwise, if you were hearing a conversation or reading a letter about an African, you might just misjudge the likely colour of their skin. If you say South African, they're more likely to be white."

"Does that matter? Jessie Owens was black. He made it. Am I going to be known as the white 400 speedo?"

"The aim should be for you just to be you. What's your surname anyway?"

"I don't use it."

"Why?"

"It's my father's name."

"But you usually do use your father's name."

"Your father usually stays by you and doesn't just screw your mother and walk out."

"So what's your mother's surname? She didn't walk out."

"No, but she didn't walk in either. She didn't want me any more than my father did. She used to say I just came along unexpectedly."

"So we've got to find you a surname for when you're famous."

"What's yours?"

"Martinez."

"OK, I'll use that."

"You can't do that."

"Why? Don't you want me to?"

"No. It's not that. I'd hope to play some part in your future. It would be better for there to be no hint of a relationship."

"So what can you suggest?"

"Well, the hospital will have played a major role in any success you have."

"Pablito Hospital doesn't sound right."

"How right you are. Look, I think Cas has got to be involved."

Pablito's face lit up. "I want her to like my new name and to still see me as she knows me."

"That's good thinking. Leave that to me. She'll love it. I'll try and create an opportunity to discuss it with her."

Chapter 5

Cas's confidence behind the wheel did not surprise Peter. She had known the hired Alfa Sud for barely two or three minutes before she had taken command of the two wing mirrors, with Peter's help on the offside, the rear view one and the layout of the gear box.

"Not driven one of these little Italian shits before," she announced.

"Not been driven in one," Peter replied.

She had stretched first into second at take-off and then built the revs up in third before the first set of traffic lights, with their amber to red warnings, advised that if she went further they'd both, the car and herself, be written off by some sleepy Spaniard coming out of their siesta. Peter silently gave her rope for perhaps the first 25 to 30 kilometres.

"Would you mind pulling up in the lay-by up ahead?" he asked, breaking the silence.

Cas shot him a glance of non-understanding, but did as he asked. "Are you sick?"

"Nope."

"Leg hurting?"

"No."

"Want a pee?"

"No."

"The map?"

"No, I'm fine. I've done the journey many times."

"What then?"

"We need to talk."

"What's to say? Not that you agree you're the biggest cheat alive?"

That surprised Peter. "We'll go into that, if you want to expand on it, but no, I just want to say that, given another 50 kilometres, there's a strong chance you'll kill both of us. This isn't just the drive of my life, I keep getting the feeling it could be my last. Maybe you're in a paddy because I haven't said I like your skirt, and more particularly your legs, which you clearly want to draw my attention to. But you're driving almost in a tantrum and I think it would be safer for both of us if we get that out into the open."

"OK. I said you were a bastard and you *are* a bastard. You go round giving lessons to lesser mortals, and then capitalise on that. I don't know what Pablito's deal is going to be on that, or whether you have some sort of repayment in mind. I've worked out, though, that because I included you in my need factor, I'm in for some sort of penalty or come-uppance."

Peter laughed, less with humour than astonishment. "Out with it, Cas. What's the problem?"

"You should bloody well know! It's one of three things, I guess, and they're all getting to me at once. Hence the mad driving. One, because I showed you a bit of need last night, you probably reckon that outside the hospital environment, I'm going to be an easy lay, and word might get out in the boys' club at the hospital that I had a weak moment. That's bastard point one.

"Two, you might not have reacted too well to having some of your own medicine administered to you by getting your arse slapped, so you're no doubt planning to get your own back.

"The third possibility," her face was becoming gaunt, and her voice trembly, "bastard point three, is that you're just a power freak who's used my genuine help to get back into physical shape, and now you're using your influence over even the Professor to turn me a servile little chauffeuse. So that, my dear Chief Executive Officer, is why I'm cross. I've been working out the odds."

Peter opened the car door and got out. Cas watched his every step from the passenger door, round the bonnet, until his firm, masculine hand was placed on the driving door handle which he jerked quickly to open the door.

"Out," he commanded, as he leant in to the car and removed the keys. "Come on out."

"Piss off!"

"Cas, you're acting worse now than Pablito, and I've no intention of doing what I'm accused of by putting you over my knee. It would prove too much of a point."

He stretched his hand out towards hers.

"OK," said Cas. "So I fall for this trick. You get me out of the car... you hop in and drive off and I'm at the mercy of the next passing truck driver."

"Wrong again. I gently lead you like this," extending his hand towards her left wrist, "or pull you if need be, out of the driving seat. Now please do as I ask."

She hesitated. Then she swung her legs out so that her feet hit the road, but not without first having caught his shins. "Well, you should have given me room," she announced tartly.

He eased her into a standing position and led her back around the bonnet, opened the passenger door and sat her down, then swung her legs in and closed the door. He locked it ominously from the outside. By the time he had completed the return journey to the driving seat, her head had fallen forward into her lap, and she was crying. He put the keys into the ignition and started the engine.

It was as though she had heard a starting pistol or the whistle to mark the commencement of a seriously competitive game.

"Peter, you can't!" she screeched.

"Can't! Don't you remember your lesson number one that everything is achievable? There's no such word as 'can't'. Your mother must have taught you that."

He engaged gear as she braced herself upright in the seat.

"Peter," she appeared calmer, "you really shouldn't drive. You've still got a crocked knee. It'll be on the accelerator. You could set yourself back."

"Not half as much as if you'd continued to build up your ridiculous imaginings about why I... well OK, I suppose I did cheat... but why I asked, not instructed, the Professor to get you to drive me to pick up a suit... and by the way, also to get you back for your date."

"What, not because you thought I'd be an easy lay after last night?"

"No, absolutely not."

"The control freak in you?"

"Definitely not."

"Because your butt is still stinging?"

"Not at all."

They remained silent. Several minutes passed, during which all of Peter's previous driving experience returned to his every muscle, as did every element of judgment, at which he was so well practised. Nothing seemed to have been impaired by the major trauma to his body.

"OK, bastard patient. Why?" Cas suddenly broke the silence, as if to say she gave up and couldn't work him out.

"Look, let's have less of the bastard, please. I have a father, albeit he's not been with us now for a long time. So I'd rather you don't call me by that name."

"Sorry! I didn't know that. Were you young when you lost him? Can I ask how he died?"

"Do you really have a genuine interest in knowing?"

"Yes, I do. Unless you're going to accuse me of having your habit of prying."

"Now that's another thing. You must get used to seeing any genuine interest not as prying but just genuine interest, an attempt to find out how to share a moment of happiness, elation or grief even. So, I don't see your interest in my father as 'prying'. It's a simple answer. He drowned, and yes, I was very young."

"Oh shit. I'm sorry."

"Don't be. It was tough at the time but it was an accident. His luck ran out at an early age."

"Like Mark's, I guess." She remained silent for a moment, then reverted to the burning question. "Back to this trip... so why? What's your agenda?"

Peter avoided his habit of giving multiple answers and categorising each one numerically.

"Put simply – you've got the best legs in the hospital. They would make good travelling companions and take my mind off your driving, which somehow I knew would be manic. I judged that I could get you back in time for your date, so whether you were an easy lay or otherwise wasn't relevant. I don't believe anybody will ever control you and I'd get no joy out of failing in that regard.

"Anyway, I'll have to save anything else I have to say till later because my place at Girasol is just round the corner. Oh, and by the way, when I introduce you to Tania, I'd like it if you could go up a gear, be a little superior. You'll probably recognise her as being the easiest 'lay' this side of the hospital. But that's not how I see the position, and you'll find I go into superior mode. I'd be obliged if you would too."

That's warned me, she thought. He pulled into the entrance to a farm.

"Why are you stopping?" she asked.

"Well, I guessed, even though the sun's going down, you'd like to patch up the mascara and lipstick... that's if you want to beat the competition."

"Bast... sorry." She pulled herself up. "Pig!" was her second choice. "My bag's in the glove box in front of you."

He passed it across as she instinctively turned down the sun visor and located the all-essential vanity mirror.

"Hell!" she exploded. "You're dead right. I don't need repairs, I need a total renovation." She wiped away the tide marks left by the flow of tears and set about rebuilding her foundation.

"Peter. I'm sorry about your father."

"It's OK. I'll tell you about it properly one day. It might help you to understand your Mark's death, and even accept it a little more."

"Oh, how I wish I could. Did you see your father... after he'd passed on... dead?"

"No."

"And... was it Anna? Your wife. She was killed in a car accident, you said. Did you see her?"

"No. My father-in-law did the identification before I reached South America."

"Have you ever seen somebody close to you dead?"

"Yes."

"Who was that?"

"You'll cry."

"I promise I won't."

"It was a baby boar, a young wild pig."

She laughed. "That doesn't count."

"It does when you've just killed it yourself. Out hunting."

"Oh, you poor thing!" She put her hand on his knee to comfort him. "But if you knew you were going to kill it, why didn't you pull back and let it go?"

"My father wanted me to toughen up. It was a lesson. Just like Pablito's, but in my case, to toughen me up rather than, in his case, calming him down."

Cas continued renovating her make-up in concentrated silence.

"How's that?" she said finally, turning to him.

"Great! You could just win."

That made her smile. "Onwards then. And tell me about your dad now."

Cas's eyes were glued to Peter's profile as he told the story, full of emotion. He really was still upset, both by his memory of the event and the telling of the story.

Now she looked ahead of her for the first time in several kilometres.

"Wow! This is beautiful."

"Thank you. Actually, we're here. Welcome to Girasol."

"Wow!"

That's what they all said. It made Peter very proud. Here was his conception, his detail, his overall planning and whoever he introduced to Girasol, it was unusual for their reaction not to be, "Wow!"

That had never been the case with Anna. He never quite knew why. She had once confided in her brother Max that she didn't like sharing Peter with anybody or any thing. Once she had made up her mind that he was to be hers, she had expected 100 per cent. Generally, that was how it was but when Girasol came on the agenda, it dropped to 50-50. There always seemed to be a small re-design for him to have to think through, or an ornament for the garden, "Just to fill that corner."

Even when they sat in the late evening sunshine, listening to the music they normally shared elsewhere in the world, he'd be somewhere distant. Enjoying the same music together at home in England, nothing would enter his mind and they would soak up the beauty of the chords almost as one person.

Suddenly Cas was emphatic. "Peter, it's a self portrait!"

He'd never heard that before. He laughed. "A Picasso, I'll bet."

"No! Even if you hadn't told me, I would have known that you had designed all this. It's calm, strong, bold yet muted. It reeks of strength yet also charm. What are the trees?"

"Original olives."

"There you are! It's where you got your skin from, Peter. It's all so beautiful."

She leant across and kissed his cheek. "Let's go and meet the lay competition."

She threw the door open and leapt out as a pedigree rabbit might, having forced an opening in its run.

Tania wasn't around, it appeared, although Peter had called her to ask her to air the rooms in the November coolness as he was coming 'with a friend'.

Another bloody girlfriend, he means, she thought. She was in no mood for this, and so soon after the other recent one. She had already decided she was unlikely to even bother to mount a night watch to see what they got up to. She hadn't believed him for one moment when he'd said that they might have to get back to Barcelona by early evening. Nobody escaped his introduction to Girasol that quickly. They'd stay over, and she'd be an intruder in her own rightful place.

In Tania's absence, Peter remembered the key wired to the underside of the letter bin at the top of the short path to the front door. Cas followed like an excited child. "If this is the outside, I can't wait to see the inside!"

"Hold on there," he instructed.

This time Peter was alert to the burglar alarm. He remembered the four digits he had stored on an anonymous piece of paper in his wallet. It was, of course, the number of the year he was born.

"OK, you can come in now," he said proudly.

The open door revealed the tasteful terrazzo floor, plain white walls as a backcloth to some Catalan tapestries. There was an animal skin over the fireplace.

"Oh my God!" Cas shrieked. A look of horror overcame her face as her hand covered her mouth. She turned and threw her arms around Peter's neck. Peter was perplexed. "The bastard!"

"Who's the bastard this time?"

"Your father."

Peter roared with laughter. "Why? Exactly why?"

"Did he make you mount the boar's skin as part of the lesson?"

Peter followed her gaze towards the stretched coat mounted on the chimney breast.

"You soppy softie! That's not a boar's skin. It's the coat of quite a dangerous wild cat, which rips through herds of lambs and defenceless chickens. No! That one deserves to be dead, and by the way, I didn't kill it. I bought it in an antique shop in South America."

There was suddenly a chill breeze. Cas turned towards where she felt it was coming from.

Tania was wearing tight red trousers, three-quarter length, and a black blouse. A wide sash embraced her waist, with tassels that fell down the side of one thigh.

"Welcome back, Mr Peter," she said through leaden gypsy eyes, distinctly ignoring Cas's presence.

"Hi Tania, thanks for opening the house up and freshening the air. This is Cas. She's another one of the angels in my life who's been sorting out the defects in this old body."

His was only a year or so older than hers, so Tania didn't take kindly to his comment – particularly when she looked at this new blonde's young physique. He should have seen her use her 'old body' on the Coca Cola guy. Then he would have chosen his words more carefully.

Tania held out a limp, impersonal hand to Cas, a gesture that hinted any friend of Peter's would only become an acquaintance of hers under duress.

"I'm pleased to meet you," Cas said politely, in reaction to the open coolness of Tania's greeting. "I've heard a lot about you."

Peter half-wished she hadn't said that.

Tania cooled a few more degrees. *Oh yes.* Her thoughts were profound as they seemed to pound against her skull. *I suppose you know that I'm the one who got his brains kicked out years ago because he'd peeped at my sister and me in our staff changing room. I'm the one who was the magnet to those bandit cousins who caused him to be shot up... and look what that's done... he's found you as a result... a new bimbo plaything... well you ought to know, chick, what he probably hasn't told you is that he's fancied me almost for more years that you've been on the planet and even without his attention I've got lots going on here... oh... and by the way, you also ought to know if you find a deep furrow in the bed, it's where Alano Carlos screwed me and said it was the best he'd ever had... So, you've a hard act to follow, blondie. If only she could have said what she'd been thinking.*

Peter was cross that Tania had shown such silence at Cas's attempt to be aloof yet friendly.

"Tania. You don't seem to be with us today. Is something wrong? Cas was attempting polite conversation."

"I'm sorry, Mr Peter. I was deep in thought." She turned to Cas and said, "Excuse me. It suddenly occurred to me that I didn't know what you might drink."

"Do I look alcoholic?" Cas said laughing. "Nothing exceptional. Why?"

"I usually stock up Mr Peter's fridge. If I said Coke, would that be one of your preferences?"

"As it happens, it would be."

"Merde!"

"Don't worry, 7-Up, orange juice. I'm really easy."

Peter chirped in. "So what's the problem? Is there a supply hitch?"

"Only that the Coca Cola salesman hasn't shown up for a couple of weeks. His wife was due a baby so I guess he's changing nappies rather than re-stocking his clients." She smiled inwardly at the innuendo, which only she would understand. "I'll slip down to the garage. They should have some."

"Please don't bother. It's not life or death."

"No. But if there's something you like, you shouldn't be made to go without," Tania pronounced, flashing a look at Peter which he knew all too well how to interpret. "By the way, how's the leg, Mr Peter?"

"It's good, thank you."

"Hey, I've got to look at that knee," Cas interjected, now back in professional mode. "Peter drove some of the way here, much against instructions. Let me have a look at it for you. Sit over there, would you."

"I'm not taking my trousers off in front of Tania, thank you."

"There'll be no need. I'll roll your trouser leg up."

He made a pretence of disappointment.

Tania decided it was time to leave. "I'll leave you to look at legs and stuff. If there's anything you need, you know where I am."

"Is chef on tonight?" Peter asked.

"Yes, of course." And then she remembered that, it being Saturday, he'd want to stay behind for an end of week night cap and some sex, if she would give it. Well she wouldn't, probably, with Peter around. He could go to his own home and wake his wife up for a change.

"Do you think he's got some fish?"

"He's sure to have."

"We'll probably have a really early supper. We're planning on getting back to the hospital, and there won't be a suitable stopping off point on the way back. What time would you like to eat, Cas?"

"Can we phone through later? We've got to discuss the logistics of the return journey, to get you back before all the doors are locked for the night."

He was suddenly disappointed that this could transpire to be a very short visit.

"That's right. Sorry, I'd forgotten. We'll give you a call, Tania. OK?"

"Fine. I'll hold a table anyway."

She bade her farewells and left in slightly better humour than when she had arrived, now knowing there was at least a chance that the bed she felt she had rights to might not be used by a new body on the circuit.

Cas forced Peter into one of the lounge chairs, took off his brown Barker slip-on shoe, and rolled up his right trouser leg. She knelt down, resting his foot on her thighs as she placed both hands behind his knee joint. Her expert fingers probed deep as she covered the full circumference of his knee, with his leg in a straight position. She adjusted his foot to a slightly lower level on her thighs and shuffled forward to bend the knee. As she did that, her thumbs exerted pressure on the ligaments and cartilages on each side. She exercised the knee backwards and forwards.

"You're always going to have some arthritis in there, you know."

He knew.

"Can we check the patella?" Peter asked knowledgeably.

She moved both hands automatically to the front and applied gentle pressure to the knee cap between her forefingers and thumbs.

"Does that feel sore?"

"Not yet, but I sense there might be a problem."

She didn't think too much about the reply, her brain was interpreting the senses transmitted through her sensitive hands.

"It all seems good. Why do you think there might be a problem? Does it ache? Does it hurt when you bend it?"

"No, not at all. It seems good enough to me."

She let his knee go and shuffled back in the kneeling position.

"Don't move away," he said softly.

"Why? Peter, you're being a little strange. First, you ask me to look at your kneecap, apparently for no reason. Then it's 'don't move away'. You're up to something in that inventive mind of yours."

"Oh, nothing really… well… it's not your problem but I've got this fixation over sex."

"Oh, here we go! A big leg-pull coming up, I suppose, or have you been having me on?"

He went into multiple explanation mode.

"Well, I need to know roughly when that knee will take my weight, that's the first thing. Secondly, and I've always said it in the most public of places, you've really got a wonderful cleavage and I needed to feast my eyes on it after the stress of the journey… and all your tantrums and stuff." He smiled his deep smile.

"You're a bugger, Mr Peter. Go look down Tania's shirt. I'd say she'd be up for that and welcome it. As for the knee, it seems good. Pity you won't get to try it out in the foreseeable future. I think you ought to sort out your suit. Show me where, not how, and I'll make us a cup of tea, then we'll head back. I'm not sure which one of us I don't trust the most," she said, seriously meaning it.

"Then we'll just have to work that out. If it's me, we'll stay on. I'll make you a promise. If it's you… well, the lady will determine the future. I'll go along with what you want."

He couldn't be fairer, she thought.

"I'll make some tea. Do you have a blue suit?"

"Yes, I think I've got one here."

"A crisp white shirt?"

"Possibly needs a press."

"Show me where and I'll choose you a tie… depending on the taste you had in the past… or did you buy for yourself or let people buy for you as presents, which you had to wear."

"Seems a deal to me. I've always bought my own. Which first?" Peter enquired.

"We'll boil the kettle and make the tea, and while that brews, we'll choose the tie, and see how bad the shirt is."

"It'll at least be clean."

He beckoned for her to follow. "Here's the kitchen." He spread his arms out as though conducting the members of a symphony orchestra to stand up and take one final bow.

The kitchen was still very modern, although probably part of the original design. Cas knew the cupboards were bound to be laid out logically. Peter seemed that sort of bloke.

Sure enough, the left hand one contained china cups with saucers, but also some serviceable mugs. The next contained tea, coffee, chocolate and, she noted, milkshakes. The next had sugar, sweeteners and biscuits. She didn't doubt if she continued in a clockwise fashion, she'd find breakfast, lunch, dinner/supper and retiring to bed cutlery and dry stored packaged food, stored in sequence for the needs of the day.

The tea was made.

"OK. Follow me to the dressing area," Peter enticed.

"Is the trust still there, or am I at risk adventuring into a dressing area, which, given your logical way with design, is no doubt close to the bedroom?"

"Well, you're right, of course. But back to the question… yes, the trust is still there and can be relied on. I'm not up for being raped two days running."

Her eyes flashed. She was hurt to be reminded in that rather cold, sordid way about the previous night.

"Peter, when do we get to talk?"

"I thought we had been."

"No, about my little wild pig."

That hit a tender note in Peter. "Why, do you have one?"

"Of sorts."

"Then it'll be your turn to tell me about it. The English would talk on any serious subject either over tea… or during coffee after dinner. Tell me when you're ready and I'll look forward to listening. I'm fairly Anglicised these days."

Stopping outside the dressing room, Peter said, "Here's where we do the choosing." He opened a door into a small room where there were two louvre-fronted wardrobes and a matching door. "Ties, shirts, suits," he said, indicating the left-hand one.

Cas pointed to the one on the right. "And this one?"

"Oh, that's a bit of a lonely one."

"Oh, come on! Now I'm more interested in that than the boring old other one."

"You might not like it."

"Now I'm even more intrigued."

He opened both the doors, exposing empty rails. "There," he said, "the loneliness of a wounded widower."

"Oh shit! I do put my foot in it, don't I? I always push just that bit too far."

Peter laughed. "To be honest, Cas, I'm playing on those emotions you've said I mustn't intrude upon. It's eight years since Anna was killed. How long for Mark?"

Cas suddenly looked shocked. Panic overtook her face. She stared at the floor. "I don't know."

Peter stepped forward and took each of her hands into his.

"Let me tell you. Year one, devastation. Year two, the grieving comes out. Year three, confusion. You can't seem to get those memories out of your mind, yet something begins to tell you life must go on. Four, you try too hard to forget the past. The fifth year, you see sense and decide to move life on, but again try too hard to find somebody emotionally suited, someone who can accept where you've been, and replace the one you've lost. Year six, you'll accept anybody, anything, any available person or persons to fill the void. Year seven, you think you've found them.

"Year eight… well, that's an interesting one. I think I only know part of the answer because I only have partial experience. But I think it must be something like you imagine you find a one-person solution. You miss the point of whether or not you read into the situation a false sense of compatibility, you don't see the gaps in each of your requirements. Security raises its head.

"Then you walk into a new scene where you meet somebody totally the reverse. Free, with their own set of problems, lost, somebody with a greater need than yourself who needs navigating through their year three and onwards. A hopeless confrontation destined by all the rule books not to be right for either party, yet… to date it has been right for both parties' requirements… the areas of mutual flattering, an interest in a common denominator and a teapot which, if it's not poured soon, is going to be a total waste of water, tea and the energy used to boil the water, which we can ill-afford.

"Cas, I'm as sure as I can be that Mark is your 'wild boar'. You're about a quarter of the way through year three. You're confused. I'm way ahead of you, so I'll have to let you be the judge of any ongoing mutual need."

Cas remained silent for a while, then: "Christ, Peter. Are you some sort of second son sent down to lead me?"

"No. Certainly not. Just somebody who's been there. The chap with the empty wardrobe. Listen, we need that tea."

He remained holding just her one hand and led her down the stairs in silence.

"The English expression is 'I'll be mother'," he said. "OK?"

"You are a bugger. I'm so confused now, yet I'm sure of the reality of what you've just said. Yes, you be mother. Mine's strong with a dash of milk."

"Good God! So is mine. That'll make it easy for me." They were back to smiling, relaxed mode.

Peter carried the tray into the living area.

"Brrh!" He gesticulated that he felt chilly. The temperature had dropped considerably since the sun went down. Peter looked instinctively at his watch. "Are you cold?"

"Yes, I am a bit."

The open fire was always prepared. He reached for the box of matches and within seconds, the dried kindle was ablaze, then the smaller pine cuttings, which emitted flames that lapped over the larger cuts of tree trunks. He stood back proudly, as no man can resist admiring the success of his pyrotechnics.

"There, madam. Warmth. That will get your blood flowing again."

"Goodness me!" Cas cried, followed by the totally honest assessment: "This must be the worst cup of tea I've ever had a part in making."

She looked at her watch. "Oh God, do you know it's just coming up to seven? The pot's been standing for over an hour. We talked for that long, did you know?"

"We talked for the sake of eight years versus two plus. It doesn't matter how long it took."

"I can't drink any more of this shit," she confessed.

"How's about a civilised gin and tonic?"

She looked at her watch again. Keeping her head bowed, she said, "Actually, I'd like to head back, Peter, please."

His stomach churned with disappointment, which he knew he shouldn't show.

"That's fine. We can get you back by 8.30. Is that OK?"

She hadn't raised her head. "Would be fine."

"OK. That doesn't answer the question of the gin and tonic."

"Well... nine o'clock would do."

There was a substantial pause while Peter dispensed the drinks from a cupboard alongside the fire, which was now well alight.

"Ice?"

"Please."

He opened the ice tray in the fridge and dropped in two of the frozen cubes using tongs as if professionally delivered. He handed her an Edinburgh cut-glass highball, which had tonic bubbling up the inner sides. There was a slice of pre-frozen lemon floating on the top.

"Cheers," he proposed. "Here's to you benefiting over the next five years, and to hell with the last three."

"The last have been alright actually, despite what you've said. But cheers anyway. Here's to you discovering about the next eight for both our benefits."

"I'm not going to argue the point of your recent past being OK or otherwise. What I'd say is it's positively year three, you have to decide now to take up a life again."

"I think I have, actually." There were too many 'actuallys'. It was a word Peter thought she was using to re-affirm a point she was not that positive about.

"Here." Peter sat down on the fur rug in front of the fire, leaning his back against the sofa. He slapped the floor with his left hand. "Come on. We can make stories out of the dancing of the flames. That's if we have enough gin to get stupid."

"Will I be the first to escape the web you've cast around Girasol?"

"What do you mean?"

"When I get away without having graced your bed."

"Cheeky bitch! Do you want some sort of confessional? Well, lump it or leave it, you're going to get one. When Anna died... oh let's stop there... the benefit of being eight years down the track is that I can now refer to Anna as having... died... you know, conjuring up satin sheets and lace-trimmed pillows, holding hands and witnessing a last shared breath together... not, as was the case when Anna was killed, a horrific tangled mess of cars upside down on their roofs, groans, blood, ambulance sirens... that, my sweet Cas, was, I understand, how it was. So when I speak retrospectively, I refer to the calm of death rather than the turmoil of being killed... having life stolen as opposed to eased away."

Cas's shoulder and upper right arm were leaning into Peter's left one. He could feel the pressure increasing as she listened.

"Can I say... ?"

"Well, I'm listening," she replied.

"Well, at the stage, you're at, if you close your eyes... you're at Mark's side. The fact is, he's dead. He's in that horrific state."

Her right arm started to shake and with it, Peter could see there were tremors crossing her chest and moving down her left-hand side. It was involuntary and uncontrollable. He put his left arm round her shoulder and pulled it firmly to steady her shaking body.

"Would you do something for me... and I know I've upset you... but just try... I want you to close your eyes... please, it won't hurt, I promise."

She was in no state to refuse, she needed Peter's help. He could see her eyes were closed.

"When did you first hear about heaven?"

"I was about eight."

"OK, that's good." He moved his hand across to hold hers. "How did it come about?"

"My rabbit died."

"So how did heaven come into play?"

"My mother told me about it. How wonderful it was..."

"How do you visualise it now you're a big girl?"

"Oh... beautiful, calm, a field of lavender and tall, shady trees."

"Can you see Mark?"

Her body jerked reactively as though she had suddenly seen a ghost. "I only see Mark one way."

"OK. We understand that."

She began to sob. "Peter... you're causing me a problem..."

"Do you want me to stop?"

"Yes... but no," she said, looking up into his open face.

"So, what's the problem?"

"You're being so kind to me. I'm susceptible."

"I won't stop till you've done your bit towards resolving the situation. Close your eyes again."

"They smart."

"Good, that's fine. They won't for long. Can you see the sand dunes?"

She shook again. "Yes!" she cried out loud, amidst tears.

"Can you see Mark?"

"Oh yes!" she said, through tears that were now heavier.

"Do you have a scarf with you? You know, one you might have put over your hair on the back of the bike."

"Christ! How do you know these things?"

"Right... gently lay it over Mark's face and head. OK, now watch his body float up to heaven... ouch, can you smell the lavender? Can you see the field? Look, there's a rabbit, there by the tree... under the tree... there's Mark... no scarf... his face, how you remember him alive... he's all healed up... Mark has just died."

Her body stopped trembling. The tears had ceased. But she was breathing heavily.

"That's it," he said with confidence, "now we've got Anna and Mark both calm and perfectly dead... oh, and your rabbit, in those wonderful heavenly surroundings... and you've got your life to get on with... I'm into mine... and that brings us back to your question. By the way, it's eight o'clock."

She stayed silent for a while. "The question... or, more correctly, the answer. We digressed," she eventually answered.

"I'll top the drinks up and try and remember the question... or maybe some other digression so that I don't have to answer it," Peter said, trying to lighten the moment.

Cas was deep in thought. Inwardly she felt comforted by Peter's encouragement to see life beyond the early years of grieving she had been through. She could understand now that it was the constant vision of Mark's smashed face and the horrendous impact of his death that had made it extra hard for her to cope.

During her moments of silence and the emotion that had been forced out of her, she felt she had gone through some form of exorcism, producing great relief. Later, she even thought of it as the sort of experience she had sometimes read about in magazines, in which she'd had no previous belief. She was now calm and her confidence had been restored through the strength Peter had imparted to her. He might be years her senior, but that was a bonus, as his maturity had helped her to understand another dimension of her grief. It was also evident in how he dealt with pain, the special way he handled Pablito, his control of situations, the way he appeared to have coped with her need for him only the night before.

This evening's needs were different. She'd wanted to make up for last night by being unavailable. But damn it, he'd got to her availability another way, not sexually but compassionately. She'd pulled herself together now with a warm inner feeling. For the first time in over two years, she no longer had the fear that around every corner there was danger and the prospect of another dead body landing in front of her. That was why she enjoyed her hospital work so much; because there she was dealing with remedying and rebuilding near-misses and would-be corpses.

Pablito must have been a mashed up mess when they cut him out from below the vehicle that had run him down. They'd allegedly had to leave his leg behind.

Peter had been pretty silent about the extent of his own wounds but by reading the case history, she could tell he must have been knocking on death's door for a while.

In body refurbishment, she was protected from the fear of the finality of death. The security of her hand in Peter's had given her time to think… if she could believe in the lavender field and its occupants, then death might not be so painful and a new understanding of life might begin.

She was transfixed in a trance of thought when Peter returned and passed the refreshed drink down to her at floor level.

"Here, pop this under your bum, terrazzo can get very hard." He threw her a tapestry-covered bean bag. It was modern in its concept but disguised to be a part of his built environment, which she might well have expected. He threw another in front of one of the leather armchairs. She felt surprised, although she was loathe to admit it; he didn't want to pre-suppose close contact with her again. Maybe he'd had his time to reflect too and had assessed her to be some sort of liability. She hoped not.

Even though he was now sitting opposite her, there was still a closeness.

"Now, young lady. What question?"

He must know what question. He was surely playing for time. But she'd go along with it, it must be part of his mature plan.

"I think I asked if I'm going to the first lady in your life to escape your web and to leave Girasol without being bedded by you?"

It seemed a more difficult and pointless question now, less easy to put because she could feel the difference two sips of refreshed gin and tonic were making. Being inwardly relaxed, she was ready not just to imbibe the drink but all the security he was prepared to pour into her. He was either, as she had suggested, a superhuman God-sent figure, or a very cunning, not untypical male, expert at getting a young lady between the sheets. Or maybe, she hoped, he was simply Peter Martinez, an unusual but sincere, straight man.

"Oh God! I remember now. That made me think of Anna… then Mark… and then we sorted you out a bit. So. The question. I remember."

Cas laughed. "If you bloody well play poker, then I'll tell you straight it would be practical for me to take all of my clothes off now…"

It was the drink, surely it must have been, she thought. "… That's not what I meant… what I meant was you're so bloody clever at ducking and diving that I wouldn't trust you with a pack of cards. Now stretch yourself. So… the answer, and don't make out you don't remember what you said last time… because you've yet to answer… and I seriously doubt whether you ever will."

"Right… my sweet Cas. The answer is no… well, almost."

She screeched again. "There you go! I told you you'd wriggle out of it."

"No, seriously…" That usually meant Peter was about to launch into a long dissertation.

"Well, it'd better be a short explanation. I need to have a pee… so, as you were, seriously…"

"Seriously… Anna and I were the only ones to come here once the development was able to have fitted out bedrooms. It was very much a second matrimonial home outside London. Actually, as I've said, Anna didn't like the place. How many times have I said that before?"

Peter wondered now whether the gin was getting to him. He hadn't really had a proper drink since before his accident.

"Anyway, since the actual development and all through my marriage, I didn't truly have to share the place with anybody as Anna avoided coming out for one reason or another. It became a bit of a sanctuary, really… whenever I needed to get right away, chill out, as the youngsters would say…"

"Remember, Peter, I *am* a youngster, so be careful…"

"Well, anyway, it was mine."

"Yours, surely, with Tania here waiting for you."

"Good God, no! Tania's my uncle's girlfriend, although I'm not supposed to know.

"Anyway, the upshot is, apart from my daughter, the first lady invitee was a bit by accident. When Jan was bringing me to Barcelona, without me having any idea whatsoever what she and my mother were letting me in for, I accept I did cheat and I diverted here. Believe me, that was for my sake, not hers. I needed to breathe in the Girasol air. Jan has been the only other non-related female to be introduced to Girasol since its development. She took a sort of maternal pity on me and, if you want me to be honest, she did share my bed, but not in the way you'd expect. It was there, or to be precise, on the way there that she announced until I was fit, there would be no sex."

"Had you before that?"

"Good God, no! You're a little pryer. But no. I'd only known Jan for two days. She interviewed me as some complex PR stunt or other and I do have to say that, at the time, we got on enormously well, which was through some commercial compatibility... when I had my... well, let's say, accident, she was in early contact and, if I'm honest with myself, she provided some much needed support, and she was female. That's no reason, I now know, for believing you should then spend your lives together. You'll learn. Or, at least I hope you do. There are, let's say, three relationships between man and woman. Maybe there are even four, five or six, as some are maybe yet to be discovered."

"What are they, Chief?"

"You haven't called me that for a while."

"You haven't been chief in my life for a while."

"Not knowing what you mean, I'll give you my version. OK. Do you want it?"

"What, here on the floor?" she said, seductively. "Christ, Peter, did you spike the drinks. I'm sorry, that was a silly innuendo. 'It' so often means... well, 'it'. I promise I'll listen and take you seriously."

Peter was suddenly overcome by the thought of laying Cas back and giving her 'it'. From two metres away, and the most relaxed he had ever seen her, he was seriously certain his knee would cope with the challenge. But an inner strength told him 'not yet'. It would be a breach of trust. Yet there was some magnetic force dragging them together. It was the positive versus negative pole attraction. Where he was strong, she was emotionally weak; where he was mature, she was not; and that was a powerful draw. Magnetically they would fuse.

He wanted any further contact, physical or conversational, to be natural and rooted in sensitivity. Not, as it had been, a lustful need to satisfy horniness. He'd go for the option of being listened to and being taken seriously.

"Forgiven," he said.

Without further explanation, she eased her back away from the couch, swung her knees under her upper torso and crawled off her cushion across the two-metre divide. She put her arms around his neck, and said, "I love you so much when you're serious," pecked his lips and then made the return journey. Tucking her legs under her, she leant back on the couch and announced, "I'm all ears!"

"You're a hopeless case," he laughed. "Where the friggin' hell was I?"

"Now! We've given up that word. You were about to postulate on the three types of relationship between man and woman – as you perceive it, presumably. Which, incidentally, I already think is bullshit but tell me and I'll then tell you how right you are."

"OK then. Tell me where I'm wrong. One: there's the maternal relationship, mother and son. A best friend, mentor, hard-pushing, should you be using a deodorant effect! That's deep and can never be taken away, I suspect, unless a mother then puts herself between either of the other two relationships."

Suddenly Cas did take him seriously. She had seen that in Mark's mother, who had never accepted her. When he died, the mother could not see it was Mark who had the wild genes, presumably generated through the male line, and was therefore shocked and angered by her son's violent, maverick death, whereas a more dignified way of dying would have caused her to grieve more reverently. She had refused to acknowledge Cas at the funeral, although Cas's grief was far deeper than the mother's wounded pride.

"Carry on," Cas said encouragingly.

"OK. Then there's the loving relationship."

Cas prickled. Was he about to knock what she had just been drawn into saying? She was confused by this entry into her life. She didn't honestly know if she loved him or not. True, she had been cocooned in his company, by necessity, for almost two weeks. He fascinated her beyond belief. Was he expanding upon these theories to prove or disapprove a point? She found it hard to understand.

"What's that?" she asked, hoping it did not sound like a plea for him suddenly to announce his undying affection to her.

"When you're there, you begin to know it. There are sparks between the long periods of stability in the relationship. The sparks, or blips, are sort of Sunday school treats during the more conservative outings of term-time. There are cementations of joint interests, mutual advising on fashion, the building of a home, perhaps a family and the shared planning that's poured into that. The bouts of sharing overtake the moments of sparking. It's a bit of a religious thing, built on respect. Respect according to the vows taught to us by the church. It's the best relationship in the long term."

Cas couldn't help but be disappointed theirs was not yet 'long term'. She wasn't sure what music she hoped to share, even whether she could respect that, but what she did know was that with her body she would worship him. True, with her body, she'd enjoyed him… only once. That was not yet long term. She supposed it was nevertheless a true spark.

"Do you want to know my view about the third?"

"Well, you've covered the 'best' and that's confused me enough to return to reality and remind myself I'm still dying for a pee."

"Upstairs. Top of stairs, straight ahead. Are you alright to get up the stairs?" he said, as he sensed her stagger a little.

"Bloody cheek! What were you going to do… lend me your crutches?"

She tried her hardest not to waver. She bounced off the banister on the fourth tread, and the wall on the eighth, and the giggles as she entered the main bedroom echoed, and brought vibrancy to the house, sufficient to cause the ghosts of the sunflower heads in the surrounding fields to lift their chins in the November chill, and cause a chuckle and a smile that passed along each carefully planted line like the connection of fuses between a string of firecrackers at Chinese New Year, designed to both ward off demons, and to excite any onlooker.

Peter looked at his watch. It was 9pm. There was no way he should now drive, and Cas was irrational enough without two gins. They would stay, he resolved, albeit maybe between separate sheets. He lifted himself from the floor and walked to the phone.

Tania answered at the other end.

"Hi." He never referred to himself as being the caller. He couldn't bring himself to say, "Hi. It's Mr Peter here." Or, "Hi, it's me." He always said, "Hi, I'm arriving tomorrow. Could you air the place?" Or similar.

Sadly, as hard as Tania might wish, it was never, "Hi, it's Peter. I'll be there at nine. Get yourself into something to please me." Tania would have been ready. So many times she had longed for it. So many times it had not transpired.

"Hi, Mr Peter."

"Tania. Could you deliver up a couple of meals?"

Once again, it was not going to be the dreamed of demand, but the request for food was quite understandable.

"Sure, what would you like the chef to prepare?"

"Parma ham and melon."

"For one?"

"No. Two."

Her back prickled.

"Then sole with a green salad for one. Cooked anyway the chef can prepare and keep hot while we eat the melon – that's just the sole, we'll have the salad cold," he said, with a chuckle at his own originality. "And a rare fillet steak, again with a green salad. Just a pot of coffee… oh and some devastatingly bad for you chocolates."

"Liqueurs?"

"No, thank you. Oh, by the way, do either you or your daughter or, in fact, anybody, have a pair of ladies' walking boots or sports shoes, about size 38?"

"Is it for the young lady?" Tania questioned, without a clue as to what the shoes might have to do with what she presumed was their intended wild night ahead.

"Yes it is," Peter said in his usual commanding manner. "Please let me know what you can fix. Let the food come up as soon as it can."

He heard a loo flush and a good five minutes passed before he heard footsteps on the top landing. Cas re-appeared, all her damaged make-up repaired again. Although there was not, to his knowledge, an iron on the upper floor, it looked as though she had pressed her blouse and skirt. She'd piled her hair up, such as that was possible, and clipped it back with what looked like a turtle shell comb, though knowing her views on conservation and non-intervention with nature, it was bound to be a plastic look-alike.

She was surprised to see Peter in the kitchen, scurrying around in the cupboards, all of which he had designed, locating plates and cutlery.

"So what's afoot?" she said. "I've been upstairs, directed myself as instructed into what I've now seen is 'your bedroom', and made the best use I could of your bathroom. While I was freshening up, I've been thinking that I can't fit into your life as the maternal influence, or even yet as the matrimonial influence. So I expected to find you standing on a soap box to explain how, and why, I'm unlikely to fit in to the rest of your bullshit."

"*You* are terrific!" Peter announced. "Absolutely great. Come here."

She felt daft enough to do as she was told.

"It's my turn," he said, and leant forward and pecked her lips. "I love you so much when you're serious."

She was amazed he'd taken the trouble to remember her own words… and reversed them onto her.

"So listen," he said, "I'm a bit pissed, you're a bit pissed. I've ordered some food for us. We're not going back to Barcelona this evening. You get the bed. I get the couch, or the spare room if it's made up. OK? The third type of relationship gets explained over dinner.

"Oh, by the way, you look lovely, all refreshed. You make me feel grubby. I'll slip up and try and match your example. If somebody from the hotel comes, the first course can be left out. The second should be in heat containers. If you could just stick both those in the oven, it's on and warming. The sweets need to go in the fridge. Pour yourself another gin but I'm chilling you a Montrachet all for yourself, and don't dare touch the bottle of red next to the fire. That's got a reserved sticker on it."

It was not that she was speechless. She was overawed by his organisational ability, his total containment whatever the situation, or so it seemed. He noticed the sort of vacant stare she was giving him as he reached the foot of the stairs. He turned back and walked towards her.

"Is everything alright?" he asked, with a worried look on his face. "Is it that you really did want to get back? Oh come on, put a fella out of his misery. What have I done wrong?"

"That's the trouble. You've done everything right. I just cannot believe the depth of your capabilities. You've completely taken me over and I'm just not used to that. I could get very used to it. But in most other dates with blokes, I've usually had to cook, or prepare a picnic… sort out the tickets for a show… make sure the car has enough fuel. With you… well, it's a sort of luxury break."

"Thank God for that. I really thought I'd dropped a clanger. I've ordered you food. Is that alright?"

"Of course."

"Trust me on that."

"Trust you on everything."

"That's great. What I'll do now is to go and strip down the spare room bed. That'll give me the option of my own bed, the spare room, or the couch. I've then got an evens chance of aching all over my body tomorrow from a night on the couch, or any of the other locations I'm not used to, so that any onlooker might think we shared a hectic sack together, or the alternative of looking well rested."

She was hardly listening to his ramblings. She'd been thinking further.

"Do you have a picture of your father?"

"Yes, I do. Why?"

"May I see it?"

He had to think where it was. It was the one of Paco and Maria on their wedding day. It was in his study. He fetched it.

"This is my father."

"God, he's handsome!"

She gazed at the photo for a moment, then addressed it, much to Peter's puzzlement. "Mr Martinez. Sir, I know you're Peter's father. The eyes, the skin, the strong bone structure, the character about the head, the hair. Certainly, there's no need for any DNA screening. So I just don't want you to take this personally. But your son is a bastard in terms of being a cheat, a sod and, as we would say in South Africa, a sneak of a snake. So don't take offence please. Oh, thanks. You don't mind? You agree, even? Now you're the one in the family I should be with."

She turned to Peter, who had been watching with total fascination. Here was a girl who, just a few hours ago, had looked at death with horror. Now this same young lady was making up her own ground rules about communicating with a being in the world beyond. Peter wouldn't interfere or take issue with that.

"OK, Peter. Your father doesn't mind me calling you a bastard. I actually think he agrees you've got all those hallmarks, all the traits of being a true son-of-a-bitch – though in saying that, I don't want to be offensive to your mother, so he's cleared the way for me to say that to you, taking no personal offence himself. So, back to the odds. The odds are, you'll be sleeping in your main bedroom in your own bed."

"… And you?" he enquired.

"The couch. Then when I'm all full of aches and pains tomorrow, any onlooker will know."

"Christ, what will they know?"

"They'll know you're a selfish, scheming bastard who lures young women into your web when they really wanted to get back to base the night before, and that I'm a nice Bok who just didn't fall for it."

"I've got an idea."

"I thought you would have. What's that?"

"I go upstairs, which I now do, and strip both the spare room bed and mine. And make them both uninhabitable."

"Where does that get you?"

"Both on the couch in front of the cinders."

"Piss off upstairs, you bastard!" she said in true frank antipodean style.

He turned to climb the stairs.

"Stop!" she commanded. He froze. There was real authority in her voice. "Come here, please."

He wasn't sure about this, so he thought best to not question, just obey.

"No, right here," she stipulated.

He stood, now almost touching her in case she was about to faint. She raised herself up on her toes and gently kissed his lips.

"Now, don't you ever dare leave me alone for even a minute without a proper goodbye. Now you can get upstairs and do whatever damage you like. I'll fix a room at the hotel when the food gets delivered."

She spent her unaccompanied time walking round the house. Picking up bits and pieces of interest, imagining what their significance was to Peter's life, and then putting them back almost exactly, she hoped, where she had found them. Peter was bound to have laid his personal memorabilia out according to a master plan. She looked into his chosen paintings long and hard. There were some signed 'un abrazzo Jaimé'. Wasn't Jaimé a male name? There was no way Peter was gay, or ever had been. She'd have to ask what the significance of that was.

She was just picking up a framed photograph of Peter and another good-looking man a few years his junior, taken on a golf course, when the chimes from the door-bell rang. They made her jump. She replaced the photograph and went to answer it. Tania was standing there, carrying a large tray supported on what appeared to be a long, slim box, which might have contained flowers. She had a paper bag slotted uncomfortably under one arm.

"Hi!" Cas greeted her, "Peter's put you to a lot of trouble, we could just as easily have come down to the hotel, I'm sure."

"Oh, he likes to eat here. I think he gets anti-social at Girasol… a bit of a hermit, really."

Tania put the box and tray down on one of the kitchen units. "This one," indicating the box, "needs to be kept warm. This one is a fridge job." She took the paper bag from under her left armpit. "Mr Peter asked if I had any walking shoes that would fit you. I hope these will do."

"Fit me?" Cas said in amazement. "He's not going to make me walk back to Barcelona, surely?"

Tania still had the problem of needing the world to know that she was the only one who could read Peter's thoughts, his plans, and that it was her God-given ability. She used it to the full especially when there were women around who kept Peter from making his future a permanent one in Girasol, where she could attend to his needs and continue to read his thoughts.

"He's probably planning to take you to the cutting."

Cas didn't know what she meant by 'the cutting'. It was not an expression she was used to in South Africa. It could have been some winter tradition of cutting down trees to provide wood during the colder months.

"What's 'the cutting'? Sorry, I don't understand."

"Where he was shot. In the woods. You know, at a clearing."

Cas understood what a clearing was. It was often where game met up to meet their mates before returning back into the jungle to start the breeding process. She hoped that wasn't Peter's intention.

"Why do you think he'd want to show me that?"

"Oh! Less show you. More take you with him for support. He won't want to go there but, knowing Mr Peter, sooner or later he'll make himself go back to relieve the pain."

"Why would he do that? Surely it's still fresh enough in his memory."

"Not our Mr Peter. He won't want the hurt and the hate to linger around. He'll go there and get the haunting out of his memory for all time."

Cas could see the logic in that. In over two years, she had not been back to the dunes. She'd almost made her mind up never to return. The memories would be too traumatic. She wondered, though, if it might in fact help. It might not all be as bad as it had seemed. Mark wouldn't be there. She now knew where he was. There'd be no bike, that went to the breakers' yard days after the accident. She doubted Mark's friends would be there either. They'd probably all grown up now and settled down with families. If Tania was right, she would see for herself how a revisit might work.

"What size are they?"

"About 38. Mr Peter guessed that was your size. And Mr Peter made a very accurate assessment, spot on, as usual."

Touché, Cas thought. Each sensed the other was bristling

"Mr Peter's freshening up upstairs. I'm sure he'd want me to thank you for all the effort you've made on our behalf."

"No more than is deserving of the man who owns the place, and all who work here," Tania said, as if turning the clock back to a century before.

Cas couldn't resist trying to influence Tania with a contemporary alternative. "Just because you own something, a business, say, doesn't mean the workers are also your property. That idea went out of fashion with the advent of European socialism or communism. So Mr Peter wouldn't want you, or chef, or anybody else, to think that he owns you."

Tania's comments, Cas thought, might have been more appropriate in South Africa, where one would purposefully employ colour and the prejudice that went with it, and in that sense one did think in terms of ownership.

Tania didn't like having been put in her place by Cas, and showed it. She bade her farewell. "I hope you sleep alright. Has Mr Peter explained about our night visitors?"

Cas wasn't good in the dark. That was a leftover from her father economising on the expensive commodity of African electricity.

"Night visitors?" she enquired.

"Yes. Well, you make sure he tells you, we have screech owls here that swoop seemingly all night. Bats, of course, and the light night breezes from off the sea turn the pantiles into veritable Pan's pipes. He'll explain. Have a pleasant stay."

If Mr Peter was constantly going to put her allegiance on trial with the current and recent female intruders to Girasol, she was blowed if she would give them an easy ride. Besides, they wouldn't last the course, as she had. She knew Mr Peter still inwardly battled with his desire for her. Her time would surely come. That was Tania's fervent belief.

"Hey, I heard voices."

Peter re-appeared. He'd found one of his favourite relax mode Lacoste polo shirts. The light blue of that combined with the Boss denim jeans took years off him. He veritably leapt down the stairs with hardly a hint of the limp he'd had on his last visit.

"Hey, babe," he said. "This knee of mine really feels good. Thank you for that."

She was so pleased. More than any compliment about her looking refreshed, or the semi-serious ritual about who might sleep where, words of praise for her professional skill were worth volumes of chocolates, or tons of sprays of flowers to her... a simple, "Thank you for making me better," was exactly what she aspired to.

"I shouldn't say it, because you've got a big head already but, to be fair, you've been a perfect patient."

"Thank you."

"So... food," she said. "I want to know what you see me as eating."

"First the wine. The lady will enjoy a chilled Montrachet, methinks."

"Yes. The lady believes she would."

"And to accompany the Montrachet, the Lord believes his Lady would enjoy Ogen melon..."

"Shit, my Lord, wouldn't I!"

"But accompanied by..." as he said that, he revealed a plate of Parma ham.

"Oh gosh, my Lord, nothing could be finer." She giggled at the game play.

They sat opposite each other at the circular table in the living room. The log fire had raised the temperature to a comfortable level.

"Oh, one thing more," Peter said as he pulled the cork from the bottle of white wine, then moved across to the window and drew the wild cotton light drapes to shut out the night. He then went to the back patio doors and repeated the formality.

When he returned, he stood to Cas's left. "Would the lady like to sample the wine?"

"Please kind Sir, do."

He poured a little. She instinctively smelt the taster of wine, as she had seen her father do. Then sampled a little.

"It's excellent," she said. "But why the drapes?"

"Well, then I can freely kiss your lips to taste the grape for myself, just in case you're being a polite house guest and the wine's really crap."

"Excuses," she said. "But really, why the drapes?"

"Well… Tania. She doesn't have a lot in her life to amuse her. She'll be out there somewhere trying to share our evening. It would be the same if I was here by myself. She's a bit of a witch, really. With a Peeping Tom trait."

"A witch?"

"Well… let's start the food," he said, sitting down, having filled both their glasses with the white wine. "Tania… she's a gypsy in gypsy's clothing but yearns to be westernised. She's got gypsy habits too, she'll sit out there on the hill and replicate hoot owls, and shrieks of suffering animals… just like she and her family did in the south when she was a child.

"But look, she's OK. She's loyal, and although you don't know about it, good for my uncle and quite a few other men of the more desperate type. But she's a mischievous gypsy deep down."

"Has she ever been good for you?"

"Good God, no! She offered years ago when I was quite a young man. But fortunately, the moment she offered, even at that age, something inside me was repelled. That's how it was, has been and ever will be. Now… how's the melon and ham?"

"The melon was a bit like you and, as it happens, the ham too."

Surprised, Peter said, "How come?"

"The melon with the lemon was a little tart and the ham as smooth as satin."

"You really do have a pleasantly unpleasant way with words."

"Well, you shouldn't be telling me about another woman who's offered you favours."

"Are you back to yesterday?"

"No. Back to now. But not that easily. Impress me, my Lord, with my next dish."

He stood up and collected the plates. She made an effort to stand and help, but he put himself behind her, placed a hand on each shoulder and pushed her down into her chair. Her right hand moved to hold his left on her shoulder.

"Kind Sir, do let me help."

"Nope. Sit and enjoy the fuss."

He broke free, collecting the plates and taking them into the open-plan kitchen. He went to the left-hand unit drawer and found his oven gloves, took the hot box out and opened one end. Only he could see the word 'pescado'. He had pre-heated some plates and onto one of those, he slid out the sole, to which chef had thoughtfully added new potatoes and mange tout. The salad Peter had ordered was covered in that newfangled cling film stuff. He delivered the course to his anxiously waiting guest.

"I really hope it's right. I guessed you might be vegetarian, but with flexibility where fish is concerned."

Cas stood up as he put the plate in front of her.

"Peter, I really don't know what wicked trick you're playing on me but, so far, you've read exactly the food I would have chosen if a full à la carte menu been put in front of me. Brilliant."

She leant forward with eyes closed and lips pouting. He took the opportunity.

"Oh, that was for Tania, by the way."

"Frig Tania."

"That's what you asked earlier. Had I ever. No!"

They both roared with laughter.

Peter set out his steak and salad, leant across the table and replenished Cas's glass with Montrachet. "Oh, this is now yours. I'm into red."

"That's quite another thing. I'm not keen on red, so I'm happy."

They ate in silence, until Peter asked, "Should I have put on some music?"

"No. We'll make our own. Besides, we don't know what we each like. Beatles? Classics? Carpenters? What would you guess?"

"No, none of those. Tell you what, after dinner, I'll pick one track. Just one, and you tell me whether it's right. Trust me?"

"Trust you? Trust you more. Yes, of course, I trust you."

After the meal, Cas insisted she clear the dishes with him.

"Peter, that was perhaps the finest banquet I've ever been entertained with."

"Thank you, miss! Now… coffee?"

"No, I wouldn't sleep."

"I'll do coffee, then."

She turned to Paco's photograph. "Please, Sir, convince him. Tell him I do intend to sleep."

"Then you'll need a cremat, my father suggests."

"A cremat? What's that?"

"It's a Catalan liqueur concoction. I'm not going to tell you the recipe, it's secret, but you chuck a couple of logs on the fire and I'll bring you a cremat. Do you set fire to Christmas pudding in South Africa?"

"No."

"Well, you'll have to believe me, we'll need the lights down for full effect."

She suddenly changed gear. "Peter. Music. Just for fun. Can you play me what you thought I'd like."

"I will, but I'm not confident. I could be a generation out."

"Go on. Try. It'll be fun."

He fumbled around in a tray of cassettes.

"OK, no looking. As I come in with the cremat, you hit that button. If it's wrong, I'm sorry now… by the way, still no looking."

He fed the cassette into the player and selected the track. He noticed Cas had taken up her pre-dinner location on her bean bag, staring into the embers.

"About now," he commanded as he left the kitchen area bearing a stainless steel dish awash with the blue flame of the ignited liquor.

Four steps towards her, he directed in full stage managed terms. "Sound… now please." There was a momentary pause.

Charles Trenet entered their world.

"*La Mer…*" his first sung words echoed around the room.

Even in the dimmed lighting, and despite the reflection of the blue flames in her face, Cas was ashen. She started to shake as though possessed by some unwanted external influence. She held out both her arms to Peter, despite his handicap of still carrying the cremat. He placed it in front of the fire, still with flames dancing on its surface. Her extended arms were in need. He knelt down, allowing her to engulf him. Her body trembled for a while. Gradually it calmed. He held her firmly. Quite what he'd stimulated he did not know. It was unintentional.

The track stopped. He still could not see her face.

"Peter," she said nervously, "I had, I thought, so much in common with Mark. I loved that song, I suppose particularly the Bobby Darin version. Mark used to joke and tell me to get a life and listen to the Stones and a few other contemporaries. How the fuck do you know all this?"

"It's an accident. It really is. I'm sorry. It wasn't meant to be like that. I thought you'd say to me that I was a square, old-fashioned romantic."

"Why on earth would I say that?"

"Anna did, anyway."

They clutched each other in an act of desperate need.

"I've decided," Cas said with great determination, sufficient to concern Peter.

"What?"

"We're not sharing."

"Oh."

"Neither of us gets the couch."

"Oh."

"It's here, now… and then we'll see."

"Should we have the cremat?"
"What a friggin' good idea. Can you replay the music?"
"Over and over again, of course, if madam wishes."

Chapter 6

Cas was ordinarily an early waker. Things, events in Girasol, seemed to relate to threes. Her senses this morning focused on three important things. Where was she? Was he asleep? And, how quickly could she get to the loo?

They had settled eventually into Peter's bed without further ado. She thought he had carried her up the staircase because she remembered expressing concern about his knee and him saying that it was a bit late for that after she'd led him astray on the floor.

She got to the loo in time, leaving Peter asleep. She had a bit of a hangover but bits and pieces were coming back into her mind. They had downed their cremats, which filled their insides with warmth. The one particular thing she did recollect was the contretemps about their positioning. It wasn't a row, as such, but it was a firm discussion she had lost. Always, she preferred to be the dominant partner, so it was not uncharacteristic for her to have pulled Peter across the bean bags and knelt above him. She remembered clearly him shaking his head before he pulled her down and rolled her onto her back.

She hadn't liked that. Peter, though, had seemed intent on knowing best, and his sheer power enabled him to win. As he took over her body, she'd looked up into his face. It was clean, it was whole, intact; it had a masculine beauty about it. Gradually, with gentle and then frantic kisses, her mind focused on the total pleasure of the situation.

With Mark, she had always had to play the superior role and since Mark, on the few occasions sex had raised its head with others, she had continued in that. She got to know that at a certain point in lovemaking, it would always be Mark's distorted face that would be grimacing up at her, not her current partner's.

That first night with Peter had been no different. He'd called it rape, in fun, but she believed it was the presence of Mark's ghost that caused her to be that way. In her mind, Mark's eyes, bright with anger, were always scrutinising her, questioning whether she'd been satisfied, haunting her. The aftermath always left her feeling sick, knowing that Mark had had the pleasure of controlling any new excitement she occasionally sampled with a make-do replacement.

With Peter just those few hours before, she had experienced none of that. Like a slide show, his face turned from kindness to a loving smile as she reacted to his pace or rhythm. Charles Trenet made her so happy, yet the lyrics were sad. She remembered being honest with Peter as they lay shattered and satisfied, gazing into the dying embers.

"I didn't see Mark once," she confessed.

"Then life is beginning. When you do see him, and you will, you'll be looking down. Force yourself to look over your shoulder and look up. That's where he is. He's all patched up and pleased to look down on you."

Through the haze of her inward explosion, that's what she remembered. She was now a totally relaxed being again.

She lifted her aching legs from the loo and crossed to the vanity unit. God, she looked awful. She couldn't have him seeing her like that, so she did some instant repair work with cold water and a little of a cream she found on the shelf. She'd have to ask him about that, she thought. She was wearing his Lacoste shirt, but appeared to have lost her pants somewhere over dinner.

Opening a louvred door, she found herself looking into an airing cupboard. From a pile of Peter's jockey shorts, she chose a white pair and was quite pleased with the fit and her reflection in the mirror.

When she crept back into the bedroom, Peter was still sound asleep. She lay on her side, contemplating his relaxed face. Her stomach churned. This was exactly the position, looking down into a face that, hours before, would have taken her back to the dunes. But her new-found mentor seemed to have effected a cure. Perhaps she really could get on with her life.

She didn't know for how long she had been looking down at Peter. Her arm, where she had rested her head on her right elbow, had gone to sleep.

Peter opened one eye. "Buenos dias."

"Buenos dias, guapo," she replied. Well, he did look handsome.

"Shit. You weather well. This isn't the little lady who was a bit squiffy last night."

"I wasn't too squiffy to remember enough to thank you this morning." She leant down and kissed him. "Thank you, thank you, thank you." She wriggled and moved over on top of him, laid her head next to his.

His hand moved onto her buttock. He suddenly realised he was not feeling the silk of the previous night. It seemed a coarser cotton material.

"What have you got on?" he asked.

"I think they're some fella's pants to replace the ones he stole off me last night."

He lifted the duvet and made a tunnel he could look down to see what she was wearing. "Hey! They're mine." He pushed his hands into the waistband and started to force them down.

Cas shot her hands down behind her and grabbed the elasticated waist band, pulling hard upwards against the force of gravity, in a vain attempt to show resistance.

Tania was furious. "That's his bed and mine," she whispered bitterly. Pulling drapes had been far from Peter's mind the night before.

Tania walked her German Shepherd almost the same route each morning. She was, by tradition, both an early riser and a lover of fresh air. Some mornings, when she felt she needed it, she would jog up the hillside but more frequently she would walk, as she had today. Either way, she would always stop and look down, surveying Peter's house. In the summer, she would look across the sea of sunflowers and then turn full circle to the ocean beyond. At this time of year, the carpet of colour had been rolled back and there was less to distract her eye.

True, whenever Peter was in residence, she would carry the mini pair of binoculars her daughter had bought her. Usually she was happy to focus on the man himself or, with luck, the focal figure getting dressed. She rarely saw his naked body, unless she caught him off-balance, typically in the seclusion of his patio garden, leading to the water's edge, when he felt the need to ask the sun to warm and bronze his body. She had never before witnessed actual 'activity' with a female.

Yes. OK. She knew what went on when Anna was with him. But their body language never gave the vibes of pent-up emotion being released. She sensed her man had been too crocked to chase the English bitch around the bed just those few weeks ago. She'd got her own back anyway, courtesy of Messrs Coca Cola and their delivery service.

Often she had smiled about the way she had enticed their man to repair the electrics. She hadn't quite realised how much she had needed the electrics of her own body clock to be released until he had stupidly out-performed his needs. Typically male, she had thought after the event. But thank God for frustrated chefs used to working on meat as a daily routine and over-fertile van delivery/sales people.

This scene, though, was just not palatable.

Squabbling under a duvet with a much younger blonde bimbo was completely out of order. Tania gave herself four minutes to jog down the hill, although she had walking gear on. Perhaps then a minute to regain her breath and composure. The way they were behaving, they would be at each other for more than five minutes, then fall back to sleep until mid-morning and then demand hotel services. So she had time to rescue the situation.

She set off back down the incline at a steady pace. Her loyal dog ran ahead, frequently slowing, allowing her to catch up, jumping up against her hips as though to encourage her to run on, then turning and charging down the hill, barking occasionally, only to smell and desensitise the odd pee from a previous dog at the base of a pine tree.

She stopped two houses away from Peter's. Vanity forced her to smooth back her black gypsy hair into the pony tail she sometimes now adopted, in the hope that it made her look younger than her Spanish tourist's doll bun, which was more natural to her. She tucked the shirt into her trousers below the light fleece she had put on to rebuff the early morning November chill. She was no longer out of breath.

"You, my dear Peter, are, without a doubt, and in deference to your lovely father, who would be ashamed of you too, a menace. You would rip off a girl's veil on her wedding night to expose the look of terror or satisfaction on the young bride's face. Likewise, you threaten to rob me of the borrowed protection to my dignity, even though the pants do, I suppose, belong to you."

Peter released all the power he had previously applied to divesting Cas of her – or rather his – underwear. He lay back and laughed like he couldn't remember laughing for years.

"My darling Bok. They're *my* friggin' pants and I want them back – even if they won't be wearable ever again. You, my sweet, are a drama queen extraordinaire. What's with the bride's veil? There aren't many girls these days who need that sort of coverage to disguise their emotions."

He stopped for a second, unsure if he'd heard the chimes of the doorbell.

"Now listen here you... I'm not a drama queen..." Cas retorted.

Peter held his forefinger to his mouth.

"What?" she said.

The chimes sounded again.

"There's someone at the door," he indicated.

"Oh yes. So you haven't got the energy to take advantage of me in your torn pants, or is it the desire that's missing?" She giggled and lay prostrate on top of him.

"No. Cas. Seriously. There's somebody at the door."

"If it's the King of Spain, does it matter?"

The chimes were insistent. This time Cas heard them too.

"Shit!" she said, "it's the police. They know I'm underage and on drugs. You must send them away."

Momentarily, and he wished he hadn't reacted, Peter said, "You're not, are you?"

"What, underage or on drugs?"

"Either," he said, realising the stupidity of the trap she had set him.

"OK," Cas said. "I agree. Go and check who it is."

Peter threw back the duvet as the chimes sounded again. She started to giggle. He had not got a stitch of clothing on. She rolled over in the uncovered bed they had shared all night.

"So what do you bid for a Lacoste polo shirt, a little crumpled and sweaty, and a ripped pair of white boxer shorts?"

"Friggin' nothing. I'll go as I am."

Cas went into serious vein. "Stay there, don't move. You've got a robe in the bathroom."

She nipped out of bed and scurried into the bathroom. Two doorbell chimes later, she was back wearing a terry-towelling blue bath robe and holding out, at full arm's length, the Lacoste polo and shredded boxer shorts.

"Here, I agree. They're yours. You can have them back."

If only, she thought, she could have snapped a photograph of the look on his face. It would have swept the awards in any amateur photography competition where the subject matter was 'shock'.

"Look, you mischievous girl, I can't open the door in these."

"Well, I really don't see why not. You seemed happy enough to feast your eyes on them when I was wearing them. I don't see the great difference. Look, if you're going to be all shy about it, I'll go to the door, but if whoever it is doesn't speak English or Afrikaans, you'll have to come down. So get ready to wrap the duvet around you, or something."

He waited until after she'd left before he burst out laughing. She'd totally upstaged him with a masterpiece of situation comedy. Hell, she seemed so much fun. More so, perhaps – though it could have been his imagination – since she'd had her 'exorcism'. Who'd know?

He could hear Tania's voice. Tania. What the hell was she doing here? She normally knew not to disturb him. It might be some emergency or other. He went to the wardrobe and hanging there was a tracksuit. He put it on, not bothering with pants, and nonchalantly ambled downstairs.

"Oh, buenos dias, Tania. What's the problem?"

Cas turned to him, her back to Tania, raising an eyebrow as she spoke. "Apparently the phone's gone crocked. Tania was trying to get a breakfast order in before the morning chef gets off. It's ten o'clock."

"God! Is it really? Let me just check the phone. Do you want to step in, Tania?"

She took the option. The curtains were still drawn. Her stomach heaved as she saw the ashes in the fireplace. Then the bean bags, clearly laid head to toe. She knew what had been their purpose. There were two liqueur glasses in the hearth, one lying on its side as though thrown or placed there in a hurry. The cremat pan was also near the fender. There was the skirt she remembered Cas wearing the day before, thrown onto one couch, and a black unpadded bra hanging over the back of one of the dining chairs. It had every sign of having been flung into the distance with carefree abandon. Tania felt quite sick as she choked back her rage.

"Looks like a cyclone went through here last night, Mr Peter."

Peter felt embarrassed.

Cas answered. "Not a cyclone at all, if my memory serves me right. There was some ingredient the chef put into that superb meal which, well…" she went into exaggerated coy mode, bending one leg across the other and dropping her hip to add emphasis, "… well… made us relax."

Tania never boasted about when she had screwed, and disliked Cas even more for baiting her. Peter, she thought, looked totally as though he wanted to be out of this equation. Tania didn't think it was fair of him to allow her to see the graphic outline of his manly bits and pieces, so tautly placed in his tracksuit bottoms.

"Look, I feel dreadful now…" she started to explain, as her eyes picked up on a little pair of black knickers hanging precariously on the parchment shade of one of the table lamps. "… I doubt if you'll need breakfast anyway. I'll leave."

"No!" Peter said firmly. "Good idea. Cas, what would you like?"

Cas had got the female vibes. Tania was jealous. She obviously had a thing about Peter and objected to Cas's intervention. It was pretty clear Peter had never romped with Tania. If he had, Cas was sure it would have shown. She decided to play the dominant role.

"Aren't we going back to bed?"

That did embarrass Peter. "No. Breakfast, and then we'll go for a lovely walk. Did you find any shoes?" he asked Tania.

"Yes, I brought them last night before the hurricane hit."

Cas nodded. "Yes, it was very kind of you. I only bought sandals. I didn't know we might go rough walking. Thank you very much."

"So, breakfast!" Peter said. "Croissants. Fruit. Loads of coffee. Cas, anything special?"

"Any chance of a boiled egg? Four minutes with toast."

Peter suddenly glimpsed the bulge in Tania's fleece as she felt around for a pen and any piece of paper. The article pulling the jacket out of shape was clearly heavy. But what?

"What size fleece do you take, Tania?"

"This one's a small medium."

"Here, slip it off. Cas, pop in the cloakroom and try it on. Then if I know your size, I can get up to the golf club and buy you one. I'm sure I didn't mention walking and there's a chill in the air. So you will need something."

Tania was just about forced into doing as he said. If she hadn't, he would have ripped the garment off her back. He so wanted to discover what was weighing down her tog.

"Gosh! What have you got in here?" Peter said, his hand diving into the pocket before Tania could prevent it. He fished out the pair of binoculars.

"You been bird-watching?" he asked.

"Yes. Gulls, actually. They're very active at this time of the year."

Bloody aren't, he thought as he remembered he and Cas were bound not to have thought to draw the drapes in the bedroom. With the power of these binoculars, Tania probably would have been able to read the label in the back of the pants they had been fighting over.

Peter walked across and picked up the phone. The ringing tone was intact. He dialled the number of the hotel. The morning waiter answered.

"Hi. It's Peter Martinez here."

"Buenos dias."

"What time does breakfast chef finish today, Manuel?"

"I'll ask, Sir."

Tania looked uncomfortable.

Manuel was back in a few seconds. "She works through lunch today. She's relieving for Juan."

"Muchas gracias," Peter said, and put the phone down. His mood had changed. "Try the fleece for size. In the cloakroom, please," he instructed Cas.

She knew that voice already. It was not one to play around with. Playschool for the day was about to end, she felt.

As the cloakroom door shut, Peter turned on Tania like a possessed boxer who has heard the bell to start the first round in a grudge re-match. He wagged his finger in her face. "Now listen! You are a peeping Tom. That's a disease. You want to get to know the hotel schedules a bit better and then you wouldn't have needed to disturb my peace... and it *is* my peace. I could have phoned for breakfast in the normal way. I'm very disappointed in you."

Silence, Tania thought, was her only defence.

Cas re-appeared. "Fine on size. Thank you."

Tania looked like a scolded cocker spaniel. Cas felt a little sorry for her.

"Am I interrupting?" was the only knife she had available to cut through the frosty atmosphere radiating from around Peter and Tania.

"No," Peter responded. "Your timing's very apt. We'd got to the point when Tania had indicated she owed you an apology."

Tania looked deeply uncomfortable. She had no idea what to say or do. Her instinct told her it was best to cry. So she did.

Cas crossed the room and took her into her arms and held her shaking body. "Now, come on. It can't be as bad as that. What do you need to apologise for?" She thought she knew the answer.

"I was out walking..." Tania said between sobs. "And I was watching the gulls out at sea and Mr Peter's house came into view. I focused on it just for a minute and couldn't help seeing into the bedroom. I'm sorry... I watched you... well... you know what I would have seen."

Cas stepped back. "But you bloody well don't!" Her mood had changed. Tania had suddenly lost a potential friend.

"Now listen. If you peep, get your facts right. Yes, of course I know what we were doing. We were having a friendly fight over a pair of Peter's boxer shorts..."

Tania then dropped the clanger of all clangers. She was actually trying to be helpful but hadn't made allowance for the fact that her brain was not functioning normally. She was like a cornered animal, with not much chance of escaping the inevitable.

"Miss. If you're looking for your knickers, they're on the table lampshade."

Peter and Cas looked across as one to where Tania was looking. Peter reacted.

"Get out! Get back to the hotel. The aggravating thing to me is that it's not me who employs you. But what I can decide is that I don't want you to have anything more to do with my house. We'll talk about this again when I'm less cross. Go back now."

Tania turned, then, remembering her fleece, returned and took it back from Cas. With her hand on the front door handle, she looked back to both of them.

"I am really sorry. There's a reason for all this but I'll let it wait till our discussion," were the last comments she directed towards Peter.

She left a sort of vacuum behind her. Cas attempted to break the ice again. She moved towards Peter and put her hands behind his head.

"I'm pleased I lost my knickers. I wish you hadn't thrown them across the room, though, and I'm sorry I stole your pants," she giggled impishly.

Peter's sternness slowly evaporated and turned into a smile. "A girl should hold on to her knickers, and a fellow his underpants. That's the moral in this sad tale." He moved back and held her hand. "I'm sorry about Tania. She's always been trouble in my life, and her whole family too. Her cousins, her father, sister. Listen, I'll tell you all about it… let's shower, and find some suitable underwear. We'll have breakfast and then I'll take you for a walk." He kissed her lightly.

"Peter. You'll have to make allowances for Tania, as I'm afraid I'd ask you to for me as well."

"Allowances? Not financial allowances?"

She laughed. "No, you clot! We've both got the same ailment."

"You're ill?" He was now coming out of this situation as the confused one.

"No, you berk! You beautiful berk. We're both in love with you… oh, and Jan too, and I don't doubt many others."

"Tania, in love with me? Oh, come on!"

"No, my darling, you come on."

"Oh, and you… ? You say!"

"Yup. I'm sorry. But I promise I won't be a burden."

"Burden?"

"Peter, do you realise you're just standing there repeating every word I say, and it's annoying."

"If I repeat what you said and say I love you too, does that annoy you?"

"Oh, Peter, darling…" She stepped forward and put her hands round the back of his neck again. "You don't have to say that."

"I'm not saying it because I have to."

"Well, if you mean it, then it would be comforting if you reassured me that you won't be a burden to me."

"What?" he said, with astonishment.

She laughed. The laugh turned into a smile. "Come on, Peter the realist. Think back to yesterday. You got as far as lesson two in what love is about. You were meant to lecture me over dinner on the third. You're very clever, I do have to say. Instead of the lecture, you taught me in the practical way. Let's call it love. That's nice. But the heat and the explosiveness between us isn't the type to last at that pace 'till death do us part'. Another fortnight of that and we'd both be dead anyway.

"Look, Peter, we've been brought together by extreme circumstances. I'm meant to be healing you but it's transpiring that you're the one doing the healing. You've transformed my life… again… that much will stay between us forever. I know that. You might not.

"There's enormous chemistry between us but in terms of fluttering hearts and church bells ringing, we have to face facts. We're suffering from mutual infatuation. OK, it may last a lifetime, if our time together is rationed, but as for sharing a toothbrush and me putting up with you leaving the toilet seat up for life, I'm too cynical to believe it would last… as much as I'd like to be wrong. So yes, I do love you… of the infatuation kind."

"You're a wise and beautiful young lady. If, as you call it, I'd 'lectured' you, it actually would have been about exactly that third type of love, infatuation. We've been through a lot since we started on that subject and my mind's buzzing with the excitement and the fun of what we've shared together."

"That's lovely to hear. Me too. But come on, statistically that's hardly going to last, day-on-day, night-on-night… and even that depends on your knee mending up again… you're limping, do you know that?"

"Bugger that. You're walking funny, too."

"Peter, my love, I don't have anything on under this robe. Any girl walks funny, given those circumstances. But now that Tania's found my knickers for us, we'll be able to get comfortable again."

That made Peter laugh again. "You're a little girl to me. So I'll just say, we'll see. We'll see what happens and play each day as it comes."

"That's right. If the fervour remains and we both bring along spare pants… who knows? But in the meantime, breakfast together. Then that walk. We can talk as we walk."

"It's a deal. Just one more thing." He took her hand and led her upstairs.

"You won't get me near that bed until you've had steel shutters fixed," she said, as they entered the bedroom.

"The trouble with you youngsters is you only think a relationship's active when you're in bed… with the prospect of making wild and passionate love," he continued, leading on into the bathroom. "You know, there's a tender side to life too."

He opened the door into the shower and moved the thermostat to just right of the middle. He turned the water on.

"I'd like my robe back," he said, as he undid the tie she had almost doubled around her waist.

"I'll be shy," Cas said, "I've never shared a shower."

"So that makes two of us."

"Oh well! What's one more experience of a lifetime in the one very short but lovely weekend? You'd best get your gear off then," she said in as practical a tone as she could pretend.

Afterwards, Peter phoned to hurry up breakfast and whilst they waited, they talked and talked.

"Who's the artist who writes 'Un abrazzo, Jaimé'?"

He explained Jaimé.

She had so many questions. "Who's in the photo?" "What's that?" "How did that come about?"

She tactfully left Tania out of the discussion as she learnt about Peter's stepbrother, José Jnr, and Jaimé. But he held back on a photograph of Malaysia.

"Can I walk round the garden?"

"I'll show you. As you can see, it's very small. You'll need a jacket."

"I'm OK. What I'd love is to borrow that Polo cardigan you've got in your wardrobe."

"Have I?"

"Yup. It'll go with my jeans, and be as warm as a fleece… and I'll feel as though it's you wrapped around me."

Peter smiled. "You ought to be in Customer Relations. You really know so well how to make a fellow feel good." He went pensive for a few moments. "That's a young fellow, of course, a contemporary, no less."

"Oh, Peter! Please don't spoil it. No young subaltern could be as deserving as my brigadier. You've led me over hills to overcome my fears and nightmares. I'll make you a promise. Nobody of my generation will ever teach me more than you… that's, of course, until the infatuation wears off and you run away with an older woman."

"I tell you what," he countered, "if, and I say if, I were to contemplate running off with such a female, it would only be so I could catch up on some sleep… and not have to fight to get my boxer shorts back."

"We're funny together, aren't we?" she said as she laughed.

"Tell you what," he said.

"What?"

"You've stopped calling me Chief."

"So I have. Well, there you go. There's another thing. We've become equal."

The chimes resounded at the front door, which they could hear from the patio garden.

"Christ! Food," she said.

"There you go. You're coming out of infatuation already and concentrating on your other needs of nature."

"No way, loverman. It is infatuation which makes me hungry."

She desperately hoped the waiter delivering the breakfast was not fluent in English, particularly when spoken rapidly with an enhanced South African accent. She wouldn't want him to understand her next little game between them. She caught up with Peter as he opened the door, and spoke at a rapid pace.

"Peter dearest, I take exception to you saying that my need for food has overtaken the desire for screwing." She held back on the use of the word 'sex' for fear it was too international these days. "Given the option, I'd choose the latter, so could you send the food away for half an hour or so, then we can get back to the less basic needs in life. Now!" she instructed.

Peter's mouth dropped open sufficiently to have enabled him to consume the boiled eggs and croissants, toast, jam and everything else on the tray in one intake.

Cas laughed aloud, and now spoke in a slow, staccato pigeon English. "OK. Me very hungry. Me eat instead of other things. Me give in. You, boss, right. OK."

His shoulders went, he was shaking with laughter. He could suddenly see the funny side of her reaction to his teasing. This young lady was winning the hands dealt between them as often as she was losing.

He took out a 500-peseta note. "Muchas gracias," he said as he graced the lad's palm with paper.

"Lady very funny," the young fellow announced, pretending to have understood every word. "Buenos dias," he added with a smile and turned to retrieve his bicycle at the front of the plot. Peter kicked the door shut.

"I nearly invited him in. You know, having somebody in to breakfast of your own age to play games with you," he announced.

"My darling, infatuating Peter. We are so funny together, aren't we? Do please say yes."

"We'll see," he replied. "Now listen, I've had enough of sex, I'm hungry. Please can we eat?"

"Of course, Chief, if you want to be really boring."

Chapter 7

They walked at a steady pace, hand-in-hand, much to Tania's disgust from her vantage point of one of the upper rooms in the hotel. They would break that contact occasionally and she would link her arm through his. Tania imagined they were talking and joking all the way.

She was totally wrong. Hardly a word passed between them. They were together, as an item, yet their thoughts were apart, though comparative.

Cas was thinking she had never walked anywhere with Mark. On the back of the bike they would never hold hands or link arms. If she put her arms around his waist, it was more often to hold on in fear. Kissing was just a precursor to him showing his hunger for late adolescent self-gratification. Rarely had such contact been for her. Certainly not in the way she had demanded of Peter.

There had not really been anybody before Mark. Education. Further education and the results her father insisted she achieve were all-embracing. She had turned to athletics in her mid to late teens for physical relief. She got a huge thrill from middle distance running, it was a real stimulation. Her expected reaction to a trainer's demands set her off on a course of achievement.

Peter was in a reflective frame of mind too. Although his vocal cords were being rested, his brain was charged. So there was no comparison between this sudden relationship and the one he'd had with Anna. Certainly he and Anna had been more stable and long term. This was short, but so was his time with Honey. He supposed with Honey he had led the way. But then, he argued with himself, he wasn't the all time leader with Cas. One would lead, then the other. Yes, he thought, it was a joint thing.

In terms of pure sexual satisfaction – the chase, the encounter, the mutuality – Marcia would always take a lot of bettering. But then, he contemplated, it was a fairly simple subject they had practised. There was no humour, no talk of it being other than an opportunity to exchange pleasure. And it had been competitive. How the hell would her new husband cope?

"Hundred pesetas for your thoughts," Cas eventually broke into the silence.

"Oh. Just contemplating the pleasures of the air. The environment. Being with you… and yours?"

"Identical," she said, staccato. Then followed quickly with the question, "Peter! Is this the walk you were on… you know… when you got shot up?"

He tensed. His grip on her hand tightened. "Don't completely remember," he said cautiously. "Pretty well, I'd think. But what's in that? That's all over and done with."

"I don't think it is."

"Why do you say that?"

"Do you know you have nightmares?"

He knew too well he did.

"Nightmares! No. Sleep like a log."

"Bloody don't," she countered.

Since the event he'd only shared a bed with Jan, and that was only once when he was clapped out. So who else would know?

"What do you mean?" he asked.

Cas changed position from holding his hand to linking his arm and leaning towards him. "During the night, you screamed out 'No! I'm not ready. Don't shoot'."

"Go on! That was to do with our encounter on the hearth rug."

"Peter. Be fair. I went through the dunes experience with you. Deep down, you're troubled too."

They walked on in silence for a time.

"What do you think you meant that you weren't ready?"

"Oh, I don't know."

"It must mean something."

"Now listen." There was just a hint of irritation creeping into his voice. "I'll do the psychoanalysis – OK?"

Anyone else would have backed off. "No!"

"No! What the frig do you mean by that?"

"Just no. I'm getting a bit fed up…"

She put on an aggravated air to match his. "You seem to think you've got the only right to go round helping people with their problems. You must have them too. Please let me help." She squeezed his hand.

They continued walking without speaking. When they came to a clearing, Peter hesitated. He continued to lead, intentionally walking on to the path cut into the woods on the far side.

Cas stopped. "It's here," she said.

"Look, one clearing looks just like any other, doesn't it? It's of no consequence."

"Then why is your pulse racing? And your blood pressure, I'd guess, has gone through the roof. Now that certainly wouldn't be good for you."

"That's amateur speculation."

"Then let me take your pulse. It would relate to your BP."

"So what if it happened to be the place?"

"Where would you have been?"

"Well, I suppose, just about where we are now. I'd walked up the hill, just as we have."

"…and the bandits?"

"There was more foliage cover, but in those bushes over there."

"Close your eyes."

"Look, Cas, I don't need this, OK. I'm fine. I've forgotten all about the experience." His shoulder was hurting more than he could remember it ever had. The strength had somehow been sapped out of his right knee.

"Close your bloody eyes," she demanded. He did as he was told. "What do you see?"

"OK, silly girl. Wanting to play games? I see bandits. OK. So you've heard what you wanted me to say. So let's walk on."

"What do you think?" He didn't answer immediately. "Come on, darling. Please pretend I'm getting it out of you. Tell you what. Do that and I'll give you a kiss."

"OK then, but I want you to know I'm only playing along for the incentive."

"Right! Eyes tight shut. What colour do you see?"

"Black… no, very dark green. Between green and black. It fades, in and out. Then red. Black fading into green, then a red flash."

"What happens when you screw your eyes up tight?"

"It goes total red… no, red and black, it fades in and out."

"What do you hear?"

"Silence."

"The whole time?"

"No. I can hear branches snapping. Sort of firecracker sounds."

"Where do they come from?"

"Straight ahead."

"What are you thinking?"

"I'm scared."

"Just scared?"

"I think I realise it's the reverse of my baby pig situation. I'm the one about to be shot."

"What do you think?"

"I'm not ready to die."

"Then?"

"Pain. Huge pain."

"And now?"

"Noise. So much noise. Then… well, now the noise is going into the distance."

"What was the noise?"

"A helicopter."

"What do you feel now?" She leant forward and put her lips onto his.

"Comforted."

"Open your eyes. It's me. Look around. No bandits. No guns. No blood… and you were absolutely right. God agreed you weren't ready to die."

"The dream I have. It's always about not being ready. Not ready for a meeting, or catching a plane… I'm paranoid these days about being ready. That could be it. I suppose I wasn't worried about being shot but I didn't want to die. I've often wondered, you know, when your chips are down, if you're really ill and in pain… then there's likely to be a time when you'll want to die. I just knew that was not my moment. You know, I'd hate to admit it but we might just have worked something out."

"There you are! You've allowed somebody to pierce your armour. It's nice to be helped."

"You're right. Not many people do help me… you know, in the sense of sharing, making a decision. I'm always… well it won't seem appropriate to say it here, but in the firing line, as it were. I always finish up making the decision. Thank you for that. Thanks for the help. Now, where's that kiss you promised?"

"You've had it."

"When?"

"Five minutes ago."

"Go on. You're kidding. You didn't."

"So you want another one."

"Yes, please."

This time she put her arms lovingly around his neck and kissed him softly and fully on his lips. She pressurised his to open slightly and fed her own lips into the gap, forcing his mouth to part further. She slid her tongue in and withdrew it as quickly, then extricated herself from the closeness to his body.

"Now," she said, "next time you're on an incentive you'll know what to expect and, for the record, that kiss was exactly the same as the one you say you don't remember."

"Go on," he said with a smile, "and it was you all the time, not part of the dream."

"You're a sod, Mr Martinez." She clenched her fist and hit him gently on his rib-cage.

He held out his hand. "Let's leave here before I have to lay you down over there and teach you a lesson."

"Would you?"

"No, I bloody won't, but I'll buy you a drink."

"What, up here?"

"Well, not exactly. If we walk on, we'll come to the golf club. You could meet my stepbrother, with any luck."

"José Jnr?"

"As in the photo."

"Do you know, I didn't know your mother had remarried either."

"Well, there you are. Learning every second."

Chapter 8

José did happen to be in the Pro's shop, there was always the chance he would have been out on the course, either playing a round or giving a lesson. The alarm buzzer announced the imminent entry of either serious golf shoppers or thieves interested in shoplifting some gear. He seemed a little taken aback by the appearance of the snappy young blonde, and particularly surprised when Peter followed her in.

Cas found José's open face welcoming as it broke into a smile, which conveyed the welcome intended, but also made a quick assessment of the "this is nice, I could fancy this… perhaps she's come for lessons" type, which men cannot prevent themselves from making.

His face changed even more when he saw Peter, and he positively rushed from behind the cash register and threw both arms around his neck. Peter reciprocated and wrapped his arms around José Jnr's waist as they exchanged bear hugs, each trying to lift the other off the ground.

"Hey, watch my bloody shoulder, you great oaf of a bear!" Peter shouted. Then, "Good to see you," he said, as he stood back and surveyed José Jnr from head to toe.

"Good… you look very good. You've lost a bit of weight. Younger. Yes, you look younger," José complimented him.

Peter returned the assessments. "You never change, you lucky bugger. It's all the golf you get to play. Good to see you too."

"Now, who is this young beauty?"

Cas's legs weakened. He might be only a stepbrother but they'd got the same style.

"This young beauty, as you so rightly say, is Cassandra White. We're a bit of an item."

Cas was inwardly shocked to hear that in such an open manner. *God, that'll get round the family circuit pretty quickly*, she thought.

José held out his hand and Cas extended hers to complete the formal introduction. Although José was coming towards her, he gave no hint of this being a stand-off. His cheek brushed hers and he pulled her body towards his. He was hugging her to him with great strength, yet promising her no harm by a certain gentleness he exuded. God, it was quick to be admitted into the Martinez family circle, she thought.

As they parted, Peter said, "And how are the lovely Carmen and the kids?"

"Great," José said. "That's not 'great' just as in terms of 'yes, Carmen and the kids are great', it's also 'great mate, thanks for taking me off the viewing list for Cas by telling her in one hit that this brother ain't available and you're the only family choice'."

"Peter *is* the only family choice." Cas spoke for the first time. She'd decide who she chose to fancy, she thought.

"OK," José smiled. "That's put me in my place. I'm very pleased to meet you anyway. Listen, why don't we go and get a drink at the bar? You still half own it anyway and the guys would be pleased to see you – after all, they'll want to see how you're mending up after the… well… what shall I say… drama. You look great to me."

"A lot of that is thanks to Cas. She's pushed me into getting the leg working."

"Well, I tell you what, brother, if ever I do my knee in, I'll go straight to wherever I'll find this young lady to get it put right… and oh," he added quickly, "I'll be sure to have a picture of Carmen and the kids and a sign that says 'SORRY! ALL THE BEST ONES ARE ALREADY MARRIED', and stick that on the bedside table."

Cas was quick to say, "And I'll add a little footnote saying 'OR GAY'."

The three laughed almost as old friends would.

José had been very shy through his teens but once he got onto the golf circuit, turned pro and started winning prize money, he gained stature, and a female following. Like most men, Cas assessed, he was of course all talk. She hoped so anyway, for his little family's sake. Tania's availability, just down the road, permanently in the hotel and on the look-out, did spring to mind.

Oh God. Surely he wouldn't fall for that, she thought.

Peter was welcomed at the bar by the golf club steward. They obviously knew each other well. They ordered a couple of Camparis with tonic for the fellows and Cas went for a pressed orange on account of her driving later, not to mention the blood alcohol level from the night before. While the steward fixed the drinks, Cas asked if Peter really did own half of the bar.

"Half of the bar?" José answered. "He bloody owns nine of the eighteen holes on the course, half the entire clubhouse, car park… half the lot. We're partners. I had all the hard work to do to save out of my winnings and this lucky fellow just put loads of people to work to earn him his fortune. That's the luck of the draw," he said with a laugh.

"Sorry to hear about your grandmother." Peter modestly changed the subject.

"Thanks, pal. Yes, it was a bit sudden. Bit of a shock." He showed his serious side. "She, of course, was a mother to me once my own one died. She brought me up. Forced me to learn table manners and study at school. Yes," he said pensively, "I loved that old lady. I'll miss her."

"Use the present tense. It'll help."

José looked puzzled. "Sorry, Peter! Don't get you."

"You said loved. As though once she died, it stopped."

José turned to Cas. "How do you cope with this funny bugger? Right, we're playing golf. OK, I miss a putt and at the point the ball dies, which it does, everybody talks about the putt I missed. Forever after it, missed, as in loved."

Peter smiled. "You always miss putts when you play with me, you'll remember. Try thinking that in your grandmother's case, she's still in play, albeit, as Cas and I have been discussing, she might be at the edge of some lavender field in another world."

"Sounds to me, Cas, you've been having a wonderful weekend. Has he been foisting all his clever philosophies on you too?"

"Only two," she answered. "The one he was absolutely right to point out, he's actually helped me come to terms with a situation I've been grappling with for a while."

"And the other?"

Cas smiled as she gazed into Peter's open, undamaged face. "Oh, that was less philosophy, more inevitability." Her smile deepened and warmed and she placed her hand over his as he sat on the adjacent swivel bar stool to hers. He simply returned her smile.

"Well, I won't press that one," José announced.

Their drinks were placed in front of them and they each lifted their glass. "Santé," José announced.

"Santé," Peter replied.

"Cheers," Cas announced.

"So how would you be for a game of golf?" José enquired.

Peter shrugged and pointed to Cas, indicating she would decide.

"I'd say in a week or two. Yes, then, but I think next week, we've got some catch-up to do. You haven't really exercised much this weekend."

José laughed. "What, old Peter not exercising with a lovely girl like you?"

"José, I don't actually find that too funny," Cas said firmly. "If I take the innuendo in the way it's meant, I'd like to see you 'exercising' as a bloke who lost his testicles in a shoot out in these very hills and coincidentally, but fortuitously under the circumstances, with a girl who has chronic cystitis."

José's lower jaw almost touched his chest. "Christ! I really do put my foot in it, don't I? Peter old chap, I didn't know."

Peter laughed. "Me neither."

José looked confused. He peered into Cas's face. "The cystitis?" he enquired.

"Me neither, but you're being bloody personal to your brother and I wanted to teach you something of a lesson now that your grandmother can't. But I'm sure she would have, if she'd heard your attitude."

"Peter, marry this one quick. She's good."

Peter looked embarrassed. "You're getting personal again. If you aren't careful, she'll tell you why we can't do that."

"Already married?"

"No. Because I'd suggested you could be best man and you're here to be vetted. Cas whispered to me that she'd rather call the wedding off."

José roared with laughter. He alighted from his stool and leant forward and kissed Cas's cheek.

"I'm so sorry I haven't been on my best behaviour. I was so pleased to see Peter, and of course to meet you, that I got over-excited. We'll meet again and review the entire situation." He looked at his watch. "I have to leave you, I'm afraid. I've a client who's booked a practice round. I get 20,000 pesetas out of it, so it's not bad for a weekend."

Cas held out her hand. "It's really nice to have met you and to have tried to re-shape your direct and personal intervention." Since it was said with the smile, he knew she had been pulling his leg. He acknowledged to himself that he had been over-excited.

The blokes exchanged bear hugs. There was a murmur between them she could not quite hear.

"I meant it," José whispered, "marry this one."

"What, with chronic cystitis?" Peter shrugged and pulled away.

Both laughed into each other's open faces.

"I'll ask what you said, José. So be careful," warned Cas.

"I'll happily tell you too," he replied. "Oh, by the way, hope it gets better." They all parted laughing.

"He's nice," she said as they walked from the clubhouse.

"Yes, I'm fond of him. You should be careful of what you say."

"Why?"

"Carmen's got chronic cystitis."

"Oh my God!" She put her hand to her mouth.

"And golfers, you'll have to understand, don't reach a great age on account of them losing their balls."

"Oh very funny," she said. "Here, get me back to Barcelona. I want to be with normal people again."

They spent a few minutes doing a superficial but systematic tidy through of the villa. By the time they had done that, Cas had satisfied Peter that he should merely choke Tania off and still entrust her to do the cleaning. For convenience, he agreed.

They went to Peter's wardrobe and took out a blue suit on a hanger, and a white shirt, and Cas chose a tie with a pink background with a blue Liberty print pattern. All the clothes and a pair of black shoes and blue socks were carefully placed into a hanging robe to be taken to the car. Peter agreed Cas could borrow the pullover she'd been wearing, provided she threw the boxer shorts they had argued over into the bin, as what he described as a penance.

They stood in the lobby just inside the house. Both paused. Neither had to suggest anything to the other.

"Thank you for infatuating me, darling, for the best weekend of my life."

"That's strong," Peter said with great feeling.

"I've loved every minute."

"Don't you mean 'love'? It's alive and still around us. True, there'll be a bit of gossiping and grumbling up in the lavender, but it goes on. It will always still be around us. Don't you remember?"

"Of course I do."

"Then let's continue to love every minute we can. When we can and where we can… and not, for God's sake, down the wires of a telephone. We don't need that every day, at the risk of running out of conversation. Just the one occasional call, OK, to tell me you're coming over to London would always be nice. Or inviting you across?"

"Peter, I'd really, really love that. It's the shops in London, you see. I've heard about them."

"Well you can't shop all night, can you?"

"True. That's better than shopping, I know."

They kissed passionately. She pushed him away from her. "Right, that's enough of that. Otherwise we'll be here all night."

"OK with me," Peter said.

"Listen, young man, we've got an under-exercised knee to get to work on. Right, we'll be brave. We'll walk straight out and not look back. We can do a 'V' sign each towards Tania's binoculars and then drive into the distance to Barcelona."

"Perfect with me, Captain," Peter responded.

"Captain? Why suddenly captain, Peter?"

"Oh, I don't know. When we arrived, I was leading you. Now we've reversed so I suppose it's that I see you as some sort of equal. I'll remember this weekend by you finishing up wearing the pants."

"Let's get out of this beautiful place before your father hears me take your relationship in vain again."

They stepped outside. Cas waited for Peter to turn back and lock the door.

"All locked?" she enquired.

"Aye, Captain," he said, as though to counter the emotion they were both feeling.

"OK," she whispered. "I'll do the driving."

"Oh shit! Not all that business all over again."

Peter pondered for a few sensible minutes, working out in his mind whether they had put everything into the car. She'd only brought a small travel case, as had he. His suit was hanging in the back of the car. There was nothing else, he thought, just an imaginary case filled with memories.

As they turned out onto the main highway Peter covered her hand, which was hovering around the gear shift, with his strong masculine one.

"Thank you so much," he said with feeling. She turned to look at him. "Please keep your eye on the road," he almost pleaded.

"I just wanted one more glimpse of you totally relaxed."

"Why do you say that?"

"Oh, I don't know, I may be wrong, but I've got that feeling you're about ready to fly again – that is, away from a proverbial nest. I would think a man who owns half a golf course, a beautiful house, probably as beautiful a house back in England, a real car, and who has the bank manager phone him – not like me, I have to make the begging calls – is going to be a different character when he's back into work mode. So I wanted another glimpse of how you should always be. How you were during the night and when we made love. It's a sad feeling that I'm now going to be exposed to another person I've yet not only to meet, but to get to know."

"You're a dramatic young thing, aren't you? I promise you you've seen me as I am. Yes, you're probably right. I'll get back into acting mode. That's the way I make money and influence people – not make friends and influence people, you'll note. Then, you see, I'm a realist, and in that mode I'll see how important you are to me. I'll accept that on your terms. You know just to call to say you want me to come out, or to ask if you want to come shopping. Maybe we'll meet on neutral territory or... you know, I've never been to South Africa. You've never been to Malaysia. We've not made the Caribbean between us. Each time I promise we'll be 'us', as we've discovered ourselves to be overnight."

"You are lovely." She meant what she felt.

They drove in silence. Peter's mind wandered. He'd need to ring William and say don't come out. He'd be back in England the following week, he reckoned. He needed to just think about the reception thing that Han had invited him to. He doubted that would be anything other than a nothing event. He'd also like to get some sort of future sorted out for Pablito.

Shit! He hadn't spoken to his mother since Thursday. She didn't even know he'd temporarily broken out of the hospital. He'd get stick from her, no doubt.

Then he'd have to say au revoir to Cas. That would be hard. The terms they'd agreed to would be fine. It was where he and Jan had got it wrong, he supposed. He needed space. He always had. But then he needed loving too. Being loved and giving love. He would place his time and experience with Cas as maybe second to Honey, although that could have been some spiritual freak at a time two young people were both susceptible. He'd never know what it could have grown into. Still, his experience with Cas was definitely special.

He wondered why. Possibly because, mixed in with the heat and passion, the mutual desire to satisfy, was the exchange of fun. Even when she'd pretended to have used him in the hospital, the overlying result had been great mutual pleasure. No way had she used him. She just thought she had and wanted him to believe that too because, at that time, she was scared of building an affection again, only to risk seeing it end in death.

He smiled to himself.

"A million pesetas for your thoughts. You've had your space. What's the outcome of all this thinking of yours?" Cas knew her man.

"Oh. Just thinking ahead. What do you know about this reception thing?"

She didn't reply immediately. "I'm not the one to ask," she eventually said.

"Oh. Why's that? You've seen them before, haven't you? Have you been to one?"

"Yes, and yes."

"Been there and done that?"

"Yes," she nodded.

"Are you going to go on Wednesday?" he asked excitedly.

"Nope."

"Oh! I'm disappointed. Then I'll probably not go either."

"I haven't actually been invited anyway, which doesn't surprise me. I'd probably always expected never to be invited again in fact."

"Why?"

"I went a couple of years back."

"So what are they like?"

"Well, it's the gathering of a bunch of old farts with the wrong agendas."

"Well, that seems a pretty precise judgment. So why is Han, do you think, inviting me along to be in the midst of a clan like that?"

"Well, I'd hope – and remember I have huge admiration for the Professor – I'd hope it's because he thinks you might kick butt and bring a little of your reality to the event."

"OK, let's suppose you're right. But why are they old farts and on the wrong agendas?"

"How long have we got? Just until we reach the hospital? Well, firstly, you'll be the youngest male by about a hundred years. But then, you see, this is all part of the Paralympic movement. OK, it's for cripples. But there's still the old boy overlap with the main Olympics and in that you have to look towards the IOC."

"The IOC?" he enquired. "Remind me again what that is."

"Sorry, the International Paralympic Committee."

"Oh yes. I think I've heard about that."

"Do you know about it?"

"No, to be honest."

"You've heard of Samaranch?"

"Yes, of course – remember I'm Spanish."

"Do you know, I actually always forget that. Of course you are. Well, look at what he's done. He effectively changed the original intentions of the IOC. As far as I can work out, a guy called Cambertin or Coubertin, maybe, who was French, set up the IOC at the turn of the century, in Paris, I think – I was never any good at history. The intention was that it would be a voluntary committee of unpaid do-gooders. But things don't always turn out as intended. Did you know Barcelona was actually fighting Berlin for the games of 1936?"

"No. I didn't. But then I wasn't born."

"Listen, are you going to take the mickey out of me, having put me into serious mode?"

"I'm sorry. No. You're right. I just have a conflict with you knowing things I don't know," Peter replied.

"Well, you asked the question. Can I carry on from my soap box from behind the wheel of this modest Seat?"

"Of course, I'm sorry. I'll take what you say seriously."

"Now, there's a good boy." She patted his left hand. "Well, it wasn't all down to the do-gooder factor when Adolf Hitler bribed more people than the Spanish were prepared to, and got the 1936 Games. We all know why, and what happened, and why Great Britain got the show in 1948."

"Cas, I'm being serious now. I don't."

"Oh, come on! Britain and her allies won the battles but Germany won the war. Look at the investment now coming in to Spain. It's German. If you look at every location Hitler wanted to dominate with his armies, they're not now occupied by soldiers, but by sons of soldiers, and their wives and offspring. They're littered with German beach towels and the right to plant them has been created by those in Germany who benefited in the longer term from re-investment in their damaged country.

"Britain, I gather, still had rationing but, so I understand, they weren't putting immediate investment into their infrastructure. They had accommodation that was erected temporarily for their troops and they needed to use it up. The international committee, which was made up of mainly European-born elected members, wanted to throw a major street party to celebrate the end of the war, albeit a bit late, so they gave the games to the UK to use its old stadia and that surplus accommodation.

"Samaranch has been angling for the Games ever since. The IOC is now allegedly made up of his cronies and others who recognise his natural leadership. It's no longer a voluntary committee. Well, it is voluntary, providing they get an occasional desk at Headquarters in Switzerland and a slug in some shape or other for casting their vote every four years to the highest bidder. So the original intention of the IOC, being structured a bit like a private and exclusive gentlemen's club, is now gone."

"Cas. Seriously, how do you know all this?"

"You're prying, as usual. At home, in South Africa, remember I was a university student. Students stir shit and one of the beefs of my time was the fact that SA was all white. We've got apartheid. So knowing that the Olympics were meant to be open to all men and women, whatever their colour, and knowing they accepted entries from South Africa where the regime didn't espouse that principle, led us to be in conflict with the Olympic movement. Hence, also anti the IOC.

"So all the student rags carried anti-international committee articles. To be fair, when Samaranch became President in 1980, he brought with him a hint of change. He'd been exposed to fascism in his teens and been Sports Minister under Franco… surely you know all this… he'd had a spell as Ambassador in Russia and with that background he'd been elected. The problem is he's still got old farts around him but that was a backlash from the 60s when, would you believe, members of the IOC were made members for life, or at least till they reached the ripe young age of 75 – 75, Peter! You're not going to change your principles that late on… I bet *you* don't, my darling.

"So anyway, from my point of view, if I was invited to be amongst the fraternity, and there's this old boy overlap between the Olympics for the fit guys and the ones for the crips, and if I'm stirred up by one or two old farts who ask why SA should be banned from the Olympics, I'm likely to explode, as I did a couple of years back. Han wasn't upset by it. In fact he came out and openly supported what I'd said. But last year I asked not to be invited and Han didn't use heavy pressure to get me to change my mind. I'm not normally welcome at Han's events… but having said that, Samaranch is making certain noises about liberalisation. So who knows? Next question?"

"Cas, that's all very interesting. You're not only bloody good on a hearth rug but you're very interesting in a car too."

"Go on like that young man and I'll embargo anything society might consider to be… well… unusual."

"OK. So that's another challenge. But why am I invited?"

"Fresh air, maybe."

"You know me, though. I wouldn't put up with all that racism crap either."

"I guess you wouldn't," she replied.

"Cas. Come with me."

She laughed. "I'm not invited."

He thought for a couple of minutes, "You're friggin' coming."

"Oh yes! How?"

"Well, if I convinced Han I couldn't get a suit off a hanger without your help… if my knee was to relapse and I needed some nursing support, surely he'd let you help me… that's if I demanded you and not Juan."

She started to laugh. "… And I come along and rip off my skirt and expose my tattoo saying 'Black is also beautiful' and we both get thrown out."

"No. You come along and hear me ask questions and show so much interest in the Games that they beg me to go on a do-gooder committee and then you lobby me, in bed or in front of a log fire, I'm not fussed, and I become the rebel within."

"Peter, that's actually pretty good thinking."

Silence followed. Peter was thinking again.

"You know, you mentioned having been pushed into athletics to take your mind off men," he said.

"Well, it wasn't completely like that. That was the result. Yes. So yes, I do remember… well, my infatuation was still there. I just burnt up my desires during training."

"So why, in your judgement, were you not successful?"

"Well, what I didn't say was that at school and club standard, I was OK. Internationally, I wasn't."

"Why?"

"Oh, I don't know. Perhaps nobody put a hare in front of me and told me to go out there and overtake it."

"So what about Pablito? How on earth could he be motivated to control his emotions and mood swings to get a medal in the Paras?"

"Shit! That's a real question."

"Would you, for example, take all your clothes off and be his bait? Run in front of him to train him up to speed?"

"Nope!"

"So we need another idea."

"I think it would be a solid keep-fit programme, encouragement and teaching him determination."

"If, and I do say if, I were to be the committee bloke… you know, get old and learn to fart, and to raise money for Pablito's training… would you be interested in training him?"

"Does that mean I'd get to see you more often?"

"I'd suppose so," Peter said condescendingly, in fun.

"OK. A question."

"Oh no. I can't stand this. Forget it," he said.

"The question. Why does an artist dedicate a wonderful painting to you signed with affection… I think that's what 'un abrazzo' means?"

"What the hell has that to do with Pablito and you training him?"

"Loads."

"It's very private."

"Is he gay? This Jaimé?"

"No. He bloody is not. Or ever was."

"Then tell me. Then I'll answer you about Pablito."

Fifteen minutes later, or so, Cas agreed to take the prospect seriously, having heard what an influence Peter had had on Jaimé's life.

"What about his name?" asked Peter.

"Sorry, what about whose name?"

"Pablito's."

"It would be Paul in English. That's all I know about his name."

"What about a surname?"

"I've actually never seen one."

"Well, if we're going to make a champion out of him, we'll need a good marketing image in order to get him sponsorship. Once his limb is sorted, the state health service won't be interested in paying your fees and expenses, for example."

"I won't charge. I'll do it in my own time."

"Perhaps, but when he starts, or if he starts running competitively, the races won't come to him. He'll have to go to them. You'll need to travel with him, London… where of course you won't have hotel expenses…" He put his hand across and squeezed hers and smiled. "Paris, Switzerland, maybe even the Far East… and if you do that, I'll come with you."

"Why do you like the Far East so much?"

"Another time, my sweet, I reckon we're 20 minutes from the hospital."

"Oh Peter, I really, really don't want to go back."

"I know. Me too. But we're heading for a new life for you and, regrettably, the old one refreshed for me. Right… the name!"

"I'll do one, then you do one."

"OK. What do you want? To choose the first or the second?"

"The second, but you go first."

"Paul."

"That was quick."

"Well, it's the natural. Pablito translated. Now you."

She thought for a while. "Yes. Definitely."

"What? Remember I've got to agree to it."

"OK. Girasol."

"What! Paul Sunflower! What are you on?"

"I'm in infatuation, remember."

"Maybe, but you can't call him that."

Cas giggled. "I love having you on. Of course that wasn't serious. Mer. Paul Mer. It's international and it will always remind me of 'us'. You don't get an opinion. It's Paul Mer."

"Paul Sea! It's close, but doesn't quite have the right ring about it. What about Paul Demer?"

"Demer? It's a bit hard. What about Demar? It's… nice and soft."

"I actually think the idea is great. We'll tell him it's to give an association with the hospital. I'm blowed if I want to take him through the whole hearthrug thing."

"Me neither. That's just for you, me and Tania."

"Not Tania, the bitch. We'd pulled those drapes."

"True. OK. Just you and me."

"Why not Paul Demar then?"

"Peter. I actually think that's great. That's a wonderful team result. But what about him?"

"He'll agree. Leave that to me."

They pulled into the hospital car park.

"How the hell do I not show I'm in love with you to all the other gawping staff and patients?"

Peter said, "Just act normally."

"What on earth do you mean by that?"

"Listen, baby. Your interest in me has been showing from the first day you were put in charge of my case, when you wanted me to get obsessed by your butt and the wiggly little walk you developed."

"I bloody well didn't."

"Sweetheart, I'm telling you. That was one of the biggest come-ons I've had put my way in my life… and boy have I had some!"

"OK. Think of me that way… and regrettably that'll cover up the truth. Do you think anybody's watching?"

"Don't care if they are."

She leant across and they kissed. Not a kiss brimming with passion. Just a kiss to express them being a bit of an item.

"Thank you, Peter, for everything."

"It's not over yet," he said with a smile.

The caretaker porter was at the desk. "Oh Sir, I'm pleased you're back. I've been working my butt off as your personal secretary while you've been away."

"What's been going on?"

"Your mother has rung four times. She started off wanting to know if you'd been moved to another hospital and were you ill as you weren't here. About half an hour ago, she left another to say she was OK now about where you are but could you call. A lady saying she's your UK secretary rang to say could you call, not too urgent. A man called William has rung twice and got a bit impatient.

"Pablito is itching to see you. He comes down to the desk every hour or so saying what time do I think you'll be back! That's about it, I think. Oh, and sorry, Miss Cas. There's a note for you."

He hadn't really been focusing on her, he was more concerned to make sure he remembered Peter's messages he'd scribbled down on a pad. "My, you look refreshed," he added. "Had a bit of sea air, have you?"

"Yes, actually. I walked Mr Peter off his feet."

"Wouldn't say that exactly," Peter said with a smile, capitalising on the fact the porter wouldn't have understood the words, let alone the innuendo.

"I'll help you up with your bags," the porter volunteered.

"No, I can do that," Cas insisted, pursuing her equal rights habit.

"You sure, miss? I can leave the desk for a few minutes."

"No, that's fine," she said. His generation would never adjust to female equality. Yes, alright, for what they said to be taken seriously, but carrying their own suitcases... never.

Back in his room, Peter settled in to the four walls, which were now beginning to depress him. Cas had been very controlled. They'd shared a taste of honey, which had to last them both until the next time. Peter felt exceptionally lost without the constant company he had shared. Shit, he thought, that was barely more than 24 hours. It seemed an eternity.

Cas was lying on her own bed with a tear-soaked handkerchief, thinking exactly the same thing. Usually after joining bodies with Mark, and the first time with Peter, she felt nothing but a vacuum. Now it was as though she and he were still physically connected. She shot upright into a sitting position.

I could be pregnant, she thought. She pressed both hands into her stomach. *And if we are, it will be Peter for a boy and Petra for a girl, and I'll be overjoyed* – little remembering Peter's first daughter had already been given the female version of her father's name.

"Yes, mother, no mother," were Peter's answers on being told off for not having informed Maria of his change of location. The permitted trip had all happened so quickly, he'd forgotten to let her know.

His mood changed. "What! She said what? She's a bitch!"

His mother had said that by late Sunday morning she was so worried about his whereabouts that she had rung round a couple of obvious places, Girasol being one of them.

"You didn't ring the house?" he said.

"Yes, I did. I got no reply. So I rang Tania."

That was all quite logical, because they were out walking or with José by late morning.

"Oh yes," he said nonchalantly, "and she said what?"

"She said something like you seemed to be trying out a new model. I said, what a new car, and she said, well similar, but no, it was another new blonde. I said no, it wouldn't be, it was Jan, who we all knew well, and that I didn't like the expression she'd used."

Hence Peter's angry reaction.

"You see, I thought Jan had gone back. Then I supposed you couldn't keep away from each other, you hot blooded Spaniard, and presumed she'd flown out for the weekend."

"Jan and I, mother, are no longer."

This bombshell didn't go down well.

"Oh, Peter! What's wrong with you? She's so nice, so good for you. I'd got real hopes of another grandchild from you both. So who *were* you with?" she emphasised.

"An equally lovely girl I've met at the hospital."

"What, an invalid?"

"No, mother. But what if she was? There are some perfectly lovely 'invalids', as you call them, who could produce you a grandchild. Anyway, she's a physiotherapist with special nursing capabilities. She's been putting my knee right."

"… And the rest of you, I don't doubt."

"Mother!"

"Well, you disappoint me. You so need to settle down again. Have somebody who'll see to it you have proper regular meals. You need a bit of caring…"

"Mother, stop clucking. Now, I'm OK. How about you?"

She went through her usual post-menopausal bit of aches and pains and how José was still travelling and working too hard, then how lovely the funeral of his mother had been and how José Jnr had such a lovely wife… and how she had wondered why Peter couldn't be settled down like him, and how Marco was creaking a bit and Virginia, come to that, and what a good year the hotel had had.

Peter eventually butted in. "Mother, they need me for some treatment."

"Well, OK. You must go for that. I'll phone you in a day or so. Do ring Jan. She's probably upset still. Love you, darling, even though you are the really bad boy that you are. But I do love you, so take care."

"I promise I'll be in touch. I'll probably be going back to the UK next week."

"Well, don't overdo it. Tania said you looked pale."

It was pointless explaining most of that was anger.

He could normally phone his previous secretaries on a Sunday, they never minded. He wasn't sure about Val though. He approached it slowly.

"Hi, Val. Sorry to disturb your Sunday but I gather you were after me."

"Hello, Sir. How are you?" She clearly hadn't minded. He had no idea whether Val was married, single or had a partner.

"Great."

"Good. Look, I thought I'd tip you off. Mr William says he's coming out on Tuesday week. There's a Board meeting on Thursday week and he feels he ought to be reporting news of you on a first-hand basis."

"What's his diary like for this coming week?"

"Full, I'd say. I'm sharing information with Vera. Apart from anything else, it's his wife's birthday on Tuesday. There's racing at Chester on Wednesday and Thursday and the rugby at Twickenham on Saturday. He never goes anywhere on Friday, so I guess he's around then."

"That's good. Then I'll save him the trouble of a journey out. You can tell him I'll be in the office in London on the afternoon of the Monday. That's if you can get me a flight. That's tomorrow week, of course."

"Gerona?"

"No, Barcelona."

"OK. I can't see a problem."

"Good. Could you send him a memo please and copy it to the Board secretary as well. Wouldn't be a bad idea to copy it across to all directors too."

"Don't tell me you've been doing some of the advanced thinking I've heard about over there? You're meant to be on holiday and getting your leg right. You shouldn't have time to think about memos to your colleagues." She hesitated about whether she should then revert to formality having proffered a personal opinion.

"It's a question I need circulated. OK, if you could take this down: *Enquiry from Peter Martinez. Could the International Division prepare a resumé of their tracking of the construction and development opportunities in France, Italy and Spain. Particular emphasis on longer term leading to activity current through to five years. Also, what slice of group turnover they are seeking to achieve.*"

"I'll read it back." Which she did.

"Yup, fine. Suggest you fax it to all parties, otherwise they'll start bleating about timescales in which to answer. OK, anything else?"

"Just a word really. It's all a bit difficult, but I might as well blurt it out. Is everything OK with Jan Roberts?" Val asked.

"Now, why do you ask that?"

"Promise, it's confidential, Sir."

"Of course," Peter said with some hesitation.

"Well, I had a strange call with Mr William. The one when he said he was coming out. Well, he indicated you'd had a relapse. Not your body. Your brain. He was sort of putting me on notice that if I didn't have a master to work for, I might face redundancy, and so to keep my eyes open. Of course, I was worried and then he explained he'd been talking to Jan Roberts, who of course I don't know, and that when she'd last met you out there, when she was helping with the private hospital deals, you'd been positive about certain things and then suddenly, for no apparent logical reason, you appeared to have had a mega mood swing and go negative. Mr William was going on to me about Pavlov's dogs and something like that. Jan concluded that you were now totally unreliable and told Mr William that she's very concerned."

"Did the prat say these views were expressed over dinner?"

"No."

"... And that Jan Roberts is not so good on drink and neither is he, so there was a strong chance of it being misinterpreted and incorrectly represented?"

"No."

"It's just not true, Val, I promise. Ask me any question you like to help me prove the point."

"I've no need. You sound fine to me. Anyway, I'm relieved. Only the fact that it reportedly came from Jan Roberts worried me."

"Oh, I shouldn't bother. What's your English expression about hell and fury?"

"Hell hath no fury like a woman scorned. Have you scorned Jan, then?" She quickly added, "Sir?" realising the question could well have been too familiar.

"Let's say there was a misunderstanding between us."

"Oh, I see."

"You can't possibly. But take my word for it."

"Listen, I'll give Mr William a call in the morning. I won't keep you any more." So she signed off as a developing, ever loyal PA to be.

His call to Jan found her very much in Sunday evening mood. She had probably visited her parents and achieved little but pressure, and would now be preparing for her forthcoming week in her usual professional way.

"Hi, it's Peter."

"Oh, hi, I hope you're not going to upset me again, this time on a Sunday evening. I've left, I suppose it must be three messages for you."

"Well, three messages and one international call with nothing left on the tape," Peter responded.

"So you got them?"

"Of course," he confessed.

"… And you didn't call back."

"What's the point? I know you well enough that if you make your mind up, it's a considered opinion and you're unlikely to change it. But I'm calling with a new point for you to contemplate. It seems you think I'm still unbalanced, and I've lost my marbles."

"When are you ever likely to do that?"

"Have you had that dinner with William yet?"

"Yes, last week."

"Do you think you could possibly have given him the idea I'd lost my way?"

"No, but he was much the worse for wear and spent most of the evening desperately trying to see down my cleavage and get the number of the coffee waitress at L'Ecu de France."

"What did you say about us?"

"Nothing. Oh well, maybe he interpreted something I said as though it was about us, but I doubt that."

"Can you remember what you said?"

"He said something like you were too stubborn to be an important leader in business because you were inflexible once your mind was made up. I said something like I didn't think that was the case normally but on a certain subject you had reversed on a previous considered opinion without clear reason, and that was possibly brought about by the pain and stress of your knee problem. Nothing more untoward than that."

"Did he comment on that?"

"No. In fact, I remember clearly he hardly heard the end of what I said, he just shot off to the gents almost as if he was about to pee himself. When he came back, he had lipstick on his collar and seemed to have a different, more successful rapport with the waitress. If they didn't bed down together that night in some seedy hotel, I'd be surprised.

"Why all this stuff, Peter? I'd hoped you were ringing to see how I am. Whether I'm still broken-hearted or not, maybe even to propose to me."

"Oh dear!" he let out in embarrassed shock.

"Oh come on, Peter. I'm pulling your leg. Look, when we spoke I was just cross and disappointed you were ditching me. I'd made up my mind we'd had an artificial relationship. I remembered you telling me when we had that lovely first night out, when you didn't get me into bed, that if ever your mother liked a girlfriend of yours, that was a clear indication of incompatibility between the girlfriend and you. Do you remember? You said your mother's idea of a match for you was a steady, reliable lady who would look after you. You told me then yours was that the lady should possess a fire and a passion, which you'd always need to hold down. My number was up the day your mother told me how fond she was of me and what a perfect couple she saw us as. That was after lunch at the hotel the day you later took the wrong turning to Barcelona. So don't worry, my darling, I love you in the most platonic way. Whether I would put up with you for the rest of my life – *no way*!"

"Jan, I'm so pleased about that. So how are you?"

"I'm really fine. Really busy. That's the love in my life."

"So, you wouldn't put a spoke in my wheel?"

"Of course not. How could I?"

"OK. So this is what William is saying." He told her about the preceding call.

"Soppy bugger," was Jan's reaction. "I'll phone him tomorrow and put him right."

"No, I don't think that's the right thing to do," Peter directed. "Leave it, I'll do it my way, using Val. She seems quick to grasp situations."

"I'll willingly speak to him."

"No, that's fine. I'm glad it's all worked out well to this point at your end. I'm back in the UK next week. I'll give you a call. Perhaps we can have dinner."

"Fine, I'll make sure I'm booked every night."

"That's not very kind."

"Well, it sounds to me that you'd be back to your primitive ultra-fit self and I don't want you saying to me that I'd be breaking a promise by sending you home when you get me to my front door and want to test out your knee!"

"Oh yes. That. Are you sure you don't want me to prove myself?"

"Sure, very sure. But give me a call."

She replaced the receiver. She wept buckets of tears.

Peter lay on the bed, taking stock of things. He was actually very tired. There was a knock at the door. He was inclined to say he didn't want any food but then realised they hadn't eaten all day. It would be 'room service'.

"OK, I'm open. Come in," he invited.

It was Cas.

"Hell, am I…"

She stopped him in full flight by putting her forefinger to her lips, against the replenished lipstick, which he noticed. There was a shuffle of shoe leather against the polished floor from behind her.

"Look what was waiting outside the door to the staff wing."

It was Pablito.

"Hi, Pablito. How's it going? Your walking looks good."

"Yes, Mr Peter. It's good."

"I got a message you wanted to see me. I was going to pop round when I'd cleared a few calls. My mother's fussing and all that, even at my age. So to what do I owe this pleasure? Particularly as you're accompanied by the prettiest nurse in Barcelona by far."

"That won't get you anywhere," Cas warned. "Prettiest in Spain, maybe. Pablito needs to talk."

"Have you eaten?" Peter asked Cas.

"Funnily enough, I'm starving. I haven't eaten since last night."

"Me neither. What about Pablito?"

"Not yet."

"Then why don't we all go to the refectory and eat and talk?"

"Suits me," Cas replied.

"OK by me," was Pablito's view.

"Then, let's go. Pablito, you lead the way. I want to see how your leg is healing up under the limb."

That gave Peter the opportunity to lag behind with Cas. He 'accidentally' brushed her hand. He whispered, "In case we don't get the chance again, slip back to my room after, if you can."

"What are you guys saying about me? I can hear you."

"I'm going to let Miss Cas tell you what we said. She's the knowledgeable one in this establishment."

"You're doing fine," she said, "pull your shoulders back. You'll do better."

Peter was impressed with her quick, confident analysis. She was right. Pablito did just that and his stride and confidence improved.

They ordered indifferent food and got stuck in at the lad's pace.

"So… why did you call this board meeting?" Peter eventually asked Pablito.

"Board meeting?"

"It's where directors of companies talk through important issues."

"Oh! Well, I'm not sure it's like that," he said. "It's simple. I'm on to become a world champion athlete, if you want me to, and if you can help me to become one."

"And you've agreed to change your name to achieve that goal?"

"Yes."

"You could adopt the name. Make it official."

"So what more do you think?"

"Right, the next one is more difficult. How would you feel about a female coach?"

"Frig that," he said, "no, I'd want a man."

"I mean Cas."

"Cas. What, this Miss Cas?"

"No, you'd just call her Cas."

"Would you coach me, miss?"

"Yes, I would. If you promised to work and train hard. You've got five years, just about."

"Five. What, then I'll die or something?"

"No, then the three of us will win a Paralympic gold."

"Oh shit!"

The deal was struck with Paul Demar.

Chapter 9

Gina's stomach always churned on a Monday morning. Saturdays and Sundays were OK. Then, she didn't have the problem of being able to see Benito Alvor's eyes over the top of a mask, or be with him in the clinical conditions of the scrubdown area, unless there was an emergency. That now did not compare with the privacy of the shower they'd shared together in Barcelona, or in the motel between Palafrugell and Lloret, to which they almost sprinted whenever they mutually decided they needed to be together.

If meeting up was off the agenda, Gina knew she had to focus on her own domestic scene, which was fine. It hadn't changed and never could. She had now found an outlet in which to be herself, let her hair down, be indulged and satisfied until the inevitable and dejected return home.

So she had come to dread the butterfly feeling, brought about by her wondering how soon she would meet up with Benito at work and whether it would be this week they could fit in their self-indulgements once more.

As she pulled in to the staff car park, she thought she glimpsed Benito's car. When the headlights flashed, she knew it was him. He made no effort to get out. Was he OK? Maybe he'd got one of his cramps and his leg had seized up again. She gave a couple of furtive looks around the other parked cars. There was nobody around. No couple to look up from being wrapped around each other, as she and Benito had done on a couple of previous occasions.

Gina instinctively went to the passenger door, which was open. She slid into the seat, semi-facing him. As she did, her button-through coat-style dress strained to expose quite an amount of her slim pale thighs. Normally Benito would have commented how nice they were and thanked her for the little show. But today he seemed glum and in a serious mood.

"Hi," he said.

"Hi. Something's wrong," she acknowledged.

"It's what we rehearsed wouldn't happen."

"Which one?" she said, not wishing to lighten the mood.

"About all three, I'd say."

"Why don't you start at the beginning?"

"OK. I got home on Friday. You'll remember we'd had those couple of difficult ops. I was really tired. My wife said we were out to dinner with friends and had I forgotten. I said I had but could we get out of it because I was exhausted. She got bitchy, you know, her usual theme of it being alright for me, I'd got my life in my job. Our social life was her life and how could I deprive her of that? I said it didn't happen often but I really did want to cry off. She then turned hysterical and said she often wondered if there was some sideline that was making me tired. 'A bit on the side' was mentioned. You'll be pleased to hear this; she said she and I hadn't indulged in sex for weeks, and that was unlike me.

"I was cross about the connotations of a 'bit on the side' and, like an idiot, I rose to the bait. I blurted out that I wouldn't blame myself if I had. Her constant demands and bickering were enough to drive a man to that. She said what did I mean by that. Was there a bit on the side? I, of course, said there wasn't but from then on, for the rest of the weekend, she never let up. It's been, 'I suppose when you go to these conferences there's a tart there to share your bed'. And 'What about the operations that take you into the evenings... I bet you're off bonking your tart in the back of the car' and 'How can you do that, what about the children?'

"The more I lied and insisted, the more her imagination ran riot. It upset me anyway that she saw me as straying with what she termed to be a tart and not my beautiful Gina. The more we argued that there was no tart around, the more she invented situations where there could be the opportunity. Opportunities, to make it worse, that *have* existed, and that we have ourselves invented together in real life.

"Gina, I've had it. I need to tell her and get out. Would you do the same? We could set up and be together permanently. OK, working together would be strange... but no stranger than now. Tell me you will. Please."

"Ben, my darling. It's not what we said, not what we planned. People would get hurt. It'll blow over at home. Give it time." She put her hand on his knee. "I'm really very, very flattered."

"So say yes. Will you join me?"

"Oh, Ben. You're asking me to make the easiest decision of my life. But it's too easy to say yes. The odds are of the two of us being satisfied but a whole chain of other lives being ruined. We need time. Time to work out the effect of that situation. The pact we have means that when we're together, we're on rationed time. We've resolved to enjoy ourselves and give pleasure to each other and laugh together. Feed into that equation a number of broken hearts, solicitors' letters and disillusioned kids, and it would take a lot for our times together, even our permanent time with each other, which might be the result, not to be changed by the new stresses we'd face. So, what seems easy and determined by natural desire and instinct is too hard to react to in an instant."

"I thought you'd say yes without hesitation."

"And so I would have done if circumstances were different. But we covered the eventuality our way by saying we'd never let it happen. We need time..."

Almost as though on cue, Benito's pager bleeped.

"Oh shit! Not now," he said, looking down at the intruding little box clipped to the waistband of his trousers.

"Take it," she said, "it may be somebody else's life at stake. Somebody this time we don't know."

The message read: *Emergency on the way. Serious Gerona road accident. Two to be dealt with. Both bad. 40 minutes probable arrival.*

"We're off," he said, without too much conviction.

Gina had never, ever seen her Sñr Alvor drop an instrument before. The theatre was cool under the recently revamped cooling system, yet he was sweating.

She felt sick. Even swabbing the blood the consultant was generating did not take her mind off the greater fear of the power they had within themselves. On the one hand, they had what it took to fight to save these two lives. It was a young man and, apparently, his fiancée, whose motorbike had been sucked in by a jack-knifing German transporter, destined to deliver its contents to make hundreds of tourists happy in next year's summer sun. On the other hand, she and Benito Alvor had control over the destiny of one disgruntled wife, unhappy with her lot; an apparently contented husband, oblivious of his inability to satisfy his seemingly happy wife; the young Alvor family; and her own two doting daughters, who would be shocked by their mother's revelations. Not to mention her parents and parents-in-law… did he have parents? She didn't know.

Gina's mind was not on her work. She was in some strange automated role. Her boss was blundering, he did not seem to be fully coordinating his brilliant mind with his deft, practised hands.

Suddenly she thought about God. How would they both explain their actions to him? They were not licensed to break their vows, just perhaps bend them… as long as nobody other than themselves got hurt. *Oh God*, she thought. The hurt she felt in trying to think negatively about Benito's sudden proposition was hurt indeed.

Anticipating Monday morning, Peter feared that first encounter with Cas's eyes. She felt likewise at the thought of their first confrontation back in nurse-patient mode.

They should have run away from Girasol together while they had the chance. It was only a matter of time now, and a little more treatment, which she would now be able to administer, before he would be away from a hospital environment. But they had come back and each was awaiting the other's re-entry onto a stage where they would now become actors.

He'd been kind and generous when she had slipped back to his room the night before. He wasn't sure she would accept his suggestion. So when she appeared, he was genuinely pleased.

"Thank you for coming back. Sunday night's always one with nothing great to do!"

She was in pretend relaxed mode. "You summoned me. Patient to nurse."

"I suppose I did. It was actually an invite. I just couldn't let a perfect weekend pass without saying goodnight to you."

"You're sweet," she said, "I'm not used to that in a man."

"I'm going to be even sweeter. I'd like to prove one more thing to ourselves at the end of this lovely day," he replied.

"What's that? That you can turn me on again?"

"In a sense," he replied. "Here," he patted the bed, "we're going to just hold each other, lie in each other's arms. Any more sex and one of us will go blind, so let's just hug and save on the optician's bill."

They wrapped their arms around each other as he had directed.

She whispered, "Shit, Peter, it's 12.30. Say goodnight gently."

"Goodnight… gently."

"I knew you wouldn't be able to say it without rising to my temptation. Goodnight gently to you too."

She was gone. Now each would wait for the other's presence while they caught up on some much needed sleep.

On that Monday morning, Peter didn't know whether she had been clever or just fortunate, but she appeared in the refectory with Pablito. Peter was able to greet the boy and then joke for all patients and staff at breakfast to hear.

"Huh," he said loudly, to get their attention. "So, you two have been out on the tiles all night, eh! I'll get Professor Han to sack you both."

The lad took it seriously. "I haven't been anywhere all night. Neither has Miss Cas."

"Morning, Miss Cas," Peter said with a deep smile and, before allowing her to answer, he mused, "and do you stick to that same story?"

"I do… and I can vouch for it too."

"How come?" Peter pretended to challenge her.

"Juan and I were just walking along the corridor when we saw you being dropped off by taxi. What was it? The casino this time or a bit of night life?"

"Neither," Peter pretended to say firmly. "Church, if you really want to know… and who knows, I'll be the only one to know if my prayers come true."

This was all beginning to backfire on Cas. She'd need to escape this rather open public display of fun, with its flirtatious undercurrent, and return the relationship to its normal level of banter between them, which those around them had got quite accustomed to.

"Let's start again. Miss Cas." He held out his hand. "Good morning."

Their touch was warm and tender, yet they knew the electricity those hands could generate.

"Good morning, Chief," she said with a glowing smile.

Peter held his same hand out to the lad. "Morning, Paul."

Pablito didn't react at first.

"Morning, Paul Demar... potential Olympic champ."

The way Peter had said 'Paul Demar' made Cas feel that her knees were going to buckle. She thought to herself *Oh my God, the cunning bugger has built in to the equation 'La Mer'. Every time we say or hear the name will be a memory jerker back to Girasol.* In a sense, it was an enormous compliment, but how hard it would be not to confuse the new-found name with their equally discovered emotions for each other.

She smiled broadly. "You big mischievous bastard!"

"Oh come on. It's just coincidental."

My God, she felt happy. So did Peter. So did Paul.

"I like Paul," he said. "Pablito was fine when I really was the young one. My mother and the other kids never graduated me to Pablo, the elder."

There was never mention in the lad's conversations of his father. Peter quietly bet to himself that he would come onto the scene if he realised the boy was a potential success, and a money earner.

"... And Demar?"

"Yes, I like that too. It'll look good in the papers," Pablito reacted.

Chapter 10

Shelagh McArthur, née Delaney, was really pleased to say goodbye to William and send him off packing to go to work. There she knew he would become Mr William in the environment where ordinarily he enjoyed the power inherited from his father's founding generation. Word, before she married him, was that his two previous wives had both reached the point of despising him before he had walked out on them.

Each time, the divorces had cost him dear and that prospect was looming again. It was beginning to cross her mind. She supposed that five years earlier he had been more boyish. He'd never needed to go to work. He just drew his pay cheque each month and filled his days with her on his arm, doing the circuit of horse race tracks, Mayfair restaurants, Barbados in January, the family villa in April into May, cricket, Henley, the round of cocktail parties and weekends as house guests of fringe aristocracy.

She was five years younger then as well, and ten years William's junior. His class impressed her above the wealth, and lack of it, which she had inherited as the female heir to the Delaney fortunes. Her grandfather had started the family empire many years before by buying two second-hand cranes from a bankrupt coal-miner. He had stripped off the four wheels, which gave them their manoeuvrability around the coalmine, and mounted them on steel stilts so that they were less dependent on being operated with the lifting bucket below ground level, and made them operational up to four storeys high on a Heath Robinson climbing frame.

Those small beginnings had been the foundation of the Delaney crane empire and her father's great wealth, made from servicing the requirements of the capital cities in the UK in the immediate post-war building boom.

William, somehow or other, had suddenly got a new message that if he didn't work at the family empire, a predator could swallow up a chunk of shares and ease the family out. No longer was the group actually family-controlled sharewise. As each shit cousin, uncle or maiden aunt ran out of their own particular brand of family silver to sell, so they had turned to paper stock. Institutions had bought embarrassingly large parts of the equity and therefore, unless William showed he was the controlling influence within, he could have been chopped and a successor put in to bat by the investors. None of that appeared to have made him any more sensible though, and that fact was what was coming home to Shelagh more and more.

Weekends in Deauville when they were courting (well, sleeping together while trying to ensure nobody knew what they were up to) used to be fun. It seemed the same crowd was still there. Jockeys with their model wives, and everybody knew why the two extremes of stature appealed to each other. The statuesque models were the epitome of physical perfection, and the little chaps could pick up big money for riding horses for owners like William. Then, if bed became part of the ride, the jockeys' ability to simultaneously service 'up-top' and 'down below' without any contortions, seemed, was a bonus.

Then there were the trainers themselves, from whom any owner's wife, or girlfriend of the day, could expect to receive enormous charm. They relied on the female influence, although, in the main, the women didn't really understand form. But an owner would often hear from his lady that, "So and so the trainer is a great bloke," which seemed in itself to create a retainer role between optimistic owner and opportunist trainer.

Shelagh had realised this past weekend that, despite the varying physical statures, and financial ones, of the 'jocks', the 'trains' and the 'bosses', put them on to a golf course, where they all boasted false handicaps in order to try and win, and they all became clones of each other. In short, they were all a bunch of plonkers.

Her husband happened to be a leading light. Totally pissed by 9.30pm on the Friday night. So utterly out of his mind as to wager £1,000 on himself winning the Stableford later that next day, which was willingly shared between two spiv turf accountants, who had somehow wheedled their way onto the guest list for the weekend. For William to then to boast he would take on all comers at £10 a point on the backgammon board the next evening was just not endearing, particularly when Shelagh could see how all those sober 'mates' were prepared to goad her husband into ever greater degrees of foolishness.

To have then only shot 14 points in the golf competition and to be pissed by six in the evening, with the pleasant formal dinner ahead of them both, was even less endearing, as was leaving him asleep on the four poster bed as she showered and poured herself into her newly acquired Chanel gown, to appear in style at the evening event, as would have been expected of a Delaney.

As one then, without the ties of a husband, she had found the French Count attentive and amusing, albeit probably gay. But at least he was sober, and fun. Not like William would be the next morning, when he had to sober up to place sensible bets for the racing programme, which they had all ostensibly come to watch.

At the end of the weekend, William had slept all the way back in the company plane. So that sobered him up sufficiently to, "Apologise, old girl... had some sort of stomach upset... bloody Frogs' food, I wouldn't wonder," which were lame excuses. As was his final insult: to lie that he was going to the club to play bridge on the late Sunday afternoon, when Shelagh knew only too well, as a result of a regular fiver to the chauffeur, that he'd be down at the stables to look after that sick mare, when the certain odds were that the mare was only 16 or 17 and enjoyed his attention, providing she was given 20 quid to, "Keep quiet and hang on to your job."

So to see his bleary eyes leaving to go to work on this Monday morning was no loss to Shelagh.

By contrast, Mr William's entrance into the office was welcomed by Vera Miles. She'd had a perfectly ordinary weekend, but could have done without Peter's phone call that morning, insisting that he knew William was in the office and that her shielding him was going just too far. Peter was, after all, the group CEO and just had to have access to the Chairman, he insisted.

"Find him!" was too strong a command for her to take. She couldn't. She didn't know where he was until he walked in.

"Morning, Vera."

"Oh! Thank God. Morning, Mr William. Peter Martinez is getting very cross and anxious to speak to you."

"Peter Martinez? Bloody cheek! Goes sick forever, leaves me to run the shop. What's he think he is?"

"He's not sick, Sir. He's on leave."

"Pull the other one. He's not bloody fit to work so, rather than get topped by the Board, in the best interests of the investors, he takes the cowardly way out and books holiday. Pull the other one. What's he want, anyway? Did you say I was going out to see him next week?"

"Yes I did," Vera said loyally.

"Well. What's he want?"

"He won't be there next week."

"What? Where's he off to now, for Christ's sake?"

"He'll be at the Board meeting."

"What?"

"As I said, he'll be at the Board meeting."

William paled. "So damn it, woman. What's he want?"

Vera was always upset by becoming 'woman' in his vocabulary. Sometimes he could be nice, kind, ask after her parents. Then when things weren't going his way, he'd reduce her to 'woman', as if to blame her for all the ills he was enduring.

"He insists on speaking to you."

"Do you know how to contact him?"

"Yes."

"Then bloody well get him," he said, with little grace.

Peter didn't have anyone to shield his calls during his coffee break/rest. Not that he got coffee, just water. Cas had given him a gentle knee treatment in the first quarter of the day.

"Seriously," she had said, "you really did overdo your knee. First the driving, then… well, you know. You have to be careful, you could do untold damage." She couldn't help but smile.

The phone rang. "Peter Martinez," he said, in his efficient, businesslike way.

"Hello, Peter. It's Vera Miles. I have the Chairman for you."

"Is he sober?"

"Mr Peter! I'll put you through."

"Hello, Peter," William greeted him, "you any better, old boy?"

"Yes, fine."

"How fine?"

"Fine enough to be back next week for the Board meeting."

"Is that wise?"

"Yes. I'm sure it is."

"Listen, Peter, old chap. Don't you think you're trying just too hard?"

"Too hard for what?"

William always had the habit, probably picked up from Harrow or Eton, or wherever it was, whereby he never ever leaked the source of his information, but always relied upon it.

"Well, old chap, and I'm saying this for your own good, word is you're not so well."

"What's my trouble?"

"May be stress. Confusion. You've taken a bashing. Told you get confused."

"Who told you that?"

That encouraged William to believe he had hit a nail on the head.

"Not who told me that. Let me put it this way, nobody has denied it."

"What, not even the waitress?"

"What? Which waitress?"

"Were there two?"

"Now listen, what do you mean?"

"No, William, old boy. You listen. I think the Board ought to be considering three things."

"Oh, so you now chair the agenda, do you? In your state of mind?"

"Yes. I think I do. Hear me out. I'll list the three things. OK, one…" Peter broke naturally into his multiple choice canter. "… Word is, I can't say from whom, that you're pissed more often than not and your brain is getting pickled. Two, I need to ask who fronts the European side of the group's operation and I expect the straight answer, 'Mr William'. Third, then, what are the prospects for the Construction and Investment in Europe, and where in particular is being targeted?"

"You on drugs or something, Peter?"

"Not at all. I have a clear head, a pretty fit body again and if you think I need to see a brain expert, then invite him, or her, to the meeting and non-Execs can decide what level of testing I need... with the option before all of us to interpret Construction and Investment, not just on the existing basis of the UK but in the expanding markets of Europe. I'll see you on Thursday week. Oh, and make sure my agenda item is tabled please, old boy."

Peter gently placed the receiver, into the cradle. He felt satisfied that, in a sense, he'd begun to stuff Mr William.

Almost on cue, it seemed, there was a knock at the door.

"Mr Peter. Are you ready?" was the formal request.

"Yes, Miss Cas," was the equally formal answer.

He opened the door.

"You look happy," she observed.

"Oh, I am *so* happy. I've just fucked."

"Peter. I hate hearing that. That sort of language. Now apologise before I really take offence. Surely you've got some understanding of my sensitivity."

"Sorry, my love. I ought to qualify. I've just fucked the Chairman, metaphorically speaking. Kicked him into touch... actually paved the way for Paul Demar's future, your own, and with a minor vested interest in my own rewards too. In short, my sweet, I sense we're on a roll. Now... I'll need my knee to be fully functional. Can you cut the offence and get on with the job... oh," he added softly. "Blow me a kiss and tell me you still infatuate me... please."

"I'm beginning to fucking not," she said... but with a soft smile.

Maria usually didn't mind Monday mornings. This one she did. She had a busy schedule ahead of her anyway; the two tour companies were arguing price and room allocation this year particularly. Places like Turkey and North Africa were competing from a base of nil. So any tourism they could attract would be the beginning of a long term investment, and they were cutting the margins enormously.

Maria and Marco were agreed. They would not compromise the service or facilities. To an extent, they would be happy not to have the tour operators and their special type of customer, but it was steady income that paid the overheads.

It wasn't so much the day ahead but the aftermath of the disappointing day before that had lowered Maria's spirits. Not only had she had a maternal panic about which hospital Peter had been carted off to because of an imagined stroke, she'd then spoken to Tania. In many respects, she treated Tania, if not as an adopted daughter, at least as a common-law sister-in-law – that is, once she had sussed out that she was her brother-in-law's long term plaything.

But Marco's visits to Tania were now certainly fewer and, as he announced at a Board meeting they had held, "Girasol can now look after itself, Tania's doing a good job and doesn't need my interference quite as much." *Interference*, Maria had thought. *You mean putting your hand up her skirt or slapping her bottom.* Maybe he was losing his sex drive or had now been told, as part of the aura of confidence Tania had developed, that he was no longer giving her the level of satisfaction he might just have done 20 years before. Not to mention that she was less dependent now on the 'pocket money' and little presents he used to buy when she was on a cleaner's wage.

The result of Maria's call to Tania was part informative and majorly mischievous. Of course, Maria knew Tania still had the sweats for her son. Who wouldn't, as Maria knew that when they were both young, Peter's head had often turned to follow Tania's provocative strut. Maria felt that nothing had ever taken place between them, but she'd never be sure with two such electric characters.

Effectively by hearing from Tania about Jan's demise, romantically speaking, had ruined her hopes of inheriting a new daughter-in-law, who she really thought would look after her son when she herself was no longer around. Someone to be the guardian angel in Peter's life. If it had been a break after a row, and Maria had seen that before with Peter, it might have got patched up. But with a new young lady on the scene already, and a blonde at that, it was clear Peter's attentions were diverted big time. Jan was undoubtedly past tense.

"Oh," Maria sighed, as her head finally hit her Sunday night pillow, "it will all turn out for the best. Perhaps I'll like her. I'll get Peter to tell me all about her." That was enough to allow her into contented sleep.

José did his best to put up with Maria's unrest. "Give it until the morning," he'd insisted, "everything becomes more clear on a new day."

She'd been up at six to pack José off to the office, which was now on a campus outside Barcelona. He'd be away again for four nights, then come home exhausted. Spend three nights with Maria and then go back. He'd reached an age when he could now retire and they'd discussed that... but against the backcloth that José actually still did like the job and the trimmings of the high position he now held, the decision was always, "We'll have to see." Maybe knowing his father was now alone would encourage him to give up the insurance world and take on a family role in the hotel.

Maria resolved early on she would just have to make the most of this day, and by ten she was pretty normal and up and running. Peter hadn't said he would be seeing her before his return to the UK. Surely they would speak again before the weekend, though. At least she hoped so.

For Cas, the morning had started full of apprehension. While she hadn't had a great deal of sleep in the last three days, Friday apart, the sleep she had had was deep and undisturbed, without a hint of a dream, let alone a nightmare.

Her stomach now churned as she showered. Would Peter be able to play things down to revert to the normality of their working relationship of just a few days before? Should she ignore him? More to the point, *could* she? She made a special point of washing her hair, unusual on a Monday. Mondays didn't ordinarily count as a day on which to look anything other than scraped together. Usually there was a new intake of patients anyway, and they were too anxious to notice a grain of dandruff or a few hairs out of place in a clip or bunches.

Her physio coat was always pristine on the first day of the week, so she didn't have to get her iron out. Gosh! Peter needed an iron to press the shirt he'd collected from Girasol. She'd remember to offer it to him. Would it look as though she was being intrusive, like Jan, she supposed, to suggest she iron the shirt for him? Yes. It would.

She set out from the staff quarters and walked quickly with a skip in her stride, through the newfangled swipe-controlled double doors onto the landing. She nearly tripped over the body leaning back against the wall with legs sprawled out, blocking her path.

"Christ!" she yelled as she did a little leap over the limbs, which she'd only just picked up in her vision before it was too late.

"Sorry, Miss Cas."

It was Pablito.

"What the hell are you doing there? Someone could have fallen over you."

"I said I was sorry, Miss," he said, agitated.

"That's OK," she humoured him, "no harm done. It does you good to get a bit of surprise exercise in the mornings. Now, what are you doing there? You surely should be at breakfast."

"I couldn't sleep."

"Why?"

"I thought it was a dream."

"What?"

"Somebody being prepared to make me into a champion athlete."

She laughed kindly. "Now listen. We can only do that if we have the right raw material. It would need you to do it for us, to help you do it."

She suddenly realised she was talking as though there was a binding partnership between her and Peter. That was a bit presumptuous. She didn't doubt he would put his all into the sponsorship and encouragement, but from a distance. After all, he had done that at least once before with Jaimé, she now knew. She hoped, however, that the project would cause Peter to have a further reason to return more frequently to Spain, or be at the other end of a phone, and travel to the parts of Europe where he had said she would have to go. She'd have to see. She would concentrate on the raw material and just let the rest fall into place.

"I will try hard for you, miss."

"I know you will." She consciously reverted to the singular. "Now, you won't even get near the starting blocks without a good breakfast in you. I'll take you to the refectory."

She'd got a hostage, a shield, a decoy to divert Peter's eyes, and any of those others who happened to be around, from direct contact with herself. That seemed good and gave her confidence. It worked.

Now she was waiting for the second half of the working morning with her more senior charge. She knew he was in business mode. He'd been talking about a sensitive conversation with this William chap, his colleague and Chairman. She hoped he would still be calm and relaxed.

Tania had gone to bed exceedingly grumpy and had tossed and turned, drifting in to sleep and jumping out of it with a desire to scream at the fact that her Peter had been cross with her. If she was banned from cleaning and stocking his house, she'd never really have time with him again.

She had needed to 'peep'. She didn't like being accused of peeping, though. It seemed perverted the way he had said it.

No! He'd have to eventually understand that she simply needed to know that he was basically just using this young intruder's body. That it was just an impulse to unload his natural needs onto this plaything. That would have shown if he'd just rolled over and gone to sleep afterwards, which she was sure he had.

Now that she could focus in daylight on the bed he'd been sharing, she realised it showed signs of more than just two people in semi-passive mode. She could tell. She'd been making up hotel beds for most of her life.

From afar, when the scene looked steamy and physical, she'd just had to intervene. She couldn't let this young bimbo arouse her man, as it appeared she was doing. She had to stop it, and in her mind she felt she had succeeded. She hadn't intended to discover the evidence of their antics out of view, behind closed curtains, the night before; she'd thought the bed would be the place they would play. But then, she told herself, the way clothes were scattered around indicated the result of them drinking the Montrachet and the sister red wine she had so carefully selected. If they were drunk, nothing serious would have happened. It would just have been scatty fun. He would have been incapable, as men in her own life had often been after too much drink.

Once she had run through those odds, she had drifted back into a shallow sleep on that Sunday night. Then suddenly she had woken again with a sinking feeling of fear, and a replay of the nightmare scene with Peter and this interloper.

She'd eventually decided, on awaking on the Monday morning, that she had had enough of this indecision and at 6.30am, she quietly took out her bicycle and rode the few hundred metres to Peter's house. She tidied and dusted the lower floor and set the dishwasher onto its cycle. She then vacuumed thoroughly, hating every strand of blonde hair she saw disappear into the cylinder. She felt like puking as she entered the bedroom. The sun was breaking into the room through the open drapes.

She stood and looked up at the hill where she had established her vantage point. Looked at in reverse view, she realised how insignificant she was, such a distant and minute presence to the occupants of the room. Nevertheless, she'd seen what she had seen and that was the sole purpose of her having been at that spot on the horizon.

She sorted the ground floor out in her usual meticulous and trained way. She'd been doing cleaning in its various forms for most of her adult life, so she knew the short cuts. Upstairs was a different matter. There was a layer of emotion, envy and a passion in the air that she had to dust and dampen down before she could fondly re-make the bed. She ripped the sheets off and threw them into a pile on the floor. She was repulsed by her thoughts.

The bathroom was quite easily sorted. There seemed a lot of clothes in the linen basket for just a one-night stopover but, thank you God, she thought, there weren't any girlie bits and pieces left behind. She looked in the mirror and glimpsed a much older woman than she should have seen. But then she had hardly slept, certainly hadn't even run a comb through her hair and only thrown on a pair of jeans and a T-shirt.

"Huh!" she said to the mirror, noticing she was wearing the Coca-Cola T-shirt giveaway. "I suppose that bastard will stay at home again changing nappies and leave me short of stock again."

The thought of Alano 'Cola' Carlos prompted her to go into the bedroom and view the made bed in a different light, through the prism of the pleasure she had given to Peter in her imagination, through the body of the other man.

There was another mirror image staring at her and in that one, below the mess of her general demeanour, she was now showing signs of having become horny. There were hints of perspiration staining the white armpits of the T-shirt. Her pants felt hot. Instinctively, she went into the bathroom, took a towel from the airing cupboard and put that over the door into the shower. She slipped the T-shirt over her head, stepped out of her jeans and removed her underwear; that would freshen up a little while she showered off the grime and her mood.

She allowed the water to stream over her hair, which would dry naturally in no time, certainly by the time she had cycled back to the hotel. She hoped the freshness on her skull would clear her fuzzy head. She wouldn't have described herself as a headache type person. She'd put this fuzziness down to the recent times. The shock of Peter being shot, his recovery. Toni going out of her life for ever. Her father…

She'd probably change back when she got into her hotel manageress clothes. A smart black skirt with a white shirt. She would change her underwear too. There was a chill around. She'd wear stockings, appropriate for the autumnal mood. That always cheered her up. The day was improving.

Refreshed and back in the hotel, she was studying the computer diary. They had three overnighters, which was good for a Monday at this time of the year, and the local Lions Club had their monthly lunch. She liked those because it brought men into the hotel. She was best with them. Inadvertently, they'd probably work out she was wearing stockings. That was always a fun turn-on.

There was suddenly a chill atmosphere. As though a ghost had entered the room. She looked up.

"Christ, you made me jump! I didn't hear you come in."

"I didn't want to disturb you. You were so engrossed in what you were doing."

"So, Alano Carlos, salesperson extraordinaire, you've decided to come back and service the requirements of all my currently undersupplied guests," she said, heavily laden with sarcasm.

"Oh dear, is it as bad as that? I've only had a couple of weeks off, actually. I came back to work on Tuesday last week, which unfortunately meant I missed calling on you. Last week was the third."

"That's right. I suppose you're going to say your wife had the child too."

"Well, yes, of course," he said with surprise.

"Well, are you going to say what it was?"

"Look. Is there something up? OK, I know we both got carried away and I haven't seen you since… and maybe you're regretting what we did. But I'd rather not be on the receiving end of this tongue that I don't recognise as the same one I discovered when I saw you last."

She was rather pulled up in her stride. She wasn't used to people speaking their minds to her – except Peter perhaps, as she quickly remembered the lash given to her by his tongue the day before. That, too, she thought, had brought about the current headache, which would not budge.

She softened somewhat. "Do you regret what we did, then?" she asked.

"Not at all. It was what we both needed. I don't actually know your reason but the effect was the same for us both. Mine was male and animal, I'm afraid – in plain terms, a shortage of supply. My wife, for the past three years, has changed her philosophy and the bed is for conceiving children, no longer for fun. So frankly, whether she is, or was, pregnant or not, there was still this shortage. Then you showed up with the same needs and I have to say, you were the best I've ever had, and I thank you for that. So no, I have no regrets, unless I'm now going to be lashed to bits by your tongue whenever we meet. So how is it with you? I might as well know the truth. Regrets, or no regrets?"

"No regrets. What did your wife have?"

"A baby boy."

"That's a second boy to go with the daughter?"

"Yes."

"Are they both well?" she asked casually.

"Pretty good. She's quite tired, it wasn't an easy birth. But she's OK. The baby is a poppet."

"And how long, in male terms of course, do you think it will be until your supply is replenished?"

He laughed. "I can't think that far ahead." She laughed too.

"Listen. Two things. Can you look in the fridge and freezers and tell me what stock I need, and then get me stocked up."

"Of course. The second thing?"

She put on a coy act. She stood up from behind the desk and walked to his side. "I'm a bit embarrassed really."

"No need to be with me. Just shout and I'll take it on board."

She brushed her hand through his hair. "Well. I'm sure it's going to sound corny but I've missed you. I thought you'd had your fling and done a runner. Tell me I'm wrong."

"You are."

"Would you like me to say sorry to you for even thinking that?"

"Well yes."

"Then stock up bloody quickly. There's an electrical fault down the road."

He grinned. "Then we can't have that, can we?"

There was less play and hesitation getting him into bed this time. They both now knew why they were there. Each was uninhibited and active, she particularly, pinning Alano Carlos down and taking a commanding role above him. She then got a thrill from turning her man over so that she could look up to the hills, and to her earlier vantage point.

How's this, you bastard? she thought, imagining Peter was there, getting his binoculars all steamed up. "How do you like your own medicine thrown in your face?" she radioed to her imaginary peeping Tom.

They crescendoed... and she froze.

"What?" Alano Carlos said, disturbed by the sudden halt in her play.

"Listen," she said.

"What to?"

"Shit. It's the phone."

It's him. Peter. He can't stand seeing me do it. He's phoning to make me answer the phone. To stop my fun, because I stopped his. Those were the clear and rational thoughts inside her brain.

Alano tried to coax her back to activity. "Let it ring. It can't be for either of us. We don't live here. It's certainly not my wife."

"No. The phone. It's probably Peter... I'll explain. Just give me two minutes. I'll be back."

Tania was out of the bed without a thought of even grabbing some clothes, or a sheet or robe to cover her bare body, and was downstairs like a shot. She picked up the phone. Her head was aching.

"Hi!" It was Peter's voice.

She paused and took a deep breath.

"Hi, are you there?" he questioned, in the silence.

"Yes, it's Tania. Sorry, I was vacuuming and didn't hear the phone. I heard this noise, I thought it was the vacuum."

"Aren't you putting too much into it? You're quite out of breath."

"Yes I know, but I ran to the phone. I thought it would stop."

"So what are you doing cleaning, when I said you were fired?"

"I wanted to leave it nice for the next person."

"And what stage have you reached?"

She realised she'd got no clothes on at all. This was going to become Peter's repayment. She had drawn the drapes back. She knew from her own experience he could get a full view of her from the hill. *Crafty*, she thought. She turned so that she was full frontal for him through the window.

His voice through the earpiece initially confused her. The words were staccato, each one like a shot from a revolver held to her temple.

"Stop. Stop now what you are doing. Leave. Leave my house. I'm calling to make it perfectly clear. You're fired. Fired. Do you hear?"

The harshness and reality in his words brought a sudden stabbing pain into the back of her head.

Alano Carlos had heard the conversation from Tania's side. At first he lay there expecting her to return quickly, fully prepared to continue their entanglement. But when he found himself looking at his watch and working out she'd been gone for six or seven minutes, he realised his fervour had, if not died, certainly waned. A further five minutes made him cross. He got up and dressed. Still she had not reappeared.

He'd been off on paternity duty now for three Mondays, so each of his early week clients needed re-stocking – though not in the sense of servicing their needs in bed. Tania's were the only ones in that category. His male urges had already delayed him by over an hour. If he didn't crack on then there would be a couple of clients who would not get re-stocked. He'd also promised his wife's mother he'd be back by five to feed and bath the older kids and free her to get back to prepare his father-in-law's supper. He was a demanding male too.

Bugger cleaning up the bedroom, Alano Carlos thought. She can do that. She's well used to it. Who the hell was sufficiently important, anyway, to drag her away from the party?

As he set out to descend the stairs, he caught a glimpse of Tania's nude body. She was lying back in a casual chair in the sort of undignified pose caught lovingly on canvas by a number of the Old Masters. As a teenager, he'd always preferred the poses set up in the well-thumbed copies of Mayfair and Penthouse that were passed between his mates, as compared with the overweight nudes depicted in the history books about art in the school library.

The pathetic sight stopped his speedy exit, and he went back to the bathroom. He'd seen a robe on the back of the door. If he was going to walk out on her mid-needs, as it were, he'd at least throw her a cover for her body, for when she realised the cost to their relationship of that one phone call.

As he reached the turn in the staircase, he came into her focus. Yet she seemed unaware of his presence. There was now an uncanny silence around her, no more conversation could be heard.

Alano Carlos was on a run. His juices would never be rekindled, he knew that. When he lost focus on a goal, he could never go back. That much about himself he understood. Had it not been for his responsibilities to keep his young family warm and fed, he certainly would have chanced a different job. That, he knew, would be going forward. But circumstances had prevented it.

Tania was still holding the receiver and appeared to be listening to the incoming call as he laid the robe over her. He kissed the forefinger and middle one of his right hand and placed them on her lips, like some revered bishop on the lips of a dying saint – except Tania was clearly no saint and had blown their shallow relationship for good.

She began to raise herself from the chair, as if to say, "No, don't go, don't leave me, it'll be no more than a minute." She clung firmly to the handset as she did.

He felt no desire to change course. He closed the front door quietly behind him. She heard the diesel engine throb and the judder of his laden van as he pulled away.

"I was sorry about not having the right cordials for you and your friend at the weekend. The Coca-Cola salespeople have gone to pot. I'll have to change suppliers. No, it's not like it used to be."

Her words fell on deaf ears. Or no ears. Peter had hung up.

A tear rolled down her cheek. She felt confused. Her focus was blurred as she fixed her gaze back up the hill. She thought she glimpsed Peter against the backdrop of the trees. She'd have a closer look. Standing up from the chair, she allowed the uninvited robe to fall to the ground as she moved towards the window, inviting him to feast on her body through the lens of the binoculars again. Like he had that time in the staff changing room of the Playa, and at the fiesta, when he couldn't keep his eyes off her, and when he'd picked her up from the ground when she fell off her bike.

She knew how he appreciated that. It was the least she could do. Maybe the tears were blurring her vision but the definition in the distance was fading.

Now she imagined she heard his voice.

"So we've sorted all that out, eh!" he was saying in a businesslike way.

She found it hard to respond. Her voice couldn't co-ordinate with her brain. She automatically blurted out the words she most associated with him.

"Yes, Mr Peter."

"Cheers, Tania."

"Cheers, Mr Peter. Take care."

"You too."

So he did care.

She continued to strain her eyes into the distance as her body grew cold. She began to shake. Was it the coolness of the day, her lack of clothing, or fear? *Where is he?* She strained to get a final glimpse of him in the hills. The trees parted, as if blown apart by a storm. She thought she saw cousin Toni.

Her mood turned to panic.

"But you're dead," she muttered, "you can't be cross with me now. I've done nothing. Don't hurt me. You'd gone so what was I expected to do? Not live? Not serve Mr Peter?"

The image of her wild cousin Toni appeared in the distance.

"Oh dear God! Please save me from this beating."

She knew no more, save that she whispered, "Peter, help."

Chapter 11

Professor Han never took work home with him, or the thought of it. His young Vietnamese wife saw to that. Home to her was a sanctuary of calm and love, and a place of learning for the son and daughter she had produced for her older, doting husband. It was the habit of her family, established before they got out of Vietnam during the troubles, to burn incense and to change the perfume as they moved through the day. She would pump calm into the air as they got up and set themselves up for the day. Then she'd light another stick which had a more stimulating effect as her husband left for the hospital and the kids for school.

Fresh air wafted through the house as she stripped back everything in sight for her daily cleaning ritual. Hers was more thorough in a day than most of the young Spanish couples, their neighbours on the pleasant estate three kilometres west of Barcelona, carried out once a year.

So when Han escaped his sanctuary and got behind the wheel of his Mercedes, which was kept gleaming by his wife every Sunday morning while he was allowed to lie in, he gently switched modes.

A smile crossed his face. Normally in his special unit there was no emotion, no passion, just the grunt of reaction to heavy physical effort. So thinking back to the week before made him laugh, although each event would have been serious, had it gone wrong.

The Pablito boy getting his arse kicked by Peter Martinez was indeed a high point. Han, of course, knew that was exactly what the boy needed but had he attempted to administer the treatment, he would doubtless have been up before a medical disciplinary committee by now. The up-side of that was that he would have been suspended on pay while an inquiry was set up. The further up-side of *that*, he thought, was that he would have been forced to be at home all day, with the kids out at school. Before they'd had the family, that's what he had most liked. Daytime relaxation with Kiki was fun and physically rewarding. How to make your man feel good seemed to be an inherited attribute of the more northern of the Oriental races. Yes, Kiki was a real find.

Anyway, he could dream on behind the wheel. There would be no inquiry. Just a report of two patients having a scrap, which ended peacefully. He did wonder if the 'bait' idea as to how Cas would tame her own bull might be going a bit far, but on balance he didn't think so. Given their differences in age and culture, she and Peter Martinez got on extremely well together, Han told himself. Prior to Peter's arrival, on many a day Han had had to sort out one of Cas's 'down' times, when she said she couldn't go on with the constant reminder of her fiancé's death ruling her planet.

In the short space of time he'd been there, Peter seemed to have lifted her out of those moods, though Han doubted he knew what had brought that about. Pablito was acting as a further catalyst between them and all that knocked on into the rest of the team, who were as high in spirits as he had ever known. That was good news, particularly this week, with the open evening for the Federation meeting.

Being a strong national organisation was important with the IPC on the horizon. All year round at hospital treatment level, he and his physio teams would usually attain their objectives, getting patients back out on the road with their various spare parts or, as in Peter's case, a review of his own essential parts. Their stimulant was to have the real hope of renovating an otherwise wrecked body to a physical level of athleticism, and to be dreams come true.

Han had previously hosted the evening that was coming up. The presence of his wife always helped. The fuddy-duddies liked her vivacity in the midst of their serious approach to performing the functions for which they had been elected. They'd meet and socialise. There would be some wine and tapas to oil the wheels. Then Han would show them a few examples of patients and progress. *God only knows how Pablito will react*, he thought. The presence of Peter, not as a patient, would no doubt be a help.

Then after that, they would get to review the plans leading up to the 1992 event. It seemed miles off but each of them was aware of how the time would fly, and of the need for them to move on beyond the social gathering stage, to hard business time. They could give input to the main Olympic Committee on things like building programmes, sponsorship and publicity, and contact with the other competing nations.

It would be an anxious week for him but it took him into a different arena every now and again. That did him good. He responded well to change.

He thought he ought to inform Peter Martinez about the way the evening might pan out. He hoped there would be enough life in the attendees to grab Peter's attention. While he did not doubt Peter's ability to turn on the charm when necessary, he perceived that he could become bored quickly.

Han pulled into his personalised parking spot. Took his very important briefcase from the boot, locked the car and made his way into the hospital through the rear door, so as not to be confronted by any of the day's outpatients, or more particularly their families or supporters. He always had a team meeting at about 8.45am on a Monday morning, just to make sure everybody had got back from their weekends away. Today they had gathered in the smaller of the three lecture rooms.

Han went first to his office, where his loyal early bird secretary was waiting with his day's agenda.

"Buenos dias, Professor."

"Buenos dias, Abril."

She was a pleasant, stable-natured 50-something, perhaps five years older than himself.

"What's the day?" he said, forgetting to enquire whether she had had a good weekend. But then he never did. She knew that once he was in the hospital, that was his life. Full-on concentration on the job in hand.

It looked pretty normal. A few intakes to assess. A ward round, which usually took the form of a walking tour of the activity areas, where he could assess progress and monitor setbacks, which usually came from patients' over-zealous desire to get back to normality earlier than was good for them.

Abril looked at her watch. "You're expected at the team meeting."

He looked at his timepiece, the one bought by his wife at the Omega duty free in Hong Kong.

"Gosh! Yes. They'll be playing cards if I keep them much longer. I'll see you after. Sometime during the day, I must find time to dictate the agenda for Wednesday."

"Will it vary much from the July one?"

They met quarterly but from January next year, it would become every two months and then in the following year, monthly. They left the options open for sub-committees then to meet weekly. He said he would think that through, but to leave the July agenda on his desk.

"Buenos dias, everybody," he announced as he entered. The partial Spanish and Oriental English used to make Guy, one of the physios, laugh. It was neither one thing nor the other, but he supposed it was courteous of Han to show that he was fluent in two words of the native tongue.

"Everybody fit?"

"Yes," echoed through the 20 or so present.

Han glimpsed Cas. She normally did stand out in a crowd.

"So... Miss South Africa survived the trial of driving Mr Martinez south."

There was mirth from all but Cas.

"You could say that," she said, "but I think you ought to advise him not to drive for a while. I think, out of our sight, he'll overdo everything. He gives the impression he thinks he's fully retrained," which was their expression for rehabbed. It sounded so much more athletic and less 'patched up'.

"Then do we all get to see his performance with his fiancée?"

Initially there was a silence. Heads turned to reconfirm it was Guy who had said that. The comment upset Cas enormously. She'd forgotten Peter's original and macho prognosis of what his aims were. In the midst of having grown to like Peter, even before the events immediately pre- and over the weekend, she'd made a point of forgiving him for his chauvinism.

"I wouldn't expect that would give you any pleasure, other than to see how the other half live," she responded.

Most thought it was said in fun. Han was a little more perceptive than that and picked up on the little hint of spite.

"Now now!" he interrupted. "We have to respect a number of things – particularly that we should not malign our patients. Without them, we wouldn't have jobs. Moreover, sometimes people when first admitted put up a defence mechanism to cover for their physical deficiencies. But, Guy, I have to say your comment, I'm sure meant in fun, would have been better not made in female company." Han half-realised he was close to dropping a clanger himself. "Let's move on," he said quickly. "We've important work to do."

He turned to his number two. "Give me a note on the valuable comment Cas has given us on her observations. Thank you, Cas, for taking the patient to his home. I'd like you all to know the importance of that. I'm not sure if you all know of Peter Martinez's normal role in life. He's quite an entrepreneur and, of course, being born a Spaniard, I'd like him to become interested in the IPC. I think, having seen his performance with the boy Pablito, that he could inject some real life into the committee. I'm asking him along to the meeting on Wednesday. Typically, he immediately said he'd need a suit, shirt and tie… so there you are… that's the sort of man he is… taking things seriously from the off. So, if she hasn't moaned to you about it yet, Cas drove him down on Saturday. So thank her for that."

One of the other girls put her hand in the air. Han beckoned it was OK for her to talk.

"Professor, next time, could I have the job?"

They all laughed, including Cas. Another hand shot in the air and, without being given permission to speak, the person did so.

"Me too," she said.

Suddenly there was a chorus in agreement. Guy pushed his luck again.

"Sir. Perhaps we all ought to put names in a hat to see who gets lucky."

There was more gentle laughter, with a hesitant overtone. Han called the meeting to order and said what the week's programme was going to be, then covered the other normal topics about shifts and patient allocations. He made no move to disrupt Cas's work with Peter, in what was probably his last full week in their care.

Just before the meeting broke up, Han enquired if there was anything else.

Cas made a movement as though putting in a hesitant bid at an auction, as if she was not sure whether she really wanted to catch his attention.

"Professor, we've got a sort of new patient."

"Really?"

"Well yes. Pablito has left."

"Left! Good God, he can't have!"

"Well, not literally. He's renamed himself."

"Renamed himself?" Han, for once, was lost.

"Yes. For when he's a national champion athlete."

"Are you serious?"

"Well, yes."

"What's he calling himself?"

"Paul Demar."

"Wow! I like that. Do you think it will stick, or is it some early adolescent fad?"

"Oh, I think it'll stick alright. Tell you what, on your round, call him Pablito. See if he reacts."

Professor Han thought for a few moments.

"You talk about him reacting. Have you got to know him that well?" That question was addressed to them all.

His regular handlers, Oliveria and Guy, openly scoffed.

"He's like a pedigree greyhound. You never quite know where you are with him."

Cas knew that was because they hadn't won his confidence.

"Is there a specific reason why you ask, Sir?" she questioned.

"Well! Just supposing. Just supposing his mind, at least, was made up and he'd got this vision of being a representative of his country in 1992 – wouldn't it be amazing if we could get him into the equation from today, as it were? Just supposing we made a point to the Federation meeting on Wednesday that we have a lad who represents the Games' target principle, somebody whose progress they too could follow, along with the necessary input for sponsorship. We're actually preparing a competitor to run on the track within the buildings where they would be inputting ideas, someone who'll actually sleep in the accommodation they'll be providing. Wouldn't that halve the difficulty of the job in hand?"

Oliveria and Guy remained sceptical. Perhaps they'd had too much difficulty in the original harnessing process. It often happened that those who broke in a pony from the wild didn't get to obtain the best ride from the tamed animal.

"Could we?" said Han. "Dare we parade the lad… what did you say he was now called… ?"

"Paul Demar."

"… This Paul Demar in the making, show him off, on Wednesday? Dare we?"

"Yes," Cas was emphatic. "It could be part of his early training. It rather pre-empts the fact that I've said I'll coach him, in my own time, and I was going to ask the department's permission to do that."

"You can all do what you like in your free time, apart from working for some unqualified masseur or chiropractor. Of course you can. On that basis, would you bring him along to the meeting?"

"Yes."

"Can we try and get his appearance away from just being a person with a dream within the hospital? You know, put him in a formal tracksuit, so that he looks the part. Also, I'd like to get you out of your white physio uniform and into your social gear, so that you blend in with the members."

"I don't know about the latter," Cas reacted.

Oliviera spoke up. "I've got a little black suit you could borrow. I live in hope of a Prince Charming inviting me out to dinner. But I doubt it'll be required this Wednesday, or ever!"

That caused laughter and an air of relaxation, which Han turned into a pretty serious issue.

"OK," he said, "let's do it." Then he thought again. "Total secrecy must apply to this plan. Nobody, *nobody* outside this room must know the surprise. We'll spring this on everybody." He thought hard. "We'll spring Paul Demar and his coach, and Peter Martinez, on them as a total surprise. In fact, make sure to keep Mr Peter out of it too. His being surprised would make the evening.

"Well, that was a good meeting. Thank you. Most constructive. Now we must deal with the root requirements... all those in need of our help... that is, the greater arena we should be aiming for, boys and girls. Back to the job in hand. Have a good day. Have a very good week, in fact."

Chapter 12

On the late afternoon of the evening event, Peter had felt strange pressing a shirt again. At home in the UK, he had his dirty linen collected each week and delivered back, either crisply folded, for his daily help to lay fondly over the bed, or on a hanger if they were not going to adorn his own body immediately. *Gosh*, he thought, it's years *since I had to iron my own shirt*. Probably back to the Prince of Wales Drive days, when he and Max had fought over who should have the first use of the iron in the mornings. Then the argument that ensued was to which one of them had left the thermostat set on 'woollens' instead of 'cottons'. He always thought his fun mate had re-set the dial incorrectly for a bit of a joke. He was in fact right in that guess.

Anna had then taken over the laundry.

Occasionally, he knew, Tania had taken it upon herself to do a bit of pressing when she cleaned Maria and Peter's family home without being asked. He thought about her now. She'd been strange during their last conversation. Pre-occupied? Maybe, as well she might have been, after her appalling behaviour. Strange, though…

Next he laid his trousers onto the ironing board. He really loved the satisfaction of burning a deep crease into them, watching the steam rise out of the damp handkerchief he traditionally used as a pressing cloth.

He was surprised Cas hadn't been across to say how she hoped he would enjoy his first grown-up evening's entertainment in weeks, and how she wished she could be there. Perhaps there was a tinge of envy that he, a relative outsider, had been invited into an inner sanctum and she, so much a part of Professor Han's 'Institute', had not. He would have liked her to be there but it was not his place to invite guests or seek that privilege. He would just have to deal with the old farts without her. Now what Han ought to have done was to get her into a plunge bra and let the old buggers have a fun night out; then the hospital would get the support he was after. But he couldn't be expected to be that good a marketeer. Peter sensed that was Han's intended short term role for him. He'd see.

The reception was due to start at 6.30pm. He'd get there about ten minutes late. That was his style.

He realised he hadn't got a full length mirror in his room, so he couldn't quite see how he looked. The shirt collar, he could see in his shaving mirror, was a tad loose. He'd shed nearly 10 kilos during his hospitalisation. It was probably the lack of alcohol, or could have been the result of Cas having put him through his paces in the gym. If he tightened his tie a touch, he felt the collar would close up, which it did. He needed a haircut, or at least his mother would have said he did, because the hair at the nape of his neck was curling. Cas had crimped it more in her excited fingers at the weekend. Maybe she didn't think the same way as Maria.

It was about time to go down, he felt. His knee had loosened up again in the three days of concentrated physiotherapy Cas had been giving him. She now talked freely to him while she manipulated his knee. It was all very professional but there was an extra sensitivity in her expressive hands now, or so he liked to think.

Peter didn't usually feel apprehensive about entering a room. In this case, the majority of conversation could well turn out to be in his native tongue, unless Han was involved, who had only perfected a couple of Spanish words in all his time in Spain.

Han had brought along a couple of secretarial staff to control the limited entry at the door.

"Buenos tardes," one pleasant, mid-30s off-duty secretary volunteered, before asking for his name.

"Peter Martinez," he responded. It almost had to be because there were only half a dozen name tags left on the temporary desk they had put up for the event. She stepped from behind the remnants of what had been a formal alphabetical layout and pinned a label on the lapel of Peter's suit jacket.

"What's it say?" he asked, as he tried to read it upside down.

"Peter Martinez – Guest."

"Oh fine. That's what I am. Muchas gracias."

The other girl, some six or seven years younger, smiled openly as she opened the doors for Peter to make his entrance. Years before, he thought, he would have earmarked that one to chat up and attempt to take home with him afterwards. Not nowadays, though. But even then, he usually froze out at the last minute and never ever had introduced any member of the opposite sex to his flat on that basis. He loved living with his own imagination.

The noise of excited conversation was close to deafening. But then that was why Peter always tried to arrive late. The ice was broken with the reception supply of wine, sparkling wine and orange juice. One of the kitchen staff, in her best black skirt and neatly pressed and laundered white blouse, stepped out into his path, indicating he should select a glass of nectar to his liking. He chose red wine.

Suddenly the Professor was in front of him. Peter's focus was immediately taken from him, however, by the lady at his side.

"This is my wife, Kiki," and, in turn, "this is one of our star patients, Peter Martinez!" he explained to her.

Kiki took his hand, and he felt a little frisson. There was always something, for Peter, in an Oriental hand. He had no doubt it took him back to Honey, and to Coco.

"It is pleasant to meet a star patient. My husband needs every one of them." It was profound and true, but softened in its seriousness by her giggle. "... And you are behind this young man I keep hearing about."

"If you mean Pablito... no. Not behind him. I'd like to think in front of him. We've all had problems in our lives, I don't doubt. Some of us have been there, overcome them and moved on. So if one can teach another how to do that, in my view, the potential result is a very good reason for being on this planet."

Kiki related to every word this opinionated man had said. She was thunderstruck, but she was not prepared to show it. She had lived through the Vietnam 'problems' and the insistence that the Americans could cure every problem with might and fire-power. That, though, had forced her family to evacuate their homeland, and to separate. Eventually, she had met Han and he had been her mentor in overcoming the loss of her family around her. They'd met when she was at a low ebb, but Han had gently led her into thinking about establishing her own family unit, with him, and dedicating herself to them.

"Well, Mr Martinez..."

He interrupted. "Peter, please."

Now that was still a hard custom for an Oriental to get to grips with – to be on Christian name terms on a first meeting. With Peter though, Kiki felt quite at ease, so she would try.

"Very well, Peter. What I was going to say is that what you said was very apt, but I think you make light of your generous efforts. After all, the boy, as I understand it, is nothing to you, yet my husband did tell me, in graphic terms, how you did what everybody else would have loved to do... and to be fair, should have done. They are his carers, not you."

Han interjected. "Now, Peter, that's enough of sharing you with my wife. Let me introduce you to some other people. My dear, you come with us too. They all like you. Actually, Peter, you'll find they far more appreciate being in the company of a beautiful woman than with you or me. You watch." They all laughed. "By the way, a name card with a red band across the top is a committee member."

"Does that mean you're saying I've got to be on my best behaviour?"

"No. Not at all. Be yourself."

The first red-banded label appeared in front of Han. The Professor knew everybody by name but Peter was almost the opposite, because as soon as he was introduced, he would lose all recollection of the name straight away. Peter knew that was a weakness.

"This is Señor Emilio Elezor. I'd like you to meet Peter Martinez. He's one of our better patients."

Emilio was rather short and a little portly. "I'm pleased to meet you."

"Actually, I'm Spanish, we could have been old-fashioned in our native language," Peter replied, presuming he'd break some ice.

"Oh, I see," Emilio said with a gentle welcoming smile. "So are you this protégé the Professor has been on about?"

Peter looked to Han for help.

Han interjected, "No. No. No. That's later. Peter is just a very special patient."

"So don't you compete?"

"Well, I'm hoping, that is, crossing my fingers, that when the team here has finished with me, I'll be mended so as not to be sufficiently disabled to qualify as a paraplegic. I'm a bit old for the principal event in the actual games."

"Now I might debate with you which are the 'actual' ones, but surely if the Professor doesn't quite achieve your full recovery, you could shoot arrows or kill clay pigeons? I've still got hopes of getting invited to compete in that myself."

They laughed at both hypothetical prospects.

A much taller, statuesque male now approached the quartet. Peter flagged up the red band. This new arrival introduced a sudden presence to the occasion. He didn't leave it for them to effect the introductions; behind his outstretched hand, which cleared a path into their midst, he announced to Peter: "I am Jorge Quinto. You must be this secret weapon of Han's. Are you his competit…" He held back on finishing the word, making out, Peter was quite sure, that he had only just seen Kiki.

"My dear Mrs Han! I didn't see you surrounded by all these big men." He took her hand and lifted it to his lips, gently kissing it.

What a prat, Peter thought. He caught Kiki's eye and winked. She let forth a little giggle.

"Nice to see you, Jorge, and how is Mrs Quinto?"

"Oh, fine. Doesn't change, but who would want to, married to me? Now I was in the middle of something… yes… so you're this chap Han reckons to get trained all the way to compete in '92, are you… ?" He thought more deeply. "What's the sport… archery… shooting… ? What!"

Peter laughed again. "Look, I'm just a patient who hopes to get sufficiently sorted out to get back to my job."

"Peter's being very modest, actually. He's big in the UK in business and I think could contribute greatly to what we're hoping to achieve. He's very experienced in life. Very worldly. Quite international, whereas most of us committee men are from professional backgrounds, with a hint of narrowness from the paths we've taken in academia."

"You're being a bit generous," Peter interjected.

Han took back the conversation. "Jorge is a lawyer, Peter. Well, Jorge… when I say a lawyer, I don't think that does you justice." He went on to explain to Peter: "Jorge entered our bar system and was a circuit judge for years. Then he got a calling into practice, a strange thing to happen, you'd think, and he joined one of the biggest law firms in Barcelona as principal partner. He's expanded that, I think I'm right in saying, Jorge, sixfold in three years, so he's no ordinary academic. I think you two have a lot in common."

Peter wasn't sure he agreed but he was not prepared to rock the boat.

"By the way, Jorge is too modest to tell you he's Chairman of this Committee."

"Really?" Peter said, ducking his head in a sign of reverence. "We must try to have a deeper chat sometime before I go back," he suggested. "I'd be pleased to contribute if such talents as the Professor says I have can be used."

"Good. That's the spirit," Jorge complimented him. "I'd best press on, I'm meant to say hello to most people here."

As he said that, there was a gentle barging to Peter's side, which made him wonder whether he should ease further towards Professor Han's wife, to prevent somebody who was obviously intent on forcing a way between them from succeeding. Or, alternatively, he could make a more friendly gesture by easing over to let the person into their little throng.

He decided to take the less contentious route and moved slightly away from Kiki.

A strange male voice broke into the conversation. "I have to say Jorge, you're keeping some pretty dubious company these days."

Han looked to his side in surprise, while Jorge Quinto did not seem too perturbed. Kiki looked decidedly put out. Peter was close to the side of the face approaching from behind from whence the seemingly derisory words had emanated. He didn't have a full view, though he could recognise a male who was about equal to his height and stature.

"Even to be seen talking to Sñr Martinez and you're likely to be in the gossip pages of the papers the next day… and it certainly won't do your legal practice or your reputation any good whatsoever."

Peter was none the wiser about the person's identity. He felt he knew the voice but not the English accent. There was now a strong arm around his one shoulder and neck, and a big hand on the shoulder still recuperating from the accident, which caused him pain. The power was pulling Peter towards the generator of this sudden force. Now an outstretched right hand wrapped itself around Peter's, exerting power firmly into what was turning out to be a surprisingly friendly handshake.

Peter stepped back, releasing himself from the shoulder hold, which enabled him to get a full frontal image of the interloper.

"Dios mio! Cómo hizo entra en un lugar así."

Both the Hans understood by the tone what had probably been said, although not the detail. It was all OK, though, because both men were suddenly laughing and bear-hugging each other like long lost brothers.

Peter reverted to English. "How the hell does a bloke like this get into such a respectable establishment?"

"He's a committee member," Han replied.

Peter stood back to take a full view. He looked at the badge, then the body, next the face, and exclaimed: "Well, well, well, Ramon Gaspard! How the hell are you? You look good. What are you up to on a committee doing good? That's not your style," he mused.

"I'm fine, Peter. I can afford to 'do good' these days but not out of the money you paid me. You were a lousy payer. Yes, I'm OK. And you? I thought you'd been shot dead or something. But who would have screwed that opportunity up!"

They both laughed again.

Kiki realised they knew each other well and that they obviously went back a long way, so she shouldn't be upset by someone joking about missing an opportunity to kill another. She'd seen too much of that in Vietnam. It made goose-pimples envelop her body.

Jorge Quinto also obviously knew Ramon Gaspard well, and hadn't minded the banter about his reputation being damaged. "Come on, then, Ramon. Tell us the whole story. How come you know each other so well? Were you in the same prison together, or something?"

"How do you like that, Peter! If I could afford the legal fees these blokes charge, I'd bring a case of defamation against Jorge here, but I know he doesn't mean it.

"Well, yes, we go back a long way. This man is actually a genius. Not only did he design a scatterbrain idea of a development before he was 20, he managed to raise the money to build it. I had just started up my building company and was pretty desperate for work and we set up a… well… less of an agreement, more of a punishment together. I said I'd build the first ten houses without invoicing. He sold them all off plan, so he was ten house sales in hand and that way we built out the whole estate. This man, by the time he was only in his 20s, was a multi-millionaire in anybody's currency. The papers said he was worth 12.5 million pesetas. That's this man."

"Has he paid you yet for the ten houses he had in hand?" Jorge asked.

"No!"

"Hey! That's not fair," Peter defended.

"True. The direct answer is he didn't pay me for the ten. He called me into the office he'd established on site and actually said he couldn't pay me for those ten. I was about to wreck the place and take my cash in kind when the soft young man explained because he'd made a pile of money and as, in effect, I had financed him, he wanted to give me a final settlement of the value of the building cost of 20 houses. Yes, the old softie put me on a bonus. To be honest, I've not looked back since. I went out and bought ten houses for myself with the surplus and you know the rest. You of all people, Jorge, ought to, because you have most of my money in legal fees anyway."

It was by now very light-hearted. The potential heat had gone out of the situation.

"Where can we go to catch up with each other?" Ramon asked Peter.

Han intervened. "Nowhere. I'm about to invite our guests to a quick tour of our facilities. We're running behind. Before that, I've an announcement to make. Stay here together. I want to see your faces when I say what I'm going to say."

"That sounds exciting, Professor," Jorge suggested. "Then under those conditions, I'll take your lady's arm and protect her from these two villains."

Han excused himself and went into the wings of the raised area in the lecture hall, which had been cleared of chairs for this event. Neither Peter, Jorge nor Ramon knew what Han was up to. Perhaps Kiki did, but she was not going to let on.

Han reappeared and walked centre stage to the lectern, from which he was well used to addressing students. He banged the mahogany top with a gavel and flicked on a microphone. He blew into it two or three times in imitation of the Barcelona-Madrid express, on which he travelled quite often. The room became hushed.

"Ladies and gentlemen. Señoras, señors. May I please welcome you to the Barcelona Hopital del Mar on behalf of the Board of Governors on what at least I hope will be a memorable occasion. You are all special guests, of course, and the form of the evening is a relaxed one. We'll break away from this reception very shortly and I'll invite you on a ward round with me. We will then reconvene here and Jorge Quinto… do you all know Jorge Quinto…?"

There were mock hisses and boos from those who did know him. He was obviously a popular figure, who Peter was now liking a little more, but there was clearly a perverse side to him, of which people liked to make fun. That was fine by Peter. To be popular you have to be fun. He knew that.

"… Jorge… could you identify yourself? Obviously some of our guests have either led too straight a life to have come across you, or don't have the sort of money to buy your advice."

Jorge was not slow to put his hand in the air. There was a little intermittent clapping.

"While you are all looking that way, could I just point out my dear wife? She allows me to partake in the behind-the-scenes activity of the POC."

There was a strong wave of impromptu applause. Kiki accepted the compliment in a dignified way.

"While you're still looking that way, there's a good-looking young man I'd like you to be able to recognise."

Alongside the platform, there was a frosted glass screen which gave a one-way view into the lecture theatre. Cas and Pablito were there, straining to see where Peter was. They inadvertently clapped when they saw him, and both giggled with pride. Peter, at a distance, looked decidedly embarrassed. What the hell was Han up to?

"Peter Martinez. Could you please make yourself known?"

Peter was hesitant. Although he was quite accustomed to ad-libbing, he still felt injured and not at his best, so found the focus on him hard to take.

He raised a hand. Nobody clapped. There was an air of expectancy hanging in a cloud over the room. Peter was as much in the dark as anybody else. Kiki was smiling. Ramon's mouth had dropped open and Jorge showed no emotion, yet was keen to know more about this man. Almost any acquaintance of Ramon would be a good bloke. He liked the story of the bonus. Would he like what he was about to hear?

"Peter Martinez is a modest man who came to us as a patient." There was a hushed surprise. Peter certainly didn't look as though he was working on one false limb. He now looked fit.

"What Peter has personified since he has been here is the guiding principle of the Paraplegic Federation. To strive, to help those whom some of the less well informed in the world consider to be cripples. Those who, without the government's assistance in supporting hospitals and medical centres throughout Spain, and the richer parts of the world, would be squatting in a gutter with a beret in front of them, asking passers-by to chip in and pay towards their next essential meal or a packet of cigarettes.

"Peter and I believe all of you in this room understand the 'cripple factor', and you all contribute generously in both financial and overall support terms to the committee's aims.

"But there's another side to this, other than just making material things available to those in need. There's the educational side, and there are psychological hurdles to overcome, which no amount of money or potential IPC support can help with. And, at times, it's beyond the capability of the medical staff at this institution to do that either. It's a long short story, but Peter Martinez has been instrumental in doing that for the benefit of one patient.

"I'm not going to bore you with his technique but suffice to say, no book could teach it. It's about having people who can naturally use their talents gained in the University of Life, and put them to good use, turn them into a unique medicine for others. You may say I'm now talking in riddles and perhaps, in Peter Martinez's view, out of turn."

Han continued to address the now captivated audience. "A young man called Paul Demar was severely injured in a road accident. He hadn't expected to face that when he woke up and saw the sun on what he presumed would be another fine day. It turned out to be a dreadful day. He lost a limb, but we have been able to make one up for him, which we believe will eventually be very much a part of his body, and which will get him to where he wants to be, with Peter's encouragement and coaching from one of our own senior physios.

"Ladies and gentlemen, may I introduce you to Paul Demar and Cassandra White, a team, a duo no less, who we hope you will follow over the next five years until they reach their goal of achieving a high quality medal in the 1992 Para Games. Paul and Cas."

Cas's knees were virtually knocking together and she thought they would surely be seen below the hemline of the borrowed skirt and above the stiletto sandals another colleague had loaned to her. Paul, for his part, seemed to be thriving on the imminent attention. They walked out to immediate rapturous applause.

Ramon turned to Peter and above the noise shouted, "Hey, mate. What a girl, eh? I'd like to be coached by her. What about that, eh! She's your type, unless you've grown out of girls."

"She wouldn't give me a second glance, mate," Peter confessed, with an inner smile.

"Oh, go on! Don't give up that quickly. We'll have to get you two talking. She won't be able to escape your charm, given a bit of a drink as a loosener."

"We'll see," Peter smiled.

The Professor held his arms in the air. He beckoned Cas to the microphone.

"Cas, how hopeful are you of helping Paul Demar to achieve his goal?"

"Totally. He's got an amazing will, if we can keep that harnessed." The three on the rostrum laughed. They all knew about that. As did Peter.

"Well, best of luck from all of us here. Now, Paul… what's going to be the best way to train you up to reach your new ambition?"

"Hard work, Professor."

"Tell us about the limb."

"It's good."

"Would you show us?"

Paul went shy. "Will the people mind it being the wrong colour? It's a prototype and they haven't perfected the plastic colour yet."

"I'm sure nobody will mind that."

He lifted his leg onto a chair just behind the lectern, and rolled up the bottom of his tracksuit trouser leg. "It's just an ordinary artificial limb," he announced to the gazing audience.

The Professor turned to those onlookers. "There you are, that's what you're up against, whether it be a leg or an arm or a hand. Modern technology and ambition teaches any of our patients that it's they who are the 'ordinary' elements in the equation. We will try to teach them to live within those parameters and have a life as close to normal as possible. Ladies and gentlemen, please feel free to come and meet some of those people with that faith – our patients."

The room filled with applause again. Peter was looking on, now speechless. That was Cas, his Cas, a grown-up, mature public relations expert. Groomed, as she was, she would raise the sponsorship money Paul needed. De-groomed, as they had been together just the weekend before, he was so infatuated by her he too would move heaven and earth for her to succeed. Wow, what a challenge the next five years would be.

"You coming, Peter?" Ramon was beckoning.

"No. I live here till next Monday, then I'm back to the UK. I'll hang around here till people get back."

Ramon Gaspard moved closer towards Peter. "Peter, I've always enjoyed reading bits and pieces about you. There was this article in a finance paper just a while back, which wrote about Malaysia and was very complimentary about Girasol. I thought then we needed to have a chat. I couldn't see why you wanted to give all your expertise to the UK. We've both grown. That's my company too. I'd like to have a chat before you go back. It's as though some strong force has brought us back together. Can I phone you here?"

"Yes. I'll give you my evening line," Peter smiled at his own bravado. "Ramon. Tell me seriously, what the shit are you doing here?"

Ramon seemed happy to explain. "Firstly, this committee has access to the plans, programmes and people involved in building what's needed to convert Barcelona into a place fit for the Olympics, and short-term homes where the competitors and support teams can live. I'd just like to keep my company in place for the maintenance, if not a slice of the construction."

His smile faded. "Just as importantly... well... you see, my lad is a spina bifida casualty. Being part of this group re-affirms to me that he's not alone. Here I learn he's ordinary, really, and then I go home and cry. Listen, Peter, you and I always told each other the truth in those good early days. We must meet before you escape again. I'll ring you," he said assertively. "By the way..."

"What's that?" Peter replied.

"You've got a problem."

"Dozens. Don't we all? Specifically though, what's that?"

"You haven't taken your eyes off the Australian since she's been on that stage."

Peter touched his nose with his forefinger. "Don't get nosey, old pal."

"Oh, I won't."

"By the way, she's not Australian. South African."

"Go on! So you still do your research."

"Phone me, if we don't talk more later. Go and look around the wards. See you later. Ramon, it's really, really good to see you," Peter said, seriously.

"Me too you."

Chapter 13

One or two people had got out of the tour and stayed behind to talk to Cas and Paul. As Peter arrived at rostrum level, one of the interested parties took Paul off for a chat. He had been an international athlete himself, apparently.

The path to speak to Cas was clear. She seemed pleased to see him.

"Hi," she greeted him, "my, aren't we the smart dude!"

"You've stolen my opening lines, I'm afraid. Listen, I've got to say this very quickly before we get interrupted. I've seen you in your physio stuff, coats with undone buttons, I've seen you in your birthday suit, and your little mini-skirt too. Each in their own way turns me on. Tonight, though, you look absolutely fantastic. Great, lovely. Beautiful."

"But I apparently don't turn you on."

"You do. So I'm beginning to think it's just you who has this spell over me."

That, Peter, is so sweet, she thought wistfully. "Peter, I'm so sorry about this, but I've just got to say it."

He looked frightened.

"I'd die for you, Peter." She leant forward and gave him a formal kiss on each cheek, then stepped back. "Be sure to leave your friggin' door unlocked."

"We don't say friggin'."

"We do, if that's what I mean, my beauty."

Peter had not been a bad judge about having to be quick. The bloke had finished telling Paul Demar all about his life and successes and had made off, so Pablito was now on his way over to Peter.

"When I'm a champion, I'm going to have a blue suit and white shirt."

"Are you just? Good for you. Well done, young man. You've already got some big support."

"Peter, may I ask you a question?"

"By all means. I just don't promise to answer it. OK. What's the question?"

"They say you're going back to the UK early next week."

"Yes, I think I am."

"So when is our race?"

"Oh, Paul. I'm sorry. I'd rather put that behind us. I'm sure you'd win anyway."

"Well, yes. So am I. But what about football?"

"You're absolutely right. What about that? Let's involve Cas."

Peter beckoned for her to come across. He explained his conversation with Paul. She had forgotten too, so her hand went up to her mouth as though to half-apologise for forgetting such an important thing.

"Relax, both of you. I've got three tickets for Saturday."

"Who's playing?" Paul asked.

"Real Madrid and Barcelona, as I promised."

"Can we go?"

"Cas? Will you come?"

"Gladly."

"Then yes, we can all go. That'll be the first of many outings. When you win, we'll wear our blue suits and sit in the directors' box together."

Paul thought deeply. "I think Miss Cas will have to wear trousers, though."

"... And why is that, Paul?" Cas asked.

"Your knees are too sexy. I find I can't stop looking at them."

"Then trousers it will be."

Paul was growing up.

Gradually the guests filed back into the lecture theatre, where the hospital caterers reached one of the pinnacles of their year by serving the canapés they had put together in between preparing the essential food for patients and staff. They circulated with an abundance of wine, intended to keep the conversation flowing.

Peter told Paul, as the first group returned, to go and socialise. "Speak when you're spoken to. Preferably answer yes and no and don't, *don't* go into any of your long philosophies about how bad the staff is here, or how I kicked your butt."

"I wouldn't do that, Peter. I'm a changed man. I see it all in a new light. Tell me you both know that."

Peter looked to Cas for agreement.

"Let's say," she said, "we'd like to believe that, and we'd encourage it, but there's always a hint of a monkey on your shoulder who pushes you into a wild streak. So part of the coaching will be overcoming those moments as they become more remote. But yes, we do know where you want to be heading."

Paul did as they suggested and moved across until he was a short distance from a gathering of four who had returned from the ward round.

"So you're aiming to compete in these games we're responsible for putting together?" invited one of the foursome with a name and a red flash.

"Yes, Sir," Paul said brightly.

"... And in which event... ?"

Now he was into the conversation and continued to be welcomed into small groups throughout the rest of the evening.

That left Cas and Peter together.

"Well!" she said. "What do you think of the old farts then?"

"Oh… they're OK. Actually, I've met up with a really old friend who's on the committee. I'll introduce you because he said, as soon as you made your gorgeous entrance, that you were exactly the type of girl I'd make a play for… that is, providing my tastes hadn't changed from the days when we knew each other well… yes, he suggested I should chat you up with a view to getting you into my bed."

"Really! So tell me. Did he also say that would be easy, in his view?"

Peter laughed. "No, of course, he didn't."

"Well, that's good. I'm beginning to like him a little better."

"No! He was the one who said you'd have too much style to fall for an approach from an old gigolo like me. I was the one who said he was wrong and that you'd be easy!"

"Now listen here, Peter Martinez, you've just talked yourself out of getting a real pleasant time later."

"Ooh! I'm sorry."

"Too late. You'll just get an average one now."

She turned to walk away.

"Don't go, Cas. Stay. We'll talk to these old fogies together. Please."

"Will that be OK? Won't it look like staff fraternising with patients?"

"No. The Professor indicated we'd got Paul in common. It would be very appropriate. Please… stay by my side."

"I'll accept the invitation, kind Sir."

A few of the groups that had set out were now returning and making a beeline for the drink trays. The food would be delivered to them. Jorge Quinto who, as Chairman, had been privileged to lead the way on the tour with Professor Han and his wife, was one of the early ones back. Whether it was Peter he was attracted to or Cas was a matter of conjecture for any onlooker. But he was there, drink in hand.

"So you're this young potential champion's coach?"

"Yes," Cas said, with the confidence of knowing Peter was by her side. She would follow his advice to Paul and try to stick with 'yes' and 'no' answers.

Actually, she had taken an instant dislike to Jorge. More so after his next question.

"Australian?"

"No."

"Then where? I'm usually good at accents."

"South Africa."

"Oh really? Now that *is* interesting."

Peter picked up on the tone of the comment as Han and his wife joined them.

"So you've met my other young protégé. Cassandra White," Han said cheerfully.

Peter interjected. "I picked up a vibe or two in your comment about the South African connection," he said, directly to Jorge.

"Well, not really," Jorge lied.

"What are you thinking? How can a South African take an interest in coaching a young Spaniard on the grounds of physical disability when her native current philosophy discerns between rich and poor in terms of colour?"

"Well, it's a question I wouldn't have been quite bold enough to have so aptly introduced. But it is something I was reflecting on. Yes, why do you feel you can coach a boy who faces discrimination due to nothing more than a body disablement when your country practises its own brand of discrimination down to colour?"

"I've got my boss here so I have to be careful." She thought that reply would give her a way out.

"No, come on. You can speak freely in front of the Professor. You see, our great fellow countryman, Samaranch, who you'll doubtless know is President of the overall governing body, the International Olympic Committee – he, for one, is trying to force the case for South Africa to mend its ways and rejoin the senior games. Did you know that? So if you're one who supports apartheid, then we who side with Samaranch's views would have a problem with your opinion. If you don't, then we would doubtless embrace your views."

"Cas, I'm sure, can answer for herself." Peter stepped in. "Maybe she's too sociable to air a view either way, but may I complicate the position further?"

Han this time interjected. "Jorge, I warned you this man would be interesting. I'd best apologise before he 'complicates' the situation. One thing you can bank on is he'll be interesting."

"I'm beginning to feel they might both be interesting. I'm having fun. Peter, what was the point you were going to make?"

"I'll level with you. I'm extremely at ease with the paraplegic side to the games, which the handicapped take part in. It seems to me to bridge over any prejudice factor. It's 'head office' that worries me, the IOC itself, which I would think your own committee would have to follow. I have to say when I see the Olympic flag and its symbol of the five continents being linked together, I do think to myself 'bullshit'. The overall ideal is that they are, but each continent has its divisions, and the Olympics mask that, rather than highlighting the needs of the nations in each of the continents.

"It's not just the split in colour in South Africa, for example, it's other issues like the political division of Germany. The IOC, and all those who compete or become spectators, in allowing divided nations to take part against each other, to me encourages the divides, which a true Olympic movement should be discouraging."

Quinto listened intently. "And what, may I ask, are you doing about that, Peter? But before you answer, to save me putting both my big feet in it, could I please go back to the unanswered question I put to Cas. How do you come to terms with apartheid, or on which side of your Berlin wall do you sit?"

Peter admired Jorge's diplomacy. Cas thought about her reply carefully. "I abhor apartheid. That has been one reason for me working in Europe. As a nurse I cannot, I will not discriminate between a white person and a black one if they're both in need of treatment. I don't see why I shouldn't offer my seat on a bus or a train to either an elderly white or black person.

"But I have to say, not that we've discussed it, I share Peter's view, as an outsider, that the Olympic movement is a bit of a sham. How do I come to terms with coaching a young lad who may not be able to run against the better black athletes in South Africa? It's easy. I'd hope sometime in the next three, four or five years to fix a competition, even if it's in some field or an arena where they still allow cock-fighting in secret after hours, and I'd bring in an athlete of black origin to compete with a contemporary with white roots, and for the one to shake the other's hand when he's beaten."

There was stunned silence.

Jorge Quinto held out his hand to her. Although she was trembling inwardly herself with emotion, even though she had felt Peter move in closer to her so that their upper arms and hips joined by touch like a Siamese twin, she allowed the elder Spanish statesman to lift her hand and gently kiss it.

"Well spoken, young lady. Well motivated, Peter. You've both echoed my own sentiments exactly. The sad thing is that the media haven't covered the good news. They've portrayed Samaranch, and his crooked old fart colleagues as lacking in ethical control and tolerating cultures that are said, and written, to be variously illegal and corrupt. It would be difficult for any media to believe in an organisation which, on the one hand, claims to promote the youth, yet on the other allows the governing body to change its rules so that members can preside until the age of 75 and, more recently, to lift that to 80. So the IOC has, or did, lose its direction and credibility.

"Out of those ashes, Samaranch has risen as a man with a new cause and a revived direction. I guess you didn't know that last year he came out in support of the African international committee members and it was he who covered a conference against apartheid in sport. He created a special commission for that cause. I think you'll find that in a few years, the emotion behind that will grow. He'll make that happen because, at one time secretly but now publicly, he sees the Barcelona games as a showcase to the world, not just in architectural achievement but in the building of new relationships, black to white and east to west."

Jorge's audience was spellbound, hugely influenced by his masterful eloquence.

"But hear me out. None of that will happen if, in the disciplines which concern us, the Paralympics don't have a league of 'pushers' with the same aims. Indeed, if we set the pace and pass it up, it'll give the so-called 'old farts' encouragement to press harder for the overall ideals.

"In a nutshell, Peter – and equally you, Cas – I'll be disappointed and furious if, when we invite you to join our committee, you let down your own ideals by refusing. Now there, before I call for another very large glass of that very good red wine, is a challenge laid down in black and white – excuse the pun."

The silence lasted for no more than five seconds before there was a solitary but emphatic hand-clapping. That one person showing their appreciation of the performance had the effect of a referee blowing a whistle for full time and pulling all the players up to a standstill. The single applause certainly brought an overall silence over the gathered assembly.

Peter turned round. It was Ramon Gaspard who had caused this disturbance.

"Well done, Jorge. Well done, Peter – and definitely well done to this beautiful young lady, about whose attributes I have already waxed lyrical."

Peter remembered, from their days of working together in the construction of Girasol, that Ramon liked a drink. He'd obviously had a couple this evening. The accolades were nevertheless sincere and spirited, you could say.

"Cas, this is the guy who said you'd be easy to pull," Peter announced, just to the three of them.

"Bloody agony," Ramon grimaced, "you still give a bloke a hard time, Peter. Young lady, I'm suffering from a misquote. What I actually said was that if I was Peter, a lone bachelor without a care in the world, I'd have a jolly good try, and that is true."

He held out his hand from behind a broad, infectious smile.

Cas took it graciously. "… And if he were to take your advice… I'd get his other leg broken so seriously he'd be strung up to the ceiling for months while it mended."

"There you are, Ramon, didn't I say I didn't stand a chance?"

The three laughed and turned back to join the conversation between Jorge and Professor and Mrs Han.

"Well, if you're going to say a few words, why don't we do that now?"

"I see you'd rather not allow me my second stiff drink I've been promising myself. OK. Cas, the Professor is dragging me off. Grab me during the evening before I go. I have one more serious piece of advice for you. Be sure you do that," Jorge said emphatically.

Han introduced Jorge to the gathering on the basis that he doubted if anyone in the room did not know he was the Chairman of the Spanish arm of their movement, and that he was going to say a few words about how the plans leading to 1992 were going, and the committee's activities in particular.

Jorge was obviously a popular figure and, despite the muted clapping, since everybody in the room had a glass in one hand, his reception showed that popularity.

"Good evening, ladies and gentlemen. You'll be pleased to hear that I'll be short. I'd like to thank you all for accepting Professor and Mrs Han's invitation to this evening's event. It is fundamental that in the paraplegic movement, we all understand the difficulties faced by those who have less well formed bodies than a lot of us. But I always say that our God is kind and generous and makes up for deficiency in one direction with a blessing in others. Those patients we have seen here tonight are blessed with great willpower and an inner strength to overcome the fact that their bodies need to be treated in a particular way, compared with those I'd call 'fully abled'. That applies whether it has suddenly been inflicted upon them, or they've known no different from birth. We have this hospital and its dedicated staff to thank for assisting them and the development of those special attributes. We've been given an example of that in Paul Demar, the Olympic champion elect for '92..."

"At least the name seems to be sticking," Cas whispered to Peter, taking the opportunity to brush the back of her hand against his, a gesture he returned. They smiled deeply into each other's faces, hoping others would not notice.

"... But for every champion who achieves gold, there are disappointments and it is those people who don't benefit in the glory who we are representing as forcefully as those who reach their pinnacles. A special thing, beyond meeting Paul, has happened this evening. As you can imagine, I spend a lot of time touring the country, at similar evenings to this, but particularly influencing sponsorship and memberships.

"Some events become exceptionally rewarding and I'm hoping this is one of them. I believe the IOC are on the brink of a major breakthrough in developing a special rapport with the equivalent body in South Africa to do something really positive about this wretched apartheid arrangement. That, from what I've learnt here, hasn't had the publicity it deserves. The initiative led by President Samaranch is less news than the fact that there are pockets of corruption being talked about in sponsorship. Time will put such things right. However, what we all need to do is to use the flag of international co-operation through sport, and the flame of the Olympiads, to ignite a great groundswell of support for a clean-out of some of the prejudices we can so clearly see.

"This evening, I've encountered a unique young man who seems to have fervent views on this subject. I think he has the physical ability and the technical knowledge to be able to dismantle parts, at least, of this Berlin Wall. Professor Han has already singled him out as one of those patients with special resolve. I've also met the young South African physio who hopes to coach Paul Demar to success. She is fervently upset by what is still happening in her home country in relation to apartheid in sport and she too has the ability to turn heads, and then get those heads to focus on her real agenda of free sport for all, with race, creed and colour being no stumbling block. In fact, and I use the English habit of making puns, she knows those issues are her starting block.

"The point of talking about Paul Demar, a Spanish national, and Cassandra White is to say we need these young people to join us older ones, and to use their beliefs and energy to speak out, and to act towards the real aims in our movement. If we're supporting young men and women of different physical capacities, then we shouldn't exclude people on the grounds that they have the 'wrong' colour of skin or were born the wrong side of a wall."

Whether everybody had put their glasses down or otherwise, there was sudden unanimous applause.

"So... and thank you... thank you... you are being generous..." Jorge put his hands up to indicate they should calm their applause. "... The upshot of that is that I, for one, and the committee here, will be furious if the South Africans don't accept our invite to join us and become our special envoys, commissioners, let them call themselves what they like, with responsibility for the removal of... and here I go again making the most of the intricacies of the English language... removal of hurdles."

There was laughter.

"I've got to say a quick word about the actual plans for 1992 in terms of the development of the venues and the orchestration of building work."

Peter was nudged from behind. It was Ramon, a further glass down the track. Peter turned to him. In response, Ramon smiled broadly, gave a pronounced wink and put one mischievous forefinger to his mouth, indicating not to say a word. He obviously knew something, unless it was the drink talking. He slipped Peter a visiting card, leant further forward.

"Give me a call. I've thought of something great. Got to go. Look forward to hearing."

Peter turned back to focus on Jorge, who was still speaking.

"... Its final plans are with the IOC now and we get to input in about a month. We're allowed two nominations in each building facility. In that way, we get to ensure design input and quality control, to make sure not all facilities are procured for 'able-bodied' sports people, but also for those of us who are handicapped. There you have it, señoras and señors, ladies and gentlemen. I hope that is progress."

There was again a generous ovation. Peter was inquisitive. He turned to Professor Han, who had been listening alongside his wife.

"What did he mean, 'those of us who are handicapped'?"

"Hadn't you noticed his limp?"

"No. He always pushes you in front of him. He never goes first. Now that's one of the crafts of an amputee."

"Really?" Peter said, with an intrigued expression.

"He's got an artificial left leg."

"Really!" echoed Cas.

"He plays tennis to regional standard, has a golf scratch handicap and swam in amputee games before there was a hint of them getting Olympic status... oh, I suppose, over 40 years ago."

"That's amazing!" Peter then regretted his next question. "How did he lose it – or was he born like that?"

"No. In a motorcycle accident."

He felt Cas's stomach churn.

"Then he's a lucky chap."

"Lucky?" Cas enquired, surprised by Peter's comment.

"Well yes, by rights he could have been lying down in a lavender field by now."

"Now that's a thought," she said, visibly releasing a sudden rush of tension. "I always tend to lose sight of that. Thank you, Peter."

"So can you see where we're heading?" Han said. "Now what about you two? Will you join us?"

"Cas?" Peter was asking her view.

"I'd only do it if I knew I had a like-minded buddy who would fend off all the elder statesmen. So will you do it?" she asked Peter.

"The two of us as a package. Yes!"

"I think I'll really enjoy that," she said.

"I'm thrilled and excited," Han reacted.

"I can say that too," Mrs Han joined in.

"What's Ramon's contribution?" Peter asked.

"Oh, he heads the development sub-committee Jorge was talking about. Bricks and mortar, ramps and chair-lifts, stuff like that. He's a wizard in the construction field."

Peter smiled. "Oh, I know that. I know that only too well."

Jorge had joined them. He had a beaming smile and a large glass of red wine.

"So chaps," he said, "have I made it sufficiently difficult yet for you to say no?"

"They've said they'll join us," Han informed him.

"Now that is good news! Really good news. I've got a feeling in my bones that will be good for us, and mutually rewarding for the two of you. Great. Thank you. I'll get the committee secretary to give you all the necessary info. Tell you what, I'll suggest you both come across to my place for a weekend and then I can really give you all the background you'll need. We can mix it with a bit of time on the water. You can meet my dedicated wife. How about that?"

Cas was excited by a bonus of enforced time with Peter.

"Will you tell me then about the 'serious piece of advice' you have for me?"

"Good. I'm glad you've said that. Yes. But it shouldn't wait. One of our many secrets is that Samaranch, apart from liberalising on the race front, is a realist and appreciates that the expenses of an individual now competing, and training for four or five years, can hardly come from a part-time Saturday job, with the odd bit of sponsorship from the local sports shop. No. We're on the verge of professionalism. No longer a bung of notes secretly left in a pair of spikes: we're talking sponsorship with logos all over pairs of gold-painted spikes, tattoos and the like, and remuneration to go with it. There'll soon be prize money in amateur events, if that's not an anomaly. Now coaches don't get accolades much and are unlikely to get any direct financial benefit in the same way as their protégés. I'm a lawyer and what I would advocate is, even this far ahead, get your Paul Demar lad into a contract with you. Pin him down now to a personal share for you in the success you might create for him. Then get yourself in line for some sponsorship too. Get Adidas across... no, forgive me. I'm a little tired and this large beautiful glass of wine is getting to me," he said, as though confused by his own conversation and embarrassed by himself. He didn't complete his sentence of what Cas should be getting 'Adidas across'.

"What?" Cas insisted, somewhat puzzled.

"Well..." Jorge turned to Mrs Han. "I do apologise, but I'm a realist. Get Adidas across your chest and you'll get every male spectator in the arena or training ground clamouring to buy the stuff."

"Jorge!" Mrs Han announced. "Now you apologise to Cas."

"It's true. And you know it. Chests sell."

They all laughed.

Peter put a seal on it. "The problem is, Cas isn't an Adidas type. I'm sure Coq Sportif would pay her more."

"Peter!" Cas scolded. "Now this joking about my body must stop."

"OK. It's stopped. But I'm a realist too."

"... And so am I," she countered, "as you'll see soon enough."

The Hans and Jorge were a little lost, not quite understanding this follow-up scenario.

"Look, I'm sorry," Jorge said.

"Don't be silly. It's this rebel patient of mine who won't be able to walk by the time I've finished with him... in physio tomorrow. It will be treadmill until he's flat on his back," was Cas's final retort.

"Oh, I'm sorry, Peter. Sorry if I've got you into that," Jorge apologised.

"Don't worry. I've been there before. It's OK actually."

Cas huffed in attempted contempt.

The gathering broke up gradually after that, and Peter and Cas eventually escaped 30 minutes or so later. They learnt Paul had left an hour before, saying he was in training and needed sleep. To get from the lecture/academic area of the hospital back to their respective sleeping areas, they had to cross the quadrangle, which at this time of night was unlit. Peter felt for Cas's hand.

"We still on?" he enquired.

"Coq Sportif," she said in a serious tone.

"Couldn't resist," he said.

He took her arm and pushed her deep into the shadow below a maple tree. He put both his strong arms around her.

"Couldn't resist. Because it was true."

"What was?"

"Coq Sportif was… was feeling sportif."

She couldn't help but laugh. "You're a bloody lucky bloke that I didn't stamp my foot and walk out on you!"

"What, the 'I've been flat on my back' bit before. Not that."

"Yes that. By the way, did you enjoy it?"

"Yes, very much."

"You've never said that before."

"You've never asked me. You've always said things like 'it wasn't for me', 'it was only for you'. Who was I to prove you wrong?"

"Peter Martinez. You are very bad for me. Very bad for yourself. Quick, let's get back to your room. The adrenalin in me is pumping so hard, if you don't release it, I'll burst."

"Then we can't have you doing that."

They believed they would be able to creep in through the porter's door without being noticed. Both thought the staff would have gone off duty, as all the patients would be settled down and any staff out would have keys. The one chap who was on duty was the one who had been there to welcome them back the previous Sunday.

Cas broke the ice. "Hi, Paco. Everything secure?"

Peter's stomach turned whenever he heard his father's name applied to others. There was only one Paco.

"Yes, as tight as a bank. Oh, is that you, Mr Peter?"

"Yes."

"Oh good. Saves me writing a note. That mother of yours is chasing you again. Three calls. Had you moved out? I said I wouldn't get to you till the morning. She said OK – reluctantly, I must add."

"Oh. That's mothers."

Chapter 14

Maria had been tired through her busy Monday morning. Nowadays she found worrying about Peter did give her extra anxiety, which went round and round in her mind and caused her to have interrupted sleep. Hence she felt almost permanently fatigued. The hotel wasn't busy in the afternoon, so she slipped back to the bungalow for a siesta. The phone woke her. To be fair, she had told reception she was working on some paperwork and to ring if there was a problem.

"It's the hotel at Girasol for you."

Perhaps she was paranoid about Girasol since that frightening day, which could have led to her only son's death. *What's this going to be?* she thought. *Peter's been stabbed by the chef because he said the food was bad, or something.* She sensed it would not be good news. It was certainly chef. Was he about to say he was sorry, and that the food was bad, and he didn't mean to do it?

"Mrs Martinez. Buenos dias."

"Buenos dias, Andres."

"It's Miss Tania."

"OK. Put her on."

The day chef was renowned for his mild panic attacks, which Maria had heard often led to a confused situation, not least because as a Greek, and with an upbringing in his native country, his Spanish had a number of 'pigeon habits'.

"Put her on? Can't put her on, we lost her."

Lost her? Maria thought. Dead... it can't be.

"Andres, please explain from the start slowly."

"I came to work. No Miss Tania here. Breakfast chef said she was cleaning Mr Peter's house. By 10.30 we not see her. We phone. Phone busy. We phone again, phone busy. We get worried. By 11, phone busy. We not allowed to go to Mr Peter's house. Tania always say no go there unless she allows. We worry but do lunch. Keep phoning, phone busy. Finish lunch, I say, I must go. Miss Tania kill me for going but is OK with me. I get there. Door shut. Her bike there. No sounds. I shout 'Miss Tania, Miss Tania'. Nobody hear. I walk round front garden. I look in through window. It was horrible. I see Miss Tania, Señora Martinez. Forgive me..." He started to weep.

"Andres, pull yourself together! What happened?"

"I see Miss Tania. Please forgive me."

"For God's sake! Why forgive you? What for? What's to forgive?"
"Miss Tania has no clothes on."
"No clothes on?"
"Si."
"What was she doing?"
"On floor. I think she is dead."
"Is she dead?"
"No. That was over one hour ago. I broke window. I am sorry I broke window. I opened and climbed in. I speak to Miss Tania, she not answer. She look cold. She look not dead. I have seen dead. The eyes go strange. I cover her with robe. I see phone. Off hook. That why no answer. I don't know what to do. Suddenly her eyes open. 'Hello Toni,' she say. I say not Toni, Andres. 'How are you my darling…?' she say."

He started to weep again.

"Please, Andres, pull yourself together. I know you've had a shock but tell me what happened and then you can cry as much as you like."

"She say 'how are you my darling Toni?' Then she look around. She not seem to know she has no clothes. 'Where am I?' she ask. I say 'Mr Peter's house'. She say 'Mr Peter's house. Who is Mr Peter?' I say 'You know Mr Peter'. She say, 'Where has Toni gone?' I say, 'Who is Toni?' and she say, 'My husband'.

"Señora Martinez, she has no husband. I think she mean Mr Toni who tried to kill Mr Peter. Mr Toni bad man. But Mr Toni dead. She keep saying 'Find me Mr Toni. He was there a while ago'. She very strange. I put phone on hook. It then work. I dial 112 and say ambulance. Give detail. Then I phone again. I say police. I think she need police. Police came. Miss Tania say to them can they find Mr Toni for her. She would like them to. Police look around house. I am sorry, Señora Martinez. My fault they look around house. Man comes back says Miss Tania in bed with man. Man not there. Police say, 'Who were you in bed with?' She say 'Toni'.

"It was all Toni, Toni, Toni. Toni, señora, is dead. I tell police that. Ambulance arrive. Man and woman. Woman does talk. 'Who were you in bed with?' She say 'Toni'. 'Where is he now?' 'He's here. He wouldn't leave me by myself'. Lady say, seems Miss Tania not know what she is doing or saying. Then says, 'Let's get you some clothes and we'll take you for a check up'. Miss Tania say she no wear clothes." Andres started to cry again.

"Come on, Andres. You've been doing well." He seemed to react to that.

"She say, 'Toni not like me in clothes'. Lady say, 'Do you know where you are?' She say, 'Toni's house'. Señora Martinez, she always know it was Peter's house. She always say she his wife when it come to looking after his house. That why no one else allowed in there. If Toni alive, he would not be allowed there. Miss Tania scared of Toni. We didn't know why she was now in bed, she say, with him but he dead. Señora Martinez, she ill. She strange. I think her brain gone funny. Man in ambulance say she go to hospital but lady must put her in robe. She say no to robe and goes mad. I am sorry I think she go mad anyway. But she say no to robe and starts to scream."

"Whose robe was it, Andres?"

"A man's."

"Was it blue?"

"Yes."

It was Peter's, Maria was pretty sure. The one she had bought him about six Christmases ago.

"Lady say to man get blanket. Miss Tania got cross. She not want blanket but man hold her and lady dress her in blanket and put her in chair from ambulance with wheels. Put her in straps like a child and push her to ambulance. Miss Tania shouting the whole time for Toni. 'Toni, help me. Toni, come to me. Toni, don't let them take me…' All about Toni."

"Was Mr Peter mentioned?"

"Mr Peter? No. Not Mr Peter."

"Marguerite, Tania's daughter?"

"No. Nobody, Señora Martinez. Nobody except Toni, and he is dead. It's not good. I say she very ill in head."

"… And did they put her in the ambulance?"

"Yes."

"Do you know… did they say where they were going?"

"Just Gerona."

"So what have you done? Did you lock the house?"

"Oh yes, Señora Martinez. All is safe. I have the key."

"Do you know where Marguerite is?" As she asked the question, Maria remembered that the daughter had gone off travelling for the winter, as the hotel in Girasol would not be busy. Where the hell would she be? Anywhere, she supposed.

"Andres. You've done very well. I'll try to find out where they've taken Miss Tania. Can you and the others run the hotel?"

"Well, yes. Until Miss Tania comes home. I think we can."

"I'll get Mr Marco to come up. I'd expect tomorrow. Can you keep things going till then?"

"Yes, of course, Señora Martinez. Miss Tania not good."

"No, I know, Andres. You've done very well. Thank you for phoning me."

"I'm scared, Señora Maria. Thank you for helping. I will pray. We will all pray."

"You do that, Andres. We'll all pray too."

She waited till she was sure he had terminated the call, then she too replaced the receiver. She'd felt jaded before. Now she felt exhausted. The drama this young lady had brought into their lives! Maria thought they had been lucky to ship her up to Girasol before Virginia found out about Marco's attentions to her.

Peter, she knew, must have been very strong-willed in those early days not to have fooled around more seriously with an obviously willing party who, by her own confession all those years ago, especially when Peter was the hotel hero when Bob Hunt had nearly died, she was besotted with her son.

Peter need not know about the current event yet. She knew he could not possibly be involved. True, he'd been there just recently but it sounded as though he'd been otherwise engaged, as it were. Perhaps that was something to do with it. Maria supposed she ought to try to find out what was going on. Tania didn't have any relatives around now who would be concerned for her well-being. She, Marco and Peter were duty bound to help out.

She'd first find Marco and tell him, and see how far he would want to get involved. She found him soaking up a little November sunshine in his favourite spot in the gardens of the Hotel Playa. Virginia was bound to be in the depths of her now daily siesta, which she appeared to depend upon to get her through the evenings until it became a respectable hour for her to retire.

Marco was a bit shocked and couldn't understand the somewhat bizarre situation of Tania having no clothes on in Peter's house, and only thinking of Toni. He agreed that if Maria was prepared to, she should try and find out Tania's whereabouts and see how far Andres had exaggerated the story, since he was prone to panic. But he agreed with Maria that Andres was unlikely to get the story so completely wrong.

Maria went back to the bungalow, had a quick wash and brush up and went to the office in the hotel. If she was to be dependent on people phoning her back, at least there she would have more than one line coming in. She thought it best to start with the ambulance service. The girl on the emergency number just kept asking what the problem was, and who was hurt, and where. Maria eventually got through to a supervisor who reluctantly, and in order to get rid of her, gave her the number of the admin section of the service. Of course, Maria didn't know the exact time of the call out so it took a while and a couple of phone calls back, before she was told Tania had been taken to Gerona General Hospital. There, when she eventually got through, they were less than helpful.

"Are you related to the patient you are enquiring about… ? We cannot give information…" Maria eventually had to speak to the assistant chief administrator who, fortunately, believed Maria's story, and the reason for her interest. Having phoned the hotel back to check out Maria's credentials, he said he was prepared to investigate.

By seven in the evening, Maria had almost given up waiting for a call with some news. She was having an aperitif with Marco and Virginia when the phone rang in their apartment. Maria took the call and, not wanting Virginia to get involved, she asked if she could call back. That didn't seem to be a problem.

She finished her sherry and excused herself from her brother and sister-in-law's company, and hurried anxiously back to the hotel. They had to page the doctor whom the administrator had identified as dealing with the case of the young lady known only as 'Miss Tania'. It appeared that was the only name Andres could pass on to them.

The doctor, Dr Ramez, seemed a kind sort of chap and, now Maria had got hold of him, there was no indication that he would rush her away, as medics sometimes did. He explained that Miss Tania was clearly deranged, and wanted to know if Maria was aware whether she had gone through a recent trauma. "Her life, in some respects, has been one permanent trauma... I don't know anything in particular that's happened recently."

Her hesitation caused Dr Ramez to anticipate a further exposé, which would have been of assistance to him. Maria was thinking, however, that what she had said was not realistic. There'd been Toni's death, her father's arrest and the way he'd treated her sister... but that would come later. Not wanting to go into the more complex Toni/Peter details yet, Maria passed on as much background information as she could to help identify the source of Tania's problems. The doctor then asked if Toni was her husband.

"No. Toni was a cousin. And not a very nice one at that. He was never particularly kind to Tania. In fact, without wanting to breach confidences, I think she would say he'd been a cruel influence in her life. He was sent to prison for molesting her."

"Oh, now I see," the doctor said knowledgably.

"What does that mean?" Maria enquired.

"Well, I ought to explain. I'm a psychiatric consultant. After the initial assessment, it was thought I might be best to deal with the case."

"Does that mean Tania's mental?"

He paused. "That's a very lay term, I'm afraid. Not one we would recognise. But from what you've told me, which has all been very helpful and in Tania's best interests, I think I now know one of the routes I'll follow to try to flush out the cause of her problem. That will be best done after a total 24-hour rest. So I think we'll sedate her. I'd guess we'll start some meaningful work on her on, say, Wednesday, depending on the rest of our patients' needs."

"Could I ask you what's bound to be a difficult question?" Maria enquired.

"Yes, but anticipating that, I doubt I'll be able to give you a considered answer. But fire away."

"Would you say she's very ill?"

"On a graph of probability, I'd say yes but we have a long way to go. I would also say that we've seen the cause of her current condition, in others, to simply be a urine infection. We're testing for that, of course, though I very much doubt we'll see what's set this off straight away."

"Thank you for your honesty. When should I ring again?"

"I'd suggest Wednesday afternoon. Call and they'll page me. You're welcome to do that."

Maria waited till after dinner and when she was alone with Marco, she relayed the position to him. He seemed genuinely concerned, but Maria had to wonder whether that concern was tinged with the fear that out of this irrationality might come some sort of confession from Tania about his relationship with her. She decided there was no point in disturbing Peter until after she had more news on Wednesday. He'd no doubt be concerned inwardly, but outwardly shrug it off.

On the Wednesday afternoon, she duly rang the hospital. They paged Dr Ramez, who said he'd call Maria back. It wasn't as if Tania was related to the Martinez family, so why should Maria be so edgy? Yet Tania had been adopted into the family, as Marco's lover, and a loyal servant in the strictest sense of the word. However, the downside had been that she had indirectly become a threat to Peter and his life. An earlier intrusion into his life he had managed to ward off. It had, in a sense, been character building.

Maria made a number of pots of tea and busied herself with paperwork to pass the time, preparing next season's forecasts if the tour operators took up their options, and then again if they did not. A couple of 'false alarm' calls had come through. José had phoned earlier than usual because he was going to a dinner in Barcelona, which Maria had declined to attend. To an extent, telling him all about the situation eased her waiting.

"Don't worry," her husband said. "That girl has been in and out of your life so much. At least on this occasion, she's in the hands of others, and that should prevent any further great influence on your or Peter's life, or Marco's... actually, all our lives, when you come to think of it. Try not to worry."

José was always a rational calming influence on her.

"Love you," she said. "Enjoy the dinner."

"I'll miss you."

"Go on. You won't. They'll probably sit you next to some young blonde."

"Yes, and I bet he's got nothing in common to talk to me about, other than insuring his chain of hairdressing salons and his pet poodles," José laughed.

"You're funny. You still make me laugh. See you Friday. Don't be late."

She was still reflecting on the happiness José had brought into her life (not that she ever felt Paco wouldn't have done the same if he'd escaped his dreadful accident) when the phone rang. She hoped it would be José to say he couldn't be bothered with his boring dinner and he was coming home for a mid-week break and a change of shirt, as he mischievously called the need to see his wife and share their bed. She picked up the receiver.

"Mrs Martinez. It's Dr Ramez at the Gerona General. Thanks for trying me. I'm sorry, I had another serious case to attend to when you rang."

Another serious case, Maria thought. Oh God, that confirmed Tania's plight. "It's kind of you to call back. Do you have any news, please?"

"Well, I do and I don't. Now I bet that sounds strange. I can tell you what we've found. I'll keep it as simple as I can, without going into too much technical and medical jargon. But I need your help to get to a level of understanding. What do you know about the brain?"

"Oh. Very little, I'm afraid."

"Do you know anyone who's ever had a stroke?"

"Yes. Actually, recently I do. My mother-in-law."

"Good. Well, not to say that's good," Dr Ramez added, realising immediately that may have had the wrong intonation. "What I mean is, then you may understand some of the symptoms. Anyway, do you know if your mother-in-law was paralysed in any way… was she…?"

"Yes, her left side was."

"OK. Was it explained that the blood clot was therefore in the right side of her brain?"

"No."

"Oh well. That doesn't help then. Take my word for it. It was. Tell me, was she left-handed?"

"Yes. I think she was."

"OK. That figures. So, fundamentally, the movements in her left hand were controlled by messages from the opposite side of the brain. Can you imagine what might happen if the brain had some sort of turmoil and decided to reverse its instructions to the muscles that controlled the hands?"

"Not really, I could only guess."

"What would you guess?"

"Well… if it was severe enough, I suppose it could control the right hand instead of the left… but that might be silly."

"Not at all. You could easily become a brain surgeon at this rate of learning! So the point of all this – we could tell from the skin on Tania's left hand that she too was left-handed. She obviously has a physical occupation, we could tell that. So when she came out of sedation, we offered her a drink. She didn't say anything but she licked her lips and passed her tongue over them, pretty well indicating the answer would be yes. But she didn't seem to be able to say yes. She was confused. So we put a beaker of water in front of her, on the bed table. She became more confused. She didn't seem to know how to pick it up. So a nurse put the cup to her mouth and tipped it slightly. Tania drank and downed all the contents. The nurse gave her the cup to hold. She took it but then dropped it. What was happening was that she'd lost control between her brain and her usual lead hand."

"Had she had a stroke then?"

"No. Not apparently. All the normal checks we'd done under sedation showed good. Blood pressure, ECG, blood quality, no diabetes from a water sample… oh, and no urine infection, I'm rather sorry to say. No, it was what we describe in un-complicated medical phraseology as, if you like, a confusion. We encouraged her to speak. We asked her who Toni is. She just smiled. 'Is there anybody else?' we asked. She didn't answer. We asked if she was left-handed, and she said she didn't think so. We asked where she works and she said, 'In Toni's house. I clean for him'. When we asked if he comes home at night, she said, 'Only sometimes.' So, Señora Martinez, does any of that relate to the reality?"

"No. Nothing does."

"Can you expand on that?"

"Well, it seems Tania was actually in my son's house. She does look after that when he's away, which is more often than not. He lives in the UK and visits infrequently. The house is in a place called Girasol."

"Yes, I've heard of that. It's on the sea, isn't it?"

"Yes, but it's got a golf course and some spectacular hills and walks. It was there, in fact, that the only Toni I know in Tania's life was killed. He was shot dead by the police."

"Would you say that was a major trauma for Tania?"

"More a relief, actually. But, thinking about it, her father became involved and… well, that's a long story, but the upshot of that was that he came close to being shot in front of her. Then he was dragged away as a common crook. But then he always was.

"That, I'm sure, was a trauma because… well… she told me once… her father made her fulfil her mother's role as a dutiful wife, from time to time. In other words, he abused her incestuously. She once told me she hated him for doing it, but loved him for what he taught her about physical relationships, which nobody else had been able to replicate. This cousin, Toni, although I never saw him, subjected her to sexual abuse too…"

"Rape?"

"As good as, I'd say."

"OK. The pattern's becoming clear. Next… a painful question!"

"I'm sure it won't be the first."

"Your son."

It was going to be a painful question. "My son?" she said, meekly.

"What was he to Tania?"

"Oh God! They were similar ages, though he's a little older. I can't disguise the fact that she worshipped him, but they're a class apart. He's extremely intelligent, whereas she's adequately worldly. She offered herself to him but he, to the best of my knowledge, resisted her. But Toni suspected my son of having used Tania, who he considered to be his property. It's another long story, which I'll have to expand on if you feel it's of significance, but Toni tried to kill Peter, the police turned up and that's how he came to his painful end."

"… And your son?"

"Thank God, he survived."

"Was Tania interested in that survival?"

"Yes, of course, we all were."

"Particularly interested?"

"Yes. As I said, she worshipped him. But she wasn't involved in his recovery, she watched from afar."

"Is your son married?"

"He's a widower. Not re-married, but he's not without female attention…"

"… And recently? Has he been to Girasol?"

"Oh, my God!"

"I'm sorry. I'm sure this is difficult for you but, to be candid, Tania's dependent on you to help us understand her problem."

"I do understand. Yes, he was there at the weekend."

"With… well, let's say a lady friend?" Dr Ramez enquired.

"Yes, so I understand."

"That's probably very significant."

"Oh my God! Is this all going to be Peter's fault?"

"Not at all. It's nature's fault and Tania's in particular. You might understand the significance if I explain a bit more. In years to come, not that far away, so they say, you'll be able to sit where you're currently sitting and access some worldwide information centre through a computer, and the research you'll be able to do would take a week or two in the local library. Do you have a medical encyclopaedia?"

"No. But I was a librarian and still go to the library for research."

"OK. Well, to make it easy, I'll explain. There was a man called, to keep it short, Pavlov, who had an interest in the human brain. To understand that, he carried out experiments on dogs, the nearest thing he could get to humans who wouldn't object to his experiments. What he basically did was to discover that any object or event that the dogs learnt to associate with food (such as the arrival of his assistant, or the ringing of a bell) would trigger the same response as food itself – even though these things hadn't always produced that response. The dogs, therefore, had learned this behaviour as a result of a neutral stimulus (the assistant or the bell), rather than only from the natural, unconditioned stimulus – the food. Are you OK with that, so far?"

"I think so," Maria replied.

"So… in Tania's case, she may have learned to associate your son's presence with something positive, just as the dogs associated the bell with food.

"But then there's a trauma, like the shootings, which she seems to have overcome, as they didn't make a huge difference to her life directly. But if, shortly after, there's another trauma, like Peter turning up with a lady friend, which openly says to Tania 'you don't have a place in my life', then her brain tells her, perhaps, to react differently, and what has always been positive to her, becomes negative. And what has been negative, that is, Toni, becomes positive. She then doesn't know whether she's left-handed, or right. She's confused and if, and I say if, her brain is frail, perhaps going back to the positive and negative confusions of her father's influence on her body and mind, the strain would be sufficiently great for her to pass out and, on recovery, find her senses, emotions and other brain-controlled functions 'confused', even reversed. That could happen. In fact that may have happened, and that may be what we have to deal with. But we'll need to find out why the brain is so frail to have allowed that to happen. Finding that out could be the problem."

"Oh, my God!" Maria understood Dr Ramez's explanation.

"Señora Martinez, you must understand… it's early days."

"Have you seen the condition cured?"

"Sometimes. But it would help if the cause of the brain's receptiveness is rectified."

"Does it help if the 'positive' influence, if you call it that, is brought in to enter the brain?"

"Are you sure you're not a brain surgeon? Again, it's a good point. Sometimes. Sometimes, though, it goes the other way and forces the rejection factor to go deeper. Then, I'm bound to say, it's irrevocable."

"So what if my son Peter went to see her?"

"I'd rule out anybody she knows seeing her for quite a while. We need to have her total attention without external influence."

"I'm going to try to find her daughter. She's travelling abroad. It would mean her coming back. Would that be sensible?"

"Well, you must obviously contact her, but I wouldn't hurry to get her back."

"Dr Ramez, you've been most helpful. Is there anything I can do?"

"Pray. That's really the only thing. For whatever reason, the damage is done."

"Should I tell Peter about it?"

"Yes, of course. But remember, I've said he personally isn't to blame in any way. He's just the innocent and uninvited subject who's caused the complex brain cells to change around."

"When could I call again? By the way, you do personally have my number, don't you?"

"Yes I do, thank you. I'd suggest not before Friday. Friday pm. We'll probably do a lumbar puncture just in case there's a disease in the brain, and a number of other tests that'll take a while to interpret. So… Friday, then. I'll tell you at least if there's any change."

"Thank you again for being so helpful, and for doing what you can for poor Tania."

"It's my job. It's a pleasure."

They bade their goodbyes to each other.

Dr Ramez reflected. Maria was obviously a bright lady, but emotionally too disturbed to pursue his lead about them finding the cause of Tania's brain frailty. He still never liked the generality of the term 'tumour', which he would have had to refer to if Maria had pressed him on the possibilities.

Maria sat semi-mesmerised for a short while. She placed her hands together under her desk. She could never break the habit of needing to do that when she prayed. She prayed for Tania's well-being and for God to know it was not Peter's fault. She prayed for Marco and then, as usual, she prayed for all those out at sea, and that God would continue to look after Paco, please, as he had done for so long now. She crossed her body in Catholic custom and did a little dip of the head and an attempt at a curtsey, although she was sitting in her leather desk chair.

Peter, she thought. She must let him know. The friendly porter whom she'd had conversations with over the previous weekend was on duty again.

"Yes, hello, Mrs Martinez, yes of course, I remember your calls. Is it the same again – you'd like to speak to your son?"

"Please."

"I think he's out. Let me try."

He went off the line, it seemed for an eternity.

"No. I'm sorry, he doesn't seem to be answering. If he's out, he'll have to come back in past me. Shall I ask him to call you?"

"Please. But I know you're busy. I'll call back anyway. I'll need to let you know when I'm going to bed as I won't want him to call me back after then."

"OK."

Hearing her warm voice talking of going to bed aroused his feelings. He bet she'd be lovely in bed – completely overlooking the fact that to be Peter's mother, she'd have to be pushing 70. He was more into young models getting in and out of bed in the magazines the porters were used to thumbing through during their long and lonely night shifts. He opened his desk drawer and took out the latest version of Knave, which was always his favourite turn-on.

Maria disturbed his thoughts twice more before saying to tell Peter to ring in the morning.

That was the message Peter got on his return from the reception with Cas. It was about five the following morning when Cas had awakened, slipped out of bed and dressed in the half-light generated from the security illuminations around the hospital. She was aware – and pleased – that Peter watched her. It showed his deeper interest in her total presence, not just a desire to roll over, spent, and go to sleep after they had made love. That was how she saw it after this third time.

It had been soft and loving. They each expressed a pride in the other by the gentle way they used their bodies. The effect was as rewarding as the previous occasions, even if the motivation had been different.

Perhaps they had both been more tired but they slept entwined in each other's arms, until Cas woke up with a start, realising she should at least take to her own bed for her colleagues to see that morning. Peter gave her his total attention until she left, but then went back to sleep.

He woke with a smile on his face. She obviously wasn't very good at retrieving her underwear. He found her pants tucked down beside him in the bed. He'd give them to her if he saw her at breakfast. That would bring both a smile to her face, for sure, and a feigned embarrassment, depending on how he presented them. He rather fancied the 'I believe these are yours' approach. Doubtless this spirited young lady would counter: "They'd bloody well better be, there'll be a row if they're not." He'd decide his actions when he saw what mood she gave off when they met, although he had to say, Cas was a very even personality. On thinking it through, she was always the same. Yes. He liked the security of that.

He'd shave and shower… oh, and he must ring his mother. What would it be this time? "I thought you might have been taken ill and moved hospitals again." He'd call in the break between breakfast and the first treatment session. And he'd ring Ramon Gaspard too. He was intrigued by all the winking and nodding. He'd touch base with his secretary in London as well, just to check on things and to re-affirm he'd be in the office by Tuesday at the latest.

They met in the refectory. Cas greeted him first. Fortunately, he was at a table by himself.

"Morning…" then, "… honey," which was whispered.

"Hi," then, "gorgeous," he whispered in return.

She winked back. God, how she would miss him after Monday. But she mustn't let it show. If it was pure infatuation, it would wear off.

"Hey," she said, "I think I left something of mine in your bed." She spoke in a hushed voice.

"Really? Give me a clue. What was that?"

"My knickers," she said, coyly. "Are you just making this difficult for me?" He couldn't reply. "Look, I don't want the cleaners to find them."

"What colour are they?"

"Black," she said, without thinking.

"Great. Yes, OK. Found those. Good. Did you leave a white pair as well?"

She smiled. "OK. Clever bastard. And I suppose you're running a bet on me saying 'no', and you'd say 'best find out', and I'd say 'you friggin' well better had'."

Peter smiled.

"… And don't you look so friggin' pleased with yourself! You, you bastard, you just get me so bloody excited that I forget about the fundamentals in life."

He sensed she was being funny, yet she could have been close to tears. He'd not press the point.

"There's a huge compliment," he said, holding out his hand.

"Not here," she said, rolling her eyes from side to side, indicating they should be aware of the presence of the others.

"I want them to know about us," Peter whispered. "I'm proud of it. Here, just shake my hand. That'll be touch enough for the beginning of the day."

"Shaking hands with the biggest bastard in the world. That's what I'm doing," she said, as she did indeed shake hands.

Paul Demar was suddenly alongside them. "Why are you shaking hands?" he asked.

"I'm congratulating your coach, young man."

"Why, what's she done? Won one of your bets or something?"

"No. She will be appointed to the IPC with a special responsibility for looking after the interests of the little black ones, once it is officially in place."

She shot a glare at him. She knew that he was alluding to her underwear.

"The little black people, please," she said, "little black ones make you sound cheap... but then you *are* cheap... would you mind letting go of my hand with your cheap, insincere white one."

"Are you two cross with each other?" Paul asked.

As one, they both replied, "Not at all."

Then they both laughed in unison at each other's immediate response.

"No. We're just having fun with each other."

"Oh. That's good. I can't bear rows."

The three talked together over breakfast like good old friends, now all heading in the same direction. They reviewed the previous evening and it was clear Paul would have no problem being in the limelight. Once they'd talked about the good bits, Paul became a little hesitant.

"Is something bothering you?" Peter eventually asked the question both he and Cas could sense needed to be asked.

"Well, I've been thinking, and I was talking to Sñr Quinto. He says do I realise how important it is to have a coach, and in fact, someone able to talk to sponsors and the like. I said I did and that's why I've got you. But then, he said I've only half got you. It's an arrangement... well, like just friends, really. He said that was dodgy and I ought to talk to you about a contract so that you'll support me right through and make me train and things like that. He says if we do OK, I might make some money and that I ought to share that with you. He says we ought to become formal agents and athletes together. Like having a contract that says that."

"He's a lawyer. Did he say if he would draw up a contract?"

"Yes, actually he did. He said if I wanted somebody to help me get the relationship right, he could see to it. He's a big name in lawyers, you know."

"Yes, we did know that," Peter replied. "What I advise is that you get together with Cas and go along and see him in his office. You could get it all fixed up and then you both have security."

Paul turned to Cas. "Don't worry either. I'll understand I'm not the only one in your life. You'll have to look after your little black ones like you both want to," he said innocently.

"Sure. Don't I want that, Cas!"

"Pig!" she said.

"Are you two arguing again?"

"No. Just joking. We'll contact Sñr Quinto and fix it up. Now let's all get on. Cas, do you want to pick up that stuff from my room? You might need it."

She thought, *You'll never let go.* "Yes. I'll come and get them now. Save later, won't it."

Cas collected her overnight leftovers and, after a suitable kiss to seal what they both agreed was a successful evening with a happy ending, she left Peter to make his three calls.

"It might be tight to do those in 20 minutes, so don't start on my body without me."

Cas responded from a practical point of view. "How could I ever dream of doing that? Tell you what, it'll give me time to catch up on my laundry. See you as soon as possible."

"Hi, is my mother available? It's Peter Martinez here," he announced. He knew he must be talking to a relatively new receptionist, as she didn't recognise his voice. Usually there was a snappy, "Yes, of course, Mr Peter."

His mother's distinctive voice came on. "So, here's my only son, raised from wherever he was when I rang."

"Hi, Mother. I'll tell you where I was. I was fixing up an appointment to be on the committee of the Spanish Paralympics Federation… I'm about to become an influence on the Olympics in '92."

"Go on! Really? Or is this one of your windups?"

"It's true. It's something the new lady in my life and I are going into. To try and encourage greater recognition of the coloured races banned from entering competitions because of their own country's entrenched position on race."

"Apartheid?" Maria enquired intelligently.

"Yes, that and East and West Germany, and a number of other issues."

"Oh well. That should keep you out of mischief." Maria hesitated, then plucked up courage to ask the question on her mind. "Peter, is your girlfriend black then?"

He roared with laughter. "No! She's beautiful and blonde. It's just that she's South African and embarrassed by her country's attitude to race. OK. I know what you're wanting to say. Why don't you come to Barcelona before I go back to the UK on Monday?"

"Are you still intent on going back to that busy world and that hectic life you lead over there?"

"Well, I'll need some money from somewhere to keep this lifestyle of mine up, which I've become accustomed to, and all that."

"Can we talk about that later? I've got some sad news."

That usually meant somebody had died. Marco, Virginia… who?

He couldn't contain himself. "Who this time, who's died?"

"Peter. It's not always that bad. In fact, no one's died. It's Tania."

Now hearing anything about Tania was always bad news. His heart sank.

"Hit me with it, Mother."

She did. In about ten minutes, while he listened intently.

"… So that's it. Nothing we can do but wait and see. But I thought you would need to know," Maria concluded.

"Of course. Thank you. It's all very strange. Why do you think she was in the house without clothes on? Do you mean absolutely nothing on?"

"Apparently, according to Andres."

"Just don't understand that. I spoke to her during the morning. Perhaps she was a bit strange but then I'd well and truly choked her off the day before. She was doing her peeping Tom thing, trying to make mischief because I had a female guest in the house.

"Well, as you say, we'll have to wait and see. Is there anything I can do, or you'd like me to do?"

"No. I don't think so. Do you pray these days?"

"Well, I did when her cousins shot me up. Sure, I pray."

"Then if you get a quiet moment, pray for her, would you?"

"OK. Now… how would it be if you come up on Sunday evening? Bring José, then he can stay over. You might like to see me off at the airport on Monday and then go back. We'll speak on Friday. Let's take it as provisionally OK because you haven't immediately said no. So is that alright?"

"Peter! You're so forceful. Yes, I'd say provisionally yes."

"Good. I've got two more calls to make and then I'm on the last lap of getting my body finally sorted."

He put the phone down and contemplated all that his mother had said. So Cas was right. Tania really did have this huge hang-up over him. But why the nude bit? That was all strange, unless she went there, to his house, to fantasise over an imaginary relationship with him. On his bed. Oh wow, that would be weird, and then for his phone call to drag her away downstairs to speak. She'd hurried. She said she had. Well, he might never know. He was just relieved he hadn't walked in and found her like that. Then again, he always rang and said when he would be arriving, so that she could get the house ready. He would pray for her, of course he would… to please his mother, but a little later. First Val, then Ramon.

"Hi Val." She had picked up his private line in his office. "I'm really fine," he answered in reply to her question as to how he was. "But then I should be when you think about the amount of time I've been away getting this old body of mine sorted out."

"That's ridiculous, Mr Peter. Everybody… well, everybody apart from Mr William… realises you were really smashed up. So it was bound to take a while to get you mended. The girls here, by the way, are saying do they get to see the scars?"

Peter held back a little. It seemed Val was going to be quite familiar. The 'Peter' bit said it all.

"Certainly not. The body of a CEO is way out of that reach. Particularly loyal servants might get to, though, if they're good."

"Is that a promise?" *She is familiar,* he thought.

"Give up the idea, Val. It's not a pretty sight, I can tell you. So… what's on?"

"Well, it looks as though your memo has let the odd rocket or two off under the backsides of the guys in the International Division. I've had one or two of my contemporaries on the phone on behalf of their line bosses, asking if I know what it's all about. I've been able genuinely to say I don't know, but I don't think they believe that too much. Mr William dropped by my desk yesterday, saying he'd like to vet any memos that come in."

"Bloody cheek! What did you say?"

"I said I'd let you know that, and you would no doubt tell me what to do… and he said, 'Listen, young lady, I'm the Chairman, I'll tell you what to do', so I just wanted you to know that."

"Yes… and then?" Peter pushed for her to complete the story.

"Effectively… well… can you tell me what I said, Peter?"

"You said 'get stuffed'."

"Of course I didn't," she said showing a hint of disappointment. He should have known better.

"Well, you should have done. OK, I expect you were nice and you said again you'd let me know his wishes."

"Spot on."

"Good girl."

"Thank you."

"Anything else?"

"Your son Alex rings pretty regularly for an update on your movements. He's been really concerned and he was talking of flying out, and he checked if that was a good idea or not. When I told him you were back next week, he was ecstatic and said he'd got a better idea – could I book you out for a quick lunch with him, or dinner if that would be easier to fix. He's desperate to see you."

"What's the problem? I'm sure you've asked."

"Yes, I did. No problem. He just wants to see you fit and well and in his words, 'have a quality hour or two' with you."

"He's a nice boy, you know," Peter said, as though reassuring himself.

"I think you're lucky to be able to say that."

"What do you mean by that?" he replied, with a hint of indignation.

"It seems... promise you won't be cross..."

"No!"

"Well, it seems he's been left to his own devices... you know, you haven't helped him along, given him nudges in any particular direction, got friends to help..."

"Look, Val, I'll always welcome your input, you should know that, but you'll have to understand I've stood off for his own benefit. I didn't have my dad nudging me in the right direction... I had to make my own ground. Alex will be all the better for that. Look at Mr William. He's been nudged in the right direction, probably even been told by his old man which influential son of the aristocracy he should lose his shirt to in order to secure the odd ministerial recommendation for the award of a contract, or even which horse to back at Newmarket to supplement the family income."

"You *are* better, Peter! You're really sparky. That's good! Oh, by the way, there's an invitation lying around on your desk. It seems you haven't accepted a lady called Marcia Hunt's wedding invite. It's Saturday week and she needs to know."

"Christ, is it that soon?"

"The invite was dated shortly after you got shot."

"Can you phone and say yes. I accept for both of us. That's myself, and my plus one, Miss Cassandra White."

Val went decidedly quiet.

"... And I suppose that's your essential nursing companion?" she said sarcastically.

"As it happens – yes." He laughed, one of his guttural utterances, depicting sheer enjoyment.

"Well, that lets my boyfriend back in with a chance, I suppose."

"Yes... and you'll be so much better off that way – after all, you *are* my good and potentially loyal PA."

He'd made his point.

"... And what shall I say to Mrs Hunt's question as to whether you can make her pre-wedding party on the Thursday before?"

"Book me up. Anything. I'm definitely not free."

This time Val had the upper hand and she ricocheted Peter's laugh straight back down the phone at him.

"Listen, call me if there's anything to say. Outside that, I'll see you Tuesday. Oh, by the way – can you find out how to set Mrs Cook up to spring clean the apartment, get some food into the fridge, you know… the usual coming home bit."

"Will that be for one or two, Sir?"

"One… of course." He supposed it was a sensible question. "Oh, and can you get a return flight out of Barcelona Friday week morning and back Sunday evening? That's business class."

"Name?"

"Miss Cassandra White. Book the ticket to collect at Barcelona Airport, if you would please. Listen, I'm actually very busy. I'll tell you why when I get back. Must go. Thanks for holding the fort."

The receiver her end clicked back to a silent reality. Val focused on the earpiece on the inanimate handset in her hand, as though staring all the way down the connecting cables to Barcelona and Peter's still attentive ear.

When Vera had offered Val the secondment, she had jumped for joy. She so wanted to be lifted out of the middle tier team in which it seemed she was stuck for life. Her fiancé was everything she could have accessed, but a bachelor CEO with worldwide visits, dinners and the like would suit her down to the ground – that was, after the obligatory trip into bed, of course.

"So there's really no chance," she confided to the plastic instrument. "Oh well! C'est la vie. I'd best stay nice to Mike. He wants me. But then he doesn't offer what that man does. Then there's always Mr William on hold!" The phone decided to stay a silent confidante.

"Sñr Gaspard, por favor."

Obviously Peter had a stronger British accent overlying his mother tongue these days than he had realised. He was noticing that anybody with an international background, on hearing his Spanish, would answer in English. But he felt a definite dual nationality, so he wasn't at all bothered.

"Who can I say is calling?" the operator enquired in perfect English.

"Would you say it's Peter Martinez, please."

"Certainly, Sir."

Ramon was the same. He was distinctly bilingual. He came on the phone.

"Hi, you lucky old bastard."

"That's some greeting. Why do you say that?"

"Well, you *are* getting old, like all of us. If you're going to pull the South African girl, you're lucky, and… well, to be fair, I know you're not a bastard but take that as a form of affection."

"That's OK then." Peter let him off the hook. He was becoming over-conscious of how freely the 'bastard' word was being lobbied around in his direction.

"Good evening last night," Ramon affirmed.

"Yes. I actually think it was. If for no other reason than to catch up with you."

"You funny old charmer!"

Peter preferred that to countering Ramon's insult with another, as men locking horns tend to do. Inwardly, Ramon was touched by Peter's comment. He didn't often receive that kind of thing.

He was a father of four, so his wife gave him 20 per cent attention. In fact that was an overstatement, because she looked after her mother too.

He got no affection within the group of companies he had established. He'd had a tough, hard ride since the days of building Girasol with Peter. Those were very happy times together, when Peter would daily nearly run out of money to pay the progress payments, and Ramon would go short on labour as his best craftsmen were attracted to easier lives as waiters or chefs to satisfy the needs of the Costa tourists, who were now flocking to Spain in their millions on package deals. So client and builder alike struggled, and in those mutually stressful circumstances, you make real friends. Mates with a true understanding which, as soon as they set eyes on each other again, had immediately been rekindled.

"Look, Ramon. I'm in this Institution and I'm meant to be getting down to two last serious days of remedial therapy before I go back to the UK on Monday. I'm intrigued by your 'nod nod, wink wink' antics last night. What have you got in mind? And you've got a very short timespan to say whether you're trying to find out if Cas has got an older sister or a young mother I can bring along to make up some wild foursome."

"Peter! You shock me. I've been married now for 21 years. You'll probably remember the girl. Used to bring lunches to the site…"

"What… not Bianca? Is it Bianca? *Bianca*?"

"That's right."

"Wow, you're the lucky old sod now! She wouldn't let anyone get near to her. She's the one we used to joke would finish up in a convent. You'll have to tell me how you did that. Good God!"

"Listen, Peter. I can't speak on the phone. If you've only got two more nights – that's weekday ones, because I devote my weekends to the family – we need to get together. Could you do an hour or so tonight, or at a push tomorrow? I promise you it'll be worth the time. I'll even buy a simple paella to share in one of those working men's bars we used to frequent because we couldn't afford anything more."

Tonight – that was OK. He thought he'd have to square it with Cas, but she'd understand. He might even be able to get young Paul Demar some sponsorship.

"Tonight… that's fine."

"I'll pick you up. Let's say seven, OK?"

"I'll wait with bated breath," Peter said with a laugh.

"You'd better do that, old son. See you then."

Peter imagined Ramon's large bricklayer's hand throwing the phone into its rest. He was pleased they were in touch. Christ! Bianca. How the hell did he do that? He'd find out.

Ramon had always been reliable. On the dot of seven, the porter rang up to say, "Su coche está aqui, Señor," as though Peter was some important aristocrat. Ramon, typically though, was parked on the restricted parking area reserved for ambulances and had just contained the attention of a police officer when Peter came out through the swing doors. Peter slid into the passenger seat and struck the leather top of the dashboard hard, twice with the flat of his hand.

"Let's go, let's go, man, don't hang around with the gendarmerie."

Being together took them both back over 20 years. They were carefree young men again. Ramon dropped the clutch and hit the accelerator. He developed wheel spin and planted a layer of rubber into the concrete surface of the layby outside the hospital.

"Can't you get this brute to move?" Peter challenged.

"Look, I value my licence too much. I'm not like you. I do still have to work, you know."

They laughed together. Peter worked out this was a smart, upper range executive Mercedes, even though he wasn't very good on foreign cars. He was a Jaguar or Bentley fan.

"So times are still hard," he joked, as he inhaled the perfume of the newish leather. He turned round to take in the full view of the back seat. "I just can't come to terms with the fact that some nights still, you actually lay that Bianca beauty across that leather."

"Wish," Ramon said. "I wish. When there are four mouths plus mine to feed, passion doesn't get that regular. I have to say a family of four, with one hyper-dependent, is a pretty full-time job and understandably gets pretty tiring."

"Where are you taking me?" Peter asked, without commenting on Ramon's moderate but pointed exposé.

"There's this simple restaurant just five kilometres into the country." He slowed the car.

"Does this old port area take you back?"

"Yes, wasn't it here that if we had any money at the weekend, we'd come to that fish stall and buy winkles as a treat?"

"That's right."

"The area's looking tired, eh!"

"Yes, but all capitals of the world have their areas like this, which at one time were the hub of industry but are now becoming derelict."

"Right, but nobody's going to rebuild berths if the water isn't deep enough for these huge ocean liners they're building these days, or tankers even."

"What about building for yachts?"

"Well… yes. Great. So, you go broke. What's a yacht owner going to pay for a slip of water?" Ramon laughed. "You see, you've got too far removed from your native land."

That actually hurt Peter. He was always conscious of the fact that he had rather run away after Girasol, taking his young man's fortune with him to invest in the more vibrant community in northern Europe.

"But you'll be telling me all about it. Eh?"

"I hope to. But you'll have to be in a listening mood."

"I'm all ears."

Ramon built up speed but only for four or 500 metres to the inland side of the waterway, across the main busy road along the quay.

"Have you got a nice pad in London?"

"Yes. It *is* nice."

"Better than here?" He'd stopped in the midst of some tenement buildings.

Peter looked across at Ramon.

"Honest opinion," Ramon requested earnestly.

"Yes," Peter responded sincerely.

"They need pulling down."

"So… that's easy. But what do you do with the land? That's difficult."

"Why? Have you lost your sense of adventure?" Ramon challenged.

"No. Not at all. But you've got the harbour on one side, blocking out the sea, and historic Barcelona spreading westward for miles, as it always has."

"OK. Let's start again," Ramon suggested. "Do you want to go back to the harbour?"

"I've no need. I know it."

"OK. Suppose you strip out all the old warehouse buildings, demolish them, leave the surrounding water, virtually as it is without deepening it, and build restaurants jutting out into the sea."

"Nobody would go there."

"OK. Restaurants and clubs, discos, places for the kids."

"OK, but where do the kids come from?"

"… And shops."

"So the kids need to come with their parents."

"That's right."

"OK, I give in. You've lost me," Peter admitted.

"The Olympics."

"Yes. I know about those."

"There will be about 10,000 athletes."

"OK, for what… three weeks?"

"… And say, one adult for each athlete."

"OK – 10,000 adults."

"Spectators."

"How many?"

"Hundreds of thousands. Do you realise the Spanish budget for the games is put at $7.5 billion?"

"No. I hadn't. 7.5 billion is one hell of a lot of money. That can't work."

"It can if you build new structures and effectively loan them to the Olympic movement and then take them back and either sell the property long term or continue to rent it out. If Barcelona gets the attention of the media in '92, then it'll be a future focal point for tourism.

"So this is what happens. We – that's as in we Catalans and IOC and International Paralympic Committee members support the idea of needing a purpose-built Olympic village, as compared with what other nations have done in the past, by using existing facilities like university campus buildings out of term. Stuff them with competitors, then clean them up and hand them back at cost after the teams have gone home with their medals. Something borrowed, nothing gained. The $7.5 billion budget is invested short term for the duration of the games but in the scenario we envisage, the designated Olympic village, once empty, then becomes available long term. If it's fashionably designed, then the locals with cash will buy a competitor's previous temporary home for real cash. If part of the village is around the harbour with restaurants, discos and shops, there'll be a constant intake of tourism. All that becomes just an extension of Las Ramblas and Barcelona could become Europe's focal point for tourists. It's got a beach, it will need hotels for the Olympic tourists anyway, it's got tradition, style, even a zoo. It may become second to Paris or London."

"Great in theory," Peter conceded, "but where does the money come from?"

"Well, for a start, the government through the international organisation will underwrite it. Then the marketing guys go to town and sell the Games' rights to world television to some pretty high bidders. Los Angeles in '84 raised $75 million in federal taxes, which the locals were happy to raise to get the city restated on the world's map. Over 30 companies contributed over $120 million in sponsorship. You're talking big, big money."

"Ramon, we've been sitting here for nigh on 30 minutes. Where does the wink and nod come from? Are you going to ask me to loan even one of those billions just for the fun of being able to buy a ticket in my home country, or to get our lad, Paul Demar, to be able to walk to his own stadium?"

Ramon laughed. "No. You build it and get paid for it."

"Build it?" Peter thought hard for a minute or two, then responded. "Sure. Build it. We could all build it. But first, you've either got to finance it, and then build it with the risks of your prognosis being wrong, or be so bloody cut-throat as to cut the arse out of the tender to get the work. Doing that, I doubt there'd be enough profit to buy tickets for the fencing or the judo, let alone the final day's athletics."

"Wise words, my good friend. But not wise enough. Let's go. I'll buy the paella."

Ramon obviously had more to say later. They drove off in silence.

"One more look," Ramon said as he backtracked past the marina. He stopped by the roadside. "Can you see that?"

There was nothing there.

"See what?"

"Oh, that's a five star plus 40-odd storey hotel."

"Go on," Peter said with a smile, "and somebody's got to build the bugger."

Ramon slapped his friend's thigh. "Now you've got it! Christ, was that your bad leg, mate?"

"I wouldn't say if it was. Take me to that paella."

Chapter 15

Ramon seemed well-known at the restaurant. They were ushered to a quiet table to one side of the main seating area. He ordered a bottle of Montrachet.

"Do you remember we had a bottle like this when we sold the first villa?"

"Too true. We certainly couldn't afford it then. How life changes!"

Ramon took charge of ordering a seafood paella, having checked if that was still OK with Peter.

"Absolutely fine," Peter said.

The waiter vanished to drum up the food from the kitchen.

"Right, let me not keep you in suspense any longer," Ramon suggested.

"I was hoping you'd say that."

"OK. Us sitting here contemplating the exact amount doesn't really matter, but probably many billions of dollars' worth of construction is what is in prospect. I've shown you some of the potential housing land and the leisure area. There are stadia, pools, halls for the gymnasts, loads and loads of infrastructure, all to be built in a tight timescale… not to mention a magnificent fountain park and a new tramway. I'm telling you, it's huge, Peter."

"How do you know about all this?" Peter asked.

Ramon touched his nose, indicating it was a secret and not to pry. "Well, old chap, the Federation/IPC have two Spanish representatives on the buildings procurement sub-committee…"

Peter now smiled. It had taken longer than it usually would have done to sink in, but better late than never. He'd worked it out.

"… And you're one of them."

"That's right."

"The other?"

"Jorge Quinto."

"Go on!" Peter was remembering how well he and Cas had got on with the Chairman. "OK. So that gives you the inside track as to what's going to happen. How do you get included in the action?"

"Well, Samaranch's roots go back a long way. A number of his supporters, left over from pre-war days, who wouldn't wish to be identified, are still mad at the way the Krauts, through that bastard Hitler, stole Barcelona's thunder in '36, disguised under the banner of peace, not world domination.

"So, very quietly, as it's the IOC's responsibility to produce the integral parts of the games, he's let it be known that he's happy for the Germans to be financing and building for short term tourism but the new foundation to the capital of Catalonia is to be built by natives. So it's been ruled if there are six tenderers for each project, at least three must be from home territory."

Peter became more pensive. "Are there three or four home-grown companies who could cope?"

"No. Two certainly. Three perhaps, but none with a great deal of strength in asset or capability terms."

"Ramon. I've only met up with you again in the last 24 hours. Tell me about your company. How has that developed?"

"Good! I'm number two on the list. We're certain to get, say, $300 million of work, if I want it."

"… And the number one company?"

"They'd get $300 million, too, 'by arrangement'."

"Number three?"

"Now there's a question. They're a very deep-seated Catholic organisation, who're not prepared to discuss strategy with the two of us. Suffice to say they are, at least on paper, a bit strapped for cash."

"OK. So what am I meant to do? Drool and say 'well done Ramon'? I envy you the prospect. Why are you telling me all this?"

"Shall we have another?" He pointed to the empty wine bottle. "Look, I usually get sent home from here in a taxi. I think it would be a good idea."

Peter felt he was out of drinking practice, but he was intrigued.

"OK with me. You have my rapt attention."

"$300 million of turnover in three years would push me a bit," Ramon continued. "We've got a number of villa developments that soak up cash. You know the form. You sell everything you've got. Have a really good holiday, then don't sell for a year or so while the mark goes under, or the rand or pound. Given that, averaged out, it's good. So I've been resolving to myself, and my co-directors who, I have to say, are excellent at constructing things but not so hot on thinking out the future, that we take, say $100 million to $150 million and not get greedy."

"Makes sense to me. Well done! Now I'll ask you again: why are you telling me all this?"

"Well, of course I've read all about your antics in the UK. I'd heard you were doing well, you're something of a local boy made good. When you got shot you were, of course, all over the local news. 'Spanish tycoon', 'multi-millionaire', 'Boss man of one of the largest construction groups in the UK', 'international entrepreneur'… I'd meant to write to you, but you know how it is…

"Then I saw you at the hospital and I worked out God had made us come together for another purpose."

"So how do you see that?"

"Well, I figure if it were your company and its equity strength bidding for the work, on financial merit you could hold all $300 million. But you won't get it because you're offshore to Spain.

"So supposing we combined and the combo was principally Spanish. Then I can't see why the two shouldn't share in $400 to $500 million, and 50 per cent of that to me would be better than I'd get ordinarily."

"Tell me more. How do you reckon we'd get together: 50-50?"

"Actually, it would have to be 51 per cent Spanish, 49 per cent other. The Krauts have been up to that one to try and get in on the work but they won't work without a majority control, so none of us Spanish contractors will give them the light of day."

"So why would you expect us to be any different?"

"You still hold a Spanish passport, don't you?"

"Yes I do."

"OK. So 49 per cent UK company, two per cent Peter Martinez the Spaniard, 49 per cent my existing company. I own 7 per cent of the existing outfit. The 25 per cent holders have wanted out for cash for years. Valued at pre-Olympic turnover, allowing for the cash flow shortages, and the heavy gearing, you could get their 25 per cent for about… do you want it in dollars, pesetas or sterling?"

"I'm lazy. Sterling," Peter replied.

"OK. You'd buy them out for £250,000," was Ramon's forecast.

"So for us to get a 51 per cent holding, then I need another 26 per cent from your 75 per cent personal holding."

"Now you're talking. I think there's a premium attaching to those," Ramon said, with a cautious smile.

"How much?"

"A million."

"Pesetas?" Peter posed.

"No, you cheeky bastard. Still sterling. So on that combination, you get 51 per cent, that includes the two per cent to you, for the all-up cost of £1.25 million. The return is, say £200 to £250 million of turnover. You're left with an asset in shares at cost of £1.25 million. We'll be a big popular company by then and so we float and you cream off on the share price representing turnover and profit within a five-year span. What do you think? That's good arithmetic, isn't it?"

"I know you well, Ramon. While it's you, I know we could settle any differences over a bottle of wine, and I trust you. Without that relationship, it's about control."

"Yes, I've thought of that. You'd be Chairman. You'd have the swinging two per cent vote. That's control."

"And you?"

"I'd fancy Chief Executive."

"So would I. That's the best role you could fill in both our interests." Peter held his hand out to shake Ramon's. "You'll have to understand I've got a Board of fuddy-duddies who're all institutionally led. But I hope I could swing that. I'm keen to broaden our base in Europe," Peter summarised.

"So there you are."

They shook hands.

"There's just one thing, Peter, I'd like to get off my chest. It's a difficult one but I cringed when you said how well you felt you knew me and that you could trust me. I need to check that out with you in greater detail."

Peter was disappointed. What was going to come out now? Embezzlement? Tax adjustments?

"Hit me with the bad news."

"Well, it's about Bianca."

"I was going to save that up for coffee. How on earth did you get to pull her, never mind marry her?"

"Actually, for the record, it was the other way round. I got to marry her first and then I can promise you, the generosity of the conjugal rights... well, let's say it made up for the year or so of courting and just holding hands, because 'Mother and Father wouldn't want it to be otherwise', as she constantly reminded me. So many times I thought, 'selfish buggers, they've been having their good time, that's how they got the beautiful Bianca after all, so why deprive me?' But I waited patiently. Believe it or not, I was mad about the girl."

"Yes, that's all very well but if I remember correctly, we both invited her out, we invited her out together and in a foursome but she was just never interested."

"Believe me, she was, but she was giving us the hard time... she preferred me... of course."

"So how did you break the ice?"

"Do you remember she'd arrive at the site and ring the bell on the back of her van? We'd all down tools and go down to choose sandwiches for our break, or a pizza or the like. Because I was the boss of the gang, I used to go down last. By that time, she was always paranoid about the amount of money in her money belt. It used to bulge full.

"So I worked out this plan. It was a Friday. I did the normal and bought my grub and asked her out, as I usually did. She was in a pleasant mood that day. She said, 'My dear sweet Ramon, will you never give up?' One day, I might have. Why she chose that day to give me hope I won't ever know, but it was too late to stop."

"You're losing me," Peter said, in puzzlement.

"Well, as I walked back to the site office, encouraged by what she had said, I heard this 250cc motorbike in the distance. It got nearer and I turned round to see the chap in leathers with his helmet on. He was talking to

Bianca with his back to me. I could see she looked worried. He had his hand in his pocket. He'd parked his bike up the road from where the van was.

"Suddenly Bianca screamed. He had pushed forward, grabbed her into a bear hug and undone her money belt. I dropped my lunch and ran like crazy, and managed to grab the bloke's shoulders from behind. He dropped the bag but with his free fist, he thumped me on the jaw and I reeled back onto the ground. I heard the motorcycle engine start and it roared off. Bianca was crouching over me. You know, in that little pelmet skirt she hardly wore? Her whole voluptuous body was surrounding me where I was lying. She was holding my head up off the ground and she was wiping my swollen lip with a lace handkerchief. She cradled my head in her lap. Wow, that was something! She was saying sweet things about me. How thankful she was, and how could she not now reward me by going out with me... just the once, of course... she was sure when her parents knew what I'd done to save their daughter, they'd allow her to go... and not to be back too late, of course.

"It wasn't lost on me that the whole time she was swooning over me, her hero of the day, she was clasping hold of the money belt. She'd lost nothing. I had the date.

"So that's it. That's how I got to marry Bianca... and produce our four beautiful children."

"OK, great story. I'm not surprised at what you did. That's you all over. I'd trust you more after that too."

"That's kind. I've been to confessional on that a number of times because it's always bothered me. But I've never told anybody outside the Box the whole story."

"There's more?"

"Yes. And I'm sorry if you're not going to like it." He took a deep breath. "Oh well, here we go. It was a put-up job. My brother said he'd act out the robbery, providing I assured him he would get away. He'd borrowed leather gear, which wouldn't be recognised and which he later burnt. It worked like clockwork, except he was just meant to push me over. Not knock me unconscious. I asked him why he did that afterwards and he said he thought it would make it look authentic. So there you are. What do you make of that?"

"Love is blind and can remain so, you cunning old bugger!"

Ramon leant across and slapped Peter on the shoulder. "Still trust me?" he asked.

"Even more so. If you want something enough I now know you'll get it."

"Too true – $500 million in turnover for 'Newco' will suit me."

"I'll drink to that," Peter concluded. He lifted his glass. "A toast to Bianca – thank God she was mugged!"

They both roared with laughter. Peter then put on his serious face.

"What about the lad?"

Ramon didn't need to ask which one. He knew Peter had a soft kernel. He'd seen him reacting like a father to a son with Jaimé many years before.

"He's fine. He's got great spirit. He'll be alright. I believe God handicaps certain people, like the club secretary treats his golf members' handicaps, so that those most penalised have to work harder to be, or stay, equal. If, and I say if, I pull off my share sale idea, I'll probably get him a racing chair to practise in. Who knows, five years down the track he might also be a competitor in a temporary pad in Port Vell."

"Port Vell?"

"It's the harbour area we've been looking at."

"Sorry, I didn't know it was called that. Too true. I'd be pleased to see that, providing the buildings are finished on time."

"No worries about that. I'll see to that."

They enjoyed each other's company through the evening, reminiscing, with Peter holding his own by taking Ramon through his Malaysian love affair and Coco's appearance on the scene, the Hunt affair... all things male, in short. But then he could feel the effect of his share of the two and a half bottles of good wine.

"So what are your thoughts on my proposition?"

Although he saw Ramon as a friend, Peter knew that he personally had a lot to gain from the proposal.

Peter forced himself to think clearly. He dared not say his heart was thumping at the idea. He had sensed there was to be a lot of building opportunity in Barcelona for the Olympic thrust. Hence his pushing William for some statistics as to how the group perceived that market had been relevant, whatever the statistics William might dummy up for the Board.

His potential deal with Ramon meant they would be able to go straight into the inside track through the new combined company. Inwardly, he was absolutely besotted with the idea. But he wouldn't let that show.

"You've got to understand when you're part of a major corporation, there are channels to go through and politics to overcome, even if you are the CEO. Give me time to work on it. I'm, let's say, optimistic because at least I like the idea."

Ramon held his hand out across the table. "Then I consider the deal to be done. You'll pull it off your end. I'll do precisely what I've said I'll do this end. What a really good evening. I'll get you back. Eh!"

"Not bloody likely! With all we've got at stake, a taxi will be a cheap and safe alternative. I'm not letting you go near a steering wheel tonight."

Peter got back to the hospital in one piece and he left Ramon in the back of the taxi, to be taken home to the open arms of Bianca.

"Any calls?" he asked the porter.

"No, Sir. Were you expecting some?"

"I always do," he said. "Good night." He swayed very slightly as he walked the corridors.

He almost fell through the door to his room. He stripped off his clothes and went to his bathroom. As he peed, he muttered, "What a waste," as he saw the wine flush into the Barcelona sewage system. He had a token wash and went back to the sleeping quarters. He threw back the duvet cover. There was a note, written on a sheet of A3 paper with large lettering.

"Good night, my darling. You're pissed. Missing you like I'm going to after Monday. Dream sweet. Cas."

He leant forward and kissed her name.

The next morning he woke to find himself virtually still face down, flat on his stomach with his head buried in the paper covering his pillow, with a three-piece, percussion-only band thumping in his head.

He opened one eye to glimpse the daylight. It closed voluntarily.

"I know you're there," he said.

There was silence. He'd expected a reply.

He opened both eyes, rolled over and sat up.

"I said I knew you were there."

"I wasn't going to say I was. I thought you might just leak out the name of the person you thought was here."

He held out both hands. "Come here, Cas. It could only have been you."

She got up from the casual chair and walked over.

"Don't get too near, my love. I think I must smell like a brewery, tinged with the air of the fishing fleet returning to port." His stomach churned at what he had said. He'd never lost the sense of that mixture of fish and salt and air he'd learnt about in his early years in Rosas.

"Wow! Garlic," she observed. "Did you have a good night?"

"Amazing. Absolutely amazing. Ramon has the deal of all deals, I tell you. I don't quite think he's aware of the potential."

"Can you do the deal?"

"I already have. Well, there's a bit of finessing to do. But it's done… bar the shouting, as they say."

"Tell me later."

"How was your evening?"

"Really great. I had time to myself without some sex-craved beast ravishing me the whole time. I had a bath. Shaved my legs, which were well overdue. Had supper with Paul, who sat opposite me and adored me for you… made a few phone calls. I spoke to Marie-Claire, an old friend from South Africa. I remembered she was a psychiatric nursing specialist somewhere in Spain. I only had her phone number. We've never discussed where. Coincidence of all coincidences, she's in Gerona. She's not in the ward where Tania is but she said she'd make some enquiries. Peter, she came back to me. Tania seems very sick."

"Oh. Sod it. On one hand, it doesn't mean a lot to me, really. On the other hand, I've known her a lifetime and I suppose of all the jinx influences in my life, she's the biggest. But I still can't see her hurt."

"You, my love, are a lovely old softie."

"I actually mean that."

"I know you do. She'll mend. Your mother will see to that…"

"Christ! I've got so much to tell you," Peter said, as he remembered he did have something to tell Cas.

"What's that?"

"Well, I told you quickly about Tania, then something happened. I didn't tell you the good news."

"I'm all ears."

"OK. We're having dinner on Sunday with my mother and José, my stepfather."

"Oh shit!"

"What's with the 'oh shit' about meeting my mother?"

"Supposing she hates me? She will. I'm partially responsible for Tania, and Jan. Oh boy! She'll go for me."

"Rubbish. She'll say to me, if I love you then she'll love you, if I don't, then she won't."

"Peter. We've agreed we don't talk love. We talk infatuation."

"That's right."

"Well?"

"Well. I've changed the rules. OK?"

She seemed stunned. In her mind she had, but she hadn't contemplated he had too.

He passed over that as though it was a statement of commercial fact.

"Then there's the other thing."

"… And what's that?"

"Can you get a day's leave Friday week?"

"I'd think so. Why?"

"We're going to a wedding."

"Where?"

"Oh. Somewhere posh, in Kensington in London."

"London?"

"Yup. I've got you an air ticket over on Friday, back on Sunday."

"… And do I know the person getting married?"

"Nobody does."

"Does the groom?"

"Certainly not."

"Do you?"

"Very partially."

"Is she a cast-off?"

He might as well lie, he thought. "No, a friend of the family. Widowed, actually. Lucky to find a new man."

"Is it what you call a 'tails' affair?"

"What, with the bloke she's marrying?"

"No, stupid! I mean, dress code. You're getting sex mad, not tail as in a little bit of alright."

"I'd think so, yes."

"What the hell will I wear? I've got jeans and a borrowed suit."

"I'll fix that. We'll choose something Friday afternoon."

"Well, I'll see."

"So that's fine, you're coming."

"Bully! Gorgeous! Listen, I'll breathe in and we'll seal that most important deal of all deals you've yet to tell me about with a soft kiss."

"Do you really mean that? No, on reflection the kiss has to be tough and strong. Like the deal."

"What about it being soft and gentle if I'd prefer?"

"No. That wouldn't be representative in this important deal. You'll see that when I explain."

"Oh shit," she said, "come on. Where's this tough bully boy's kiss?"

"What next?" Peter asked as they broke from what did finish up with gentleness.

"What the hell do I wear to meet your mother?"

"We'll go to a fancy dress shop and get you a nun's outfit."

"I'm not being funny."

"We'll choose something together. Say Saturday morning."

"Peter. Can I be truthful?"

"I hope you always are."

"I'm not ready for this. I am really not ready for this."

"I think you are."

Chapter 16

"Here, I always bring plenty."

Maria offered Cas her box of Kleenex tissues. It was debatable which one of them had held back the tears the longest. Now they were both letting rip.

"Is that the first time you've waved him off?"

"Yes. It is. I thought I'd be alright," Cas said with surprise.

Maria laughed. "I always do. From experience, if it helps, it's not so bad once he's gone. That son of mine creates such a presence, as he leaves there seems to be a huge vacuum cleaner behind him, which pulls out all the emotion he builds up when you're with him. It all dies down and then, certainly in my case, I think back and use the next couple of days to mull over what we did, what he said, what he said he's going to do and then gradually my stomach calms down and I start to focus on when he says he'll be back, or when we'll see each other again."

"I hope that happens to me too. At the moment, woman to woman, I can't see that happening."

They were two very different women, almost two generations apart, but temporarily bonded by the same man.

Maria linked her arm through Cas's. "Here, I'll buy us some coffee."

Peter and Cas had agreed they'd say goodbye at the hospital but Han, who wasn't stupid, said he wasn't happy about a patient who had been in their care, and who no doubt was being released a couple of weeks early, being allowed to get to an airport under his own steam. So he had asked Cas if she'd be happy to be deputed to nurse him to the airport. She felt he must have worked their relationship out. She didn't know how, because she thought they had been very careful. After all, she had broken most of the rules by allowing a personal involvement in a patient's life and could well lose her job because of it, if they were found out.

If the Professor had worked it out, would he wait till Peter had left the hospital and then fire her? She'd have to work out the strategy to follow, either way. Whatever, she doubted she would want to deny it; her feelings were strong enough for her to be prepared to go up onto the hospital roof and announce their infatuation for each other to the whole world.

"If you're like this after, what, three weeks, how do you think I feel after all these years?"

"It's less than three weeks, in fact – I hadn't realised that. Wow, that son of yours has given me so much in that time. He's changed my life completely."

"That's his talent, my dear. I've heard so many, both male and female, to be fair, who've said that…"

She put her hand onto Cas's knee. "Oh, and to make it clear in the male cases, in case you're wondering, they weren't gay; and apart from perhaps in a couple of instances, the girls have not had an 'involvement' with him in the boyfriend/girlfriend way. I remember Michelle, who I still see with her grown-up family. She was heavily into drugs and he got her on to remedial therapy, which in the space of a few weeks brought her life back to normal. So look back on your three weeks with very happy memories."

"I will. Don't worry."

"Don't worry?" Maria repeated.

"Well, you must be thinking Peter's old enough to be my own father… well very nearly, but he would actually have been sowing his oats a bit early in life if that had been the case. But he's unlikely to have got to meet my mother, and anyway, she had stringent morals. So don't worry, I'm not likely to steal him from you… I mean marry him and claim I want all his love.

"We're not the marrying kind and anyway, you have hold on him by natural instincts, so that any other female will get the secondary share of that love."

"Oh come on, Cas," Maria laughed. "Any love Peter has for me is from a particular part of his heart. It's a caring, appreciative type of love, which does nothing for a fellow between the sheets. That type of hot love is available to any lady of whatever age. That's for that lady and Peter to evaluate. I'll be full of praise for any of my equals of the frailer sex who can provide that element of love to him, with a hope of a bit of tender loving care thrown in. In your case, if I can mark your card, I can see that he's opened up that special extra sense behind the façade of a young lady with a stunning figure, blonde hair, a sense of humour and a caring way. That means to me you're complicated enough for him to puzzle over. I'll tell you. Peter's besotted by you, but you're wise to talk about not being the marrying kind. A bit of paper doesn't necessarily make a marriage. A burning furnace needs constant stoking. A bit of distance, having to wait, seeing each other sparingly will keep the embers smouldering… don't rush to be fuelling the fire day and night."

"Where did you learn your philosophy, Maria… may I call you Maria?"

"Yes. Everybody does. Oh, the learning. I've attended the University of Life for many years. And I have to say with some pride, I loved Peter's father enormously. More when he was out at sea for a couple of nights at a time. Even more when that same sea stole him from me.

"Don't ever tell Peter, he'd say it was outrageous, but with José and myself, it's still very hot beneath the duvet. He's away four nights pretty well every week, so we appreciate the joy of jumping back into bed together, as compared to what could be seen as the obvious benefit of a daily ritual. You've tried to level with me. May I reciprocate?"

"Please," Cas replied sincerely. She felt she suddenly needed all the help she could get.

"I like you very much. I can see you're very good for Peter. I've not seen him this happy in years. Just take it slowly. Hang back. Make him do a lot of running. Nothing keeps his juices more active than the thrill of the chase. He and his father used to hunt. That taught Peter a lot."

"He's explained that. Thank you for saying what you have. I'll give him a really hard time." Cas threw back her head in rapturous laughter.

Maria suddenly said, "Talking about the little bugger has dried up our tears. There, I told you it got better."

They finished their cold coffee and walked across the concourse with linked arms. Each had a bit of a skip in their step. They set off in different directions, to Maria's car and Cas's hospital one, vowing they would speak on the phone, and both accepting Peter would have to divide his time between them, and a number of others.

Peter had made himself wave once and then march off at pace, forcing himself not to limp. He was deeply sad to leave them both. His mother, as always, had been so supportive after the shooting. Apart from the nurses, Gina in particular, she had been his principal female companion all the while until Jan had flown out. That had been a mistake, but he'd see her in England and all would be reinstated, and they'd be thoroughly good business friends.

Then Cas had taken over. In a big way.

He would be seeing her in just four days' time so that would not be too bad. He jerked back a tear, knowing both sets of female eyes, albeit blurred too, would probably have been attempting to pierce his thick male skin from behind, to force him into one final wave. No, they all had to accept an au revoir was an au revoir. A pact to meet again soon. As they would.

"Champagne or orange juice?" the fresh-faced young British Airways stewardess asked.

"Why not?" Peter said, forcing himself back from recent but now already distant memories.

"Sorry, Sir. 'Why not' says nothing. Champagne or orange?"

"Oh, I'm sorry. Champagne."

She poured the glass professionally.

"Are we going to be on time?" he asked, not that he was at all interested. He thought polite conversation was called for.

"We were spot on landing to the minute on the outward leg. I suppose we should be on schedule." Then she shrugged. "Air traffic control," she said. It meant nothing but everything. So Peter agreed.

"That's right, air traffic control." He agreed, and she seemed content with that.

The champagne was fresh on his tongue. It was only 11am, which was a bit early for alcohol, at least for his disciplined approach to treats.

He was worn. Not tired, because he'd had so much to pump the adrenalin in the previous three days, take away any feeling of fatigue. The drink intake with Ramon on the Thursday had most certainly had an impact. Then Cas had worked him hard on his last official treatment day on the Friday in the hospital. It seemed she wanted to pour into him additional treatment so that he had a reserve for the weeks to come. Like the competitor he naturally was, he took everything that was given. That is until about 4.30pm. She had him doing press-ups, which he'd hated even before his accident. Now he dreaded them. "I expect 20," she said in her sergeant-major voice.

On three, Paul Demar came into the room. "Go for it, Peter," he'd said. Peter did two more, and Han's assistant was there. "Lock the arms, Peter. It'll take the strain out of the toes and in turn the knees," he advised.

Then there were two of Cas's nursing colleagues... *What's the gay coming to watch for?* Peter had thought, somewhat angrily. And what the hell was the woman from the kitchen doing here, then the porter, who believed he was Peter's secretary.

"Fifteen, I'm told. Sixteen. Seventeen." It was Han's voice.

Then Cas. "Come on, Peter. Three more for me."

"Great. Two."

Then, as one, they all shouted, "Twenty!"

He collapsed face down. He ensured he had recovered quickly and did a victory roll onto his back, with hands behind his head.

"Mr Peter. We're all so pleased to have had your presence in this hospital, we couldn't resist seeing Cas put you through your final paces. Paul Demar has something he wants to say to you on behalf of us. Paul Demar," Professor Han announced with an outstretched arm.

"Mr Peter. You've been a great inspiration to me in particular. You hit butt harder than anyone else on this planet. But below that strength is a kindness and a warmth that I, and others, will never forget."

Peter was touched and embarrassed and, as he so often had when he received an unexpected credit, he attacked back.

"Who told you to say that, Paul?"

The lad looked towards Cas. Peter thought that was a major giveaway.

"Would you tell him, Miss Cas, the Professor said I could say what I liked and those were my words."

"They were, Peter."

"Then that, my man, is good enough for me."

Peter sat up on the couch. "Come here and give me a hug, you soft old para."

My man, Pablito thought. *He called me my man. Not 'my boy', or 'my lad', he promoted me to his level.* So he stepped forward and gave Peter the hug he'd invited.

Professor Han looked on at the seriousness of the occasion.

"We've had a small collection to get you a going away, or leaving, present."

One of the nurses produced a wrapped parcel with an envelope, which presumably contained an explanatory card.

"We'd like you to accept this from a number of people who've been pleased – very pleased, I might add, in my case – to have met you. We'd like to think that you'll come back and see us and slap a few more butts, if invited so to do."

There was a ripple of impromptu applause. Han passed the parcel to Peter. By now Peter had swung his legs over the edge of the exercising bed on which Cas had forced his final exercises in that hospital.

"I'm overcome," he said. "The thanks ought to come from me. I have to start with the boss." They either laughed or giggled, depending on their sexual persuasion, the girls being joined by Juan.

"So… to Cas, the real boss." They all laughed or giggled, this time in shock, expecting that the accolade was to be directed to Professor Han. "She has been inspirational."

Cas dropped her head, initially, it seemed to all those watching, in embarrassment. She was thinking that, coming from Peter, it was really an unjustified comment. She knew it was she who should have been saying how influential he had been on her.

"I've a lot to thank Cas for, and that I now publicly do. To the second-in-command, and all his team – Professor Han and his 'A' team and supporting staff – thank you each and every one.

"As for you, Paul Demar. I'll thank you only when you show me a pretty senior medal in 1992. That indeed will be the mark of a thank you. For whatever there is inside this box, thank you enormously. May I open it later?" He was following the advice of his dear friend Max, who had once said, "Don't ever open a gift in public. You might hate it."

There was a lot of almost end-of-term laughter and one by one they bade their au revoirs. Han was the last but one to leave.

"Peter. I know I'll see you frequently on the Paralympic Committee. It really has been a pleasure to have met you and renovated you."

Then there was just him and Cas.

"Cas. Thank you. Thank you for many things. The treatment, the care, the bullying and for being 'the bait' which I'd almost forgotten. Did I rise to it as you'd hoped? Thank you for the extra-curricular activities. For allowing us to fall into infatuation… and beyond."

She threw both arms around his neck and sobbed into his chest.

"A top up, Sir?" Peter shook himself out of his daydream.

"How far are we from take-off?"

"Oh, there's some delay with French air traffic control, as I informed there so often is. Can't actually say but I think there's time for another glass. The captain's asked for a cup of tea," she confided, "so it will be a while."

The seat next to him was unoccupied, which made him all the more lonely. He supposed if they hadn't taken off he could get off and speed away to find Cas, and never return to the rigours that faced him back in the UK ever again. But that wouldn't be him. He needed to put the deal together with Ramon and get loads of sponsorship for Paul and Cas so that she could retain her independence, should she so desire. That was obvious, from the previous Saturday morning's confession.

They'd risen, in their respective quarters, in the normal way. Apart from the night porter, nobody was meant to know she had left his room at just before midnight. But the night porter felt duty bound to spread the gossip throughout the rest of the weekend, unbeknown to Peter or Cas, that he had worked out what was going on between them.

They had met in the refectory on that last Saturday and agreed to leave early. They would be back to pick Paul up for the football at around 1.30pm for a 3pm kick-off. So theirs was a short shopping spree and, unbeknown to Cas, a quick trip in a taxi to soak up the views from Montjuïc, before the planned intrusion of the Olympic stadium, and where they would take in the view from the hill out to the sea and Port Vell, allowing Peter to explain what he hoped would be the future scenario for him and Ramon.

They'd taken in the view from Montjuïc first. It was a clear morning and, with the sun coming up from the sea, the city and the hills and their trees were awash with deep shadows. The power station puffed out a little papal smoke against the dark blue backcloth provided by the sea. Cas had not been to that side of Barcelona before.

"This city has everything, Peter. It's got its history, the sea, the harbours… I've begun to call it home."

"Do you know, I actually don't know if you've ever been to London?" Peter realised.

"Only when I was about nine. I did London and Paris with my parents and grandparents. I really don't remember it much. They made me do tours of museums and I wanted to do things like run in the parks and active stuff like that."

"Tell you what. Next weekend, put your trainers in. I'll take you on my favourite jog. Down by the Thames and a park called Battersea Park. You'll like it."

He talked about their weekend and, if he was serious about adding all that to the agenda, she reckoned he'd just run out of time – that's if some sleep was contemplated.

They went from the hills to El Corte Inglés, a fashionable store at the top end of the Ramblas. Peter was allowed to sit in a leather chair just outside the changing room.

"No, you can't," she ruled, when he suggested he go into the cubicle with her like the other young men were. "They're probably married and anyway, we'd want to screw and we'd get thrown out," she said honestly.

She appeared three times and on each occasion, she could easily have turned heads on a catwalk. As it was, Peter witnessed two of the 'married' and privileged young men ask an assistant which rack the suit had come from so that they could get their other halves to try and look as attractive as they had found Cas. When one of them said he needed a size 16, Peter guessed 'no chance'. Another's partner was an eight, but when she appeared to view the creation in a long mirror, the trousers were about four inches too long, the seat of the pants was nearly down to the backs of her knees and you couldn't see her hands in the sleeves of the jacket. She was only about 150cms tall.

Cas's 170cms, plus the high heels she wore away from work, made all the difference. Peter realised they had been short on having to give each other opinions on personal appearance; to date they had been as one on everything.

"So which do you like? And don't say all of them just like the other wimps I can hear through the walls of the cubicles."

"It's up to you, what you feel comfortable in."

"That's not much help to a girl who hasn't yet met your mother."

"Oh, for Mother's benefit. Anything. Any one that you've tried would do," Peter conceded.

"Now that's what I said not to do."

"OK. Sunday night supper. The denim jacket and matching jeans."

"Good, that's exactly right. It was my favourite. I like the black number, it made me feel really smart but I agree it might be over the top for a casual supper."

"Have them both."

"Good God, no! That would be extravagant. Besides, I'll only wear them when you're around, and wanting to show me off somewhere. Would it do for the wedding?"

Peter thought about that prospect. "No. I know where we'll go for that."

"Well, just remember a nurse isn't on a TV star's pay. It'll have to be affordable."

He would never have contemplated that she'd think she needed to spend her own money on decorating herself largely for his benefit. He'd be buying anyway. But she didn't seem to realise that.

"Right, denim suit. Last chance. OK." She asked the assistant to follow her back to the changing room. "Make out you're helping me change out of these things, would you. But what I really wanted to do was to pay you now from in here. If I don't, my boyfriend is bound, I think, to take over and pay, and I don't want that."

"No problem, dear. But if that was me, I'd let him pay. That sort of thing never comes my way."

"Well, I won't," she said, firmly. If she was to meet Peter's mother, it would be on her own terms.

Peter caught the arm of the assistant as she came through. "Has the young lady chosen just the denim?"

"I'm not sure if I'm meant to say, Sir."

"Of course you are. We're together."

"Well... yes."

"Just the denim?"

"Yes."

"Well, will you wrap them both up and I'll settle the bill."

"I'm sorry, Sir. I can't do that."

Peter was amazed. "Why on earth not?"

"Madam has already bought the denim suit."

"Bought it? I was going to buy it."

"La señora didn't seem to think that was the idea. She was certain it was to be her purchase."

Well, that had never happened to him before. Cas was different. He'd have to question that.

"Then I'll buy the other suit as a present."

"Actually Sir, I wouldn't do that."

"Now, listen. If I want to buy a present, I don't expect you to have a view on that."

"Look, Sir, my job could be on the line here. Of course I'll sell you the suit. But if la señora had wanted this one, I'm sure she would have bought it. She liked the other one for a particular purpose. If I might say so, if you buy this one for her, it just says her money is of less value than your money. She might not be able to afford them both but she wants to make the point, I humbly believe, that she can be self-sufficient. Tell me, Sir, do you know what the event is, the one she's chosen the denim suit for?"

"Yes, I bloody well do. It's to meet my mother."

"Then the black one. Why would you buy that?"

"Look, this is none of your business, but as I intend to report you to your line manager, you might as well know. It's for her to wear to have dinner with me tonight."

"Sir, I've never had the luxury of a boyfriend who had enough money to buy me a suit anyway. But if I had, I would take what you're suggesting as a statement that you're not satisfied with my wardrobe. Does she know about the dinner date?"

"No."

"But she does know about the date with your mother?"

"Yes."

"Then let the young lady, Sir, be comfortable."

"So I mustn't, in your view, buy her the present?"

"Really, I'd say that. Tell her she looks ideal on the date with your mother."

Peter wanted to think he was right. Yet maybe it would be wrong to intervene. He could quite easily say, "OK, you've spent your pocket money. Here, I've done a two for the price of one deal." But he wouldn't.

The assistant went back to the cubicle with the bill.

Cas wrote out a cheque, placed her name and address on the back and asked for the suit to be wrapped. The assistant hovered.

"Can I help you with anything else?"

"What's your wedding section like?"

"What, a wedding dress?"

"No. Guests 'going to a wedding' dresses."

"What sort of wedding?"

"Well, it's actually in London."

"Then if I were you, I'd buy something there. Things in Spain suit Spain. When in London, wear what the Londoners do, is what I say. Are they your friends or his?"

"His."

"Then you know the rule, do you?"

"No. I don't think so. What's that?"

"Well if it's his friends, you say 'what would you like me to wear? Will you choose something for me?' Then he'll be so pleased and he'll pay."

"I don't like that idea. I like to pay my way."

"Then there's the risk that what you can afford might not match what his friends can afford and you'll feel awful. They'll be older, too mature to be thinking denim. Let him choose for you, I'd think he wouldn't be too bothered about paying. In fact he may be very pleased to. Leave it to me."

They left the changing room together. Peter stood up from the chair he had become well accustomed to, and automatically took Cas by the hand.

"La señora is asking if I can show her something to wear to a friend's wedding. Do you have time?"

"Oh. No. Thank you. No, we don't have time. We'll get something in London."

"Oh. Sir, do you know the cost of fashion in London?"

"Look, miss. Would you leave that to me? That's going to be my treat. Isn't it, Cas?"

"Well…"

"No arguments. It is. You'll just have to agree."

"Well, madam, have a wonderful trip. If a boyfriend of mine said that to me, I'd be very excited."

"I *am* very excited."

"Then job done," the assistant said, winking at Peter.

"You've been kind," he said, to his own surprise. He held out his hand and took hold of hers. She felt the crisp 1000-peseta note in his palm, which she slid into hers with some proficiency. She'd done it before, he knew.

"It's been a real pleasure to serve such a lovely couple."

They rushed around after that. While she was in the store, Cas said she needed some make-up.

Peter said, "I didn't think you wore any."

"Your mother will think I'm underdressed if I don't."

"OK. I'll leave the lady to get herself sorted. I'll see you over there. By the watch stand in ten minutes, OK?"

Once Cas had gone, Peter went over to the perfume counter. "I'd like a bottle of Chanel Number 5, please."

"Yes, of course, Sir – 100mls or 50?"

It was the way she said it that made him think 50 would be underdoing it.

"Oh – 100, of course."

"Thank you, Sir. Anything else?"

"No. Thank you. That's fine."

Chapter 17

"I'll have to take your glass, Sir. Would you like to finish it?"

Peter awoke from his recent memories. "Oh, sure. I understand. Thanks. Does this mean we're on for take-off?"

"It certainly seems that way."

He wondered if, once his mother and Cas had seen him off, they had just gone their separate ways. Probably not. He had a feeling his mother would use the opportunity to whip his new girlfriend away into some quiet corner of a café and ask what her intentions were towards her son.

What are her intentions? he thought.

"Seat-belt, Sir."

"Oh yes, sorry." Peter was not his usual organised self. He knew this journey was a link away from a time of cocoonment and, thinking more about it, two emotional disturbances too – quite apart from the trauma of the shooting, which suddenly jogged his memory. The time with Jan had led him down the wrong path, which he'd discovered once they were apart. Then Cas. God, he hoped their absence from each other wouldn't expose frailties in that relationship. Then he mustn't forget Tania.

He'd rechecked with his mother that it still wasn't advisable to go to see Tania. Maria hadn't exactly been specific. Something about them wanting her brain to take her into the future and not be clouded by the past. As it happened, that was just as well because he wouldn't have had the time. His Saturday morning had been planned around Cas's shopping. The afternoon was Paul's at the football and he had booked himself and Cas into the Palace Hotel for the night, with the plan to take every advantage of each of its five stars.

Sunday morning, he reckoned, would take care of itself. Then the afternoon and evening would be spent with Maria and José. Then an early start to break with Spain for a while and re-enter the cauldron awaiting him in the UK.

Late on the Saturday morning they had gone back to the hospital to grab a cafeteria sandwich and collect young Paul, who was waiting for them in the entrance lobby. He refused to eat anything, saying he was too excited and would be sick. Peter told him he had half an hour to be ready and that he'd need an anorak.

That gave him the chance to tell Cas of his Palace Hotel plans. "Let's pick up some things from my room. You'll need something warm too, there's a chill in the air. Oh, by the way, chuck some smalls into your overnight bag, something that will go with this…" He threw her the gift-wrapped perfume. "I've got a surprise for you later."

He'd noticed a mood coming over Cas which he hadn't seen before. She'd always been what he thought of as 'level', no swings, no ups and downs. He'd perceived earlier there was the odd down and a touch of snappiness in some of the things she had said during their shopping trip. Maybe she was like a lot of other girls when they get into the retail world.

He should have realised that once she had bought the suit, and the cosmetics, it might have come home to her that she had been set up on some sort of trial. Meeting the parents. Seeking to be approved. Of course, she would want to be, not just for her sake but for Peter's. That would have made her wonder how Peter would go down with her own parents. He was exactly the reverse of every other fellow she had taken home before. Rolling rich and possibly her parents' ages. Cultured, kind and considerate. What else could they want? Probably less of an age and someone who would not interfere with their long term plans that their daughter should be sufficiently well qualified to support herself independently at any time in her life. Her mother had given up her career in favour of raising a family in difficult times in South Africa. In her grandparents' day, both grandfather and grandmother were able to work in their chosen professions by having a house staff of three. All black. That was not available, by political edict, for her parents, and hence her mother had no means of support other than that which her husband happily provided.

Those thoughts had in fact made Cas edgy. Peter's organisational abilities were closing in on her a bit. They'd been wonderfully involved with each other every day, and recently some nights, for almost three weeks. She just needed a little space. She knew there would be plenty of that after Monday, yet that was depressing her. So she reacted to his command to throw a few things into a bag.

"What's that for, Peter?"

"After the game, we'll get Paul back and then I've organised a bit of pampering."

She knew the signs. She was hormonal and the thought of somebody slopping creams and lotions over her body, if that was the pampering he had got in mind, wasn't really appealing. Suddenly she didn't like the thought of being told where she was going to sleep, if that too was what he had in mind.

"Pampering, Peter? Tell me more."

"Oh come on, it's a surprise."

"I'd like to know."

Peter knew she meant it.

"Well… I thought it would be nice to have a quiet evening, which will be one of our last for nearly a week… and I've booked a room at the Palace Hotel. You'll like it. It's old and has character."

She thought: *And were all the other women you've discovered these delights with old and with character, or just young bimbos doing what they were told?* There had seemed to be no pre-planning before they fell into bed together in Girasol. This was all too... well... too organised... too Peter.

She didn't show her true feelings.

"I'd worked that out too," she said. "I'd planned just what we've ordinarily been doing – no ground-breaking new routines of 'pampering' each other into moods of artificial relaxation and having to find out which way the shower works, or having to put on smart pyjamas in case there's a fire rehearsal during the night. I'd just seen it as you and me here. Then for me to finish up in my own bed. I'll probably be sad and I'd rather wash the mascara off my own pillow than for you to have to give the chambermaid a tip to do it in some plush hotel, where I might not even feel comfortable."

She'd got a point. He'd best reassure her on that too, otherwise it would be, "Look, let's give it a miss. We'll meet up in the morning and have a lovely new day."

If he'd had a sister, he would have been better able to cope. He would have recognised the signs she was now showing. *Of course she is,* Peter told himself. *I should have seen this coming. What a berk.* If he'd known her intimately for three weeks and he hadn't seen this before, then it was bound to be imminent in a healthy young woman. After all, that was something he'd learnt from marriage to Anna when, in the earlier years, she'd had a couple of uncontrollable emotional days each month.

Unless, he suddenly thought, *she's pregnant and missed her date in her diary.* He'd just assumed she was on the pill. Yes, she was bound to be. He beckoned her to him for a hug.

"That's fine. Absolutely fine. You're right. We'll have a lovely night in. But I'd like you to open the little present."

He was kind. He was alright. He understood. She felt better.

"Oh wow, Peter! I've never had good perfume before. You're wicked to spoil me. I'll wear it tomorrow for your mother."

"Tonight, please. For us."

"Well... OK. But I don't want to get too used to it or waste it. I'd like it to last forever."

"There's plenty more where that came from," he advised.

Now that was wrong. It cheapened the idea totally. She wished he'd said, "And that's the right idea... it's the only bottle in the world, specially and carefully and lovingly chosen for you. There isn't any more where that came from." He hadn't, but she wouldn't make a big deal out of it. She let it pass. Gosh! How she too knew she was tetchy.

They had been in Peter's room, sorting him out some warmer clothes to wear to the match. His problem, now that he was getting away from the balanced internal climate of the hospital, was that he had a limited wardrobe to choose from. He'd just about got by. His blue suit had come in useful to wear a second time, this time on the journey home, in order to bring a bit of formality back into the relationship with his chauffeur, Fred Perry, who was due to pick him up at Heathrow.

He and Cas had left the room. He was going to the refectory to get the sandwiches and she to her quarters to do as she had been told, to get something warm.

Han wasn't usually at the hospital on a Saturday. They met him in the corridor.

"Morning, Professor," Peter addressed him. "Isn't it unusual for you to be in on a Saturday?"

"Yes. I had a sudden concern about young Paul. He's going to do more walking than he's done in hospital and there will be stairs and ramps and other obstacles." He turned to Cas. "I think he should have a forearm crutch, just to take some weight off the limb when he needs it. He'll go mad but I think he ought to."

Cas agreed.

"So you'll tell him, eh! Peter?"

"Me! Why ruin *my* day!" he had said. "OK. I'll have a go. It must be sensible."

"That conveniently leads me to a question," Han continued. "What about you when you leave? How would you feel about a light stick?"

"I'd break the bloody thing across my knee!" Peter said shortly.

"Peter," Cas interjected, "if you get told we recommend a stick, then you'd be very silly not to take that advice."

That pulled Peter up in his tracks.

"OK. You know my capabilities. What do you think? Do you recommend it?"

She thought. "Actually no. But that's conditional."

"On what?"

"On you promising to follow a disciplined morning routine."

He smiled a smile she knew to be full of innuendo.

"I'll go and organise the crutch for Paul," Han said, tactfully.

"So are you going to show me the routine?"

"Yes. I bloody well will! Tomorrow morning."

"So that's a promise?"

"It really is." And she meant it.

The 'seat belts fastened' sign flicked off and the hostess appeared with her trolley laden with beverages.

"Can I pour you a drink, Sir?"

"Oh boy! I've enjoyed your champagne. Perhaps a Campari and tonic please, no ice."

"Tonic, Sir, not soda?"

"Yes, that's right. Please."

She put down the paper coaster and placed the highball glass carefully on it. She then placed a small packet of obligatory peanuts on the side.

She found the Campari and a tonic in her trolley and deftly, in accordance with training standards, poured his order, remembering no ice and a slice of orange.

"Enjoy your drink, Sir." And off she went, merrily dispensing her wares to his fellow travellers.

I bet Cas and Mother aren't into the Campari stakes. It'll be coffee and maybe a biscuit, he thought.

He didn't quite know why, but he then thought back to the football. Maybe it was that Paul had asked if he could have a San Miguel. Peter wasn't too sure at the time and conferred with Cas.

"Why not? We'll all have one. It'll roughen our taste buds up for the coarseness of the match."

"It won't be like that," Peter informed her. "These two teams will just glide gracefully at each other. They're the best pros in the world. There won't be any fisticuffs out there," he added, indicating the pitch.

They each had a can of beer and took to their seats.

In the seventh minute the Real Madrid left full back was red-carded for cuffing one of the Barcelona forwards with a determined strike with his left elbow on the blind side of the referee, but in full view of the linesman.

The crowd supporting each side went berserk. Barcelona's because their man, by all accounts, was seriously injured (well, so it seemed for five proud moments), and the Real Madrid supporters, because 75 per cent of them were blind side too, and on what they saw they felt the referee had been unfair.

Cas tapped Peter on the knee, leaning across in front of Paul, whom they had sat between them.

"So that was a Real Madrid professional glide?"

Peter could not hold back a smile. "Well, let me put it this way... you won't see Barcelona get up to those tricks."

True. Not until midway through the second half, when the Real Madrid centre striker was hacked to the ground with just the goalkeeper between him, the ball and the wide open net. A penalty was awarded. Cas leant across Paul and said something Peter could not hear, or did not want to hear. Who'd know?

Peter reflected, as he now realised he was looking down on the Pyrenees, on the fact that it had been a good game for Paul to have seen. The lad favoured Real Madrid and was therefore quite satisfied to go home with a 2-1 win to them, a Real Madrid scarf and a number eight replica shirt. Peter, wisely under the circumstances, suggested they wait for the crowd to disperse a bit before making tracks. Paul appeared to be breathing in the atmosphere even though the numbers around the stadium were thinning. He had soaked it all in.

"At the Olympics, how many people will watch?"

"Oh I'd say, 100 million."

"What! You're joking. They'd never get into the stadium."

"No, you twit. On TV."

"Really?"

"I'd say so."

"Wow! You'd be famous then."

"If you're in the winning three. If you're an also-ran, then you'd be known at home, probably, but not internationally."

"So how many people will watch live? Like here."

"About 60,000, I'd say."

"How many here today?"

"Oh, about 60,000."

"Wow! That's going to be great, isn't it?" He addressed that comment to Cas. Then he thought deeply again. "How far would you say 400 metres is?"

"Well, if you ran right round the edge of the outside of the pitch and put curves at each end, that would be about it."

"… And 800 metres."

"Twice round the outside of the pitch."

"Do you have a minute hand on your watch, Peter?"

"Yes, I do."

"Could I borrow it?"

Peter took the watch off, which Anna had bought him for one of their wedding anniversaries, and passed it to Paul.

Paul looked down at the face and suddenly said, "Wow!"

He looked up and visualised his running stride; counted up each metre he ran before completing the circuit and passing the imaginary finishing line, and then on to a repeat lap. He imagined the length and speed of his every stride until his eyes fixed a focus at the top corner of the pitch, which to him was the beginning of the home straight. Cas could see that in his mind, he was running longer strides and at a faster pace.

"Now!" he shouted as he looked down into the face of the borrowed watch. "Two minutes. I can run that in two minutes. How would that be?" he asked Cas, who was now to him the important person in their trio. She was to be his coach. His mentor.

"Bloody good for an amateur. Very good indeed."

"But I'll be an amateur, won't I?"

"We've got to talk about that eventually," Peter chipped in. "But aim at two minutes, with five years to improve, and you'll be famous, for sure."

"Come on, let's go. There aren't so many people now."

"Paul. Going down you'll need your pole."

"If you'd said crutch, I would have thrown it onto the pitch. Pole is good. It's got athletics about it."

"OK. I'm OK with that. I agree. There, it's nice not to have a fuss," smiled Cas, who had come round from her usual stance that you call a spade a spade and a crutch a crutch.

The three shuffled out of the row of seats and quite naturally, as if by instinct, Paul linked arms with Cas on one side and Peter on the other, as he grasped his pole in his left hand.

"You can be my crutches if you like."

"But you throw crutches away, that's not very nice," Peter responded, semi-seriously.

"But not you two! You're special."

Chapter 18

"Would you like to order a light lunch, Sir?" The hostess broke into his thoughts.

She presented him with a plastic tray. As usual, it had been laid out and pre-packed without leaving a centimetre of space for anything other than a sophisticated game of chess with the various pieces – but not until you had discarded one of the pieces or played Russian dolls by placing one plastic container into another.

As though the stewardess was part of a team checking his tray layout, she asked, "Would you like wine, Sir?" focusing on his patiently waiting empty glass.

"Please," he said, smugly satisfied that he was keeping ahead of their cabin service.

"Red or white?"

"Red."

He was a seasoned enough traveller to pre-empt the next question. "…And if you have a Rioja, I'd prefer that to the French."

"Yes we do, Sir."

"That's excellent."

As she leant across, she realised he had redesigned his tray layout.

"There, Sir?" she asked, rather intelligently reading his planning precisely.

"That's fine," he said, with a hint of a compliment in his voice. "You've picked the spot," he added with a boyish grin, "as they say!"

She seemed pleased anyway. Then, with just a hint of a girlish smile, she struck her killer blow.

"Would you like any water, Sir?" she almost demanded, hovering over him with a plastic beaker in one hand and a jug of iced water in the other.

He always forgot this option. He'd have to give in. Game over.

After he'd had coffee he dozed off, waking to find his tray had been removed. He looked out of the window and down through the clouds. Mid-Provence, he thought, maybe Toulouse. His mind drifted back to the time he'd driven Marcia and Bob back to England. He smiled, thinking of their first time, him and Marcia, and how he was now intending to duck out of her pre-wedding 'party'. He knew that 'party' would just involve the two of them, but he wouldn't allow that to get in the way of Cas's first visit to him in London.

Full circle and he was thinking of Cas again, and how they had merely slept together on that slightly emotional Saturday night. If she didn't want to play around then, as he had learnt from previous experience, it was not worth pursuing. As she had left for her own room shortly before dusk, she had actually whispered that she knew she was being a pain, how sorry she was, and thanked him for his understanding. He was fine with that. She was back by eight in a much better frame of mind.

"Up you get, you lazy gorgeous bugger! We need some colour in our cheeks. We'll have breakfast and then walk down Las Ramblas. She had dragged the duvet off his bed. "I certainly want some colour in my cheeks when I meet your mother."

She hurried him through breakfast and into a taxi to the Plaça de Catalunya, to take advantage of the downhill walk. Normally, on previous visits, he never had known there not to be a sea of people, locals taking in the walk down Las Ramblas. The promenaders always seemed happy, and choosing and buying their bouquets of flowers for their loved ones, or people they were going to share Sunday lunch with, was their favoured retail art to match the ambience around them.

The artists appeared fewer though at this time of year. Many had gone until the tourists returned again the following year, but there were still some who lingered, to offer hastily sketched portraits or caricatures to passers-by, rather than taking their summer earnings to some far corner of the world.

Peter had forgotten that about halfway down, where the road to the left widened out in front of the Church, the local Sardana troupes would swirl together on these typical Sunday mornings. He picked up the echo of the flute and the beat of the drummers some 300 metres away.

"Have you ever danced the Sardana?" he asked Cas.

"No. I've never even heard of it. What is it?"

"It's a local Catalan dance, typically brought out at fiesta time. It's wonderfully emotional. We'll see some shortly. Can you hear the music?"

She could. It made her shudder slightly because to her ears, it was slightly off-key.

It made the hairs on the back of Peter's neck stand on end. For most of his life, whenever he had heard the music, he was reminded of the night when his father went to sea and didn't return. More recently, there was that painful one when he had stopped and seen Tania and Beth celebrating in the village square. Both events reminded him of periods of extreme unhappiness in his life. Yet the music and the beat still held a magnetic attraction to him.

They stopped at the top of three or four steps, from which they could look down on the concentrated movements of the outer circle, and its two inner ones. There was a swirl of jumping people, linked by pairs of joined hands held high.

"It looks fun," Cas admitted. "Is it hard to learn?"

"No. You just try to keep an eye on what the person to the left or right of you is doing."

"Can anyone do it?"

"It depends. In some villages they frown on outsiders joining them. They feel it breaks the concept of Christian unity and like-mindedness, which the circles represent.

"But the group there will accept that tourists'll be attracted to the novelty of dancing at any time of the day, and they'll make allowances if you don't know what you're doing. But you soon pick it up anyway."

"Shall we do it? Is there a break between dances? How do you join in?"

"It's pretty physical," Peter said.

"Oh, come on. I'm pretty physical anyway."

"I was thinking you'd get cross with me if I strained the old knee."

"If you felt that happening, you'd have to stop. Come on! Let's have a go. It'll be fun."

The music crescendoed to a halt. The square broke out into frantic Spanish chatter as couples explained to neighbouring couples how well it had gone, or how amusing it had been when somebody had gone wrong. The lead pipe player indicated a rally call for participants to form up again. Cas dragged Peter's hand and in less than 20 strides, it seemed, they'd reached the outer circle.

"Let's go in the middle," Cas suggested.

"It's not the best place to be," Peter advised.

"Nobody will see me in there."

"Here, you stay here with me. I'll guide you." He moved to break the chain to his right, and they were welcomed.

She was a natural. She held her head high, a throwback from her school ballet days and, she hoped, perhaps a touch of a beat behind her tutor. As she swirled, her hands went involuntarily high, towards the sky, as Peter and the young man to her left dictated. The emotion built up inside her as the music led her to the edge of oblivion and back, quickening so the flow of her blood followed suit.

As it slowed she became sad, as the composer had planned. It had lasted for eight minutes, four of which were painful for Peter, and sad for her, before the orchestra climaxed to a sudden silence. The other hundred or so participants all clapped politely. They had been there before. They were not just clapping the musicians. They were clapping themselves.

Cas stopped, momentarily stunned. She looked up into Peter's face and threw both arms around his neck. She was crying hard. She kissed his cheek.

"Hey, Chief." She hadn't called him that for many days. "Say, we'll do that again one day."

He held her tight. She half-pulled herself back from him so that she could see more of his face. More of his eyes.

"Tell me there's no such thing as a last Sardana, please Peter."

"Of course there's not. Why should there be?"

The thoughts caused tears to stream down his face. One of them was for Benito Alvor, as it was he, and his particular level of expertise, which had enabled Peter to once more breathe in the emotion and excitement of that traditional dance.

Peter camouflaged his tears at the sudden reappearance of the air hostess.

"Are you alright, Sir?"

"Yes, of course. I think the air con has gone haywire. My eyes can't take the dry air."

"We're losing height, actually. It's probably combined with the change in pressure. Hold your nose and blow hard. That will clear your ears and your tear ducts will sort themselves out too. I'll get you a hot towel. Can't have you looking as though you're crying when we land you back home."

"I've just left 'back home', actually."

"Sorry… what do you mean?"

"I'm Spanish. I've just left home again."

"Well, I'm sorry. You would have fooled me. I would have put you at being as English as I am. Now… let me get you that flannel."

Chapter 19

Fred was pleased to see him, at least he said he was, and was parked in his usual good position in the multi-storey by having gone up one floor higher than anyone else had. So they were clear of Customs and away from the airport by close to 1pm, so Peter thought.

"Have you adjusted the hour, Sir?"

"Good God, no! I'd clean forgotten."

"Home, Sir?"

"What do I look like?"

The chauffeur looked in the rear view mirror of the Bentley Continental, which Peter hadn't sat in since he went through the reverse procedure on the journey out. Then he had been emotionally disturbed by Coco's sudden departure and Marcia's reaction to his call for her to satisfy his needs.

Christ, he thought, *so much has happened in such a short space of time!*

"Fred, don't take so bloody long setting me up. I either look OK or could do with a freshen-up."

"I'd say, Sir, a freshen-up."

"If you'd lied, I would have fired you, you know that."

"Yes I do," Fred replied emphatically.

"OK, home, as they call it," Peter said, morosely. "I'll take a shower, change my crumpled suit, quick electric shave and get to the office by 1.45pm – that's on adjusted time."

"That seems precise timing, Sir. Why not 2pm?"

"Fred, you always pry. I don't want to walk into the office and have the receptionist gawp at me and phone ahead and say to Val and any others who're in that I've lost weight, or got a limp, or look older."

"You're none of those things, Sir. But I know what you mean. We'll be there, as you wish. So Val's told you about the new receptionist?"

"No. Is there one?"

"Wow! Do you have a treat in store for you! I tell you, Sir, we get couriers coming in with no deliveries just to see her a second time. Between you and me, George, Mr William's London chauffeur, says Mr William almost tosses himself off as he leaves the London office nowadays."

"Fred! You mustn't say things like that. You know that. You're talking about the Chairman."

"I'd only say that to you, Sir. It's the talk of the pool car garage, though – not because I've told them, but because George has."

"OK. But I don't want to hear mention of that again."

"Right, Sir!"

They had passed Shannons Corner, which they usually reckoned to be the halfway point back to the Kings Road, Eaton Terrace area – Peter's London home, and which had so recently been rejuvenated by Coco but would now be so dead again, until perhaps the coming Friday, when Cas would grace it with her presence.

Peter started to wonder if Cas would be back at the hospital by now, and his mother in Calella.

"She's South American, I think."

Peter came to, out of one of those flashes back in time which he had been having recently.

"Who's South American, Fred?"

"Oh, sorry, Sir. The new receptionist."

"Fred. Exactly who else apart from Mr William is erotically aroused by this new girl? If I'd known this, I clearly wouldn't have allowed her to be taken on."

"Sorry, Sir. What do you mean?"

"Well, are you?"

"Good God, Sir! If I even thought about it, Mrs Perry would chop me balls off with a carving knife."

"Well Fred, I think you ought to know. It shows your trousers don't look as though they're made for you anymore."

"Go on, Sir, is this one of your jokes?"

"No. It's all to do with that old English phrase of yours… to look at home first."

"Go on, Sir."

Those were Fred's final words until they pulled up outside the apartment and he volunteered to bring the baggage up.

"Don't bother. It's just the one case. You make sure you're here by 1.30… and that, I believe, is the first request in the form of an order you've had for far too long."

"Go on, Sir, really. Don't worry, Sir. Here at 1.30. The office by 1.45 and a quiet secret entrance. I'll see to that. By the way, Sir, if I might say Sir, it's good to have you back. We've all missed you."

As Peter had set off for the airport those few hours and nearly a thousand miles back in time, Gina had set off on her fateful Monday morning journey too.

She'd pondered what had been intended as Benito's final question: whether she would move out and join him. All weekend, the more she fought with the question, the more it appeared to be an ultimatum. Not only from the standpoint of Benito's insistence that he could not accept the position any longer, that of loving her and being driven into breaking their original pact, but also from the other point of view: that at her time and place in life, she was being offered a second – and almost certainly last – opportunity to start again with what she now knew to be the great love of her life.

On Saturday morning, when she'd asked Miguel over breakfast what he had in mind for the weekend, if he'd said she should bung a few things into a suitcase as he was taking her away to some romantic destination where they could catch up on their lives, he would have made her mind up for her.

"You'll probably need to go to the superstore so I'll finish chopping those logs that were delivered," was not the answer she had needed.

That decided her. She was off.

Then, totally out of character over their standard bread and cheese Saturday lunch, by which time she had pretty well decided what to pack, out of the blue he read out of the local paper that The Mission, which had won an Oscar the previous year, was showing in the Palafrugell cinema.

"How would you fancy seeing that?"

"OK," she said, with an element of reactive surprise. *Why the Hell would I fancy seeing that when I now have focus on what I need and enjoy?* she thought. But then it might take her mind off the upcoming Monday.

There were showings at 6pm and 9pm.

"Tell you what. You buy the tickets for the early evening performance and I'll treat us to supper at Il Paloma afterwards," she suggested. That, she thought, would be a parting gesture.

She was always content to concentrate on the girls and their schooling, using her income to subsidise the extra classes they needed, and the clothes, and their modest holidays to Majorca. During the year, if she and Marcel got themselves an evening out to the cinema, a travelling show or an anniversary dinner, she had been happy. So this was going to be like old times, but then she had never known or expected there to be much of a life beyond marriage, and anything other than old times repeated.

It gave her the reason she needed to pull herself together.

She'd got into the routine of washing her hair for the days she saw Benito and manicuring her nails midweek, when she thought she would have her hand held in the motel they were in the habit of frequenting on their early finish day. Afterwards, they would each tell their respective spouses that they had been at the same late operation, a schedule they'd introduced to clear the backlog.

She'd wash her hair late that afternoon and put colour on her nails, which wasn't allowed in the operating theatre and which Benito had therefore rarely seen. She'd wear her knee-length skirt. Marcel might semi-hold her hand but never now rested it onto his or her knee like he used to.

She slowly moved the hangers holding her half a dozen or so blouses. Yes. That was the one. It was a cerise colour. She'd only worn it once, at the first seminar she had attended with Benito. Marcel had seen it on the washing line and commented that it was a lovely colour but had never had the gumption to suggest she slip it on and he'd drive her to some reachable venue to show her off to the world. Benito had, of course. So just wearing it would make Ben part of their outing.

They had good seats. Marcel had felt for her hand as the adverts were finishing and did place the back of his on her bare knee for support. She should have worn tights. There was a chill around. But she decided she'd suffer that.

She was surprisingly relaxed. Monday morning loomed into her mind. How could she leave him? She snuggled her shoulder into his and covered his hand with her free one. She looked at him and smiled. He squeezed her hand. She knew nothing about the film prior to going. That didn't matter; it had often been the case. However, this one was different. The opening was stunning. The music was beautiful and very moving. She cried through most of it. The moments of brutality and hatred she so related to herself that she was sure she would never get the music out of her head.

Over dinner, she was quiet. Was this to be their last supper? Had she both the courage and the resolve to be their Judas? Marcel tried to lift her from the depths of her thoughts.

"I'm really, really sorry. The film was so brilliant but it's upset me. It's made me feel unsettled. All that hatred and the stalwart attempts to protect the religious beliefs they'd attempted to plant in the rainforests. I just can't get the music out of my head."

He had enjoyed the film. He was right in his appraisal. It was brilliantly made and the conception was original and amazing. Why Gina had taken it so much to heart he couldn't say.

They had both eaten sole, which was what Marcel said he fancied. Gina had got used to Benito choosing her food for her in restaurants, and she'd never had the courage to confess to not liking a particular choice. So it seemed the easy solution to just agree with the idea of sole, and to drink the white house Rioja, rather than having to decide on red or white, by the glass or the bottle.

Benito would be choosing now if they were together, she kept saying to herself. Then the thought crossed her mind that for all she knew, he and his wife were having their own last supper. How would he be feeling? How should she be feeling? If Marcel told her once more she was, "Edgy,", "Seemed not to be there," or enquired, "is everything alright?" she felt she would snap and confront him with the situation. Just one sentence would make the rest of her life so easy: "I'm leaving you."

If she could just say it, it would be out. They'd argue, no doubt, then reason that they hadn't a great deal left between them and that the girls were now old enough to understand. The bit she would find hard coming to terms with was that she'd been cheating on him – only for a few months, she consoled herself, but that didn't change the fact that it was wrong. Then she'd have to defend against the argument Marcel was bound to put forward: that a chap in a trusted position, in charge of saving lives, was a shit and a danger to the world, and surely no animal to change to after all he had provided for her.

Countering that, as she would have to, would devastate his life. "Yes. I agree. You've provided me with logs and money for the basic housekeeping, and the odd treat like tonight. But you haven't ignited the smouldering fire in me. It's that loving that a girl needs. Not being provided with something that leaves behind a load of empty paper bags and boxes that finish up in the recycling bin to make some other housewife happy with her provisions. You've never left me 'spent'. Emotionally exhausted, bruised and even slightly battered, and thanked me for that, and allowed me to say my thanks will be the next time, giving a firm indication I'm up for more." Those were the sentiments she was rehearsing within.

"So what are you thinking?" Marcel was quite grumpy now, a feeling that was perhaps justified by Gina's apparent distance while they ate. In his mind he wanted to be brave and ask, *"Is the fish OK? The wine? It can't be anything I've said. I haven't dared say anything."* But couldn't quite let the words out.

Here was the opportunity. She also ran through it in her mind. *"Look. I know you won't like this. But I'm going to leave you."* But held back.

He slid his hand across the table and held hers. "I've got to be brave," he said, "is it us? Is it me? OK, I've noticed we're both working hard. But that's for the girls and hopefully, university. We haven't given each other time. Your hours and mine. You know. Tell me. Is it us?" His tone was soft and sincere.

"I've told you. It's the film and the music." And then she had a brainwave, "And I may be becoming menopausal." She squeezed his hand.

"Well, that's alright then," he said with relief.

Not here. Not now, she thought. That he should be told was not in dispute. But not now. Not here. Another place. A different time.

When they got to bed, he tried to light her fire as she might once have wanted. He was as keen as ever. She couldn't, however, stop thinking in comparative terms of the recent intruder into her mundane existence.

On Sunday morning, he was back to logs. She was catching up with the washing and household chores.

She'd say to Benito in the morning it was yes. Oh, how delighted he would be.

Chapter 20

North of where Gina was on that Monday morning, Maria left Cas, thinking happy thoughts about her. The young South African was pleasant, obviously besotted by her only son, as so many had been; but she seemed a kind girl with strong career ambitions.

Maria had decided she ought to go up to Girasol and had arranged to meet Marco there at 11. They had discussed the prospect of how to run the hotel with Andres, the senior day chef who had always seemed almost as managerial as Tania herself. So they were meeting him too.

The hospital were talking months if there was to be a recovery at all for Tania. She had apparently gone into a state they described as 'openly comatose'.

"What's that mean?" Maria had asked.

"Well, she has the appearance of being in a coma but she's wide awake, or conscious at least, but isn't influenced by anything going on around her," the consultant said. "She doesn't converse as such, but keeps talking with this Toni figure, or talking about when she expects him to come. Next week, we'll bring in bits of the past into her sights to see what happens. You've said you think she would most react to the names Peter, Marco, Maria and Marguerite, her daughter?"

"Yes. I'd think so. You could say 'Hotel Playa' or 'Girasol' – they would be close to her heart."

So that was for next week. Today was to follow through Andres's idea that his wife could help out in the mornings, which were the busy times really, because that was when casuals booked in and over-nighters checked out. Anybody who stayed after lunch was usually as a result of some commercial traveller having brought a buyer from the local chemist's chain or a lonely housewife a jolly good lunch, and then that had led to the question of whether a couple of hours romping before they returned to their place of business or got home to do the old man's meal could be on the agenda. That didn't take much administration. Afternoon trade seemed dependent on that.

Evenings were in the combined control of the chef of that particular stint and the head waiter. The waiter could check in late arrivals. It was only a matter of taking a passport, less writing than taking down a dinner order, and then finding the right key, and wishing the customer a happy stay. Andres's wife Andretta had had hotel experience before she had the baby. In fact they had met when they were both working at the Maria Elena Palace Hotel in Madrid. Her mother would have the child every weekday morning and Andres could take over on Saturdays and Sundays when his shifts moved around. She was a pleasant young lady who spoke good English and said she would be prepared to turn her hand to most things. So Maria and Marco hired Andretta on a temporary to permanent basis.

Maria and Marco took a quick stock check as they realised they were in comparative strangers' hands, although Andres had been in the hotel for quite a while. There were three boxes of Coca Cola and one of Seven Up just by the reception counter.

"Are these stock or going out or something?"

"Oh. They're new stock. The Coke delivery man came this morning. He does every Monday. He's alright. Or at least Miss Tania always said he was. He looks in the fridge and stocks it up with what's needed. Then the invoice comes in from head office in a couple of weeks. Then we have to pay."

"So we'll count it as stock as of today. We can revise that weekly, depending on the delivery note." Turning to Andretta, Maria continued. "What you'll have to do is adjust the stock figure weekly in this case."

"Yes, Mrs Martinez. I agree."

"The Coca-Cola man was shocked," Andres said to Maria.

"Sorry. Why?"

"Well, he delivers every Monday."

"What time?"

"Usually we're his first call."

"OK, so did he see Miss Tania last week?"

"Yes, he must have done. This Monday, he said she was alright when he saw her. He'd apparently had to get her to sign the ticket and the breakfast chef said she was cleaning Mr Peter's house and he was to go down there to collect the signature."

"I suppose then he might have been the last one to see Miss Tania."

"Maybe," Andres said.

Maria thought she ought to bear that in mind.

Marcel had tried to be attentive for the rest of Sunday, but it annoyed Gina all the more. The daughters were home for tea and both had been squabbling over the use of the washing machine. At the height of their argument, Gina had worked through the speech she intended to deliver at the right moment later that evening. She would be sorry about what she was going to tell them. But she'd explain that they were now adult enough to understand, and that she was off to get a deeper spiritual satisfaction elsewhere. They'd no doubt cry but they'd surely understand.

The opportunity didn't seem to arise all evening. She had got to a stage, she realised, that she accepted each of their goodnight kisses as a matter of habit. The norm. They'd occasionally say, "Love you, Mother," but she found she didn't actually hear that any more. So that night, when she heard those words from each of them, she inwardly heaved, realising that, in the future, if ever they were to be said again, it would be over a long-distance phone. Benito had indicated he'd apply for a posting abroad, and take Gina with him. She suddenly awakened to that reality. She couldn't leave them. She just couldn't.

Tonight she was first into bed while Marcel busied himself with his dental hygiene. It took an age and Gina usually dropped off to sleep waiting for him. But she'd stay awake tonight. It would probably be the last time they would share a bed together. He had a habit of throwing back the duvet, introducing a blast of cold air into her side of the bed. Nothing changed on this night.

"Are you feeling any better?" he asked.

"Marginally. I'm sorry, I seem to have a lot on my mind at the moment."

"Here?"

"No! At the hospital."

"Want to tell me about it?"

That was kind. She could now tell him. It might be the calmest way to deal with it. She thought the words through again.

"Would it help if I relaxed you?"

That meant he would throw himself on top of her, clumsily carry out a sequence of standard procedures he called 'making love', grunt a couple of times, ask if it was good for her and within minutes, be asleep. Relaxing it was not. But she knew his intentions. If this was the last time he would want her to say yes, then her conscience said she had to say yes.

"That would be nice," she said.

"Do you really mean that?"

"Yes, of course I do."

Six or seven minutes later, he was asleep. She was awake all night.

She'd arranged to meet Benito in the hospital car park at 7.30, before anyone else arrived at eight.

She pulled in to find him already sitting reading a paper behind the steering wheel of his Mercedes. He released the locked door control and leant across to let her in. She slid into the passenger seat. He checked around them to see if anyone was watching, perhaps even a private detective hired by his warring wife. He kissed his hand and planted the kiss on her lips.

"Well, my darling. I've had a dreadful weekend waiting for your answer."

"So have I."

"So keep me in suspense no longer."

"You know the answer."

"That's cruel. I'm hoping I do. Are you saying it's yes?"

Suddenly it felt as though Gina's head was going to explode. She hoped it wouldn't show but her hands were trembling. The music from The Mission sounded in her ears as though the full orchestra was closing in on her, like one of those great big lion-catching nets she'd seen as a kid in cartoons at the local flea-pit cinema. She closed her eyes to deaden the pain of the music and the glare of the erupting volcano behind each eye. Her thoughts rushed into the inevitable future. Her younger daughter kissing her cheek, her lips hard and cold. "Remember I'll always love you, Mummy." Then her elder daughter: "I'm not going to say I'm not disappointed. You and Daddy are my greatest institution. I'll still love you, though."

Gina's eyelids were close to being unable to hold back the flood of tears that had welled up. Then there was a voice. No face attached to it.

"Have a good day, darling. I hope the hospital isn't too hard on you. I've been thinking... perhaps we can escape to Puerto Soller for a weekend, without the kids... you know, rekindle some flames, see a happy film to cheer you up..."

They were a repeat of the last words Marcel had said as she left for work.

"You're too bloody late," she said to herself as she waved and drove away, "too damned bloody late, Marcel."

"I can't wait any more, darling," Benito said.

She opened her eyes and the tears cascaded down her cheeks.

"That's the trouble," she said, "you can't bloody wait. But I have to. I know how much I'm loved by three people. I'm learning how much I'm wanted by one. It's maybe a need rather than a love, but it's suited me because in satisfying that need, I've quenched a need of my own, one I wasn't totally aware of. Pitting those three loves against my own selfish love for you suddenly seems a catastrophic prospect." Her mind was made up. "It's no. I can't leave. I can't join you. I'm afraid my love for you would turn to hate for encouraging me to destroy those three loves."

Benito was stunned. She wiped her eyes. She was suddenly resigned, and brave enough to accept the consequences.

"That's it. That's bloody it!" She laughed a helpless, slightly hysterical laugh. "You now say, of course, that you'll wait. Then I'll say it's too late. I've had to decide in the today timeframe you offered me. You'll then say, 'But we can continue to be friends', maybe you'll say lovers, and I'll say, 'Let's see how it works out'.

"Benito, this is a moment we've both shared so many times before. The anaesthetist looks at you and you shrug in helpless agreement. The patient dies. In this case, I really do believe God has administered this anaesthetic with a major purpose, and I hope you'll join me in thanking him."

"How would we continue to work together?" he asked.

"That we'll have to see. I'm sure if I temporarily sprain a wrist, you get a stand-in. Time will cure this. Here, let me go, my darling. It's for the best. I'll have to accept I'm losing you, however reluctantly. You are a person I truly love for the fire you brought out of me. I must go. I intend to sprain my wrist in penance."

Chapter 21

When Cas got back from the airport, she had a lot of catching up to do. The Professor had not resisted her taking a day's leave on the coming Friday, so she had to fit her work into the remaining three-and-a-half days and induct a patient due in on the Tuesday.

During the lunch break, Guy told her that Paul had been in a foul mood and nobody could deal with him. "In fact," he said, "we nearly phoned the airport to say 'Come back Peter, all is forgiven'."

"No chance of that," Cas said. "But I'll have a word over lunch."

Paul was sitting behind a plate of spaghetti, just playing with it. Cas slipped into the seat beside him.

"Eat up, Paul. You need a regular diet."

"Friggin' don't if you feel sick."

"Now that's a word we decided was out."

"That was only when Peter was here."

"So the rules change when Peter leaves, eh!"

"What do you think?"

"I think not."

"So if he's gone, he's gone. Yes. Out of everybody's mind."

"Yes. I'd say so. But never completely."

"OK then. Here's a question. Will you share anybody's bed who asks? That's if he's gone, and isn't asking any more?"

"What!" She was furious. "What exactly do you mean by that?"

"I wanted to thank Peter for the football and so I went along to his room. I heard you thanking him. In bed. I could see through the keyhole."

Cas lost control. She let the impulse of the moment power her right hand from her side, up in a looping arc to land high on Paul's left temple.

"You little Peeping Tom of a sod!"

Paul's face replicated his expression when Peter had similarly lost it with him.

"Now listen here, you, young man!" Cas was shouting in a whisper. "Peter and I happen to have unexpectedly fallen in love with each other. If you hadn't noticed that at the football or at the meeting the other evening, then you've got to start learning a bit more about life. Some do but I, in particular, do not lightly go to share a man's bed and… I certainly won't be looking for a replacement, even if there is an empty and inviting bed."

"Miss. You're the one…"

"What? I just don't understand you today."

"You're the one who wants to start learning more about life," the lad said earnestly.

"… And what the hell do you mean by that?"

"You haven't noticed *me*."

"Of course, I have. If I hadn't noticed you're not eating, I wouldn't be here now."

"I'm not eating because… when the cleaner cleared my plate yesterday lunchtime, I hadn't touched the food and she said, 'Are you in love or something?' Then last night with supper, she said the same. She said, 'listen, you'll do yourself harm if you don't eat. No girlfriend's worth starving for.' Then I realised I was in love with you."

"Oh, Paul." Cas took both his hands. "How sweet. Listen, you're not in love with me. You don't know yet what love between a man and a woman is about, what it's like. I tell you, when you're really in love, you eat like a horse. What's happening is you're growing up. Has anybody explained a thing called 'the birds and the bees' to you?"

"No, miss. I know what they are. But there's never been any more to it."

"How old are you?"

"Nobody knows. I think about 12 or 13, maybe more. My mother didn't file the right piece of paper when I was born."

"OK. We'll have to find out about that. So have you ever heard the word puberty?"

"No."

"Have you noticed you're growing hairs under your arms?"

He looked embarrassed. "Yes, but when I start shaving, I'll shave under there too."

She peered at his face. "Have you never shaved?"

"Christ, no! And I don't friggin' want to. You can cut yourself."

"Have you got hairs on your balls?"

"Look, miss. That's up to me. That's got nothing to do with me loving you."

"Yes it has. Look, I'll get one of the male nurses to explain. I'll ask Guy. Oh! No, I won't. I'll find somebody."

"Why not get Peter back?"

"Because he's a very busy man and he's going to get you sponsorship from England. No, I'll find somebody. Now, get this clear. I promise you that you don't love me and that you certainly don't want me in your bed, and I wouldn't want to be there if it's the last bed in the world… and anyway, if I did do things with you it would be illegal. More importantly, you'll sit there until you finish that bowl of spaghetti, otherwise I'll say I don't love you enough to coach you to the heights."

"So do you love me that much?"

"Listen, Paul. There are types of love. There's the love a mother or father has for a child. That's the type I have for you. Then there's the type of love you have for each other when you're much older and that type of love leads people to get married and become mothers and fathers. To get to that stage, I bet you need to be shaving. OK, now eat. Mine's getting cold too."

They ate together in silence.

I'm missing you Peter, she thought.

Chapter 22

Fred had given Peter his spare apartment key, which he always kept in the glove pocket of the car in case it was needed. Somewhere between leaving the UK and his return trip, Peter had mislaid his own key. Probably, he thought, thrown away in his blood-stained trousers by the staff who admitted him at the hospital. There, at some stages, Peter had thought he might never get to put his key into the lock of his door again. He hadn't realised how those two things meant so much to him: performing the Sardana again, and opening his own door. He'd been left with a heavy limp from his dance in the square. He hoped he wouldn't now get tennis elbow from opening the door.

It smelt exactly the same as it always did. It was probably the Crabtree and Evelyn soaps and accompaniments that Anna had introduced, which he had never had the heart to change. The Oriental perfume exuded by Coco had faded.

He went first into the large lounge. It was spotless. Mrs Brown, who 'did' for him, had been in every day, he knew. Val had been paying her bills. Obviously she'd had a quadruple spring clean. The dining room was absolutely pristine, and his bedroom, the en suite, the visitor's bedroom and the visitor's bathroom. The kitchen was always his least favourite room, or at least the one he did not perform well in, but that was spotless too.

There on the kitchen table were three piles of post. One was clearly a small pile of bills. Again, Mrs Brown had been getting those across to Val via Perry. But there were a few yet to go. Then there was a pile of formal-looking envelopes. Mrs Brown thought of those as being adverts or promotions. The third appeared to all be handwritten envelopes of a personal nature. Peter picked that pile up and expertly dealt them into a number of smaller piles.

There were four with South American postmarks from his daughter, the same number from Malaysia, with those pretty floral stamps. He bet those would be interesting. Coco would be spraying out all her emotions to him, as she did, and eventually finishing up by saying she hoped he was well. Then there were a number of envelopes where he thought he knew the writing but didn't know whose it was. He'd have a good read this evening.

The heating was ticking over but it was a sunny autumnal day, so the flat held its warmth pretty well. He had 30 minutes: time for a quick whip round with his good friend, his Braun electric razor, a shower and then, God bless

Mrs Brown for it, into one of her crisply ironed shirts she had hung in the wardrobe. He always chose his suit before he showered and, without fail, put his intended trousers into his Corby trouser press. He must remember, he thought, to treat Girasol to one of those if he was likely to spend more time out there with the POC and Ramon connections. He never felt smart unless his trousers were well-pressed and his Church's or Cheney shoes spit and polished.

They left at 1.30pm exactly, though not before he'd noticed the answer machine showed "20", which he knew was the maximum number of calls that could be stored – two hours' worth of left messages, he remembered for some obscure reason.

He could see his evening was going to be a game of catch-up. Suddenly he felt the buzz of the pace of UK life. He'd become institutionalised, he thought.

Peter turned and looked through the rear window of what was probably the favourite of all his toys depicting affluence: his pride and joy Bentley. He doubted that he would have felt comfortable to drive it himself. The plane journey had caused his previously well exercised joints to become a bit fixed.

He looked back on to the front façade of Buckingham Palace. The flowerbeds encircling the Queen Victoria monument still had a lot of colour for the time of year. The plane trees aligning the Mall and hiding Clarence House from the gawping flocks of tourists, hoping to glimpse the Queen Mother, were showing signs of awareness that autumn was about to give way to the onset of winter. The colours of the parchment-type leaves were changing from their varying shades of green to browns and orange. Across into St James's Park, there were still a large number of foreign visitors, mingling with British schoolchildren on their half-term treats to feed the ducks and then walk on over that carpet of history, Horse Guards Parade.

Gosh, it's good to be back, he thought. In fact he said just that to Perry.

"Good to have you back, Sir," Fred responded, then, not being one to miss the opportunity to start up a conversation, he went on to say, "They said, Sir, you were badly damaged. According to George, Mr William's driver, the Chairman was most concerned that it looked as though fate had called you home to Spain and that by all accounts you'd have to stay over there."

"Did he?" Peter said caustically. "What did you think?"

He'd obviously put Perry on the spot. Fred was initially quiet and flashed a glance at Peter to see if he had a grin on his face, or whether it was a question to which he really expected an answer.

"No. I knew you'd be back, Sir. I said it would take more than some bandits to put you down."

"Did you, Fred? Who mentioned bandits to you?"

"George, Sir."

"Well that was wrong. This Spanish lady's husband returned unexpectedly and didn't like seeing me there in his home, and it was he who got out the shotgun."

Perry was glancing so hard into the mirror that he was nearly responsible for causing the speedy return of a number of tourists to their various homelands. After breaking fiercely and pulling away slowly, he said, "Go on, Sir." The puzzled look was likely to stay with him a day or so as he passed this story through the drivers' pool.

"Tell you what, Fred. Drop me under Admiralty Arch, would you, and I'll walk to the office."

"What about your key, Sir?"

"Oh, I expect I can still remember the password to get in."

"Beware the inquisition of the new receptionist. As I said, all the blokes have fallen for her, but she's no easy touch, she'll put you through your paces to get in."

"Go on, Fred. I expect I'll do it."

"I'll get some new keys cut while you're there, Sir. If that's alright."

"Perfect."

Trafalgar Square looked good. The pigeons were having a field day, the fountains were in full flow. *We must have some water feature in Barcelona for the games*, Peter thought. He was in touch with the planners and architects at this early stage. He'd make a note to raise the idea.

The thought of Barcelona also made him think about Cas, and seeing the turning that lead into the cul-de-sac where his office was made him think about his first-floor location and the period style, and how it was there that he had first met Jan… and, of course, Coco.

A grin lit up his whole face. What the hell would Coco say if she knew that in three weeks, he had gone from almost a celibate life since Anna's death to what some might say was a promiscuous razzle?

"Whoa! Slow down!" he said to Coco in his mind, some 8,000 miles away on the other side of the globe.

If challenged, he would have explained he hadn't exactly been celibate. There had been Marcia, but only when one or the other of them felt the need for a jolly good, meaningless romp. There'd been plenty of intention but no real meaning.

He had avoided pretty well every concierge's suggestion of providing him with 'company' in every one of the five-star hotels he'd stayed in on his globe-trotting visits, once they had seen that he was typically a businessman away from home, by the fact he checked in just one small piece of baggage.

So that was not a bad record to have, he would be pleased to let Coco know.

Suddenly though, like buses when you least expect then to turn up, Jan and Cas had come along at virtually the same time. Anyway, the one was very close to the other.

Jan was not really any more than a temporary infatuation. Peter knew that himself well. It started when he still had a touch of post-operative delirium about him. She was there and he needed to be brave and a bit macho, to disguise the fact that he inwardly really did not think he would walk unaided again.

Sadly, he thought to himself, he had this obsession about proving his masculinity with somebody. That someone had to be female, and Jan had been there, it was as simple as that. Then it apparently got out of hand when his mother had all but proposed for him. But as one door closed so another opened when Cas had come on the scene.

He crossed the road on the west side of the square, which he always did carefully because it was one-way traffic going north and most drivers saw the gentle slope of the hill as an opportunity to put some revs into the engine, which would have been idling for a major part of the journey up Whitehall or in from the Mall.

Cas he thought differently about once she had transferred from being bait, by her own admission. She was also extremely good in bed and Peter saw that as something that could last him a lifetime.

He'd be seeing her on Friday. He hoped he'd not find that when she came into his 'proper' environment, she would freeze to ensure she stayed firmly on the hook until they sorted themselves out in the real world beyond the somewhat artificial one in which their bond had initially been formed. He was walking surprisingly well, he thought, bearing in mind the fears he'd had in Palafrugell. Indeed very well, accounting for the fact also there was no bait.

A taxi pulled up about 40 yards in front of him at the bottom of Duke of York Street. The driver's arm came out of the window and, in a well-practised manner, grabbed the lever handle to the rear passenger door, which then flew open as a result of the slope in the road.

The rear of what was clearly a very shapely female body stepped out backwards and side-stepped to level with the driver, slamming the rear door shut as she did so. The lady delved into a black patent leather handbag as Peter slowed to take in the spectacle opening up before him. "If this is more bait, I've got the light on my roof set to 'Not for hire' like the taxi driver now has," he told himself.

He continued to take in the vision, starting at pavement level: black patent high-heeled shoes with a touch of black tights, possibly even stockings. She had class, he thought.

A carefully chosen wide black belt seemed designed less to hold up her grey pencil skirt and more to dress the waistband, into which was tucked a crisp white working shirt. The autumn chill was kept at bay by a cheeky short bomber jacket, which was clearly not fur – probably on account of her aversion to the killing of animals for the sake of fashion. Her black hair was in a neat bun and maybe she had used some of her boyfriend's Brylcream to make it shine.

Peter wanted to pinch himself. Perhaps when he was under sedation somebody had slipped him a slow-releasing testosterone capsule. It had certainly worked with Jan, but he would have expected it to have worn itself out during his time with Cas. However, he was now suffering a distinct distraction from this total stranger who had caught his eye.

"You're a friggin' flirt," he chided himself.

He stopped, as though to look around and get his bearings in an area not known to him. It was in fact to look around and see if every male within 100 metres was also fascinated by the sequence in this newly released make believe movie, which the director had titled 'Paying The Fare'. He was horrified with himself. He could see no such other male interest.

Stopping also gave him the chance to allow the lady, who to that point had only shown her rear side to him, to move on to her intended destination. If she turned and walked towards him, he could perhaps ask her if she knew where the Institute of Directors was. At least that would be a plausible basis from which to proposition her in some way or another.

This was not the Peter Martinez he knew. Perhaps part of his brain had been dislodged during the operation. He wasn't happy about himself, though. For years, yes, he'd admired many attractive things — but this was disloyal. Cas was on the brink of arriving. He was likely to be in touch with Jan, if only for business reasons, and Marcia was pushing him for an adiós to her days of merry widowhood.

Maybe it was the ambience of London and the close proximity of the real world of BCG, but he had to put flirtatious thoughts out of this mind. He was about to turn right at the cul-de-sac in which his HQ was situated. She would walk on, never to know that she had been in his thoughts, on the planet which they separately shared.

Ms whoever — maybe even Mrs, how the hell was he to know? — moved on ahead of him. She walked briskly and was obviously very fit, determined in her stride and totally used to the height of her heels.

"This isn't bloody fair," he said to himself, as, without warning, she turned into Duke of York Street. Not pulled by some magnetic force or for any other reason than getting to his office, so did he.

Perhaps she was a neighbour. Could well be, he thought, because there were a couple of European consulates who had offices close to his own. He consoled himself that he might see her again in days to come.

"Christ!" This time he muttered it out loud and stopped, and did a pseudo military precision about-turn, but not at a standard to match those executed by the Guards on duty at the other end of Pall Mall, outside St. James's Palace. He retraced the steps he had already taken in this particular street. He needed time to think this situation through.

She was bait for sure. She had turned in towards the eight-panelled reproduction door, effectively his door which he knew to be backed by a steel sheet, which they'd had fitted to their offices when security in London had had to be increased during a spate of letter-bomb threats.

Of course he had stopped and turned away before seeing if she rang the bell or had a key or a code to get in. Now he collected his thoughts. He was annoyed to suddenly remember what Perry had said about a new receptionist.

No, that couldn't be, he told himself. He couldn't envisage the likes of the company chauffeurs fancying a lady like that; they would know they'd never stand a chance of someone with that sort of style even entering their wildest dreams after a night on the beer.

He turned and started walking back up the slight incline. It was now five to two. If she had entered the building, as a visitor she would be sitting with finishing school poise on the deep tan leather Chesterfield. He'd be able to walk in, say good afternoon with authority and just walk on. He'd find out who she was later. What about her face, though? He'd find out if the front elevation was as good, or better, than the rear one, as was so often the case with the tangible properties Peter Martinez was more used to handling.

If she happened to be the new receptionist, he'd certainly have to introduce himself but not take too much of an interest in her. If there was any other option, he would have time, in the 30 seconds it would take him to reach the office, to find out where she was in the building and work something out.

Good God! Surely she couldn't be one of Mr William's daughters? Peter knew he had two but had never met either, or seen photographs, even in the issues of Tatler he read when he visited the barbers or dentist.

"Oh no! Shit!" Of course he didn't have a key, and he couldn't for the life of him remember the code for the keypad. He would be forced to ring the bell. That he did.

As he waited, he turned away from the door and, somewhat nonchalantly looked across the street to one of the similar regency properties.

A voice with the slightest hint of a Spanish accent – not mainland Spain, which he knew very well, but likely from his former wife's birthplace in South America said – "Good afternoon, Sir," through the entryphone speaker. *He'd have fun,* he thought.

"I'm here to see your Mr Martinez."

She was thrown. She was always given a list of visitors to Executives for the day. Delivery people and so forth came and went very regularly and had to be checked, but no receptionist was meant to quiz a visitor to somebody at a high level of responsibility in the company.

"May I have your name, Sir?"

"Not if I don't have yours."

"Sorry, Sir?"

"Not if I don't have yours. Look, if I'm allowed in I'll explain. I'm a surprise visitor."

"Is it for any legal purpose, Sir?"

My, she was bright! He could be carrying a summons.

This time Peter laughed. "No, it's purely very personal, as you'll see."

"Very well, Sir!"

She immediately phoned Val and quickly said, "Stranger at door. Won't identify. I'm letting him in."

The heavy door swung open easily once the electronic release impulse had been given. The back view of Peter, all six foot plus of him, clad in an obviously expensive dark blue suit, and the groomed hair curling up slightly in the nape of his neck, relaxed her.

He turned. *Wow!* was her inward reaction. He was really nice, perhaps it was a permanently tanned skin, possibly, though naturally, Mediterranean. It was certainly a genuine smile, with just a hint of mischief about it. The eyes were blue and the type that still made her knees go weak.

His photographic snapshot of her was a welcoming open face, shielding a bit of hurt, which made her hesitate until she too smiled with her light blue eyes. She had little make-up on but it was quality, particularly on her lips, which, if he was not mistaken, was freshly applied after her break.

"Who speaks first?" he said.

She giggled, but then stopped immediately, showing that in retrospect she felt it was not appropriate. Then she outraged herself.

"You just did, Sir," she replied.

Why? Why? What on earth even made me say that? It was cheeky in the extreme. It was unlike her, she thought, for her vocal chords to allow impulsive comment.

"Oh, I'm sorry, Sir. I didn't mean to say that." Why? Why? Why did she say that? Of course he would think she was most unprofessional. Yet she must have meant to say that. Words don't just spill out automatically.

Peter's smile was now broader. "Look. Shall we start again? You go back to your desk. I'll ring the bell. You answer and ask who it is and this time, I'll be honest and tell you…" As he reached that element of his 'I'm back' speech, he advanced his right hand, open and ready to envelope hers. "…I'm Peter Martinez… and then I'd say, 'And you must be the young lady who's turning the heads of all the drivers in the car pool, no doubt all the young engineers, accountants and others here and, not least, the Chairman's'."

He leant his head back and laughed noisily, but was stopped as he felt her hand link with his and heard her say, "Well, yes I know, Sir. I think that's why I went a bit to pieces. You weren't expected… it was a shock. I don't know, I just sort of screwed up. But can I say welcome back? You look well, Sir, I hope you're mended."

"Good God, woman! Who the hell are you? You ought to be on the stage or something. I've never felt more welcome in my own office in the whole of my life."

"I'm Sylvia Pez, sometimes called Sylvie."

A girl had now appeared behind Sylvia. Peter had a rough idea he knew the face and took a wild stab. "Hi... I'm guessing you're Val."

"That's right, Peter."

What a difference, he thought. *I'm not Peter to you until we've bonded a little bit more.* But he contained his words.

"But you're not booked in until tomorrow!"

"Who says?"

"Well... Mr William did, for one." Peter's mood had suddenly changed. "I probably shouldn't say this in front of you both, but how the hell would he know? I'm not a racehorse working to a training programme and only due to turn up at the course tomorrow."

Sylvia came to the rescue. "Look, Sir, shouldn't you step inside? If it was early morning, my notes tell me you'd have a coffee. Is it too early for tea? Whichever. One of us will bring you something in your office."

"Thank you, Sylvia. Tea would be excellent... I have..."

"Earl Grey, touch of milk only in a small jug, sweeteners but the option of the sugar bowl and perhaps a ginger biscuit, just one, nothing fancy just put on the saucer."

"You *are* well informed. Excellent."

Peter walked through the door across the heavy coconut matting and headed towards the stairs. He stopped and looked back towards both surprised ladies. He singled out Sylvia in his vision.

"You said you knew who I was. How was that? We haven't met before, I know."

"Your photograph, Sir. Magazine in Val's office."

He turned to Val. "In your office?"

"Yes, it was there."

"There?"

"Well... yes. I think Jo always had it there."

"No way! I'd best look at this."

Sylvia and Val sort of sniggered in mild female amusement.

"Sorry, but why's it funny?"

Val answered. She recognised his mood change. "You'd best judge for yourself, Sir. I'll show you." She turned as though to go to the lift on the left.

"I'll walk, if you don't mind."

Val showed embarrassment. "That's fine. I'll walk with you."

"No. You carry on. You do your thing. I'll see you up there."

"... And I'll follow shortly with some tea, Sir." Sylvia was trying to cut the atmosphere that had developed with an imaginary knife.

The door leading to the staircase closed behind Peter. Val blew out her cheeks, turning to Sylvia.

"Did I see his attitude change?"

"Yes. For sure."

"What happened?"

"Well, I'd assess that Mr Martinez is one of those very private people, and I have to say he's entitled to be. Again, I'd guess that's a new photo, probably planted by your predecessor, Jo. I do have to say the outer office you're in doesn't quite fit the ambience of the building, and I'd guess he doesn't approve of anything other than a Constable or perhaps a Monet on the walls. You'd best hurry. I'm afraid he'll go berserk when he sees how the photo has been defaced."

"Defaced? Why do you say that? It has a hint of lipstick on it but surely he must have noticed that before."

"Not if it wasn't there before he left."

Val didn't wait any longer for the lift but ran to the door leading to the stairs and sprinted up two at a time to her office. She must have been just seconds late as, by the time she entered the area leading to Peter's quarters, the picture on the wall had gone.

"Bloody agony… the photo's disappeared," she whispered.

Peter's office door was open. Val had not yet established a protocol with her Chief Executive about when to freely enter and when not to, and there had been no formal handover between the previous incumbent and herself.

She eased the door open sufficiently to let her enter. Peter was half-turned away from her, bending over the old brass wire wastepaper basket. Val saw that he had torn the photograph into four or five pieces and was in the process of dispatching it to waste.

"Oh dear. I'm sorry, Peter. It seems there's been a dreadful mistake. Don't tell me you haven't seen that before?"

"I certainly have not."

"I don't know what to say."

"You can tell me why you didn't ask questions about it."

She was quite shocked. "Questions? To who?"

"Well what about starting with the cleaners? They would know if it was new…"

Val felt speechless.

"… And answer me one thing: whose was the lipstick?"

"Jo's, I imagined."

"And who else's?"

"I don't know what you mean."

Peter stooped back down lowering himself to the level of the basket to reclaim parts of the photo.

"There." He beckoned her closer to his desk, encouraging her to lean forward and look at an area of the photo he was pointing at with his right hand forefinger.

"There. See that? That's one colour lipstick. There. That's another and there, on the end of my nose, is another. Jo rarely wore lipstick, so maybe one is hers but I'm guessing that while the cat's been away, there's been a lot of play. Can you shed any light on that?"

Val usually believed that her make-up camouflaged her lifelong habit of blushing. Sometimes that was caused by embarrassment, at others when she felt guilt. This time, she was sure that the high flush of colour would blast through any foundation she might have hurriedly applied earlier in the day.

"One is mine, Peter."

"The other?"

"I'm hating this."

"Go on then, you'd best tell me. This Sylvia?"

"Good God, no! No. She's nice, she wouldn't do that. No, it was Jan Roberts. Jo must have left the photo and she started it, I guess, by planting a goodbye kiss on it."

"The one apparently full on my lips?"

"Yes. That was always there. Then Jan Roberts came in one day and we slipped out after work for a drink. As we left, she remembered she'd left a manuscript in my office, so we came back in. The cleaners were here. As she was leaving, she made some personal comment about you, confidential, which I would never repeat. She kissed the fingers on one of her hands and planted an imaginary kiss."

"… And the third?"

Christ! Was this Sherlock Holmes she'd been seconded to?

Peter answered for her. "The third… was yours. Presumably inebriated."

She bowed her head low and nodded.

"Val. Let's just say our first physical contact has been a disaster. But what you should know, and should have been told, is that working with me, or the Chairman, come to that, there's a degree of decorum required. Our images are not to be defiled by those who ought to know better, and be able to pass the message down that there are certain things which are taboo."

"I'm sorry. I can see I've let you down. But I do have to say that what you've explained is all very well, but as you know, I have… oh dear… worked for the Chairman when Vera's been away, and his ideas are that when you're privileged to work close to those at Executive level, you're part of the inner circle and… as he explained… when you're in the castle and the drawbridge is up, you can relax, and almost party.

"I can see I'm in deep trouble, but I'm not going to be put down without a fight. There are two or three things you must be told, and some I more or less believed.

"Mr William started my first secondment by welcoming me into his office. His first words were, 'So you're the young lady sent in as my relief secretary'. I said, 'Yes Sir' and… well, I won't say too much but some would say he was on the way to exposing himself to me. I was quick to step back and say that I didn't know what he meant but I didn't like the suggestion… if I'd got it right.

"He told me Jo had apparently started that way with you. You know, I mean being offended… but he assured me she'd 'come round', as he put it, and had managed to hold her job on a balanced business and social basis…"

Peter interrupted. "Did you actually believe that?"

"I had no alternative. That was months ago. I wouldn't have known if it was true or otherwise. But then when Jo, I was told, upped and left because somebody in the office was caught with you, I thought it probably was all true.

"Then Jan Roberts… being in love with you… although that may have been all drink, I don't know. Then there was the Chairman with Sylvia Pez."

"What the hell about her?" Peter said crossly.

"Well I'd rather not tell you about that but all this is coming out unexpectedly. So here goes. There was a day when you were away and the Chairman told Sylvia he was expecting some visitors that evening in the office, and asked if she could stay late for a short while and help out with some translating, because they were Spanish. Sylvia's all right and doesn't seem to have any serious ties, and she said she would oblige.

"The next morning she told me what had happened. She was still a bit distressed, and I'd say she's pretty worldly. A girl as attractive as her is bound to have been chased around the odd desk or two, or even, with her style, or around some yacht in St Tropez.

"Anyway, the visitors hadn't turned up by about 7 o'clock, so Sylvia buzzed the Chairman to see what she should do and how long to wait. She got no answer so she came up to see if he was alright.

"He was alright and proceeded to tell her what she should really have been waiting for, if she'd used her loaf. Apparently he staggered from behind his desk and thrust his arms around her. She pushed him away but he kept going, saying that he would fire her if she didn't play ball, and how else did she expect to get her Christmas bonus. He's apparently quite strong and was close to forcing her to the ground."

"How did she get out of that, or are you going to tell me she didn't?"

"Put bluntly… she apparently kneed him in the balls, and ran."

"… And the next day?"

"Well, he told personnel to fire her. She came and saw me and told me all about it… I spoke to him and although he was very grumpy about it, he said he'd had too much to drink and it had worked adversely with some tablets he was taking, and he didn't remember a thing about it. Although, strangely, he remembered enough to want to fire Sylvia.

"In the end, he said she could stay, providing she showed him the respect he deserved. And she has stayed, I'm pleased to say. That's another story, because she really has to work."

They sat in silence for a while. Val was hoping that her pulse rate would calm down, while Peter was trying to work out how best he could use the tales, which he felt sure she'd told correctly and for his best interests.

Val broke the silence. "Does Mr William know you're back?"

"No. Not as far as I know, that's unless Perry's passed the word around."

"What about Jan Roberts?"

"I don't think so."

"So you don't know they're both in the boardroom with sandwiches and wine and probably a cauldron, which they're sitting round plotting, for the good of BCG and bad news for you, I would say."

"I'll go and say hi. That'll surprise them."

"Jan asks if you're back every time she rings. She obviously needs you for something. I hinted you may be back tomorrow when she asked this morning."

"OK. So… is there anything I should see on my desk?"

"There's loads, and there's a paper produced by International to be added to the agenda for Thursday."

"Where? Be a pal and find it quickly, could you please."

Peter realised it would take a while to gel with Val, and she was off to quite a difficult start.

She walked in front of him and laid her hands straight on a bound copy in which there were about ten one-sided A4 sheets of paper.

"I'll look at this quickly."

"You hadn't noticed Sylvia came up with your tea but tactfully left it in my office. It'll be cold. I'll make you another pot."

It seemed Peter wasn't listening. Val left, centre stage, tightly closing the double doors.

The paper was headed 'Five years in Europe – a summary to date'. The last page had the summary. In a snapshot, it showed a range of £1 million to £3 million in turnover contributions to the Group. There were no overheads or profit figures, as far as Peter could see. He thought to himself, *I'll have to do one called five weeks in a part of Europe – a forecast to date*, and smiled at the prospect.

He tugged his jacket, straightened his tie and set off to surprise William.

"What about your tea?" Val said as he passed back out through her office.

"I'll be back."

"Please stay and drink your tea."

There was something of a plea in her tone. He waited. She must have a reason.

"I've got something that will help."

"How can you have that? Unless you know what agenda William and Jan Roberts are hatching up."

"It's only girl talk, you'll understand. But its reasonably common knowledge that Jan is hurt by the disappointing end the two of you came to in Spain."

"How did you know about that?"

"I told you, she called in here one day when she got back. I'd say she wanted to do some bonding with me as the new incumbent, and one thing led to another and she sat having tea with me fairly late into the afternoon. She wanted to talk. She suggested we go to the wine bar and have a glass of wine. I was feeling down too, so we popped across to Hunters. I said how I was worried about how Mr William was ganging up against you... she surprised me by saying you deserved it... I didn't agree, and out poured her disappointment at having looked after you in Palafrugell and how, quite frankly, you could look after yourself from now on.

"Then I think we both got pissed and it ended up with her telling me how she was scared for you too, and that Mr William was concerned at how you'd got your feet under each of the divisional tables. Housing was your natural ability, and that's why you're here, but you've got too much say in construction already. Now the old guard believe you're making inroads into engineering and it looks plain for anybody to see, after the private funded hospital deals, that you fancy Europe and International overall. You've got blood in the Far East and South America, you seem to know the USA, and all that is what Mr William sees as his domain. Jan told me all that and capped it by saying something quite weird."

"What was that, or is it a girlie secret?"

"Let's say I'm worried you're going to get the wrong impression of me and that if I sneak on Jan Roberts so soon, I might do the same to you."

"I think I would have to say that's a bit over the top. Look, Val. I accept you're in a position of trust. I'll take my chances about where I expect your loyalties to lie."

"Then you ought to know I'll be glad to tell you to get it off my chest." Her habit of blushing became more evident. "What Jan said was that William won't give up Europe because of the trips. I immediately thought drugs, but she said I would undoubtedly notice. When there's racing at Longchamps, he had an enforced business trip to France. Coinciding with the Grand Prix in Monaco, his mates down in the south of France would arrange for him to meet some mayor in charge of a road project down on the Riviera, subject to EEC funding. He apparently never has business meetings. Which leads one to believe there's no business to deal with, and the trips are pure pleasure. In anybody else in the company, it would be lies. But it's apparently, so I was told, his way of getting some petty cash out and some perks."

"But Val, he's got enough money to live abroad all year if he wanted to."

"Well, apparently, years back, he got into heavy gambling debts and his mother bailed him out, without his father or anyone else knowing."

"Except you now!"

"No. Except a disgruntled ex-employee who spilt the beans to Jan before you came on the scene."

"Female?" Peter enquired.

"Yes."

"That figures. What's your English expression about fury?" Peter asked.

"Hell hath no fury like a woman scorned," she replied.

"That's it."

"Well, whatever... anyway, his mother said 'Be a good boy, never gamble again' and they had a pact to keep it from his father, I suppose."

"No. Never go to the races again," Peter corrected her. "So he then convinced his old man the French he'd learnt at Harrow made him the heir apparent to Europe, and off he'd go on a series of gambling jollies with all his mates, letting his father believe it's business calling. Now he still hangs on to International, which gets him to Barbados with the trainers and jockeys in January, Antigua for the cricket, Australia for the Melbourne Cup. He does the trips. Never totally declares, if you think back, where he's going and talks about speculating for two or three years' hence, but that never comes. That's certainly got a ring of truth about it, Val."

"That's right, but in your absence, since I've been a bit bored, I've been a bad girl."

"What now?" Peter asked, with a hint of trepidation. What else was about to be revealed?

"Well, I think I'd plucked up courage to tell you about those trips anyway, but I thought I would try and check whether what Jan Roberts had said was completely true, since she'd been slightly under the influence of drink. So I've told a chap in accounts that Mr William has asked me if I can help him out. I told him a tale about the Chairman not wanting to get Vera to do it because she'd already given him the information and he'd lost it."

"What information?"

"His expense details for the last two years because the accountants needed to do his PIIDs."

"How would that help?"

"How did it help! I got all the dates for his tickets and things and... because I was intrigued to find out... I've backtracked through the reference library behind Trafalgar Square, and I can relate a sporting event to each trip."

"That falls down sometimes, surely. After all, he was coming to Spain to see me."

"No! That's not the only reason. There's a new casino opened in Malaga."

"Come on, Barcelona's miles from Malaga!"

"Not now that we've got the King Air jet. The plan was he'd fly down there and meet up with Hugo Wolf... well, he's a young man who's inherited his father's title, boat and all... I'll keep him a bit private, but it's true! If you don't trust me, ask the two stable girls who got as far as getting their return tickets paid to Barcelona. Their job was to entertain the 'boys' on their trip between Barcelona and Malaga over a slow three-day journey... and, I might add, to be on board waiting when the casino closed or the sun came up, when the boys collected their winnings or were forced to cut their losses and return to the boat to take comfort in the cabin berths with the 'girls'. That's of course off at the moment, because you're no longer there."

"Val, you amaze me! You ought to be a spy or something. But how does it help for me to know this?"

"Well, I believe you'll find Mr William is sowing the seeds with Jan Roberts to get you 'tin-tacked', in his vernacular."

"How?"

"Simply by saying you've lost your marbles and it's outrageous for you to be bidding for his part of the empire when he has International sewn up. He's apparently enraged by your questioning his division's success strike rate in Europe."

Peter thought for a moment or two. "And Jan Roberts' role?" he asked. "The woman scorned? So she'll join in the chopping process, I expect."

Val shook her head. "She's got a real soft spot for you. She's furious about some South African girl. I don't know the whole story behind that... but at the end of the day... Jan's a nice person... she won't, I think, see you put down. She doesn't like Mr William. She calls him the lecher."

Peter was amazed. It was a lot to take in.

"Well, it's good to be back, about to be tin-tacked. I'd best get in to see the Chairman."

"Do you want these?"

Val opened her second drawer down and held out a whole ream or so of A4 paper, held together with two or three bulldog clips.

"What the hell are those?"

"William's expense reimbursement claim forms."

"Bloody agony! You're turning out to be wonder woman."

Peter readjusted his suit. Checked his tie and smoothed his hair.

"The second tea has met the fate of Sylvia's earlier one. They're both cold. I'll make you a fresh one when you come back."

At the boardroom door, Peter knocked lightly and had just turned the polished brass door handle when a somewhat startled William answered simply, "Yes," to whoever was going to interrupt him.

Peter entered quickly. He spoke first. "Heard you were here, William, couldn't not say hi and I'm pleased to be back." He feigned total surprise to see Jan. "Ah Jan! Now this really is a pleasant surprise! Bastard Spanish engineers cut my bloody phone off because the bill hadn't got through, so couldn't let you know I was coming back. No… don't tell me. I look a wreck. But I've been travelling. You look a million dollars." He took both her hands as she involuntarily stood up to greet him, and also brushed his cheek with hers. "You look *so* good. What a double surprise."

Her stomach had filled with every butterfly she had ever seen and felt in her life.

William's inner parts were far from being overtaken by the Papillon families. They were more like a bad night in Delhi with too much beer with his old school mates, who had been sent abroad so as not to further to disgrace their families and ancestors. William's hand was sweaty by comparison with Jan's cool cheek. No perspiration broke on her brow but it did on William's.

"You're back," William said in surprise, taking Peter's outstretched hand without attempting to hide his natural habit of boasting at being a Freemason and checking if the person he was greeting was too.

Peter and Jan flashed each other a glance on an intellectually much higher plateau, a glance that said 'obviously'.

"Obviously… you weren't expecting me. So what great plot are you two concocting?" Peter said with a cheeky grin.

William was not at his best when he had not rehearsed a particular scenario. He tended to bluster his way into an area of quicksand, which he only survived if he had supporters to save him from sinking further.

"Plot? Concocting… none of that. We were just talking through a release about the International Division, which I must say was stimulated by your presence over there in that corner of Europe, where obviously you've been fuelled by our level of activity already with our EEC neighbours."

"Balls," Peter said firmly.

Jan looked surprised. William countered with a, "What?"

Peter returned with a volley. "Balls! It's all very disappointing, in fact. If it wasn't for what Jan set up in Spain, with the hospital deals, it would all look a very bleak return for the time and overheads being spent."

"What?" William said on impulse, as though Harrow had not exactly stretched him on the vocabulary front.

"You say I've been fuelled by our level of activity with our EEC neighbours. William, old chap, there's not even enough going on to give the village fire brigades anything to stop playing pétanque over."

"Now come on, Peter. It's early days, and five million, I'd say, is no mere contribution to the group. It's five per cent we would miss, as with any element of turnover."

"Jan, make sure you only write down the good stuff, would you? For a start, if it were £5 million, that's sterling not pesetas, it would be two and a half per cent of turnover. But it's nowhere near five. I'd say more in the range of between £1 million in an ordinary year and three at the most. I doubt we've grossed £10 million in as many years… and I'm talking

International Division, which includes the Middle East water treatment deal, which we still haven't been paid for, and there's doubt as to whether the bond will pay up. Take two per cent net profit out of that and it doesn't even pay for your play weekends."

Jan saw William prickle.

"Now look here, Peter. I'll make allowance for you still being ill. I'll cover your backside while you're away, but I will not have you making wild allegations and dragging me into comments like that! I'm telling you, keep your nose out of International. It's my responsibility and I'm happy with its performance. It's not an agenda item. There'll be a report. If the Board want it to become an item for Board discussion at the following meeting, OK, but once an individual element of the Group comes up for scrutiny, then the whole activity of each division must be treated similarly."

"And that's exactly what I'd ask. That means I'll have to raise issues my way. We'll be talking resignations on Thursday."

"What! What the hell are you on, Peter? I'd heard your brain had slipped. Who's up for 'resignation'? I'm certainly not up for that sort of talk. I want you to know I've been in the group as an integral player for 36 years and I'll damn well see another equal span if I have my way."

Peter laughed. "It's called paranoia, or 'persecution complex', in the psychology books. I'm not talking your resignation. I'm talking mine."

Jan looked horrified. "But you can't, Peter!"

"Can't? Don't you English say there's no such word as can't?"

"Well, there is, and you can't. Can he, William?"

"Look, Jan. The Group ran well before he came in. I don't doubt it will continue to run if he leaves the ship."

"It's not a question of leaving the ship. The bloody ship is fine, solid, safe as houses. It's just we've got too many captains and some don't steer in the right lanes."

"You've really lost it, Peter. You had such a good brain. We'll get you all the help we can through the insurance policies. We'll put welfare on your case. We'll get you sorted, old son. We'll do it gradually so as not to create a furore. Jan, you'll see to that, won't you?"

Peter fired with all cannons. "No we bloody well won't! I go in to the meeting on Thursday and I either walk out, if that's the wish of the Board, and Jan goes into the market talking and sees our share price drop by 50 per cent. Now the Board won't be easily convinced, I agree, by a bloke with brain damage. So if it can't be achieved, yes, I do the decent thing and go. Leaving you, as I've said, with all your playthings. You can even get to Malaga with your boys and girls without needing to drop off and deliver my bunch of grapes and a few magazines."

William's mouth dropped open. "What the hell do you mean by that?"

"Don't press me, Chairman. Enough said. You know that."

"No, you don't say something clearly mischievous without amplifying it. It needs to be seen that you're saying unbalanced things."

"Jan, you'd best take this down. Your trip, which is already funded, is to Barcelona at the cost of International. You have one appointment now in the City, or to be precise on the outskirts, that's to pick up Miranda and Tracy, stable girls who happen to be a Group overhead... yes and flown out with tickets bought by the Group, although they don't service company property or goods. Neither will there be horses for them to attend to on your cosy mate's gin palace, quietly floating down the coast from Barcelona. You can then do your normal sort of report to the Board when you get back, on the prospects of business for the Group in Spain. But you'll find I've already wrapped everything up."

William turned towards Jan. "Jan, can you see he's deranged?"

"No, William. What I see is the Peter who always was. He's got something up his sleeve and he needs access to the Board to inform them what he's got in mind. If you want to convince me otherwise, you tell me your version of the reason for your Malaga trip. Make no mistake, it's of no concern to me, financially. I'm not a shareholder and your expense account is none of my business. If, however, Peter's version is right, then if I were in your shoes, I'd hear him out on Thursday and beg him to let you join in with him on whatever he says he's already sewn up.

"One thing seems clear. He hasn't been wasting away in some hospital having his knee bent all day long... and as for being deranged... I don't think so. On the other front, about you playing around, we all know you do. Let's ask... who were they, Miranda and Tracy... if they've got plans for the weekend. If they giggle, then wherever and whoever spilled the beans has it right."

William was exceedingly red-faced by now. His blood pressure was well up... but he soon calmed down. Jan's voice had lulled him out of his tantrum.

"What's the deal you're looking for, Peter?"

"Just for International to be put on an aggressive footing, out there winning real growth in a Europe that has far more going for it than many of the other places you visit where, I'm sure, personal pleasures have been more important than business ones."

"The deal?" William demanded, with raised tones.

"The deal would be if I hold the Board's attention to my European plans, International comes under my wing. You move over to a pivotal figurehead role, say president, or something like that. We bring in one of the non-Executive knights as Chairman. We strengthen the accounting function and marketing, and we go for real growth. 100 per cent increase in three years. Turnover and higher profit earnings by acquisition and territorial expansion."

William had remained silent for one of those embarrassing two minutes or so, which seem a lifetime.

"Suppose I'll have to hand it to you, you've got more spies out there than I have. So if you really do know what's going on, your plans must be good for my family interests. We're major shareholders and to double the worth of that would indeed gain the president brownie points in the eyes of my blood relatives. I'll listen on Thursday with an open mind. If your plan is as good as you say, I'll move over... it will be my idea, you understand. My move to strengthen the Group... you'd see to that in the papers, wouldn't you, Jan?"

She looked at Peter. He didn't need to nod. She read every page of him like a book, and cursed herself for still loving him so much.

"Yes. There's a deal, Chairman. Now, if you two stags have used my presence enough, I must go. I'm due somewhere by four. I'll just make it. Can I presume we'll all be friends again?"

"William, what do you say?" Peter asked.

"Yes, of course. You're too lovely to be an enemy," said William, directing his comments to Jan.

"Peter?"

"William stole my line."

Jan smiled. She took William's hand and squeezed it. "Get home. Get some rest. Pack in these young bits of fluff." She moved round to Peter. "Good to have you back." She said no more.

"Don't I get any worldly advice?"

"I've given you yours."

He stood, mesmerised. "What was that?"

"If you can't remember that, I'd say your brain *has* gone and you must really be deranged."

She turned and left, disguising the joy she felt at confusing Peter totally.

"What was that about, Peter?" William too was intrigued.

"To be honest, William, I have no idea at all. Absolutely no idea. But I'll work it out. That's for sure."

Peter reported back some of the points of the discussion to Val. She'd been very supportive, but he wasn't sufficiently assured of her loyalty or, more precisely, not convinced she would not sell out to a higher bidder to tell her all.

"Well, Jan Roberts seemed pleased with the way the meeting went. She put her head round the door as she left, winked and gave me the thumbs up. What was that all about?"

"I've actually got no idea," said Peter, thinking back to Jan's words.

He did another hour or so in the office. He phoned each of the non-Execs and said he was back and looking forward to bending their ears on Thursday. They liked that approach. He was cavalier by the standards of the other directors, who tended to report fact and more fact. Peter preached impulse, feel, emotion, which, they felt sure, spelt out excitement and growth.

Chapter 23

Fred had pulled up at exactly at 4.45pm, as Peter had requested. Peter thanked Val for her support, then walked down the heavily carpeted stairs, avoiding the lift. One part of him said he needed the exercise, the other that his knee hurt... and inwardly he was perplexed not quite knowing why Val was so keen to drop William in the cart. He wasn't sure about her.

Sylvia looked surprised to see him enter reception through the staircase door. Most were bone idle, she worked out, and used the lift just through the one storey. She smiled and he returned the sentiment.

In three strides, he was towering over her. On instinct, she stood up to try to level the second encounter of the day.

"Do you have a coat, Sir?"

"No. I can't afford one." Which was something he often said when he found himself underdressed for the climatic conditions. London was an appreciable 15 degrees Fahrenheit lower in temperature than Barcelona.

"You mustn't catch cold. There's more of a chill here than in Barcelona."

She was obviously a very kind person, he thought.

"Listen," he said confidentially, "I've been catching up on little bits and pieces of goings-on in my absence. Could I apologise on behalf of the Board?"

Sylvia looked puzzled. She didn't want to look silly, nor did she want to show that she didn't know what he meant. Peter thought he read that situation too. So he explained to put her at ease.

"About the Chairman's advances to you."

"Oh," she said, now embarrassed and not knowing what to say.

"I just hope you understand that's not how we all behave..."

Why the hell not? she thought silently.

"But he's been under a lot of pressure lately and... well, I don't know what your experience of men is, but... occasionally we do silly things."

"Not you, Sir, though, I'm sure," she said in a complimentary way.

This time he laughed. "Haven't you heard I've got a shot-up leg?"

"They say you've mended up well," she said with a broad smile, half-wishing she had just kept quiet.

"Listen, if we go on like this, you'll be suggesting you give me a three-metre start around the desk..."

She decided not to respond and returned in a serious vein. "Sir, I really don't think you're doing yourself justice… but I hugely appreciate the apology."

"That's OK… Sylvia, isn't it?"

"Yes."

"Which part of South America?"

"Buenos Aires."

"Oh shit!"

"I don't often hear that reaction."

"I'm sorry. My wife is from there too. I'll see you in the morning. Good night."

Sylvia was about to ring Val on the intercom when the lift doors parted. William was standing there, smiling a false, embarrassed smile.

"So how's my beauty?" he asked.

Her tone was very different from the one she had with Peter. "Sir. I don't consider myself to be your beauty. Would you mind, Sir, showing me the courtesy of that."

"Bitch!" he muttered under his breath. "I'd sack her, if it was down to me." Fortunately this was drowned out by the desk phone ringing. Sylvia's monitor indicated it was Val calling.

"Hi!" Sylvia was animated.

"Hi," came the reply. "So you've met the chief now, eh?"

"Yes, and he seems a very fine Englishman." Then, remembering that he wasn't English, she corrected herself by saying, "A gentleman is what I mean."

"Keep your eyes off, honey. He doesn't know it yet but he'll be buying me dinner."

"So lucky you. Seriously, he's the most gentleman of any here."

"True," Val said, "I bet he's been laying on the charm with you to get that sort of accolade though, and you've fallen for it."

"Did he divorce his wife?"

"Good God, no!"

"Oh. He spoke of her but I've been told he's now a bachelor."

"He would. He always speaks of her in the present tense, I understand. She's dead."

"Oh God! No!" Sylvia pondered while she took in the pain of that. "Poor man," she said sadly.

"Come on. I think he milks that one quite effectively."

"How did she die?"

"I think in a car smash in South America."

"Oh hell!"

"Listen, as I've said, he's on to buy me dinner," Val said defensively.

"Good. Well done," Sylvia said, as though Val had won the Oscar of that day.

The beauty about living where Peter did was that, despite the traffic, he was home within 15 minutes. It felt good to put the key Perry had had cut, whilst he had been at the office, into the door he felt led to home. He'd been in other beds for too long.

He boiled some water in the kettle, made a peppermint tea and took it through into the spacious lounge. There was his favourite chair and he put what he believed to be personal mail on the leather inlaid side table. He'd turned again to the answerphone with its 20 waiting messages. He'd have to leave those and the mail until later. He was bushwhacked, but then, he told himself, he had been travelling and then gone through that harrowing time with William.

And what the hell had Jan meant? Knowing her, it would all become clear eventually.

He came to with a start. The French antique clock looked as though it said 6.40pm. His watch said 7.40pm, but then he realised he was still on European time. His empty cup sat on its saucer on the floor by the side of the chair. He got up and went to his en suite bathroom to use the loo.

He took The Times and the Financial Times with him as he passed the coffee table, where they had been laid out by Mrs Brown. He hadn't checked the Group's share price for weeks. 230p wasn't good. At that level, there was a danger of there being a predator around. They would really have to do better than that. Ramon's deal would certainly help, and so would William being shunted out of an operational role, he was sure.

Peter was back to the start of his usual routine. Abluting and reading. He rinsed his hands, took out his toilet bag from his light travel holdall and located his electric razor. That, run around the curves of his face and chin for a couple of minutes, would freshen him up. He took his Cartier balm from one of the glass shelves alongside the vanity unit and smoothed it into the permanent creases in his face. They used to be laughter lines, he thought. No longer. They were there for good. He was ageing.

He went back to the lounge. Poured out a whisky with just ice from the fridge built into the side unit, and settled down to a good read, and to listen to his messages. He knew Coco's letters would be full of feeling, so he dealt those out to himself as though setting up a hand of bridge. Wow, he thought. I could probably get a game in one hand. He'd have to see about that.

"My darling Peter

You poor darling, dear papa. Who could do that to you? If I'd stayed on, this wouldn't have happened. Don't worry, if you don't get better, I'll kill myself and join you and look after you and care for you and love you in heaven."

He could hear her saying every word in her rapid Oriental pitch. Soppy little thing. *There was never any way I was going to be dead and to think of her killing herself...* he thought.

She'd obviously seen Madame Butterfly again. That always made her over-emotional, over-protective, he thought.

Coco went on to say how she couldn't concentrate on work, wasn't eating and spent most of the day praying when her colleagues thought she was preparing the regional figures. *"Don't worry, I've still done the figures and they are right because they check out. I'm like you, I can multi-task. Thank you for implanting that ability into my body."*

Her body, he thought. *Christ, her body, and her mother's*. He thought of Cas, and then Jan, Marcia and then way back through visions of previous flesh he'd had the privilege and joy to encounter. Anna he had never seen in that powerfully physical way. No one compared with that Malaysian mother and daughter.

I'll continue to pray for you and cry a lot and I know God will see me unhappy and will make you better to make me happy.

Dearest daddy Peter, God bless you. You'll be better soon. As he opened Coco's second letter, perfume wafted into his nostrils.

"My darling Peter.

I hope the Chanel will cheer you up and make you feel better (and don't go dragging that nurse into bed with you).

I've spoken to Maria..."

She had heard that Peter was beginning to make good progress and how that was God being kind to her.

The third was tracking him out of bed and when he was walking more, she'd obviously spoken to Maria again, and that was followed by, *I heard you are going to Batholona*. She had picked up the Catalan lisp and written what she had learned phonetically, which made Peter laugh.

What appeared to be the last letter in the pile from her wafted of perfume again.

'I hope you won't be cross with me for writing about myself (but to be fair, all my other ones were mainly about you and our kind God) but He's now influencing my life and I feel so happy about that because He is moving me nearer to you. Well, a couple of hours nearer anyway.

The Bank have been taken over by Hong Kong and Shanghai, you'll know it as HSBC, and I was interviewed with all the other staff and this really dishy Englishman, I think he was but he may, they say, be from Scotland. I made him fancy me! Bitch, I hear you say, but I'll do anything to get back closer to you. Anyway, he asked me if I wanted to change roles and move to the Malaysian Head office in Kuala Lumpur. What do you think? I said. I haven't got that many ties up here, friends yes, but they will always write or even love to come and see me.

Anyway…" She wrote excitedly as she would have spoken. "*… I move next week. I'll go down at the weekend and rent a flat, then I might look around to buy something, a little flat in one of the new high rises. I'm very excited. I earn a lot more money and maybe get taken out to dinner more like you showed me how. Smile! Did you smile? Do I make you smile?*

Darling Peter, I nearly didn't say, Maria says you are much better. What you should do is come to KL and recuperate. I'll make sure there is no one else staying over in the flat and we can just be with each other and sit and talk together all night… and it would be up to me to invite you into my bed and I'd slap your butt if you misbehave or lie to me!

I love you, my darling Papa. I'm so excited. I'll give you an address.
See you soon.
All my love.
Coco xxxxxx"

She made him feel so happy. She was so natural. Just like her mother. He reflected on the tragedy of that situation. One thought led to another. Cas he'd need to phone, she had said she'd be on the staff line waiting to hear. Maria he'd have to phone too.

He thought long and hard about Jan. To be fair, she'd looked good. Trimmer perhaps, and intellectually rewarding. Maybe he'd ring her and thank her.

William sprang to mind too and in that context, new girl Sylvia. It suddenly occurred to him that it was Petra, his daughter, she reminded him of. God, he must speak to her and Alex, who he knew was trying to arrange dinner in the next couple of days. *What's that about?* he thought. He was busy again.

He thumbed through the rest of the envelopes. Those where he recognised the handwriting he opened.

Max's letter was cheerful. "*So the great man up above nearly got you this time…*"

Jaimé took the emotional approach. "*… And I never imagined potential sadness could come out of the beautiful garden of Eden we created.*" He always saw it as a joint effort.

There were even a couple of get well soon cards signed on a multiple basis. *All at BCG* was one. *All in Housing* another, and similar from the secretary at the Girasol golf club. One very proper one said: *…we send you every best wish from all of us. Sincerely, Major J Hackett at the bridge club.*

Peter's tailor asked if he would need to change the cut of his suit. That was Jewish humour for you. The girls at the hairdressers had seen it as 'the news' and hoped to see him soon, and all sent a mixture of hugs, kisses and love in varying degrees of sincerity.

When Peter reached her, Cas seemed a bit flat.

"What's your news?" she had said. "I've got very little here," as though to record that Peter had been the life and soul of the place in the relatively short time he had been there. She seemed, disappointingly to Peter, to say she was more scared about the forthcoming weekend than excited. Now if that had been Coco, he thought, it would be all about what she'd wear, where they'd go, what she'd eat. What a difference a few shifts in latitude and longitude made. Still, Cas said her plane would get in at 3.30pm and yes, she seemed excited when he said he would be at the airport.

When Peter spoke to Maria, she was fine and said she had already left three messages on the answerphone because he hadn't rung and she thought the plane might have crashed. Which, he reassured her, it hadn't. Tania was no better. The hotel staffing had been temporarily sorted out and the hospital where Tania was were still advising no visitors. Marco was pretty down, so was Virginia. Maria and José had enjoyed meeting with him and Cas (which actually meant she hadn't gone down too well, otherwise Maria would have tried to marry them off on the spot so that her boy was well catered for), he should say hi to Jan when he saw her (which meant Maria still approved of her, as she had intimated)... "Oh, and wish all the best to Marcia at the wedding. Let me know what she wears... take some photos even... and of Cas too."

They exchanged their undying love for each other, mother to son and the reverse, and she was gone, satisfied they'd had their chat.

Peter next caught up with Jan. He'd checked his watch, which was now well back on UK time, which won him an hour yet told him he was one hour more tired than his timepiece led him to believe. It was eight. She'd either be out, on the phone or in the bath, which was her way of switching off and relaxing.

The phone rang about six or seven rings and he braced himself for the answerphone. It was always a hurried message. "Hi, it's Jan. I'm out. Love a message. Call you." Then two or three beeps. Peter didn't like it because it made him leave a message at the same sort of pace.

"Hi..." There was no message.

"Hi, is that Jan's answerphone?"

"Funny," she replied in person. "I field calls at home most of the time. I saw it was you. So yes, it's Jan in person."

"Hi. I didn't really get the chance earlier to say hello and how are you?"

"Oh, that doesn't matter. You were straight into 'stags at war mode'. I understand."

"Wow. Tell me about it. The knives are out, aren't they?"

"You could say that."

"Anyway. The question. How are you? You looked good."

"Thank you. I am good." Little did she want to say she'd found a new gym with a personal fitness trainer, and a new hairdresser, which the bugger hadn't noticed.

"Good. I'm pleased about that. Jan, I appreciate I upset you."

"Oh. That was at the time. You were right." She gritted her teeth as she said it. "Anyway, enough of that. What can I do for you? Not a post mortem on the afternoon, I hope."

So what was Peter phoning her about? He wondered too.

"Was it that bad?"

"Let's put it this way: there was so much testosterone being splashed around, I'm still quite randy."

"Hey. That's not like you to say things like that."

"Oh come on. I'm joking."

"Have you eaten?"

"No."

"What say you to a quick bite and a chat?"

"What, because I'm randy? Lovely idea, Peter, but I'm about to go out to eat. I'd love to. But I'm pre-booked."

"By a he or she?"

"Hey, mind your own business."

"Then it's a she. Why not stand her up?"

"Cheeky bugger. It's a he."

He was surprised. "Does he know you're a danger if you're randy?"

"Listen, my sweet. I'm still a lady at heart, despite what you'd like me to be, and I'm unlikely to tell him that. I might just scare him off. Hey, listen. He's here. Must fly. Give me a call after Thursday."

"Jan, just quickly… what was the worldly advice?"

She laughed, "Pull the other one. You know bloody well."

"I'd say 'love you', it's trendy. But I'd best keep it to 'see you!' Take care."

"OK. See you."

She was gone. He was no more the wiser.

From her end of the connection, he was gone too, even though she'd been the one to hang up. She could have talked on. She might have even accepted to see him for dinner, perhaps to unwind her pent-up emotions. It wasn't being present at the fight, it was seeing him again that had stimulated her emotions… to an extent, it was that which had overcome the hurt caused at a distance.

She brushed tears away from both cheeks. *Sod it*, she thought. That would ruin the contact lenses she still was not completely used to since the Friday before. She flicked the answerphone on to record; the zero digit showed again, which she had so often hoped would change to any other number, as long as it contained his voice. His call.

Jan loosened her blouse and walked solemnly towards the bedroom and her modernised en suite. She'd have a bath. Relax, and cry a little. Nobody was calling round this evening. Unless, of course, he called her bluff and appeared at the door. So she'd best put her hair up in combs, to keep it away from too much moisture, just in case.

Peter felt alone for the first time in many months. He could shoot off in a taxi for a game of bridge. Was Jan making up the tale about the date? Why the hell should she? She wasn't dependent on his call, certainly not after him letting her down as he had…

He suddenly realised she hadn't enquired after 'the Bok'. Did she not care? *Christ*, he thought, *she was full of it a couple of weeks back*. Hell, he'd been through a lifetime in the last couple of months. Coco, Jan, Cas and now William. He leant back in the chair.

The phone rang. Jan! She'd put off the girlfriend.

"Hi," he said chirpily, not wanting her to know she'd confused him.

"Oh. You can sound so happy but you can't return any one of my ten or a dozen calls, can you?"

"Bloody hell, Marcia! I've only been back a few hours. I haven't played my messages back yet."

"Well, listen darling. Don't bother. They all say what the fuck are you doing not saying you'll come to my special night for you."

Peter laughed. "My darling, sweet, beloved Marcia. We've done your 'special' night so many times we could have more chickens than Buxton has turkeys. Besides, you've said yes to your new man and I want you to save yourself for the honeymoon."

"Look, sweetheart, there's no way anyone would get near to replacing you on a honeymoon. Think of your poor Marcia. Back into wedded bliss and having to make all the right noises about being satisfied. You must know this isn't going to be anything other than a marriage of convenience."

"Marcia. That's tragic."

"Not half as tragic as the marriage not being to you."

"We've been down that route so many times. It's not news."

"So… Thursday. The last time. I promise."

"Marcia. I've got heavy Board meetings and I'm away mostly for them."

"OK. For you darling – special. I'll change arrangements. Wednesday. You can't have an excuse for that night if you're just back."

"Excuse, no! I'm seeing Alex." Which prompted him to call his personal line in the office which Val would pick up an answerphone message to fix with Alex, to make what he'd said true.

"Shit. Why?"

"He's my son."

"What about daytime? We've done that. Lunch at Langan's, I'll get a room. Please. Help me make this wedding thing more palatable… you've got to say yes." Suddenly her tone changed. "Shit, Peter darling. Have to go. I'll call you."

So God was looking down on him. He presumed the fiancé had returned early or unexpectedly.

He leant deep back into his chair and laughed. She wouldn't change. "So what now?" he said out loud. He'd call Alex and fix up dinner for

Wednesday. It seemed pretty important, according to Val. Then why not do what all the females in his life would do under similar lone circumstances: have a bath and go to bed.

He was immediately into his regular 'just minutes before nine' slot. So was Sylvia. She was obviously a morning and evening person. She looked sparkling and uncreased, as she had yesterday. No wonder William couldn't contain himself. But she had a certain dignified style about her. It certainly was not brazen enough for one to expect the body to be supported by white stiletto heels, or to speak without an 'h' at the beginning or a 'g' at the end of their words, or be prepared to make a living from mucking out horses.

It crossed his mind yet again that William had no understanding of people, and... yes... he was a plonker.

They greeted each other in Spanish, which gave them common ground over which to giggle. Peter left for his office by the stairs, with a brief, "Have a good day."

"Yusted, señor," Sylvia replied with a smile.

Val was already in the outer office. "Morning, Peter," she said heartily. "You've got a skip in your step."

"Do you know, Val, I've had the best night's sleep for months. I really do feel refreshed."

"Good, because you've got a bit of a week ahead."

"I've fixed dinner with Alex for Wednesday."

"Good, he'll be pleased about that."

"You need to speak to all the non-Execs. Oh, maybe Jan too... she seems as though she'd got a new skip in her step as well, doesn't she?"

"I think maybe there's a new man around. It makes girls dance a bit. You must know that, surely."

"Sure. Who's the guy?" Peter often agreed with people in order to flush out the next piece of information.

"Oh. You know Jan. She heaps publicity all day, but when it gets to her own life, the shutters come down."

"True," Peter said, in a preoccupied way. The thought of some other fellow stimulating Jan's taste buds didn't appeal to him.

He gave Val his preferred batting order for the three knighted non-Execs. Sir Bob Hall was the most influential and, in Peter's view, the most use to the Board. If there was to be a new Chairman from within, he would be Peter's man. The fact that Sir Bob was good was a bit of an accident. Peter was sure that William had chosen the non-Execs on the basis of whether they had boxes in the places where he hadn't. One certainly did have that arrangement at Goodwood and the Royal Albert Hall, the other was exceedingly 'in' at the Royal Yacht Club and always had pleasant parties during Cowes Week and Henley. Sir Bob just had keys to very many situations through his directorships with other major companies, and a long history in banking.

As he waited to be connected to Sir Bob, Peter remembered he'd actually been, or even was, on the Board of HSBC... it would be too early, and not the point of his conversation, to warn him to watch out for his job because there was a new young lady in the organisation destined to take the rug from under his feet. The thought of that made him smile. In fact, the thought of Coco made him happy.

Sir Bob always started a conversation somewhat formally and with the appearance of being aloof. Then his army days would filter through him and he became quite a mucker, keen to talk about some current affair or other, be it cricket, the political scandal of the day or simply the weather... and what he had seen in his Berkshire garden at six o'clock on that summer's morning.

"Hello, Peter. Now, how mended up are you? Not going to overdo it, eh! You've had a bashing, by all accounts. William wants you to ease up. Anyway, how are you?"

Peter also reciprocated formally and then lapsed. "Nice of you to ask, Sir Bob. Look, I hope you know me well enough that if I was crocked, I'd know it was in my own best interests, and foremost the Group's, to lay up for a while, or even be honest enough to move out. Would you agree?"

"Yes. I would, Peter."

"OK. Well, if I say I'm mentally at something like 99.99 per cent, physically 80-85 per cent and climbing, and in terms of disappointment with our share price, 100 per cent, how would you assess me?"

"Well, they're interesting stats. I'm pleased about the brain and the body bits. Why do you say you're so unhappy with the share price?"

"When I was brought into BCG, the price steadied. As I took more executive control, the shares rose through a cautious five-ten per cent, then 20 per cent, and were 30 per cent and rising. Four weeks ago, the price sank dramatically and Jan Roberts says the word on the street was that I'd had it and the old regime would take everything back that they'd given up in their previous wisdom, which was a sop to the pressure from the institutional shareholders to get to a better level of performance. Having a mare who was winning on the various racecourses was no mark by which the Group could any longer be judged by the young Execs who'd come out of their Harvards and Henleys with brighter ideas and larger aspirations in terms of their personal bonuses.

"The market doesn't know yet that Housing is going to come through stronger than forecast by the year end. We should be 300 completions ahead of target. That's ten per cent up in just nine months, which of course, they'll be told. Construction turnover is up but profit margins are up relatively more... everything else is OK, so we should have at least held our price. So why not?

"I don't have a PhD or certificate from a business school but my nose tells me that the punters got it wrong." Peter continued, "Maybe they over-reacted to my premature death but I know bloody well that, if asked, William has been saying that even if I do get back, I've lost my marbles. Why? Purely personal. He wants back in. He's the axed England cricket captain scorned and wanting to do anything to redress the position.

"So, in my view, the market sees that coming, and I know our PR team has been encouraged to promote that prospect; but, thank God, they won't without recourse to yours truly now. But to an extent they've been brainwashed and International has again been swept, thus far, under the family carpet. If they knew the sort of performance being returned in the one area where the old guard family retains control and responsibility, International, they would doubt the wisdom of William's view and see that has to be the growth area. Now that's why I've asked for some interim figures. Have you seen them?"

"Actually, Peter. Yes. I wondered why they'd been produced. If I'd had a part to play in them I wouldn't have wanted them exposed. They're crap."

"Well, that's right. William... and look, I'll explain by the end of this chat why I'm not on some sort of deranged witch hunt... is that OK with you? I'll come to that... but it has to be said, William's team internationally have just lost the drift. They see Europe particularly as an unstable collection of unmatched countries where the only areas without risk are activities in the square miles of Paris, Rome, and perhaps even Bonn, et cetera. They just don't appreciate that the natives are happy to allow that work, certainly construction, to be fought over by the Germans, the Japs, the Taiwanese and Americans, the Brits and others.

"While they're all fighting for slim margins, there's farm land being developed with EEC grants and it's the locals who know the local influential mayors and know where to take them for their perks... and it's certainly not Longchamps, Monte Carlo or some yacht in a Marina in Malaga or St Tropez. Those guys like tavernas, local wine in jugs and randy women who speak their own tongue and keep quiet about what goes on in the bedroom upstairs. So Europe isn't an extension of London, or even England at best. Our strategy is wrong. Our figures, look at them, rather prove that the rest of Europe is not showing they welcome our presence with open arms."

"Peter, supposing I say I agree with you, and would ask the question on Thursday as to what our marketing team costs are in Hong Kong, Kuala Lumpur, and elsewhere. Yet I now know, because of the report, the investment is close to nil. I'll be told we're not incurring such costs, with a degree of pride of achievement in not having made a decision to invest in such activity in those unreliable places. Who's behind asking for that report anyway? It's an eye opener to me."

"I am. For reasons other than to topple or discredit a founding family member of the Group," Peter responded.

"So, Peter, I actually do agree with you totally, and I'm pleased that you've flushed the position out for us. Oh, and by the way, the share price is lousy, I agree, and the effect that'll have on the share option scheme you've put in place for Senior Executives will be huge, fuelled with disappointment. Enthusiasm will wane and Construction, Housing, Development will slow, if not reverse. So, knowing you, you have a plan. Yes?"

"I've been in my home country Spain now, in the land of the living, for, say, four weeks. Have you heard about the funded hospital schemes?"

"Yes. Excellent."

"Well, that's come from local knowledge. But more seriously, I've stumbled on something huge. The problem I have is that it's been put to me personally, intentionally for me to arrange to give up what I'm doing here and return to Spain. The shortened version of a long story is that I have a much respected long term business friend, who I developed my first major scheme with, and a couple of others subsequently. We know each other like brothers. He's got an entrée to the paraplegic caring world over there and, by quirk of a few bent votes, I'd guess, in Switzerland, they've got the Olympics going to Barcelona."

"So they have. Not next time, the time after. Yes, I think I knew that," Sir Bob responded.

"Well, he's on the Olympic Committee and, as of Wednesday only last week, so am I. Strictly in a personal capacity, of course. Now that committee are hell bent on all construction work for the Olympic events to go to companies where the majority shareholding is held by nationals."

"Makes sense. We ought to do more of that. The Far East work that way. Carry on, Peter."

"He'd be stretched to get his share of work alone without financial support. He'd be restricted to the housing developments in the overall scheme of things. His company doesn't have the craneage and facilities for the stadia and environmental stuff. He's asked for my financial help and for me to put a hand on the tiller with him."

"Oh. That's not good news for us. Is it?"

"Well, it could be. I've got total allegiance already to what we *are* doing at BCG, should be doing, and disappointment in the current results showing areas of what we *have* been doing. I've said I would only consider going in with him if I had 51 per cent control. Now to bring that back in to BCG would mean we couldn't win contract awards as the criteria for obtaining the appointments is that the majority of shares in the appointed company have to be in native hands. But if, for example, I took 51 per cent and by agreement passed a 49 per cent stake to BGC, then my pal Ramon's, and my own 'native holding' would be 51 per cent. The benefit of having BCG behind us both is that we would become eligible, from an expertise point of view, to build everything from the starter's hut on the river for the canoeing events to the major athletics arena on Montjuic Hill.

"We're then talking potential available actual turnover of $500 million, that is at 49 per cent, about $250 million to BCG over about three years. Now what would that do to the share price? Incidentally, upfront investment would be £1 million, subject to that being made against orders received. No awards, no investment needed."

"You'd give up that 49 per cent opportunity to BCG?"

"Yes. Maybe against a personal bonus based on profitability."

Sir Bob was clearly thinking. Peter could hear the cogs churning and didn't want to interfere with that. Finally, Sir Bob cleared his throat in his nervous way.

"William is going to get in the way of all that, isn't he, if he still has his much loved International?"

"Yes."

"So we have to move him."

Peter was surprised. "It's my turn to ask: how?"

"Not sure," Sir Bob confessed. "The conventional way is promotion."

Peter smiled.

"You see, my role is as much to keep the family silver polished as to sell the odd spoon or two. No..." which is what Peter noticed he often said when he'd reasoned something through, "... I'd think offer him presidency. After all, you're not going to give this personal opportunity up in any event. You get 51 per cent, or two per cent and a fat bonus, and benefit hugely from an uplift in share price. William has more family interest in shares than anybody, so he becomes a mini hero on that side of the shareholding front and all the cousins say 'Hail to the King'."

Peter hoped his satisfaction was not showing.

"Sir Bob. You're very innovative. An asset and a joy to have the pleasure of bouncing this predicament off. There's a finesse. Oh yes, and I've seen some of those from you around the bridge table."

"What's that?"

"You become Chairman. Non-Executive, because of your other interests and time availability."

"Oh, I don't know about that," the older man said modestly, "we'd have to see."

"Look, I'm down to ring the other two non-Execs..."

"Don't do that," Bob interrupted. "If I say I'm 101 per cent behind the whole idea, would you trust me to sell it to the rest of the Board... and then deal with my finesse with William?"

"Yes, of course. But I ought to tell you I had a bit of a ding-dong with William yesterday. Principally in saying the results I'd seen on International were such that if any other Executive in the group had produced similar, in a discipline that Executive had responsibility for, he'd be toppled... and I think I hinted that might be necessary."

"Yes, I know. He told me. Then I had no idea of the game plan. Now, as I've said, I'm 100 per cent behind the idea. Topple as well. Oh Peter! By the way, I'm pleased you told me about yesterday's confrontation. I like being told what I already know, it reassures me. So… I'll see you on Thursday. London, is it, or Manchester? I haven't looked yet."

"London."

"Thank God for that! I won't have to go in that bloody toy plane. I dread that. Glad you're so much better. Show us the scars on Thursday, eh!" And he was gone.

Wow! That went well, Peter thought.

Chapter 24

The rest of Tuesday morning slipped away and with the time saved by not having to talk to the other two non-Execs, Peter slipped across to Harrods to see if he could find something as a wedding present for Marcia and William Forrester. This was when he missed Anna's influence. She would have come up with a lovely original idea. He could only think about pairs of glasses, flutes, brandy, and similar joints things. The female assistant with roots from either India, Pakistan or Sri Lanka – he could never tell – wasn't the most inspirational, so he went to the silver department just a few galleries away. That was always a safe bet.

He bought a pair of Carrs photo frames, and asked for them to be cleaned and gift wrapped. Job done, he returned to the office having ordered a sandwich through Val, which he would settle down to eat at his desk, and read the papers for the up-coming meeting. Board reports needed some studying as he always tried to do justice to them. He had also tried phoning Jan a couple of times and left a message the first time but not the second. She'd ring when she was ready.

There was a knock on the door. Usually a close colleague would walk straight in. The second knock made him realise nobody had actually followed up their presence being known by entering.

"Oh, come in," he said, in a slightly raised tone.

The door opened and Sylvia was there, silhouetted by the soft early afternoon sun entering Val's office behind her.

"Hello," Peter said quite gently, as his mood changed. "Rule number whatever: if you work here and know I'm not with anybody, you can always just knock…" he thought about it. "… To check if I'm awake, or indeed to wake me up," he said with a smile, "and then just come in."

"I'm sorry, Sir. I didn't know that. It's just that your sandwich has been delivered."

"That's fine."

He had stood up and come around from behind his desk to take the tray from her. He looked at the layout.

"Well, Sylvia, it didn't come set out like this. I usually have my sandwich in the paper bag."

She had taken a couple of plates from the cupboard in the kitchen and cut the sandwich into smaller portions, then put a paper serviette on the tray along with an empty glass and a cup and saucer.

"You've laid me out a banquet."

"Not really. I didn't know what you'd want to drink. You might have some wine hidden in your office but we have orange juice and water downstairs, or I could make you tea or coffee."

He suddenly realised that, although they normally closed for lunch from 1pm to 2pm, she was still there.

"Why aren't you at lunch?"

"Oh... I'm not going out today. I've had a sandwich and then these arrived."

"You're very kind. I don't want to get in the way of your break. I'll have an orange juice if it's not too much trouble."

"Not at all, Sir."

"Sylvia, I have a problem."

Oh hell, she thought. Why did all the men in her life have problems? Somewhat gingerly, she asked. "What is that, Sir?"

"I hate being called Sir."

"Oh, I'm sorry. What should I call you?"

"Now that's a very good point. There I have an even greater problem. Generally, the closer we work together, or one works with one another, it gets on to Christian name terms. But that's a bit early if you and I are naturally at the 'Sir' and 'Mrs Pez' stage. It *is* Sylvia Pez, isn't it?"

She was a bit flattered that he had bothered to remember her name. He'd only been back one busy afternoon and morning. He didn't quite know why he had done it, but he had checked the personnel list. *Mrs Sylvia Pez. London Office Reception* – that had to be her.

"I think the solution is simply for you to drop the 'Sir' when you address me. After all, my knowledge of South American 'stock', if I might call it that without offending you, is that in your case your family background was not in farming or one of the service industries, where servility and touching one's cap was the order of the day. I would have thought it was the other way round, with the family being on the receiving end of respect. People referring to your father and mother as Sir and madam, and yourself as Miss Sylvia."

She went coy. "Well... yes, actually."

"OK. So just drop the Sir. Think of me in your mind as Peter, I'll call you Sylvia and that will overcome my embarrassment. Mine was indeed modest Spanish stock and I doubt my father ever expected any of the family to be addressed as 'Sir'."

Sylvia laughed and turned to get the orange. She looked puzzled to hear a phone ring.

"I should be answering that. How's it come through here? The switchboard isn't on to night service."

She headed across to one of the two extensions on his desk and was about to pick the one up that appeared to be ringing.

"It's my private line."

"Oh, I'm sorry," she said, withdrawing her hand. "I'll get the orange," she added, returning towards the door.

"No. Stay, please," Peter said, as though her presence was needed.

She hesitated but did as he had asked.

"Peter Martinez," he announced into the phone, quite expecting it to be one of the non-Execs following up on Sir Bob's earlier call.

"Hi. It's good to hear your voice, knowing you're not as far away as you have been of late."

"Hi. How are you?"

"Listen, I'm rushing. That invite to eat last night… I'm sorry about that, I hope you understand."

"Of course."

"Would it be pushy if I asked if it was on offer for tonight?"

"Not at all. Can you just hold for about 30 seconds?"

"Yes, of course."

He put the phone on to mute mode. "Sylvia. Could you have a really unpretentious dinner with me tonight?"

She looked shocked.

"I'll explain later. You'll save me being a liar and being turned to stone if you say yes. Please."

"Er! I don't really know what to say."

"So that's a yes?"

"Yes."

"Great."

He pressed the mute key. "Listen, Jan, I'm really so sorry, I'm arranged. Blast it, and tomorrow I'm seeing Alex. He's desperate to talk something over with me. Thursday will be the aftermath of the Board meeting, as you well know. Friday… well, it's the lead in to a wedding… could we have a rain check early next week?"

"Bugger it. I'm away. Business trip. Look, I'll call you, OK?"

The way she put the phone down, she was either truly disappointed, angry or showing again that she needed to be number one focus. He leant back in his swivel chair and smiled broadly at Sylvia.

"Well, that's that," he said. "Thank you. I didn't have to lie. I suddenly felt I'd rather have dinner with you, finding out all about that cultured upbringing of yours, than that person."

"Was that a young lady?"

"What's the point! Yes, actually. But I meant what I said. I really would prefer to have dinner with you. Am I creating a problem? I have no idea. Is there a Mr Pez?"

"No."

"Then I undertake faithfully to mean what I say. We'll talk about South America and I promise there won't be a hint of the usual male over female conquest to see how quickly I can get you into bed. Like Mr William. Would that be a deal?"

She laughed. "I'm regretting you having hinted that you'd need a three metre handicap start but if I save you from being turned into a pillar of stone, then it sounds fun."

He remembered, he admitted to himself, that in their earlier conversation about Mr William chasing her round the desk, he had mentioned if it was him, he'd need a start in order to catch her. It was, of course, a joke but he hardly expected her to remind him.

"Where do I pick you up from?"

"Could I meet you?"

"Sure. Do you know Langan's Brasserie?"

"I've noticed it's in the contact book."

"OK. Eight o'clock."

"Yes, ideal. Will a little black dress do?"

"Absolutely. I'll give you a clue. I won't wear a tie."

"Then I'll leave off the tiara. Oh… one other thing," she added.

"What's that?"

"Could it not be too much public knowledge?"

"Of course."

"Only if it was, I think your very loyal PA might walk out on you. She says you've promised her dinner."

"What? I bloody haven't. That's not happening. I'll book a private booth. No… of course not. I'll book a quiet table. Leave it to me."

"This is all a great surprise," Sylvia said earnestly, now relaxed again, as private booths conjured up visions of the old gangster films she had watched at home as a girl, where the military leader had young defenceless women brought to him for his pleasure behind a curtained-off area in the salon.

"Actually, it is to me too," Peter confessed.

"Oh, dash it! Your sandwich will be curling up. I'll get your orange."

As Peter set out for his seven o'clock dinner date on the Wednesday night, he decided to walk the length of Pall Mall to the RAC, where he had arranged to meet Alex. He didn't doubt that, in a vastly different way, he would enjoy the evening as much as the night before.

Of course, he was greatly looking forward to seeing his son and keen to discover the reason for all the urgency. But the sudden date with Sylvia had been different.

The moment she had appeared at his table at, he noted, about 8.10pm – not too late and not too early – showing the style and upbringing that appeared so natural to her, he somehow knew this was going to be a pleasurable and uncomplicated evening.

Her dress summed that up. Black it was, plain it was also, and the only adornment was the set of her long arms, well-honed shoulders and regal neck, which supported a face that was even more radiant by night than by day. Perhaps it had a little more make-up, and her hair was groomed to just cover the nape of her neck. Simple diamond stud earrings, or a damn good imitation, were her only jewellery.

On such an occasion, gender was not an issue. Peter was as interested in her and her background as he would have been with a male acquaintance.

When asked what she would drink, she knew exactly what she wanted and no amount of influence from Peter would have changed her choice.

"Would you have a La Ina?" she asked the waiter, as if to say she didn't want to cause a problem.

"Of course, madam. An aperitif for you, Sir?"

"Yes, please. Whisky and ice."

"Of course, Mr Martinez." He was obviously well-known.

As he crossed from New Zealand House towards the RAC, Peter glanced towards one of his favourite views over the top of Duke of York steps. If the old Duke had really had 10,000 men, it would have been a pretty tight squeeze, and Peter expected that the then young-middle-aged-nouveau-riche-going-places Executives who were members of the Institute of Directors might have complained about the noise from the continuous *thump-thump-thump*, *left-right-left-right* of the boots shaking the club's renovated facade as they made their way to wherever the Grand Old Duke was marching them. Only then, of course, to be devastated and to resign their memberships as the lads having been marched back up to the top and marched down to the bottom again, on some meaningless exercise.

The previous evening came back into his mind. He supposed what was different was that they had just sat and talked, he being as interested in her life as she, reservedly, was in his. There was the sense of a slight barrier in the way she did her, "And what about yours?" enquiring into the past of the second most senior person at BCG. It was a pity, she had thought, that they hadn't just been brought together by some mutual friend who assured, "Absolutely darling, you'll love him," because then they would have been on equal terms.

Tomorrow morning she would need to be respectful, if not reverent. If she relaxed her guard too much it would just be like a shallow date between the boss and the young, impressionable office girl who would wake up having been used, but to find a bunch of flowers delivered; or, if she was to be relatively unlucky, a farewell bracelet.

Peter sensed that slightly reserved approach. Reflecting back, he was sure it was simply respect for their relative positions, not in life but at BCG. Certainly, there was no apparent fear from her, no doubt regarding his promised intention of there being no 'conquest in mind'.

To be fair, Peter thought, he wasn't really the conquest type. Certainly if some private detective had followed his recent activities, he would have reported some bedroom encounters, but nothing that could be called 'conquest'. Jan had been something of a non-event, and with Cas it was a meeting of equals in many ways.

Prior to that there had been Marcia. Well, that had been rape and education. Then Honey, and that was at least a loving event, even if it had not been subjected to the time test as to whether it was of the 'till death do us part' type, or infatuation.

Anna, without a shadow of a doubt, was of that former quality and indeed her death had temporarily parted them. That fact was about to be highlighted when he sat down with Alex. They always talked naturally of Anna and the love each man had for her. *That's an interesting thought*, Peter reflected. Alex had never spoken of his love for Peter. Vice-versa too, now that he came to think about it.

Peter's thoughts returned to the Bok. He was pretty certain that was pure infatuation, plus the fact that he had always had a soft spot for lame ducks. Cas had certainly been that until Peter put her through those paces. She might suddenly come to terms with that and her ardour might be tempered. Marginally that had begun to show as he left Barcelona, but he'd put money on the fact she'd been hormonal and a bit fed up about him moving so far away. He'd sense more at the forthcoming weekend.

Thinking back to the previous night, he recalled Sylvia's hesitation when he suddenly, but not clumsily, posed the question she had been so used to answering.

"So what about Mr Pez?"

"Mr Pez was… and please don't take offence… a fairly typical male. I was 18, he was 23 and just out of the army, where he'd been commissioned and had earned high accolades. I, of course, was impressionable and the whole world was talking about liberation, the pill and how the Catholic Church should be considering its position.

So I was a typical early 70s role model, literally. I was just starting my modelling career. I found his approaches flattering and, well, I became pregnant. His father, and mine, as it happened, held pistols at his head and we got married. Our daughter Caridad – Cari – was born and for some reason or other, Mr Pez thought that was the point at which marriage naturally ended, and he cemented the fact by going off with another woman.

"So that is 'what about Mr Pez'. Where is he now? I have no idea. His father settled up his dues to his son's wife and family and he was allowed to ride into the sunset. My father was in the diplomatic corps. Mother had died when I was 12, and we came to England… and lived here ever after."

"Is there another Mr Pez in waiting?"

"Good God, no! There have been friends, but I'm sure you know what it's like, their thoughts eventually out, and pillow talk comes into the equation. Then I run."

Peter had replied he wasn't sure he did know what it was like as there hadn't been that much pillow talk in his life.

"Oh go on!" The Chablis had given her a little extra courage. She put on an attractive young girlie voice. "Well, do you know the girls in the office say… you're one of the most eligible bachelors on the circuit and the girls chasing a slice of that reputation are bound to be laundering their best satin pillow slips in case you should call round. I was just pleased I didn't have to rush out to Peter Jones to buy some to keep pace, because of our deal that we're just doing as we are doing, chatting, enjoying superb food and, as is beginning to show, I think, this lovely soft wine." She laughed aloud and so did he.

"Listen, Mrs Pez, I'll prove how wrong your impression of me is one day but there's a bigger issue… and it's not part of a camouflaged 'conquest'. You say 'and then I run'. Why's that?"

Suddenly, she was silent.

"If you weren't one of the bosses I could tell you to piss off, and say it's none of your business."

"Look, Sylvia, this isn't boss and receptionist time out. I'm just interested in receiving an emphatic view from a young lady who shouldn't be so bloody selfish with her body to this queue of suitors."

"Well, if nothing else, I shall take that extremely clever chat-up line away with me and put it into one of my books." Now she laughed again. "I'll take it as a compliment anyway."

"Chat-up line?" Peter asked, with a degree of bewilderment.

"Oh, come on! Man meets girl. Man is generous with compliments. Girl becomes flattered. Man says, 'Can I get between your satin sheets or are you going to be bloody selfish with your body?'

"Look, Peter, it's a great line. I'm sorry. I think the wine is relaxing me. Mr Martinez, Sir, I just think it's so refreshingly male. To be exact, what all those suitors say –and it's not many, I assure you – is normally the other way round. They usually say, 'Now, how about you letting me satisfy you between the sheets? I've bought you two dinners, the cinema, a show and this is usually how I like to round it off.' They're the ones being unselfish and spreading their rewards – that is, in their eyes."

They both roared.

"So is it really like that in the girls' world? By the way. It's Peter. One to one socially, Mrs Pez."

She greeted that again with laughter.

However, she soon began to say 'Peter' quite naturally. Under social conditions she was obviously able to see him as an equal.

"OK, Peter, what about the gorgeous young Malaysian girl who was besotted by you? Are you going to tell me there was no pillow talk?"

"No, she moved in with me."

The pit of her stomach churned, but she retained her composure.

"There you are then."

"But then, what the girls and boys in the office don't know is, she's my daughter."

"Daughter? Your daughter is Coco, is she?"

"I'll tell you one thing."

"What's that?"

"There's been too much time for idle chit-chat whilst I've been away."

"Please don't be cross. There's been so much talk about you. I've been at BCG a month now, and you've been news most of the time. I was bound to ask questions to see why you had so much of a newsworthy following. I actually thought, on the birds of a feather probability, you were bound to be a Mr William crony. I couldn't see him working with anybody who has the charisma you have. As I can now see."

Peter guffawed, as was his habit.

"Now listen, now you're into new chat-up approaches yourself. Let's move the issue away. So it's none of my business but I'm going to presume you run on the principle that if Mr Right came along, you'd hang around and think about testing the water, but *caveat emptor*, buyer beware – once bitten twice shy."

"I can see why you are where you are. You've hit that in one."

"Then I'll drink to that," Peter responded. "Cheers. Now… sweets. What do you fancy?"

He'd not really had to explain Coco's existence before, he realised. Feeling at ease, he now more than happily recounted his meeting with Honey, but had a twinge of guilt that he'd not told Maria, or Alex and Petra that story. To explain it to Sylvia seemed quite a straightforward piece of history.

"So there you are," Sylvia said gleefully, when he'd finished. "You're as typical as Mr Pez, if you get a willing participant, and I'm not condemning that. But isn't that exactly the same as my situation except, I do say, you're obviously around to give your daughter the love and affection of a father, whereas my bastard ex isn't."

He'd then explained how he'd totally lost contact with Honey… and the rest of that tale. A tear ran down her cheek.

"I'll have to go to the ladies. Oh, that's so sweet. I'm so sorry. I take it back. You're no Mr Pez."

So yes, he did show love and affection to Coco and he ought, to be fair, to show a little more of that to Alex and Petra than, he realised, he had done, now that he'd discovered he did have a heart within.

What was all that realisation to do with his recent rehabilitation experience? he asked himself, as this new young entrant to his life exited side of stage to the ladies.

Peter had realised he was tired, yet refreshed.

Chapter 25

They always met in the Long Bar, and usually ate in the Great Gallery at the RAC.

Alex arrived within five minutes of his father. He tapped him on the shoulder. Peter turned, showing his pleasure at seeing him, as always, and extended both arms into which his grown-up little boy stepped. They hugged each other for enough seconds to communicate a blood bond.

Alex was the one to break the embrace. "Dad, I've been telling you for years now we shouldn't do that in public, they'll think we're gay."

"Balls! Not at the RAC. They'll know we're father and son. Besides, you really are looking more like me every time we meet. Look at you. Plain blue double-breasted suit, pink tie. What are you on, some sort of clone tablet or something?"

"No. I just happen to like it."

Peter ordered a small lager for his son. "So tell me how you've been."

"No way. I want to know all about you first. We thought, on the first reports, we were going to lose you."

"Balls," he said again. "They checked with your mother to see if she needed me up there yet and she came back with the answer that she was having the time of her life, spending her days in this lovely lavender field, and she didn't want me going up there with my grandiose schemes of developing the area and bringing her another few years of stress and flak."

Momentarily, he saw Cas's fiancé leaning up against the hedge.

Alex had been listening intently, as he always did. "I've been thinking. It's funny you should say that, but working back through all the places where I grew up, where the family grew up, I reckon you finished up developing all our previous homes. So we don't really have a heritage. I'll explain how those thoughts have come about later. But I think it's true."

Peter thought for a minute or two. "Do you know… I actually think you're right. Certainly Tulse Hill I did, and Dulwich. Come to think of it, Selsdon and Keston."

"Anyway, you look good. It's good news mother rejected the application."

Peter was touched by the sentiment and slightly worried that Alex saw all his family homes as being precursors and excuses for developments. It was simply that Peter had tried to choose houses which needed doing up and which also had space for a football goal and cricket pitch for his son and friends, and a netball goal for his daughter. That conjured up visions of Petra and Anna practising, practising, practising in the build-up to inter-school matches.

"Shall we go in and order? We can do some serious catching up while we wait. We've got loads of time together."

"Sure." That pleased Alex. He was always short of time with his father. Always had been.

Eating together leisurely was bound to be a pleasure. They both raved about the RAC smoked salmon. Usually they were able to negotiate a couple of good fillet steaks by Peter saying to the maître d'hôtel that he knew about the slabs of flesh he and the chefs had put aside for their own dinners the following night, and it would suit him and his son to have those, please. Contrary to club policy, Peter had a knack of palming a couple of £5 notes and slipping them to the maitre d'hôtel as they left, through his parting handshake. He never knew whether that was of greater influence in getting him a prime steak the next time than the approach of those other members who relied on the transmission of a Masonic handshake to book a little extra favouritism on their next visit.

Despite the invitations, Peter had avoided joining Freemasonry. He had a passion for all things at all times to be treated on a common basis rather than through a network of privilege. That's why he'd had some problems coming to terms with Ramon's prediction regarding potential turnover, but if the rules Samaranch had laid down were that the opportunities were to be for Spanish-owned companies alone, then if you were Spanish and Catholic, as opposed to Mason or Jew, there was a more than equal chance of getting the work. So it seemed OK.

Unusually, tonight Peter left the wine choice to the wine waiter. "We're in your hands completely," he said to the sommelier.

"That's unusual for you, Dad."

"I'm in an unusual mood. Now tell me, how's the job?"

Peter was always keen to follow Alex's career. He respected that, in the accidentally same way that Peter had not followed his father into fishing for a living, so his son had pursued the course he wanted at university, which happened to be English, with marketing in mind. He now found himself in a small niche market PR company, unusually doing what he'd set out to do.

"That's one of the bits of news."

Peter showed his concern. "Good or bad?"

"Good, I hope you'll think. They've offered me a partnership."

"Wow! There's only two partners, aren't there?"

Typical, Alex thought. *Straight into finite detail*, which he saw as a compliment.

"Yes. Russell and Jonathan."

"Then what's the deal?"

"A full partnership."

"At what cost?"

"Twenty per cent of my commission to them personally over five years."

"… And then?"

"I'd say they might both want out."

"Any idea of what your commission will be?"

"Yes, a third of profit."

"So you in effect get 26-27 per cent of profit."

"You haven't lost your quick brain in this shake-up your body's been given, have you?" he complimented his father.

"I hope not. Hey, that's excellent, isn't it? How did you do that?"

"I went and saw them and said I had itchy feet and I wanted to tell them in advance that if an opportunity came my way, I'd look at it seriously."

All Peter did was smile and wave his hand to get the sommelier's attention.

"Before you bring us the wine of your choice, could we have a bottle of Roederer, please?"

"Of course, Sir, vintage or non?"

"Crystal Brut."

"Hey, Dad, it's not that good a celebration! But there is more."

"Then as long as it's equally good news, it'll be a cheap investment."

The waiter went hurrying off.

"Well, the next news is – I'm planning to get married."

"What? I didn't even know there *was* a prospective Mrs Martinez."

"I didn't like to tell you, in case you told Grandmama Maria. She might not approve. We've been living together for a couple of years. You've met her. Anne Marie."

"Wow! Is that the one with a bit of French in her and a figure like an hour-glass?"

"Yes. But I have to say you haven't lost the knack of making it easy to help someone break news. The figure, Dad, is beginning to change."

"What? Pregnant?"

"Put plainly, yes. Put our way, we'd like to invite you to be a grandfather."

Peter's world suddenly opened up. He'd never contemplated the thrills his mother had pestered him about over all those years, both before and after his marriage to Anna. A grandfather! A patriarchal figure, not this time to a son, with all the closeness that entailed, but an older generation figure to a fledgling he could spoil and get excited, like he never had with his own children, and then just hand them back and leave the parents to do the bathing and singing to sleep.

Peter suddenly felt totally alone. There would be no partner with whom to share the joy. Although his thoughts put him into contact with Anna, there would be no one around physically to share those joyful moments of seeing a grandchild develop.

The champagne arrived. They chinked glasses. Peter suggested they do it three times.

"Here's to the partnership. Here's to the wedding. Here's to my grandchild."

"Thanks, Dad. But you've gone quiet."

"I know. I suddenly miss your mother so very, very much. All this should be 50 per cent her joy."

"Come on, Dad. It is. You know that. Anne Marie knows that. She's got a problem too, you know."

"What's that?"

"She doesn't have a father. He died ages ago. So our child will have only one grandmother and one grandfather."

"I'll take a chance," Peter said with a grin. "I'll marry the mother. If she's anything like Anne Marie, that wouldn't be so bad."

"Yes. Good idea, and each of our religions would excommunicate us. We'd be stepbrothers and sisters getting married. I'm sure that would be wrong."

"True. Then I tell you what… I'll get Anna's OK to taking a wife for the sake of the child."

"Dad, you know very well Mum would always have wanted you to remarry. Not too pretty or sexy, mind you, and it's always been our fear, Petra's and mine, that it might be you sitting in this chair saying you're pregnant and telling us about an intended, maybe accidental brother or sister. We're sure you're not celibate."

"Thank you. So you think I put it around, do you?"

"We expect you to. You're still young enough. We've just always had the fear that you might marry the dreadful Marcia."

"Oh, don't worry. She's getting married on Saturday. But you've given me a new resolve. I really don't want to be a lonely old grandfather who has to come and live with you and become a burden."

"Thank God for that!"

"Right, I'm advertising for a wife."

"Then make her beautiful in the image of Mother."

Peter went quiet again. Then: "Both of them actually are."

"What?"

"Exactly that. Each of them is."

"Christ! You never do things by half. What, you've got two suitors in tow? Well, you get one invite to the wedding, which says '… and guest' and one to the christening, similarly labelled. We don't want two beautiful women scratching each other's eyes out, do we? Seriously, Dad, *are* there two candidates?"

"I'd say there are. Each for a different reason. But I'm realistic enough to say there might not ever be a third."

"Right. That's a job for Anne Marie and Petra. They'll do the choosing."

"Then that's unfair. I want a bit of sexiness next to me in bed."

"I'll bet any candidate of yours is that already."

"I'm not sure that you've got a very high opinion of me…"

The waiter intervened. "Smoked salmon for both gentlemen. Pepper, Sir? Pepper, Sir? Enjoy your meal."

The interruption had gone.

"Dad, it's times like this, and when you force this quality nectar down me, that I can feel we can exchange… well… just talk. Some of it sensible stuff and some drivel… and particularly the serious shock of a couple of months back. In fact, it could well have been my need for Anne Marie to comfort me that made us a little less careful and got us into this happy state. So thanks, Dad.

"But back to the statement. Of course we have a high opinion of you. I'm very proud of everything you've ever done, although I've never quite understood you for leaving me alone to grow up."

"Do you feel I did that? Was it that obvious?"

"A bit. But no harm done. Thus far, I've got myself sorted. I've chosen a career that keeps me in touch with sport, people, gives me job satisfaction and a high income judged by results. What more could a young fellow with a beautiful wife-elect wish for?"

"A bit more loving between the ages of say, 11, I'd guess, and now?" Peter proffered.

"Do you actually know that?"

"I'm afraid so. It was a bit by design. The boarding school bit, the apparent lack of interest in your choice of studies, etcetera. Yes, I'd say that was by design." Alex looked gobsmacked. "Wasn't that a bit cruel? Didn't you know that even a fellow with a hard beard stubble needs to be told by his father that he actually loves him?"

"Yes, but life is a great university. A better place to learn than any set of books or the readings of any philosophers. My university was a world that suddenly, at about the age I mentioned, was fatherless too. That turned me, I think, into a man. Then, because I didn't, like you, have a father pestering me every time I scored a goal, or in your case scored a century at cricket, I, and you, have been allowed to develop character and a pining for that love. It gave me a purpose and now, with a son or daughter coming along, you'll develop your own way of showing the extent of your affection."

"Are you going to give me the benefit again of the shooting of that little pig exercise, or me having to bat on with two broken bloody fingers, which I have to say was hell?"

"Either. They're both lessons learnt. It was because I loved you so much, I was able to do it… and it was because your dear mother loved you so much that she allowed me to do it.

"If you're about to reach fatherhood and enter this high-flying job spree, then I'll do a deal. I'll go soft from now on."

Alex put his hand across the table and shook Peter's. "I've always seen us as bloody good friends who don't get in the way of each other."

"Thank you so much, Alex." Peter was deeply touched. "Tell you what. I'll find you a stepmother who makes me soften right up."

"Now there's a deal," Alex proposed.

Both steaks were medium rare. Both had the same vegetables. Both men ate in almost total silence.

"Was it good?" Peter asked his son.

"Excellent."

"The wine?"

"I'm just a bit squiffy."

Peter had heard that before. They ordered just coffee.

"Tell me how your job keeps you in touch with sport."

"Jonathan does theatre and the arts. Russell is gay. Not that that has any bearing on his ability... the reverse... oh, sorry if there's a pun there somewhere." They both laughed. "So Russell does music... pop through to the classics... and I suggested we had a huge gap by not covering sport.

"Footballers are beginning to earn good money, and cricketers, and they're all trying to build their profiles. Golfers too... we're at the beginning of a huge industry that needs PR and imaging. After all, you don't get the profile you need as Chelsea or Manchester United's top goal-scorer by just driving around in a Ferrari with a miniature pair of football boots hanging from the rear view mirror."

"Do you know anything about the Olympics?" Peter asked.

"Dad, of course I do."

"No. Perhaps I phrased that badly. The forthcoming Olympics."

"Seoul, next year, isn't it?"

"Yes, and after that?"

"I'm not sure." Alex suddenly changed his mind. "Yes, I bloody am, because I was wondering if I could borrow Girasol for a couple of weeks but I've never got round to it, and anyway it's a long way off. Yes... Barcelona then, isn't it?"

Peter spent coffee time telling Alex all about his plans, particularly the paraplegic side of things and Paul Demar.

"Christ! That's all staggering," Alex said after listening, riveted.

"How's your Spanish?" Peter asked his son.

"You didn't make me work hard enough at it for me to say 'good'. Conversationally, it's OK. The written stuff is naff. Why?"

"This, my son, is where a father comes out of the woodwork and at last works with his son."

"On what basis?"

"Really! Now *you* have a way of raising subjects to pave an easier route to discussion. You're on 26 per cent odd profit. I'll introduce you to somebody whose Spanish is brilliant, conceptual ability is fantastic and she's an absolute stunner who could do your PR for you as an Olympic specialist. She'd need about £20,000 salary. A car. Expenses and five per cent commission of the Olympian side of the business."

"What have you always said? 'You've got to speculate to grow'. I'll look at it. I'll look at her."

"The flip side is that you, with her backing, could handle all the BCG Spanish PR."

"Christ!"

"That's you alone. I don't want that Jonathan hanging around my stage door, or Russell turning the exercise into some operatic masterpiece."

Alex had learnt to guffaw just like his father. Their combined laughter rocked through the now emptying restaurant, turning the odd RAC member's head. They'd arrange to meet to discuss things on a business footing. They'd get together with Anne Marie, and Peter would look over the mother-in-law, with no promises, and they would love each other more dearly over each bottle of Roederer they could afford to buy. They were a nearly pickled father and son, perhaps for the first time.

Chapter 26

Peter had the third best night's sleep he could remember. He wasn't sure if he was finding the flat a little lonely; although he rarely slept later than seven, he was conscious that this morning he had beaten the alarm radio to its sudden burst into music. He was fine with that once he got going, he initially resented it for bringing him out of his secret fantasy world of dreams and into the reality of day.

He automatically turned up the volume so that he might hear a tune he could relate to for the rest of the day. Rarely did that happen. He'd missed out on the pop scene and truly did appreciate the music Anna had helped him to understand.

Anyway, he decided to get out of bed and make himself a cup of tea and then, to please Cas, would do the exercises to keep her good work going, as he had promised.

By seven o'clock, he realised it would be eight in Spain so he called Maria while he sipped his tea.

She was delighted to hear from him. "You're a good boy," she said. "Do you know this is the first time in about six weeks that you've called me without me forcing you to return a call?"

"Now is that a fact?" Peter said sarcastically.

"Yes. It really is, which tells me that you're feeling better…"

Peter had to say no more. His mother went into full download about the hotel, Marco, Virginia, Sñr Martin being edgy still. She had met Miguel and Michelle and the kids…

"Oh Hell!" Peter interjected.

"Peter. What's that expletive for?"

"Oh, just something silly came into my head," he said. He had just thought: what if he ever had cause to introduce Sylvia Pez to his mother? She'd be sure he was going to introduce her to another Michelle, whom she always blamed, he was still sure, for forcing Peter to sleep with her when she was under the influence of some terrible drug, which she might have, in time, introduced to him.

Maybe that will never happen, he thought.

They finally said their fond farewells.

"Have a good day. Don't overdo it," were Maria's final words of wisdom.

For some reason that reminded him it was the date of the Board meeting.

He hoped her wishes came true and that he did have a good day. That would mean he had fought off the Mr William demons.

He was in the office before nine. Sylvia, looking as crisp as ever, was already there. Peter was really pleased to see her but her usual smile was not naturally there.

"You OK?" he asked.

She looked all around her, as if to make sure there was nobody within earshot to hear her say something really important.

Actually, she was about to.

"Mr Peter..." she chose as her opener.

"Mrs Sylvia," he replied.

"Please be kind to me. Don't joke. I'm about to show you a very sad side of myself and... no... I don't think the worst... I'm thinking about your best interests when I say that."

"Sylvia, I'm sure there's no sad or bad side in you. Why don't you just spill it out?"

"Mr William was in the office by 7.45."

"He's not usually early for a Board meeting." Peter frowned as he contemplated what she had said. "OK, so he couldn't sleep."

"That's it... he probably hasn't slept but in the other sense, he's had a sleepover."

"Sleepover? You have those when you're on school holidays and you plan to have a midnight feast but sleep through the alarm clock and never actually get to the feast bit. So what do you mean?"

"Well, I arrived as usual at about 8.30 and Mr William's car was just up the road on a meter. Now that seemed unusual. As soon as I opened up, there was something quite strange. The stale smell of the old leather furniture didn't seem quite as forceful as it usually is. The scent of perfume was hanging in the air, far richer than any of the airsprays the cleaners use overnight, and it was quality perfume. Actually, I'm a cheat. I recognised the brand. It was one of the heavy but subtle Cartier ones, which I actually quite like."

"His aftershave?"

"No. Her after-sleepover present, I now know."

"Whose?"

"The lady he'd arrived with."

Peter always seemed to have a tan but it suddenly visibly faded.

"So they'd slept over, on your diagnosis?"

"I thought so."

"Thought so?"

"Yes, but not now."

"You're losing me."

"Now I know so."

"How?"

"George."

"George?"

"George the chauffeur."

"Christ, of course! He couldn't keep a secret for the incentive of 100 quid."

Sylvia was the one to now look surprised. "That's precisely what he'd been paid."

"How the hell do you know that?"

"'Funny isn't it, miss,' George confided in me, 'what an old bloke does to date a young girl'. 'Is it?' I said. 'Why do you say that?' He said, 'Well, if you were a bloke, miss, do you think it would be worth giving somebody 100 quid not to split about what he might know about a little assignation you wouldn't want your wife to know about?' I said, 'No I don't, but you presumably know someone who does'. And he said, 'Well miss, I shouldn't say but here's the proof'.

"Then he showed me a wad of pretty grubby notes. 'Good for you,' I said, 'who gave you that?' 'Swear you won't say this miss,' he said. I told him if he gave me 50 quid, I wouldn't and then I did something really wicked. I went closer to him and I pinched his cheek between my thumb and forefinger and promised I wouldn't tell, and that I wasn't serious about the share.

"He put his forefinger to his lips and then pointed directly up above the ceiling of the reception area to Mr William's office."

"Wow!" Peter exclaimed.

"There's more!"

"Do we need more? So he's had a bit of fun before the meeting, where he's likely to resign in favour of a presidency."

Sylvia looked down at the floor. "All the Executive Directors are already in," she confided.

"What? It's barely nine."

"According to George, they've all been summoned at five-minute intervals for an audience with the Chairman. He reckons Mr William's going to give them each a piece of silver as a memento of growing up with him. In fact George said that the Chairman had previously told him that he was going to be well looked after, and he'd heard Mr William say to the overnight girl the first thing he would do would be to take her for some sunshine.

"George said it was pretty obvious the Chairman wouldn't be working for a while and the young lady said she couldn't get abroad because she didn't have the right clothes.

"'Do you know what?' George said. 'The soppy old codger said she wouldn't need much to wear during the day, but for the evenings he'd get her fitted out with some nice things. It was in the back of my car,' George said, with some distaste, 'just as we were coming out of Knightsbridge, that Mr William said he'd got a token of how it was going to be in the future and gave her the bleedin' perfume, which she opened in great excitement and splashed all over herself and the seats in the car.'"

"So how's the smell got into the reception?"

"Haven't you guessed?"

"No way."

"She came here with him. In fact she's still here."

"What, for the bloody Board meeting? She can't! It's directors only."

"Oh Peter. I'm sorry. I thought you being the worldly one... you, with your eyes and ears all over the place, you would have known. Didn't Fred tell you on the way back from the airport? He asked me if he thought he should, and I said yes."

"Hit me, Sylvia. What? Tell me what?"

"About Val! Val's been a plaything to William for a while."

It took Peter a few seconds.

"You know... I wasn't exactly taken with her. Well, well, well! But she was happy to be stitching William up. She gave me all sorts of incriminating bits of paper."

"Well, yes... they'd fallen out. She was promised to go to Spain with the Chairman when he came out to see you. But he suddenly said not on that trip. She enquired why and found out about the girls from the stables.

"There, dear CEO, was the scorning of yet another damsel. On the strength of William becoming all powerful, and needing her in tow, she'd jilted her fiancé to free herself for this new life, but was then ditched herself. She was furious.

"But now everything is lovey-dovey again. Mr William has probably put all the Execs on a promise and he's hoping to get you binned."

"How long have I got before the meeting?"

"Best part of two and a half hours."

"How can I get rid of Val for that period of time? I'm presuming she'll be working as usual in my office."

"You're her boss. Send her on an errand."

"Where?"

Sylvia thought for a few moments. "Shopping."

"What for?"

"Say it's your mother's birthday and you need to buy her a present. Say it has to be from Harrods and she'll spend ten minutes on your mother and then get carried away on herself. She'll slip into Mr William somehow, once you've instructed her, and he'll give her some spending money. By the time she gets back, your meeting will be on.

"I sincerely hope, Peter, that you come out of this with Mr William 'tin-tacked'. Val will go with him, then you'll have to find a reliable PA... but let's make it 100 per cent clear I'm not up for grabs in that role, and I haven't spilt the beans with an ulterior motive. I just want to show my support for you."

"Sylvia… you're great! Let's go for all of that. I'll send Val out to shop… and what I'll have to ask you is if you wouldn't mind speaking to the Executive Directors to allocate ten minutes to each of them for me to put my counter-deal to them. By the way, the non-Executives are on board already.

Mr William quit his role as Chairman of the Board at 12.20pm. Peter Martinez had proposed that the former Chairman should become president of BCG but resisted an amendment that the presidency should be for life.

At the CEO's magnanimous suggestion, he volunteered that the former Chairman's secretary should be made redundant and receive twice her statutory entitlement, and that a new post should be created: PA to the president. Amidst suggestions that he was making a huge personal sacrifice, he nominated Val Armstrong for the position, leaving himself again without a PA.

The presidency, not for life, and the appropriate level of assistance were favourably and unanimously voted.

The position of Chairman would be decided, after considered discussion, at the next Board meeting. In the meantime leave was granted for Peter Martinez to act in both Chairman and CEO positions. As CEO, he was appropriately put into the important expansion area of International.

Max faxed Peter later that day. *I have to hand it to you. I've just seen your, well actually, our share price. It looks up 35 per cent. Do I sell our shares?*

Peter faxed back. *Hold, you soppy bugger, they've got another 25 per cent to go. Leave that to me, my dear brother-in-law.*

Chapter 27
MID-SUMMER 1989

Sir Bob Hall had turned out to be just the leader and inspirational success Peter had expected. His great attribute appeared to be that he let Peter play along in his slightly more cavalier way than the institutional one which any of the top 100 quoted boards would have preferred. Sir Bob focused on what he knew would appeal to the establishment. That was Peter at the helm, lifting their 7,000 employees to new heights of personal expectation and a level of success which the City enjoyed.

At the May Board meeting, Sir Bob had ruled that they had a lot to write home about. The UK housing market had gone bananas leading up to Margaret Thatcher's big mortgage-restricting proposals of 1988, and had not looked back since. You hardly needed to actually lay bricks and mortar to reap profit. Construction and Commercial Development had followed suit. International, particularly in Europe and through their Spanish joint venture, was doing really well. But then Peter always knew it would.

"We need exposure," Sir Bob announced, "but the City won't be expecting any until the half year results in July."

If they could lift the share price again, then the anticipated reaction after the results would lift the share price from a higher base. Ergo, the guy with the share options, which included Sir Bob and Peter, would make a lot of money. William saw that too.

As president, he was still as unimaginative as he had ever been, except for the fact that early on in his presidential role, he worked out that Val didn't bring much with her outside of bed. She was a let-down when William had needed an escort to a formal function now that the divorce his wife was pushing through took her out of the equation, from previously having been the right pedigree to be able to mingle in most company.

He wasn't awfully sure about Jan Roberts after she appeared to go against him in the fatal months of 1987. Still, he had little alternative, as it were, and some of his close friends were predicting a knighthood for him, so Jan would be the girl to milk the most publicity and dinner invites out of that.

"Chairman. Let's bring Jan Roberts in. She could profile Peter, and myself even. Do you remember a few years back? She did a corker then. Ask her for some more of that."

The more worldly Board members sniggered. Mr President William was still out of touch. They all knew the form. Why was it he was always a couple of decades behind?

Sir Bob did a partial rescue. "I doubt it's appropriate for Jan to interview Peter. Don't lose sight of the fact the wedding is round the corner… and I'd expect Hello magazine to take that one on," he said in fun.

"I see. What do you say, Peter?"

Peter held court, effectively by delaying his response.

"Can't see myself how Jan could be unbiased. I'll talk to Gordon Jones, who'll talk to Martin Kemp, Jan's agent, and see if he's got some up-and-coming fledgling who could do a piece. But, yes, it's OK by me. We've a lot to talk about."

"Let's get it into the market, I say," William said with determination, realising he'd just make the 2.30 at Sandown Park. "Well, if we all go along with that, that'll be the plan."

Gordon Jones, the group PR man, had been around a while. He had a soft spot for Peter and, of course, Jan, as had all the chaps she had put pen to paper about. He indeed did put it to Martin Kemp that the group were ready for a Peter exposé again, but did he agree Jan wouldn't want to do it.

"Christ! Unless you want to get me fired as her agent, for God's sake, don't make me ask her. She's jitters personified about going down the aisle. She might just not be able to portray Peter in a saintly manner, or want to!"

"Who else have you got?"

Martin thought. "Jan hogs it, really. But there's a freelancer we use. She's OK. But I'm not sure she'd gel with Peter."

"Why's that?"

"She's lesbian."

"Christ, don't tell Peter that! I think he's going through a phase of fancying anything in a skirt… or trousers, come to that."

"Actually, she's a really pretty young thing. What happened to her genes, who knows."

"Blonde?"

"Yes."

"Slim?"

"Yes."

"Blue eyes?"

"Yes."

"She's a must. He mustn't know. He'll show off well in front of her."

"… And Jan… does she know about her genes?"

"Christ, yes. Dominic, 'Dom', apparently made a pass at Jan when they both got pissed at the Shell bash."

"Really?"

"Well, at that time Jan seemed all alone in the world. No rings, or apparent ties, but then she hadn't come to grips with her man by then."

"They're OK now about each other?"
"Yes. Sure. Actually, Dom thinks professionally Jan's very good."
"Surname?"
"Dominic Hall."
"Is she the boy or the girl?"
"Oh, female, definitely."

Overall, Gordon Jones trusted Martin Kemp's judgment in these professional situations. But he'd let himself down, although one had to say he'd acted typically like an agent, when Jan had so publicly let it be known her working relationship had been marred by an 'ill-conceived' personal one with Peter. A year earlier the Board had instructed Gordon to engage Jan for a repeat interview, and she had declined but remained silent as to her reasons. William must have been away at the time or had his mind on other things. He didn't seem to remember the incident, so Gordon asked Martin Kemp to engage Dominic Hall.

"Martin reckons Jan's 'off limits'… Peter agreed it wouldn't be an independent interview. He explained to Peter he'd got a nice young thing who might do him justice. Dominic Hall. 'Dom', apparently," Gordon informed Peter.

"Fine, as long as she doesn't treat me as if she was Bernard Levin, she'll do. I'll tell her what to focus on, OK?"

"Don't think I'd do that."

"She might know better?"

"Might just. She's quite reliable analytically."

"OK. Then speak to Di and get her to fix up wheeling her along."

Di seemed to be fitting in well as Val's replacement in Peter's office. She had too much acting ability to show she wasn't very happy when Dominic showed up: blonde, beautiful, confident and skirted. If only she knew how that was bound to distract Peter.

"Dominic Hall," Di announced, more formally than ever. The only thing to indicate that she wasn't being paid as part of a different profession was that she wasn't wearing red tails, a wing collar and a row of medals. Otherwise, she could almost have passed for a member of the Red Coat Brigade who had officiated at Masonic, Lions, and Knights of the Order of St John functions, but could do weddings and international group interviews as well.

Peter assessed Dominic in seconds. So he put on his younger, co-operative voice.

"Hi."

"Hello, Mr Martinez."

"Peter, please."

"Could we stay formal? I don't want us to be particularly cosy with each other. I'd feel best if we have moments of complexity, out of which comes a strong final opinion, I promise in your favour, because you're paying the bill. I want there to be a degree of aloofness to the interview."

"Is that wise?"

"I believe so."

"Whose idea? Martin, Jan or a chap called Mr William?"

She was tumbled. "I'll have to leave that to your imagination."

"I'll bet on Jan. I'm presuming you know her if you're part of Martin's stable."

She looked more uncomfortable.

"OK. I'm aloof. What can I do for you?" he said voluntarily, as if giving in to her first demand. "Come on. Time's short. First topic please."

She was floored. He'd got to her. She was cross. No man outwitted her. She looked at her notes.

Her organised brain went to pieces. She thought, *What the fuck do we focus on?*

"So... what should we look at? Your business success, your family, your interest in the Paraplegics, your deputy Chairmanship of one of the Committee's Olympic Paraplegic Body? Your protégé Paul Demar and, allegedly, close friend and confidante, his trainer? Your demands for racial equality, your hatred of a divided Europe, East to West... ?"

"Forget your notes. All of them, Dominic. I'm told you're reliably analytical."

"Mr Martinez, I don't have the time for that."

"Then that's not my fault, talk to Martin and Gordon. Because with me it's all or nothing."

"Which interests you the most?" she asked.

"Can I be honest?" Peter enquired.

"It would be better if you are."

"I think equality."

"Good. Then I'm into that one too. My pen is ready." She indicated that by tapping her shorthand notebook firmly. "I don't believe in Orwell."

"Orwell. George Orwell?"

"Yes. Animal Farm... all men are equal, it's just some are more equal than others," she reminded him. "Yes. That's right. So how does that affect your life?"

"Simple. But you don't list religion as being on your list of topics I'm interested in."

"Well, no! At college, you're taught don't talk religion, politics or sexual persuasion."

"Right, then, religion has a place in the Orwell equation. If God had not wanted one man or woman to be more equal than the others, He wouldn't have only sent one man down."

"Christ?"

"Sorry, is that an exclamation you learnt at college, or a question?"

She smiled for the first time. "Jan said you'd tie me up into knots."

"Is that a promise?" he joked.

"Not with the white of a wedding around the corner. I'll leave others to do the knot thing."

"You're quick. I'll give you that."

"OK. So you don't have a problem with acknowledging equality... so how come you're a leader then?"

"There's more to equality than that."

"Right, then the other equality then. What about the black and white factor... the disadvantaged, the paraplegic... this young potential Olympic..." She looked at her notes. "... Paul Demar? How did that come about?"

"I've learnt to hate discrimination. You're born what you are, who you are and the only variation to that is if you happen to be born poor. If you are, it seems it helps if you're Jewish."

"That's profound."

"Show me it's wrong. A lot of successful Jews were born poor."

"Were you born poor?"

"No," he said emphatically. "I had a reasonably comfortable upbringing and a pink skin."

"How did you become rich, then, without being Jewish?"

"Bloody hard work."

"And how does discrimination feature in that?"

"I fell in love with a principle that being black or white, or crippled, has been horribly affected by ill-educated prejudice and has been turned from something of a birthright to a handicap. A handicap is something to overcome and if you have someone to hold your hand through that, then that fortunate helper can develop a deep affection in what one is achieving."

"Have you done that?"

"Yes, in many walks of life. In the case you mention, I've provided support by collecting sponsorship for the young man you refer to, Paul Demar, who will, I assure you, win a medal in a couple of years. Through that I've developed a love for the young lady who's achieved the results so far required, to allow him to qualify for Barcelona 1992."

"Do you mean love, or is that an excuse?"

"Tell me, Dominic..."

"Dom."

"Oh no! Let's be cold, Dominic. You tell me how many people can you love at a time, that's on the premise you've got blood in your heart, of course. Is it a commodity precious enough to be heaped on to one person alone or, like life, are there degrees or qualities of love that enable you to be more expansive?"

"Well, I suppose love can be as generous as you want or need it to be. I love my current partner and my mother and father, sisters too. So yes. It can be wide," she said earnestly.

"Paul Demar's coach is a lovely young lady from South Africa."

It was here that Dominic screwed up. "Is this a bride-to-be in place of Jan?" she asked.

"Jan clearly didn't tell you that if you're dealing with me, you get your research right."

"Well, I thought I had!"

"In Jan's first interview with me, she screwed up, too. She hadn't got her research straight either. Let me help you. If you're lucky, I'll come back to that question."

Peter looked at his watch. "Coffee. Then I think we ought to set a time limit. Let's agree the subjects to be covered. We'll get off the personal bit. Business I suggest first, and that will roll into the Spanish news quite nicely. Maybe we'll touch on my Olympic role and we can fade out on the wedding perhaps, if you get bored with all the rest."

"Oh! Good. At least we're back on form. Jan said she bet you'd finish up telling me what to focus on… so here we are!"

The mention of South Africa and brides-to-be was clearly dangerous ground, which was no doubt being trodden under Jan's influence.

Jan hadn't ever been able to get rid of the 'Bok' factor. Peter hadn't really understood her sudden narrowness; she was normally such a broad-thinking person. But he supposed that in every respect, Cas had caused the change in Jan's potential history by coming on the scene when she did.

There always seemed to be a rebel in Peter's life who distracted him from anything decent which was around, except during his years with Anna. Marcia Hunt's infrequent intrusions kept his taste buds open for the short, intense infatuations he had encountered.

Three days, and the following week with Cas, had sent him back to the UK anxious to see her again, and to enjoy each other's bodies. Realistically, if Peter's allocated physio had been some butch Spanish ex-PE instructor out of the army, he would not have been distracted from the relationship he had set up with Jan – much, he had to remember, to his mother's satisfaction.

Marcia's wedding weekend had actually been sufficiently disappointing to make Peter rethink the Bok relationship. But he wasn't to realise he hadn't made the right allowances in coming to any finite judgement.

Meeting Cas at the airport, he saw she was distinctly low. She seemed unappreciative of him standing at the barrier with a small posy of roses. In fact, although she had meant to be funny, it didn't come over that way.

"Oh Peter, darling. Flowers. How generous! I hope you're not going to do the 'proper' thing all weekend."

She was good at taking the mickey out of the English accent and 'properness', as she described it. That came over loud and clear as a semi-public announcement. When Peter had said he'd got a table at Mirabelle for the Friday evening, she made a point of saying she had only brought jeans, although he knew that wasn't true because he'd peeped into the wardrobe he'd said she could use in the spare room. However, she'd misinterpreted that because it had led her to ask if that was her bed too.

"Come on, sweetheart. Of course not. I just thought it would be nice for you to have partially your own set-up."

When confronted with the Mirabelle prospect, she'd said wasn't there a good fish and chip shop in the area. "Is Pimlico too far?" she'd asked when Peter said there was and it was in Pimlico. So they'd had fish and chips and both had worn jeans.

"There," Cas said, "I don't want you getting all proper and conventional when you're out of my sight."

Sleeping together was pleasant; there were no fireworks or shooting sparks as there had been in Barcelona and Girasol.

"You were subdued," he mentioned over breakfast.

"I'd wanted to be…"

He interrupted. "Are you going to say your word of the moment?"

"Which one is that?"

"Well it seems you packed just the one and brought it with you: 'proper'!"

Cas hadn't appreciated her mood was coming through that way. She'd been distinctly off about having to be taken to Harrods to get something to wear to a wedding where she hadn't met the bride or groom previously, so they wouldn't know what she really looked like anyway.

"I'll wear my physio coat. You liked that."

"Not to a bloody wedding."

"Well it suited you when I was your bait, if I remember rightly."

"Cas. Please," he'd eventually said, in the changing cubicle in Harrods. "Let's enjoy our time together. I want you to look beautiful and be the star of the show."

"OK then. Give me space. You get back to the catwalk area. I'll try these three on, but I won't do that with you sitting there gawping at me. I'll come outside and strut."

Peter took the strong hint and returned to the ever-present leather chair alongside the patiently waiting till.

Cas looked at her side silhouette in the full-length mirror, clad in her bikini pants and silk bra. It was undoubtedly her imagination as she muttered, "It fucking shows already. Oh Christ! What do I do now? He'll want to do the 'proper' thing. Am I ready for that?"

Anyway, to miss just the one period, and only by a week, was too soon to have to think seriously about the consequences. But it was unlike her to miss a day. Instinctively, she just knew.

The reality was that she would have to think of moving across to these new surroundings. She'd been accustomed, at best, to her parents' modest bungalow near the beach on the outskirts of Cape Town. Here in the UK with Peter, it was one big film set where the other players knew their parts, but she didn't.

Six weeks later, when Peter had gone out to Barcelona for his third committee meeting, she told him. To be fair, he said he was absolutely delighted, and thoroughly pleased to know now why she'd been grumpy. He, of course, knew even more about the preambles of childbirth than she did. The closest she had got was an early miscarriage with Mark. At the time, thank God, a relief.

He understood morning sickness, and knew this 'herbal remedy'. He knew about body soreness and moved his attentions from her chest to her back and neck. He was a natural father-to-be. But, as she told herself, he was also a father-who'd-been. Then, of course, when it dawned on her that their child would be a brother or sister to Alex and Petra, whom he had told her about with joy, plus the generation factor, it all flashed ahead of her in Broadway lights.

She acted her way through his weekend of celebrating their great mistake, mishap or perhaps love child. That, at least, gave her temporary security. In the following three months, she had indeed agreed to be Peter's South African bride. Dominic had got that right. She was just out of date, as in the following two months they'd shared hell together. Where would they settle? If it was London, how would she continue to coach Paul? If it was Spain, how would Peter continue with BCG?

Then Peter got the letter. When he recognised the writing, he didn't have to read it.

She loved him enormously... cherished the security he'd offered, but wanted to retain her independence... there were plenty of single-parent families. Her little baby wouldn't be one of those... he'd be the father... have time with her and the baby when in Spain... that way he'd keep his independence too... the one half of his life would be young and slightly bohemian because she'd get a modest pad in Barcelona, close to a crèche, so that she could still work, and travel for Paul... the other would be when he was suited and booted in his 'proper' land. They'd always be in love, though apart, and when together their needs could be fulfilled...

His mistake was to confide in Jan, and he'd paid the penalty for that. The bloody Bok was always going to be his downfall... couldn't he see that coming at the beginning? "... Classes apart... different cultures..." It had been quite a lecture, and obviously Jan had included some detail in her briefing to Dominic, though not all.

The coffee Di brought in caused a natural break between his more personal life and business, and gave Dominic the fresh opening she needed.

"OK. Business UK. How's it going?" she resumed.

Peter ran through the patter he put to the Institutional investors and a couple of the tame analysts in the Construction Property sector on the stock market, as he did on a regular basis.

"What about the international activities? Wasn't there some 'Night of the Long Knives' a couple of years back, where the Chairman got moved across?"

The official line was that there hadn't been and that Mr William had wanted Peter to use his European upbringing to better effect in Europe, and his knowledge and contacts in the Far East likewise.

"… And I gather, on a personal note, you're an active contributor to the Paralympic movement."

That was accurate enough for Peter. "That's right, but that, as you say, is a personal thing."

"Why the paraplegic side of things? Normally that would suggest you have a disabled child and you want to promote a world of equality for that child to live in."

"That, young lady, is outrageous! As it happens, I have four perfectly fit, lovely children. It just happens to be that I met people who were able to show a great need for motivation and an injection of business acumen. At the time, I had a bit of time spare and the rest is history… and incidentally, my family's now involved. My son does all the PR for the forthcoming Olympics."

"… And BCG are doing major construction projects in Barcelona. Isn't that a bit coincidental?"

"Again, your research is lacking. BCG have a minority stake in a Spanish consortium, which has been able to tender for Olympic construction-related work. Currently we're 25 per cent of the way through a $500 million programme that will last a further two years. The impact that has on the UK group in turnover and profit is strong. The word is 'strong', not 'tremendous' or any other journalese."

"OK. Strong… and the Far East?"

"We have, again 'strong' connections through bankers in Malaysia and Hong Kong and again, there, we're major shareholders in locally based companies. We're using their local knowledge as to how to build and our international ability to bring finance and management to their table. It works well. We get approaching 50 per cent of joint international trading with a very small injection of overseas personnel. It's the way forward internationally. We're setting up similar associations in the States."

Dominic scribbled shorthand notes and surreptitiously looked at her watch.

"Well, I think I've covered most things in the time you allocated. There's just that final question you said I'd be able to ask if I'd been a good girl, or words to that effect. What about the wedding?"

Peter paused, and thought deeply for a few moments. He didn't want her to be the witness to him being turned into stone.

"You level with me and I'll level with you. Oh, and by the way, it's ladies first."

"I'm not sure that I like such an open question. But try me."

"OK. So if it's ladies first, do we both read the same vibes about Jan's wedding?"

He and Jan couldn't have helped but keep in touch, despite the silly competition that had built up between them as to who was the least available to meet. Clearly Jan was intending to play the woman scorned for life, although when they did get together, she soon relaxed into the close sharing of personal interests, which they both did genuinely have in each other.

After the 'Bok' episode, Jan had made access for Peter difficult, to say the least. He was as sure as he needed to be that some of her reasons for being unable to meet – the 'this hot date', the 'you'll like him, I'm sure' and 'I've got to meet his parents' scenarios could have been fabricated to liven up his taste buds.

But they did eventually negotiate some dinner dates together. When they met, she always seemingly waited until she'd just had a taste too much of drink before she enquired after the Bok and his daughter. Her interest was more in his love child than the perpetrator herself. Peter tended to play down any information when asked the question. "… And I suppose Cas hasn't found a more suitable male to marry yet?" He had got used to replying on the, "Good God, no, why would she need to do that?" basis… and that seemed to inflame Jan into launching into tales about her own current associations.

Three months previously, when he had received Cas's *"Darling Peter… this is my newsletter"*, he had kept the contents from everybody, even his son – all except Sylvia.

He knew she would understand. As she did.

"You'll probably be shocked, but darling, don't be," wrote Cas. *"I've been wanting to get this out of my system for six months or so. When Paul and I went to Jo'berg for the Southern Hemisphere games, I met an old friend of Mark's. A friend of mine too. He's now coaching a couple of black girls and his aims are so close to mine, except his girls aren't handicapped, that we immediately gelled.*

Darling, don't be upset. Don't hate me but he's asked me to marry him. I can't, I feel, without your consent because it would mean he would gain title, in part (nothing can ever replace you), in Petula's life. You'll be pleased to hear there's no volcanic reaction between us. He's a lovely Mr Steady, so it's not infatuation. I think this is the one at a level you and I would never have wanted to stoop to. I just love his company, his reasoned conversation, his middle class ambitions, but not so much as to have those compared with my high flying 'proper' lover.

Would you, my darling Peter, hate me for marrying him, in this case, till death us do part? I have of course told him about the beautiful you!
With all my love,
Cas"

Of course, it had brought a lump to Peter's throat. He did love Cas, and he was mad about Petula. He'd never been over-blessed with the ability to accept that there were certain things in life he just could not have. In this case, it was made worse by the fact that he'd apparently been so easily replaced as a security provider to Cas.

But Peter was a realist, as was his mother. When he told her that she was a grandmother again, Maria said this was all because he hadn't had a father to bring him up and beat hell out of him to teach him the values of life. However, she had then softened, saying she had grown to like Cas, and would welcome Petula as a Martinez family member. They had met and Maria was besotted with the dear little girl who had introduced blonde hair into the Martinez gene pool. She'd never met Coco, which would undoubtedly have introduced another thought process to her about Oriental blood.

So Peter received Cas's letter with some pain, but also a degree of relief.

Sylvia was now closely in touch with Cas through her PR coverage of the Paras, and a full partner in Alex's organisation since Russell, the partner doing 'music', had succumbed to some debilitating illness, possibly a form of cancer or AIDS, which had put him into a convent-sponsored hospice and had proved to be terminal.

Neither Peter, Alex nor Sylvia had quite anticipated how Peter's impulsive suggestion to his son, that he knew somebody who could speak and write in Spanish who might co-ordinate the BCG/Paraplegic and Olympic messages building up to 1992, would work out. Just the one dinner with Sylvia had shown Peter she was no ordinary receptionist. She confessed to having taken the job to help with her father's subsidy of her daughter Cari's school fees, while she herself finished a book she was writing. It transpired she had been in PR but had temporarily 'got out' to focus on her daughter and her writing in a complex conundrum of priorities. Peter had brought Alex and Sylvia together to see if they had common ground. That led to Sylvia acting as Peter's PA for a while, while he used the time to set up the whole marketing scenario.

Sylvia took to that like a duck to water, secretly driven on by Peter's enthusiasm and now considerable experience.

It cost Peter a number of extra dinners to enhance the briefings. When it was known the full reason for Sylvia joining Peter's son in a business relationship, Jan surfaced again big time.

In her first, "Is what I hear true?" phone call, she said, "Tell me, Peter, a girl comes in as a receptionist... and hey! Bingo, you're off and in bed with her. A girl comes in, a talented journalist, and interviews you, and there are fireworks, and the two of you go nowhere. I was there day, and night, if needed, in your sickness and your health, dedicated… and… nothing. I didn't even get my bottom pinched."

"Jan, my sweet," Peter said in a condescending tone, "you were too important to me to be sidetracked into bed and then for me to have to hop back in at every behest, just to get my PR image enhanced."

"I'd always do your write-ups, Peter, my sweet. I just wouldn't have minded a little action. You can't blame a girl, she sees how easy it is and, obviously, how good you are, but can't get you even to fumble with the goods to see how they'd suit you."

"There's another thing," Peter had now replied, on more than the one occasion. "The receptionist you refer to, and yours truly, have not been to bed. The interviewer is, to be honest, another story."

There had been more than one occasion during an enforced and extended period of celibacy, and a pile-up of work, that he had pondered the probability of calling on Marcia's open offers. Tania was now totally out of the equation. The poor thing had had a tumour diagnosed which, due to its position in the brain and its rate of growth, was going to be terminal. As for him and Jan, that had simply been a temptation of a lustful, needy nature.

Now though – which Jan seemed to be completely ignoring – was the question of her planned wedding. In the closing stages of his interview with Dominic, that began to take on an element of spoof.

"So about the wedding?" Peter asked Dominic. "Tell me, is it genuine?"

Dominic seemed surprised. "You're not confusing your own research, are you?" she asked. "She's not gay. You know that."

"Yes. I didn't mean that. Just… is there an actual man?" he asked.

"Yes, and parents." She fumbled in her briefcase. "Don't you have one of these?"

It was a formal invite.

Mr & Mrs Stephen Roberts
invite
Miss Dominic Hall
to
The Wedding of their Daughter
Janet Elizabeth
to
John Gordon Austin
at
St Marks Church, Cobham
Mid-day on 16th June 1990
and afterwards
At
The Fairmile Hotel
RSVP

"Are you not invited?" Dominic asked with surprise.

Peter's slightly hurt response was, "Jan said would I like to go and I actually said not. But I'd best organise a present."

"They say... well you, know that expression, I'm sure. Well, they say it's because you're getting married as well that Jan actually thought 'sod it', and sooner rather than later, as she didn't want to be an old spinster. She succumbed to a proposal she'd had quite a while ago, which she'd asked to be given time to think over. So. That's my answer. Now, do I get to be told about your plans, which perhaps have brought about hers?"

"Yes. It's in early July. In Spain."

"... And the lady?"

"You'll have to see the press after the secret's out."

"Now that, Mr Martinez, is not fair," Dominic answered spontaneously. "I said I'd get back to Jan with that side of the equation."

"Tell Jan from me that instead of having a hen night, she ought to get the video out of The Graduate."

Jan had set Dominic up. She'd let the cat slip out of the bag.

Now he had set Dominic's active brain racing. "What's the point?"

"Time's up, young lady. Tell Martin I'd like to see a proof."

"We don't do that. You know that. But I can't let The Graduate thing go."

"Don't you remember the ending?"

"What, in the church? Dustin Hoffman on the balcony when the bride's about to complete her vows with the groom... you wouldn't... would you? What the hell do I tell Jan?"

"Say it would seem I'm intent on re-marriage. That's my considered opinion. What seems yet to be determined is with which one of three it's going to be... and as the chosen one hasn't yet been asked for her hand, I'm too much of a gentleman to tell you who it will be."

"Is Jan one of them?"

Peter leant forward and patted the end of her nose with his forefinger. "Sorry. Let me make it plain. I see a proof, please. If not, Martin'll never work with us again. It's been a pleasure meeting with you. Thank you."

They shook hands and parted without a great deal of love lost between them.

"How did it go with that blonde?" Di asked.

"Difficult. We didn't relate."

"Good." Di was just getting to know how familiar she could be and thought she now knew how to make Peter smile.

"Di! Be a friend. A cup of tea, then a bit of space please." That normally meant he had something private to consider.

"Sure. But by the way, your mother rang. Could you phone her urgently."

The hairs on the back of his neck prickled. He knew what that would be. At one point in his chat with Dominic, he'd suddenly felt as though somebody had walked over his grave. Perhaps they had.

"Hi, mother! You can't believe how busy I am."
"Oh! I'm really sorry about that."
He listened while Maria explained it had been peaceful, even if inevitable.
"Well, that's a troublesome era over. If it's Tuesday I'll try to be there. If I'm not, then the lilies are from me."
Tania had died.
Peter said he was sorry. In fact he was sorry. He contemplated the past for a while.
He dialled out on his private line. He knew she'd be there between five and six Spanish time. She usually was. He was working private line to private line.
Her heart always fluttered when that phone rang. Nine times out of ten it would be Peter. Five times out of those nine it would be business. Four times it would not be.
"Hi!" It was his voice.
"Hi. How are you?"
"Really great. Hey! Have you got one of those desk diaries that tell you what major events took place on certain days?"
"Yes I have, but it's not something I bother with. What's the purpose? Is this some trick or other?"
"Nope. What's down for today, first of June?"
"I know it's the first of June, I don't need to know what other day it is as a point in history."
"Go on, please. I want to see if yours says the same as mine."
"Oh, OK. You're a little boy at heart. OK, it's St Justin's Feast Day."
"Oh!" he said with surprise.
"Why, what's yours say?"
"It says it's an anniversary of when I got engaged."
Her heart sank. "Which one was that?"
"Don't know. What's your fourth of July say?"
"I doubt I even have to look. It's Independence Day."
"Can you check that? Mine doesn't say that."
She flipped over a couple of pages, and as she did, she exuded a sigh of boredom. He could hear it down the length of the cable.
"Yes, I'm right. It is. Independence Day."
"Mine isn't."
"Peter, my darling. What's all this waste of time about?"
"Look. Do me a favour, could you scratch that out and make it 'Give up Independence Day'."
"Peter, are you drunk?"

"Please, my darling. Do as I ask."

"OK." She added the words. "Right, I've done that."

"So is that a yes?"

"Peter, what are you on?"

"Are you prepared to give up your independence on the fourth of July?"

Silence was her best tactic, she thought.

"Listen, you difficult lady. Today's the day that Peter proposes. The fourth of July is the day we both give up our independence. For Christ's sake, woman! I can't ask you to marry me in a more direct way."

She went for silence, but this time it was no act. It was enforced upon her. He thought they'd been cut off.

"For Christ's sake!" he bellowed down the phone. "Sylvia... Sylvia formerly Pez... Will you marry me on the fourth of July?"

If he could have seen her face. It was a picture.

"Look, I can actually be free that day. There's a strong chance the answer is yes, but if you're not hugging me and blotting up the tears before midnight tonight at Barcelona Airport, my slipper will fall off and I'll return home, and then you can take that as a firm refusal."

"So here, my darling, is the plan. I'm leaving now. I'm coming scheduled BA jet, it's more reliable than our own. If you're not there, the invite will be off."

"Peter, I so love you."

"Sylvia, I so love you too. See you then. I must rush. I've an important plane to catch... oh, by the way..."

"What?"

"If in the meantime you contact my mother, which would be the same as giving a complete exposé to the paparazzi, the invite's off."

"Peter, darling, I want you so much. I just want selfishly to indulge the shock until I see that you're not pissed or high on some wonder drug at 9pm. No mother release, no press co-operation."

"Good! Then this one, Mrs Pez, will be the full treatment. In sickness and in health, for richer or for poorer, until we die together on the same minute of the same day, so that neither of us is alone again."

She passed the first of the four hours of waiting crying her heart out.

Chapter 28

Peter would have been first off the plane but he had left his pen on the meal tray and the hostess had tipped everything into a waste sack for disposal. Luckily she found it, but it held him back a little.

He'd cleared customs and, as always, only had hand baggage. He maintained a partial wardrobe at Sylvia's place.

Ahead of him, passengers from other flights were moving quickly. There was quite a large commuting traffic between London and Barcelona and a number would be back on the early morning flight the following Monday.

Suddenly the fast-flowing battalion of passengers slowed, as drivers do when there's been a motorway accident, or like discerning people hesitating on their intended route before walking gingerly around dog mess.

Peter reached the point at the exit route that was causing the sudden blockage. He didn't just slow; he stopped dead, causing some of those behind him to also halt, and even to bump into the rear of the person in front. He jostled for position to see what lay ahead. Normally such a delay would have little or no effect on him. But on this occasion, it was getting in the way of him being with Sylvia.

Ahead of him, held at eye-level above the barrier around the exit, was a large red sign, cut to the shape of a heart. It must have been 900 centimetres high.

All the other signs were for the Mr Joneses of the world being met by Hertz, and Spaniards coming back to see their loved ones but being picked up by transportation from the airport. A handful were for Cosmos and Thomas Cook holidaymakers, due to be collected and distributed elsewhere.

The heart-shaped notice, which was causing smiles and laughter, had its message in bold black letters, all very professionally put together:

TRANSPORTATION FOR
MR PETER MARTINEZ
THE FUTURE INTENDED HUSBAND OF
SYLVIA PEZ
(WAITING WITH LOVE)

Sylvia had cut in a couple of holes to provide her with a clear view of Peter's arrival, and his shock-horror as he read the sign.

Thank God, she thought with relief, *he laughed!* But then, she'd known he would.

Her beaming head surfaced over the top of the sign as she lowered it, and she rested her chin in the cleavage at the top of the heart. She was able to lean forward over the barrier and offer him the welcome kiss the sign was all about.

"Sod it!" he said. "I was going to tell you I was drunk when I phoned and that I can't go through with it, but OK, now that all these people know about it, I'll do the decent thing and ask you again on Spanish soil. ¿quieres casarte conmigo?"

"Yes. With all my heart."

The kiss to seal the deal was a bit clumsy because of the sign, and the still intervening barrier. So Sylvia let go of it, allowing it to fall to the ground, and threw both her free arms around Peter's neck as they entered into a long welcome-home embrace.

They went straight to the apartment, having held hands all the way while she was driving. Sylvia said to Peter to dump his case in their bedroom and change, and there'd be a cup of tea on the terrace when he came through.

He entered the bedroom and stopped as quickly as he had when he saw the sign at the airport.

There must have been 50 hearts of varying sizes hanging from the central light. Some were on a thin string and secured to the ceiling with blue tack. The duvet was pulled down, exposing two pillows covered in heart-shaped confetti. He thought that the smile on his face brought about by the antics of this apparently 16-year-old excited child would crack his cheeks.

He almost ripped his clothes off, at least down to his underpants, and went to the bedroom door. He bellowed out, "Sylvia!" as if in pain.

She reacted instantly. *What the hell has he done?* she thought. There was no smile on her face. This was the beginning of a disappointing weekend.

She entered the room in a hurry. There, under the duvet, was Peter, lying with both hands behind his head on the right-hand side of the bed (as he faced the ceiling), where he always slept. This had been the subject of early discord when they'd first gone to bed together, because Sylvia had always slept on the right-hand side too.

She had given in on that first occasion, which Peter then said had created a precedent, and if he was to stay with her in a more permanent way, that was to be the way it was. It was always said in a good-humoured way, and if, after lovemaking, Sylvia found herself looking up at the ceiling from the right-hand side of the bed, she would rule that God had worked it that way, on that night, and his plans should never be challenged.

The first time that happened, the next morning she had congratulated Peter on being ambidextrous. That had ended in a near-fight for position during an early morning repeat of the previous night's entwinement, after which, as Peter had put it, she was back in her rightful place.

"I got the message," Peter said now, extending an outstretched hand as an invitation into bed.

"Look, darling, I know you haven't had time to notice I'm wearing a new dress but I'm not getting in there to get it ruined. You'll have to give me a minute."

She feigned a striptease... well, almost. For some reason, they had at some time each agreed the other would keep their pants on. Peter thought it was because, with Sylvia being virtually an employee at the time, she was shy about her boss seeing her nude. It was always a possibility, of course, that she might be topless on a beach which, by chance, Peter could be on, and they might meet. It would be perfectly natural for a boss to say nothing to his female employee about her attire, or lack of. But completely nude would be outrageous.

The habit had stuck.

Afterwards, they showered and Sylvia slipped into a pair of pedal-pushers and a T-shirt and Peter, his Boss jeans and a cotton shirt.

The tea Sylvia had made earlier was ruined. So they decided to have a bottle of champagne instead, and then Sylvia said to Peter that, just in case he was serious about the proposal, she had in fact bought a case of 12, "Because it was cheaper that way, and although I don't know the exact timing of this arrangement you've proposed, I thought we may need the odd bottle here and there to keep us moving towards the ceremony... or whatever you have in mind."

Quite cleverly, but not the slightest bit surprisingly, she had thereby, in that short resumé as to why they had a stock of Roederer Champagne greater than most local restaurants, set the agenda for the remainder of the evening, if not the whole weekend.

Over the champagne they prepared that agenda. The piece of paper merely listed:

When?
Where?
Communication – immediate:
Alex
Petra
Cari
Mother
Others
Type of ceremony/celebration
Guests
Announcements
New Spanish Married Quarters.

As an afterthought, Sylvia had asked if she was to get an engagement ring. The list was amended and it then started:
Engagement ring – Saturday early.
When?
Where?
Communication etc., etc., and followed the previous format.

Not surprisingly, by mutual agreement they decided to call Maria and break the news to her there and then.

The receptionist in the hotel had said Señora Martinez was still in the hotel and had not yet returned to the cottage before the evening's work. If he could hold, she would try and locate her. The girl, who knew Peter's calls quite well, grimaced, waiting for the answer that he couldn't wait and would call back. Whenever that happened, Maria always got disappointed with the receptionist for not saying she would locate her within 30 seconds. That should always be possible. Missing Peter's calls might mean she would have to wait a couple of days before he had time to call again.

But on this occasion he simply said, "OK. I'll wait. I've got all the time in the world."

A few minutes later, Maria was on the line. "What's this, favourite son, that you'll wait for me to be found because, what was it, you've got time on your hands, my receptionist thought you said?"

"Mother. It does me no good to be your favourite son. Favourite out of a one-horse race wouldn't gain favour with the bookmakers. But anyway, how are you?"

Maria thought she had heard those words before. Yes, she remembered. Alex said almost the same.

At this point, Peter leant forward and pressed the speakerphone button, laying the handset on the coffee table for Sylvia to share, as Maria went through the ritual of Marco being no better, it appearing that Virginia was thriving on that as her inheritance was getting closer. The hotel was full. Chef's wife had another baby… the full set of fairly standard repetitive information about her life.

She eventually got round to asking after Peter's health, which was a sign for him to pick up the handset. When he said he was in Spain, Maria almost jumped for joy. She asked if she was on his visiting list and was over the moon when he said he and Sylvia were planning lunch at the hotel on Sunday.

"… And how is darling Sylvia, my dear?"
"That's why I'm calling."
"Don't tell me she's ill?"
"No. She's the reverse."

There was a hint of her being silenced in the background. Then Maria spoke quietly, "Pregnant."

"Mother, no. I've asked her to marry me and I'm waiting to get her answer."

"Wonderful, darling! But how long do you have to wait? That would be such good news. She's really excellent for you. I like her far more than I ever liked Anna…"

Peter caught Sylvia's eyes and they both laughed. Sylvia did a thumbs-up sign.

"… Well you know, Peter, I liked Anna because you loved her but Sylvia would be my ideal choice for you."

"Mother. If that's the case, have a word with her and see if you can get me put out of my misery, having to wait to know if she'll say yes."

"Is she with you?"

"Yes."

"Then do put her on…"

"Hello, Sylvia."

"Hello, Maria."

"Now what's all this I hear about my wayward son wanting to marry you?"

"Well, Maria. It came as such a surprise. I always thought I was just another one of his bimbos. A mere plaything."

"He doesn't have those, does he?"

"Well… he's in London by himself for weeks at a time."

"Yes. Well, I can see that. But, darling, he's always talking about you. Jan is right out of the picture…"

Peter and Sylvia caught each other's eye again. Peter just nodded and shrugged.

"Was Jan a serious contender?" Sylvia sought Maria's opinion mainly in fun, as she knew the answer.

"My darling Sylvia. You must know, and if you don't and you're going to get married, you should know, Peter's always had a following of women… well, girls even… when he was younger, but I think he's always been very selective. No! I don't think he's got a load of bimbos. Jan thought she was for him but I just don't know what happened… I think… no, I don't know what happened."

Sylvia and Peter smiled at each other again.

"So… do you think you'll accept?"

"Yes. A hundred per cent."

"Oh, wonderful Sylvia! So tell the darling man. Put him out of his misery."

"I'll see. Look, until I've said yes, if I do, it's a secret. OK?"

"Darling, of course. Who would I tell anyway?"

"OK. I'll promise you'll be the first to be told, apart from Peter. Then you can put the news on the back of that plane which flies up and down the

Costa Brava advertising sun cream. You could get that changed to 'Sylvia and Peter – Engaged'."

"What a wonderful idea! Please let me know soon. I want to be so happy."

Sylvia switched the speakerphone off and then the phone itself. She'd been caught out once before by leaving the speaker device on and the person on the other end of the call heard her subsequent conversation with a colleague, which had not been too complimentary.

She and Peter burst into laughter.

"Poor Maria! She so wants you looked after. I'll try to ring her back today after we've worked a few more things out. We'll wait for breakfast and then do a campaign plan. OK. Oh, and Peter… by the way, I've decided we shouldn't make love again until we're married."

"What? Outrageous! The wedding's off. I can't wait that long. Why the hell that?"

"I want our wedding night to mean something special."

"Look. I can easily still make it special. But the better plan would be not to consummate our marriage on the actual day, when we'll both be tired, I expect, and we'll have had a big meal and plenty to drink. Yes. I think that's the better plan."

"No, Peter. You have to respect the wishes of the bride."

"So what the hell do we do tonight?"

"We can talk. We ought to talk more." And she burst out laughing. They always acted as though they were both 20 years younger.

"We'll see how it goes."

Sylvia had defrosted some croissants and she had a large stock of English Ledbury jams. She knew Peter liked cheese for breakfast and so, while he shaved and showered, she had set the table on the terrace for the two of them. Her apartment was unusual. It had a dual aspect with the terrace facing south, benefitting from virtually all-day sun, so she had a collection of umbrellas scattered in strategic places. The bedroom and kitchen faced north, across the city of Barcelona and the hills beyond.

Sylvia only had a bowl of fruit for her early morning sustenance and she ate that while the croissants were made edible and the coffee brewed. They had an early newspaper delivery and so Peter was allowed to settle down to some valuable quiet time while Sylvia showered and got ready. She took a little more time that day, wanting to look her very best when they sat down on the customer side of a counter somewhere to choose an engagement ring. With that in mind, she touched up her recently manicured nails.

Peter was likely to ask her where she would like to go to look at rings. She'd never been present when one had been bought before, so she had no idea, or what she would like. She'd ask to see a selection. Not a solitaire. Possibly quite big, maybe quite plain, something set with a central feature stone. She wasn't a gold person. She'd probably ask to see platinum. Suddenly she was able to relax. Subconsciously, she did know what she'd like.

She chose a white two-piece suit she had bought on impulse just two or three weeks before, thinking then it was bound to come in useful. When she appeared on the terrace in high black sandals, Peter reacted to the stilettos impacting on the timber overlay to the flat roof.

He looked towards her over the top of the newspaper he was into.

"Bloody agony! You look a million dollars. Come here. Give me a kiss."

"I'll come here, certainly. But that's another thing. Until we're married, we won't kiss anymore."

"What? That would be daft! You can't do that. No sex. No kissing now. I'm quite near to calling it off. At least life should remain as pleasurable as it has been." He allowed a smile to develop. He was pretty sure she was pulling his leg. "Anyway, why no kissing?"

"When whoever marries us is satisfied that you've understood the vows – or the citizen's promises, if we find no priest will allow you to go through his ceremony – we'll be invited to kiss. I'd like that embrace to be pure. Virginal really, although sadly I know we can't turn the clock back, it's too late for that. So we'll save up for that kiss."

"By the time the ceremony arrives, I doubt even a registrar will be prepared to marry me because I'll have been off kissing and having sex all over the place… word would get out… you watch." The smile was there again.

"OK. Then we'll see. Just one now and a definite one as a thank you for the ring. That's if the invitation's still there."

"It's only just still there. It's a close thing, so I wouldn't suggest cutting anything else out."

"Cheese for breakfast?"

"That's it. It's off."

She moved over in front of him and put a hand on each of his shoulders, ensuring she was making a play from the high ground. She wrapped both arms around his neck and leant down and kissed him very fully on the lips. Then she drew back.

"I know it's going to be hard, the sexual withdrawal, but I'm happy to review the occasional kiss."

They both found the situation comedy funny.

"So where do we go for this wretched love token of a ring?" said Peter.

"Lansky? Lansky, just off the Passeig De La Saint Joan. That would be a really lovely place to go. By the way, I'd like to buy you a wedding ring."

Peter hesitated. "Could we say a signet ring? I'd really love that."

"A wedding ring's better for what I have in mind. A new shining wedding ring says 'SOLD, KEEP OFF'."

He laughed. "You don't need to go to all that trouble."

"I know. But you do."

"What about a signet ring and the label left on?"

"Again, we'll see. We've suddenly got so many options between us. Darling, could we go to Lansky now? I'm so excited. I'm really, *really* excited, and I can't get there fast enough."

"OK. But first could we perhaps review the celibacy bit? Might I suggest it starts next Wednesday?"

"When do you intend going back to the UK?"

"Wednesday morning on the 11am flight."

"OK. It can start at 10am Wednesday." Sylvia stepped across to him, still sitting at the table, and replicated the previous kiss. "Please can we go to Lansky?" she asked in her pleading little girl's voice.

"Yes but do you agree those new rules about Wednesday."

"Yes. As I remember, that will be kissing is allowed. Sex is still off limits."

"Come on. Hurry up or all the good rings will be sold. We'll review the whole list of ground rules once you've got a ring on your finger."

Lansky were pleased to see them both. They were told how they could help and the young salesman appeared with a tray of variously beautiful rings. He had asked Peter his price range and was surprised at the reply: whatever pleased his fiancée was alright. The assistant had then taken Sylvia's finger size with greater interest.

"There, señora, all these are in your range and every one is your finger size." The young man gave her an effeminate smile. "You'll want to take it with you, I'm sure."

Peter took an active part in talking through the pros and cons of the rings his new wife-to-be picked out. He noticed she resisted the stones that were a solid tone. The amethysts, ruby ones, emerald, anything green, he predicted, she would avoid, as he knew she thought green was an unlucky colour. She started to hover between the aquamarine and sapphire ranges.

"What do you think, darling? Do help me, please."

Peter said all were lovely but, typically, he said there was one stone that summed up Sylvia's personality, and shapewise it would sit really well on her long, slim finger.

"Don't be cruel. Which one is it?" she asked.

"It's completely your choice. Tell you what, I'll pop over there and write down what I think. You put the rings on your finger – the right hand, if you're being superstitious about it – and I'll wager a cancellation of the terms of our engagement you settled on me this morning, by a day, that you'll choose the one I've singled out…" She smiled a deep and loving smile. "… And I hope I bloody well get it right."

He went away and sat on a plush chair in front of a glass-topped table that had a sort of lace pattern etched around the overlapping edge of the glass on its lime-whited undercarriage, which sat on a simple wrought iron base. He scribbled down *The single oval star sapphire one*, then picked up the paper the attractive young lady assistant handed to him.

"Can I get you some coffee, Sir? Or water?"

"Is it too early for a gin and tonic?"

"Not if you'd like one, Sir. But we don't do alcohol. I'm so sorry."

"Then it's water please."

Thirty minutes later, Sylvia called across to him and to come and help her finally choose. She was sitting with her left hand covered by her right.

"Peter, I've chosen but I'm scared."

"Scared because it might not be the one I have in mind?"

"Precisely."

"It'll be the same."

"… And if it's not? I'll feel it's all my fault if we have some bad luck."

"Tell you what. Show me. If it's not the same choice, I'll quickly screw my piece of paper up and swallow it. It's not particularly important."

"OK," she said hesitantly. "Only I've put this one on the finger I never want it to leave." She removed her right hand.

"Huh!" he said in a derisory way. "The star sapphire oval… single. Eh!"

She jumped off her chair with joy. "Show me, show me… quick!"

He produced the notelet-sized paper and handed it to her. It confirmed what he had said. She jumped up in the air and threw her arms around his neck for the umpteenth time that day, so far.

"So you get your extra day, my love."

After paying by cheque supported by his gold Banker's card, and hearing the equally excited salesperson extolling their virtues (he had never, ever seen a couple be that close in choice, because usually the bloke would just agree with whatever his fiancée had chosen), there were handshakes all round and Peter and Sylvia left arm in arm.

"Coffee?" she suggested.

"Sagrada," he said. "It's not far."

"Familia," she followed.

Together they repeated, "Sagrada Familia," both knowing the other meant the bar and open café opposite the masterpiece Gaudi had started, and others were now finishing. Antonio Gaudi had started the frowned upon modern Catholic cathedral at the age of 31, over a century before their engagement.

"Wow!" Sylvia said. "We can choose the same ring, the place we both want to go for coffee… what next?"

"Bed. To celebrate."

"Why do you always have to spoil it? Do you mean my bed?"

"Of course."

"Funny, isn't it? It's quite amazing."

"You thought that too."

"No. Wrong! I had in mind that park bench over there. And we're not formally engaged yet because you haven't asked me face to face. What future do we have before us?"

Peter swung her whole body, pulling her round to change direction. He increased their walking pace and caught up with the small queue waiting to go into the cathedral in its incomplete state. He pulled her to the head of the line and then explained something to the guide at the entrance, in extremely pigeon English so that he could understand. He had said that he and the young lady wanted to go into the cathedral as an emergency, because he was going to propose to her.

Those who understood, including the guide, all clapped and moved around to give them easy access. Peter whisked Sylvia along the stone aisles until they stopped under the recently installed, emphatically coloured stained-glass windows. He knelt in a pool of red and deep blue with yellow tinted sunlight hitting the stone.

"¿quieres casarte conmigo?"

"Sí, Peter lo haré."

Their romantic moment was suddenly disturbed. It was as though somebody had clapped their hands to disturb pigeons roosting up in the massive arched roof framing. The habit seemed to catch on with another bird harasser, but in seconds there must have been 20 or so tourists, there to see the creative work of one slightly eccentric architect, all clapping in unison watching another carve out his destiny for the future. The fact that he was kneeling on one knee gave the game away.

Both Peter and Sylvia were initially embarrassed but then together saw the humorous side of it all. They jointly acknowledged the encouragement of what was a particularly romantic crowd visiting the cathedral that day.

Peter moved as if to raise himself. There were occasions when his previously injured knee gave him jip. He'd have to remember not to propose too often in an environment with a hard stone floor.

"Stay there. Surely you haven't finished?" she said.

He hoped he had; he really needed to stretch his leg.

"Here, you'll need this." She had slipped the ring off her finger and held it out in her clenched fist.

"You're right. Thank you." He returned the pressure onto his knee and, taking her left hand in his, slipped the ring onto her engagement finger.

She cried.

He stood up and consoled her, even as he knew it was happiness, and everybody clapped again, including two stonemasons high up with the gods where they had been chipping away at a moulded cornice, set to last for many, many years more than the results of Peter and Sylvia's exercise down at ground level could possibly exist, due to man's limited time allowance on the planet.

Their coffee break was remarkably silent. They just people-watched and studied the cut stonework gaining height up each of the four towers, which still had cranes in attendance the other side of the square… and when, as they seemed to frequently, they caught each other's eye, they just smiled happily at one another.

They agreed that their next discussion as to 'when' and 'where' could be left to be talked out over lunch, so they walked hand in hand to a taxi, and though the short journey would normally have been an amble, they had taken the faster option to create time to walk in the Gaudi Park. Fortunately they both enjoyed the quirky designs.

It was a lovely summer's day and one they would both remember.

Lunch was light in an outside restaurant they liked to go to, just off the Ramblas. Sylvia had a tomato salad starter and a small sole with salad, explaining that she would start eating less because she'd need to be a little slimmer to be the bride she wanted to be. Peter, who had a big appetite, said he didn't care what he looked like, which she said was a really naughty thing to say and that she hadn't liked to mention it before but wouldn't it be a good idea for him to start going to a gym again?

He had a half portion of moules marinières and a thin entrecôte with salad. He also ordered French fried chipped potatoes and had to put up with Sylvia's stern expression from the other side of the table. They shared a bottle of Montrachet.

They followed tradition and, after ordering coffee, they got round to the business part of the lunch. Peter tried to establish some ground rules on the date side of the agenda.

"Roughly how long do you think we should wait before actually getting married?"

"Do you think before Christmas would be too soon?"

"Not at all. In some respects sooner is better."

Sylvia seemed surprised. "Why?"

"Before one of us changes our mind."

"OK. What about Monday, because I'd die if you changed your mind."

"Would it help if I said OK? But to be practical, when we get round to inviting people we'll have to give them about six weeks' notice."

She said right. "Three months' time, the fifth of October."

"What day of the week would that be?"

She always kept a neat handbag. There was no fumbling. She easily found her diary and thumbed through. "A Monday."

"That's not so good."

"How would you feel about a Friday then? Saturday's the usual day for weddings. I don't see ours as being quite usual."

"I agree."

"Friday's good. I have the cleaner come to the flat that day. If it's in the afternoon, I could get the week finished off before the weekend. Yes, I quite like a Friday."

"OK. The second or the ninth?"

She started counting frantically on her fingers.

"What's that for, for Heaven's sake?"

"A girl needs to know."

"Oh, I see." He never counted lunar days. He thought that was probably because he'd never had a sister.

"The ninth would be better."

"That's really thoughtful."

"Why do you say that?"

"Well, it obviously is… well, you know, a good day," he said, merely adding to the conversation but not wishing to become too involved.

"No, not at all. It's when I'm definitely off games." His pretty face, she thought, was an absolute picture. "So OK. It's really perfect." Then she quickly added, "I was only pulling your leg to see how you'd react."

"… And my reaction?"

"Predictable, my sweet."

"So we aim at Friday, the ninth of October."

"Yes, that's it." She went quiet.

"Are you OK?"

"Yes, fine."

"There's something wrong."

"No. It's OK."

"Tell me."

"Oh, Peter. I've cheated on you already."

His face dropped. "Going to tell me about it?"

"You won't be cross?"

"How can I say that?"

"Trust me."

"What, when you've confessed to being a pretty low-down cheat on the day we got engaged?" He was playing along, suspecting this was not going to turn out to be too serious.

"It's only two months away."

"What is?"

"Our wedding day."

"We said three."

"Yes, I've cheated. I really feel I can't wait. I made a deliberate mistake in turning over the pages in my diary. But there's another thing… the ninth of October was the date you returned from your treatment in Barcelona. So it's our anniversary and I thought if I suggested that, you'd think I was being superstitious again."

"Sylvia, I'm delighted it's the ninth of October. It's the monthly mid-week medal competition at the golf club. I can get an early tee time and be here by, say, 4pm. They'll still be doing weddings at that time, won't they?"

They celebrated agreeing the date by breaking with their intended controlled intake of food and ordering a crema Catalan with two spoons.

"Shall we go home and have a siesta and then talk about where?"

Peter thought through his answer carefully before responding.

"I think if we could establish some ground rules it might be a little more creative. There's a subject we've never discussed. I suppose it's because we're quite adult and we've never sat on bean bags playing hip music with other contemporaries, putting the world right, or attempting to. I've no idea if you're a communist. But I'd say you're not. I'm sure you're not atheist either, because we went to Alex's little chap's christening and that seemed alright to us both. However, we've both been through a marriage and I'd say you've no idea if I was married in a cathedral or a register office or even a synagogue. Likewise you. But if we find we were both married in a church, we might jointly agree that was sufficiently perfect to do it again."

"Or the reverse," Sylvia chipped in.

"Precisely."

"OK. I'll serve," Sylvia volunteered. "I was married in a Catholic church. We each pledged our vows. He broke his. It wouldn't matter to me if I got married in a wigwam, do you call it, or in a field with no witnesses. If I promise to do something, I don't need an environment to put the fear of God into me if I don't keep to it."

"Great! Ours was in a really big Catholic church, very much under the eyes of God. I'm OK with religion but when you make a vow that gives you a let out to cheat if the bond ceases at death, and death is forced upon you without godly protection, I'm inclined to agree with you. But if you say the location should be a church, I'll be there, of course. On balance, the field with nobody there might be the most sincere place, because our vows will be one-to-one anyway and if they have to be witnessed to make them work, then it's a pretty sad day."

"So... no church?"

"I'd agree," Peter leant across the table and kissed his fiancée.

"A register office as it would be known in the UK?" she suggested.

"Now that I know your view, could I be allowed to make some enquiries? I've an idea. However – and it's a big however – if we're too informal, we won't be having the problem with God. It will be with my mother."

"Oh, Peter! For our own sake, I hadn't thought of that. You're really all she's got and I would seriously like to be a worthwhile appendage to that. I'd change my principles to assist that."

"You're lovely, my darling. Let me work on it. This idea I've got could involve mother's help. Leave the venue to me for a while. There *is* one big question, though."

"Not another one, surely?"
"Yes. It's fundamental too."
"What's that?"
"Where?"
"What, the issue between the park bench and bed options?"
"No! Where? Spain, South America, England, maybe on a cruise liner?"
"Oh! Yes, I see… I fancy Spain."
"OK. It's Spain then. That's where I would have said anyway."
"Right, we're getting somewhere. I feel exhausted. I think carrying the weight of this ring around is probably wearing me out."
"Shall I pay the bill and we'll go to siesta?"
"Yes… and I mean siesta."
"Actually, me too. I'm whacked."

Chapter 29

Maria was excited, frustrated and altogether knocked for six.

She very much liked Sylvia. Thinking back on all the others, Sylvia was definitely the most sincere. She had quality, yet warmth. Maria doubted that they'd have more children… oh dear, she was having trouble as it was remembering birthdays. Two more or so would be very difficult.

Just as she made her mind up that further grandchildren were an unlikely prospect, and as she was thinking that now that it was about five o'clock in the late afternoon and, since the hotel had a busy Saturday night coming up, she would take a couple of hours off, the phone in her office rang.

Having decided not to answer it, she then thought it might just be Peter or Sylvia. She hesitated. She'd risk it not being a booking enquiry for next year. She just couldn't take that.

"Maria Martinez."

Suddenly it occurred to Sylvia she was going to become a Martinez also. Somehow or other, she blurted out to Maria what she was thinking.

"Mrs Martinez, this is the Mrs Martinez Jnr to be."

"What, dear?" Maria kicked herself because although it sounded like Sylvia, suppose it was an enquiry and she'd called the person 'dear'?

"Maria, it's me. Sylvia. What I've just realised is that in accepting Peter's proposal…"

"Accepting! Oh! Now I'm really excited. Was it very difficult?"

"Maria. Please, not at all. I made your lovely son wait for an answer just to keep him in check. I'm so, so thrilled…"

"So am I."

"But what I was saying was that I'm Mrs Martinez Jnr, to be, because I'd realised I would change from a Pez to a Martinez."

"Sylvia Martinez," Maria said. "That does go very nicely. It's because your name ends in a vowel, like mine does, that makes it set properly. So when do you think you'll marry?"

"I'm not risking him change his mind. In a couple of months, I'd say."

"Dare I ask, where?"

"In Spain."

"Oh lovely, because Marco and Virginia won't travel far." Then Maria thought that might have been a little presumptuous. "That's if you *are* going to have people there." She gritted her teeth. "You really don't need hordes of people getting in the way when it's really your day. Anyway, we'll all have to see who gets invited."

"Maria, you will be there, of course, and José, and I'm sure Marco and Virginia. Peter wouldn't want it any different from that and even if he were to see it differently, I'd invite you."

"Sylvia. You're lovely. I think my son was born lucky. He's very, very, fortunate to have found you... when I think of the others... oh, he could have been in so much trouble."

"Maria, you'll have to get used to modern technology. Peter's listening in on the call."

"I don't care. Peter, you know very well some of your... well... let's say lady friends have been really dreadful, even you must see that, darling."

"Yes, Mother."

Sylvia gave him an understanding smile and with that they brought the call to an end.

"What about the children? Don't you think we ought to let them know before your mother breaks the news?" Sylvia suggested in a serious tone.

"I think that's the right thing to do. Who first?"

"Long distance, I'd suggest. Maria is a bit closer with Petra than Alex."

Peter glanced at his watch. Round about lunchtime in Buenos Aires. "Do you have her number handy? She'd automatically be on our invite list, obviously. We'll need to talk about that bit of our day, but let's get in and say keep it free."

Sylvia looked in her home telephone book and gave Peter the number and the code. The phone seemed to ring for an age.

"Not there, I think," was Peter's view.

Then the ringing tone stopped as an out-of-breath Petra answered. Her immediate reaction, although not knowing who was calling, was to apologise to the world that she was, "... Sorry. We've got a barbecue on the go by the pool..."

"Smells good. We can smell it from here."

"Papa!" she screeched. "But you don't call. Something's wrong. Maria? Marco? Quick, tell me."

"You're a funny but dear daughter. No, it's not bad news. We hope you'll see it as good."

We?" she thought. *What's he going to say?*

"I'm ringing to say that Sylvia and I are getting married."

"At last. Good," she replied in a serious voice, but it had an undercurrent of disappointment.

Peter was quick to pick up on that and, in his normal reactive style, flushed her thoughts out for her.

"Sylvia's on the line with me..."

"Hi, Sylvia."

"Hi, Petra."

"Many congratulations."

"Thank you, that's kind. We haven't rehearsed this but I suspect our next call is to Cari… she'll be in the same boat as you."

Peter came on the line. "That tells you what good news this is, insofar as, like Sylvia said, we haven't discussed what we're going to say. But I know you'll be feeling hurt for Mama, in some protective way, and that's right. However, I feel sure she wouldn't object, she would have a pang of regret perhaps, that would be natural, but she was always one to say 'life goes on'. We hope you'll see it that way."

"Papa. I do. I'm sorry I didn't disguise my thoughts for Mama but I assure you, I've been thinking of the prospect of you and Sylvia becoming a more formal partnership rather than the very close, I think the current expression is, item,

"… And Sylvia, I can tell you it's an absolute relief in many respects. Papa's had some pretty dodgy lady friends."

"Petra! You and your grandmother. What the hell is this all about? You're both making my life seem as if it's been one of debauchery! I've just had to wait for some real quality to come back into it. That's all."

Petra wouldn't have seen it but he stretched his free hand over and squeezed Sylvia's.

He passed on the date, in anticipation that, "We'd love you to be able to come across," and, "… by the way, we'd split the fare with you in some way."

No they didn't know where the wedding would be or what sort of service they'd have… and yes, she had a ring and Peter let Sylvia describe that. Inwardly he was petrified. He couldn't remember the detail of Anna's ring but the stone Sylvia had chosen was so unusual that he was sure he'd remember if there was any similarity.

The call to Cari was altogether different. Peter had, of course, met the infamous misbehaving Miss Pez.

Her mother had hardly finished breaking the news before she interrupted.

"And about bloody time too! I really don't know why you didn't do this the day after you met. You're the peas in the pod. The perfect pair. When's the wedding… ?"

The remainder was standard. The ring? The date? The place? And quite naturally, "What will you wear?"

Sylvia said in all honesty she had not got a clue. She would have to think about the weather and needed to talk all sorts of things through with Peter.

Peter's call to Alex was a cinch. It was quite factual man-to-man. Alex was all for making an honest woman out of his business partner, though he was concerned the wedding was to be on a Friday because they normally worked that day. But he supposed they'd all go in on the Saturday, if that was alright with Peter, and also, would they be expecting to honeymoon? Only he wasn't sure if Sylvia had holiday owing.

He did ask if Petra would be coming and asked if she had shown her disappointment for their mother, which in a sort of perverse way Peter was pleased to hear, as it broke the ice on that situation.

Alex proposed they all meet for a drink at Sunday lunchtime and Peter said that was a lovely idea but they would ring in the morning to see what could be arranged.

Next Peter thought he'd call Max. He was, after all, his best mate and brother-in-law. He wondered if that status would change just because Peter was remarrying. Then he kicked himself for being so stupid as to even ask himself the question.

Before he made that call, the thought did come into his mind as to whether Max being his best mate led him to be the natural choice as Peter's best man. Max had been the first time round, so all the associations with that and the loss of his twin sister might just be pushing him too far. Max might just prefer not to be asked this time, because Peter was sure he would find it hard to decline the invite. So he wouldn't put that on the agenda.

Peter's hand was inches from the phone when it rang. That confused him momentarily. Instinctively he picked it up but was slow to speak.

Before he could announce himself the caller asked, "Well, which one of you is it?"

"Your darling loving son, mother."

"Oh! Good. I thought for a moment I had the wrong number. Peter, darling. Will you invite children to the wedding?"

"Hold on, mother. I've no idea. Let me ask Sylvia... it's mother, dear." Not that Maria could see the grimace on his face. "She's saying are we going to have children?"

Sylvia could hear Maria's outraged reaction without Peter being on speaker phone.

"Peter, I said nothing of the sort!" Maria screeched down the phone. "You are a naughty, mischievous boy. Put me on to Sylvia."

"Here, Sylvia. Mother won't talk to me."

"Hello, darling. I wasn't prying into your intentions as to having a family, I asked if you'll be inviting children."

"We haven't even thought about discussing that."

"Oh! So what should I tell Petra then?"

Oh God, Sylvia thought, *this is suddenly getting too detailed.*

"Peter and I will be talking all the arrangements through, time of day and all that. We can't answer too much detail at the moment."

"I understand dear..." (which Sylvia believed to be dubious) "... but could you bear in mind that the children in South America go back to school at the end of September so if you could bring the date forward a little, that would mean they could come… which they'd love to. If they can't come, I doubt Petra would travel without them and she'd so want to be there."

"I understand." (Maria wasn't so sure that she did.) "Must fly, Maria. Thanks for thinking about that. One of us will get back to you."

"Yes. When, darling?"

Oh dear, Sylvia had suddenly been awakened to the hard fact. *I have a mother-in-law.*

"I'd say it may be a couple of weeks."

"Oh! I see." Maria was obviously disappointed. "We'll have to wait then. OK, darling. I'll be in touch. If you do make your minds up earlier, let me know and I'll pass it on."

"Or it will be on the invite, of course."

"Oh yes. Of course. Adiós. Lots of love."

After Sylvia had hung up, Peter came over and hugged her. "Something's upset you," he said with a degree of certainty.

"Darling husband-to-be, it's no longer our wedding."

Chapter 30

Following a very busy day, Sylvia's elation had now turned to the reality that this had suddenly become more of an organisational event.

But the next morning, they woke revived by sleep. They were motivated again to take their plans forward over a casual Sunday morning breakfast which, unusually, included Peter's request for a boiled egg.

"A boiled egg?" Sylvia said behind a laugh and a frown. "Does this mean marriage is going to change my master's taste buds as well?"

Peter couldn't see what was so strange, it was just that he fancied it. Fortunately there were three eggs in the fridge, so five minutes of boiling water, a teaspoon and putting the salt dispenser on the table was no big deal.

His next surprise could have been, though.

"I was thinking…"

Normally Sylvia would have cut in with some quip or other, but now there was no real reaction, so he continued.

"… if we were to drive down to see mother, I wouldn't mind popping in to the church."

Sylvia very nearly said, "What, on a Sunday?" as she would have done if he had suggested going to the supermarket or some equally boring chore. They usually liked to drive out into the country surrounding Barcelona and London, and perhaps walk and have a pleasant lunch, maybe take the Sunday papers with them and catch up on the news and all the interesting supplements, like the homes and interior design pages, recipes for Sylvia, who liked to dabble in the kitchen, and, of course, the travel pages.

In fact Sylvia rather hoped to raise the subject of a honeymoon, because she had thought about it in the middle of the night when she realised it wasn't on their agenda of things to plan.

What, she had thought, *If Petra and family don't get across for the wedding but invite us to go out to see them as a married couple instead*? She'd have to get in before that happened, she resolved.

Her thoughts were delaying her response. Tact was the best approach.

"OK. That would be nice. We could go to one of those less complicated services with your mother. Do you have any particular reason?"

"Only to think through venues. If we're not careful, Mother will press-gang us into getting married where my father's buried, sort of as a family tradition, as it were. When she remarried, it was a civil wedding with a blessing in the church because José isn't Catholic.

"So I'd suggest that might be the least of her 'good ideas'."

Both Peter and Sylvia had developed the annoying habit that, when they quoted something which, had it been written, would have been enclosed by inverted commas, they put both their hands in the air and tweaked two fingers on each in the sign of an apostrophe.

"So what's the purpose of going to church? Wouldn't that give her false hope? And besides, I thought we were heading along the civil route."

"Silvie. Look, you're edgy. I know why. It's all about Petra's or my mother's needs, not ours. But trust me. I'd like to speak to the priest. Quite informally, with your very best interests at heart. I'll try to come up with the sort of wedding I'm sure we'll both enjoy. Please… just trust me. It's one of my boiled egg-stimulated ideas."

"OK." Sylvia laughed at the boiled egg idea. She stood up and walked around the kitchen table, and pecked him on the forehead. "I think I'm hormonal, darling. I'll make some fresh coffee. However or wherever, we're going to get married, and whoever's there, it will be perfect."

"Thanks for those lovely sentiments. I promise, though, I'm working on something I know you'll like, and it'll be happy, and when I know if it's possible or not, I'll explain the idea to you. If you like it, we'll do it. If you don't, we won't. Is that OK?"

"Perfect. So let's do just a small domestic sort-out and we'll head down to Calella."

"Great. We'll leave about midday."

"Maria will probably go to church at nine. Why don't we make a bigger effort and tell her we'll go to the 11.30 family service, which is less heavy anyway, and she'll either come a second time with us or decide to skip the earlier communion service."

"Good thinking. Shall I call her?"

"Equally good thinking," said Sylvia. She seemed to have cheered up.

When Peter explained their plans, Maria was over the moon. She did decide to skip the early service. Peter said they would drive and park at the hotel, then walk to the church. He always preferred that route anyway and it's what Maria would have done.

Their drive was OK. Sylvia was much more relaxed.

"I'm apologising for the grumpy patch."

She confessed she was beginning to feel that she needed a holiday. They had not had a break since Easter due to all the Olympic presentational activity they had been involved in, taking account of advertisers' needs to gear up for at least a year ahead. That, conveniently, led her into the subject of a honeymoon.

"Peter, do you think we'll manage a honeymoon?"

"What? Do you mean that, after all the fervour and passion of our wedding ceremony and all the exposure of our love, and the knowledge that you'll thereafter obey me, it's going to be necessary to consummate our marriage in some foreign location?"

"Hey! We're not doing that obey vow. It's left out at most weddings these days. Women want equality, and most males won't say publicly that it's actually they who'll do what they're told by their other half."

"Do you know, I think I do obey you anyway," Peter announced.

Sylvia was non-committal, indicating she probably didn't agree. But there was little or no point in pursuing it because she didn't want a henpecked husband. She was more than happy for Peter to lead the pack. But obeying him by agreement in public would be a step too far.

Driving along, they agreed they found the sun-bleached fields attractive. A number of fields had already been harvested and Peter forecast that there would be a good second crop to cheer up the ever-disappointed farming community. They talked about some fields of sunflowers in the distance, which reminded Peter that he ought to really have a look in on Girasol and see how Marguerite was coping with the hotel.

A comfortable silence settled over them as each grabbed a few minutes' thinking time. Peter was planning in his mind how best to approach the priest. Sylvia was running through her choice of words to raise the topic again, which Peter hadn't directly answered.

"Going back to the topic of a honeymoon… we're agreed over the consummation but we'll really love to be in a foreign place, as our romps are going to take on a different meaning…"

That was clever, Peter thought. He recalled those old jokes his friends had told on their stag nights: "What's the best birth control once you're married?"

The sensible husband-to-be would confess he didn't know, but had an unhappy moment when experienced married blokes explained it was wedding cake, because after the ceremony, and the cake in particular, he'd find his bride loses interest in sex and therefore lessens the risk of child birth.

Here, Sylvia was saying the reverse. There was a hidden promise of that aspect of their relationship becoming more intense. Clever girl.

Reverting to the honeymoon, Peter confirmed it should have been high on their agenda.

"Where would you like to go?"

Sylvia responded in her most tactful way, thereby killing two birds with one stone.

"Somewhere really quiet. Where there are no other people. Where we don't have to be sociable with anyone other than ourselves. Where there's no phone. So that we won't be disturbed by dramas in places we've left behind. Warm. Well… hot by day but romantically cool at night… and it doesn't matter what language they speak because we won't need to communicate other than to order some delicious food."

"Would you have anywhere in mind?"

"Not really. You're my ideas man. On this issue, I'll obey what you say."

"OK. I'd say some sort of oasis in the middle of the Sahara desert, with a short landing strip and a private jet."

"How does that fit the bill?"

"Well it would be hot, bloody hot. No one else in their right minds would go there. Communications don't exist… I think it would do the job."

"What's the landing strip for?"

"Well, we'd probably have to leave the oasis at about midday and fly on somewhere where it's going to be cool at night."

"Look, if you can't take my one request about having a honeymoon seriously, I'm not the slightest bothered about hearing what your conversation with the priest is all about."

They both knew not to take the other seriously.

"So… shall I put the honeymoon on my list to think about?"

"Yes, darling do." Peter was happy with that.

Maria was overjoyed to see them both, although, probably predictably, her immediate focus was more on Sylvia than Peter.

Peter had often noticed that whenever there was a hint that he was having a serious relationship with a young lady, his mother's focus shifted to the new incumbent. That was abundantly clear when she was foisting Jan's availability, and suitability, down his throat.

On the one hand, he found it a little hurtful; but on the other, he'd always realised Maria only had himself as an offspring and a daughter would surely have given her additional companionship.

She and Sylvia walked slightly behind Peter on their way to the church. Again Peter was very happy with that. He had no concerns as to where Sylvia or indeed Maria were going to buy their wedding outfits, as he had heard them both say they would probably get them in London, which clearly meant additional welcome time with Sylvia, but probably a pain in the neck with his mother.

Peter thought he'd send his mother off, by appointment, to one of the stores and arrange for her to be taken care of by a personal shopping consultant. He would pre-arrange an account.

Sylvia was quite self-contained in that direction and did her shopping on the three or four weekend trips she made to London during the year – principally, she always said, because there was so much more choice in England and they didn't have a Marks and Spencer or equivalent in Barcelona.

The church service was indeed light as the congregation, which consisted mainly of parents and children, were treated to a sermon founded on moral issues. The priest had put something together along the lines of 'loving thy neighbour', but aimed at a school child's age. If it had been taken too literally, all games against other schools would either be draws or would not take place at all as, in tennis, for example, the server would love the receiver too much to consider hurting their pride by delivering an ace, or beating them. Inter-school athletics would comprise lines of competitors running in a line abreast, not with a leader and a following pack, and the winning tape would not get broken but would be carried across the line intact as all the non-winners embraced a show of love for each other.

Unfortunately, Peter thought, the delivery of the sermon carried too much fear and retribution. He smiled inwardly on hearing that the penalty for lying was still that the offender would be turned to stone. Peter wondered about telling the priest that the Church should not be too draconian on the cheating issue and its penalty, otherwise his industry would run out of stone with which to embellish the homes they were building in their endeavour to create family units in which parents could continue to influence their children in the Catholic way of life.

The priest took up his traditional Sunday morning after-service position in the porchway to the ancient little coast-side church, which attracted its congregation from many kilometres around. They were sent home with a message from the service to keep in their minds. The priest seemed to know all his flock by name, probably, Peter thought, as a result of the more liberalised community now drifting into non-allowed activities and having to seek relief via more frequent visits to the confessional.

"Maria, my dearest," the priest said as she approached him to say her au revoir until the following weekend. "You're well, my friend?"

"Very, thank you, Father. You know Peter, don't you, Father?"

"Of course I do. Hello, Peter. You look well and I trust you've been refreshed by your visit to us…" He turned to Sylvia. "I know you're not Petra, Peter's dear daughter."

Peter just beat Maria to the introduction. "Father Ascendo, I'd like you to meet my fiancée. We're celebrating the second day of our engagement by joining my mother in prayer."

"And how right to do that too. But since this is what I take to be your family church, will we lose you to the competition of your fiancée's own parish?"

Peter simply said, "Let me formally introduce you. This is Sylvia Pez."

"Sylvia, all I can say is that God has brought you into one of the most charming family environments I have the pleasure over which to show God's influence. So where would home be for you?"

"Barcelona and with Peter now, but my roots are in South America."

"Well, I'm overjoyed that you have Catholic blood in you, albeit not totally of the Roman strain," Father Ascendo said, finding his own humour decidedly funny.

"Father, it seems we're the last of the congregation to leave. Could I have a few minutes of your time while we're here, now that our main family topic is our wedding in early October?"

The priest, probably sensing he was going to be asked to officiate, was beginning to let the flattery overcome him.

"Peter, I doubt your mother would visit the church without speaking with Paco, your father, who was so dear to her. I didn't have the pleasure of meeting him in life, only through death and the requirement for me to flood your mother with compassion when she arrived here in the care of your uncle."

Peter noted Marco was not on the priest's list of 'dears' and 'much loveds', which was quite reasonable under all the circumstances. He'd have thought the odd confession from Marco might have done more for the priest than an adult-only film at the local cinema in Palafrugell.

Maria took the hint. "Sylvia, you've met Paco before, in a way, but let me take you to him as Peter's fiancée and our proud addition to the Martinez family tree."

Peter was alone with the priest.

"Now, my son, what are these secrets you wish to out to me?"

"Not secrets, Father. Hopes. You see, what I didn't say is that Sylvia Pez is in fact more fully named *Mrs* Sylvia Pez."

"Oh, Peter. How appropriate! God intends to join our famous entrepreneurial travelling widower with a child widowed herself by the callings of our dear God and Jesus Christ."

"No. Not exactly. She's divorced."

The priest appeared not to know how on earth he could tell Peter that her status would not allow him to officiate at the joining together of a vow-breaker with one of his flock.

"If you wish to ask me if I would make an exception and marry you despite, let us say, the contemporary position of the bride–to-be, the answer is simply that Rome would not allow it. As for me, well… I have to abide by that doctrine, and I would not be prepared to apply for a dispensation."

"That's completely as I thought. But you mention contemporary circumstances and Sylvia's ones certainly are of that nature. She was influenced to marry a disaster and life with him wasn't made untenable by the mere failure of their relationship. You see, her husband ran away without trace. Their divorce came about after a series of adverts and other formalities, to notify the world of the end of the formal marriage.

"Technically, I see that less as a divorce but more a sort of annulment. Anyway, none of that is an issue. Sylvia and I respect the Church's thinking and consider that a civil ceremony is the correct solution.

"However, I know my mother would like our marriage to be blessed by the Church, and this is why I'm discussing the matter with your good self, perhaps more in, as you say, my entrepreneurial style, almost as a commercial business arrangement.

"I'm proposing we go through a civil ceremony and I believe I'm in a position to arrange for the registrar to perform the legal proceedings outside the walls of their own office. The Barcelona Registration Department has apparently always been a little rebellious in what they do, and has allowed such variations before.

"Normally, civil ceremonies follow one after the other at 30-minute intervals, allowing no opportunity for travel time to a place outside the registrar's office, or for the official to be mobile to any extent. I believe I can overcome that. That being the case, and with a Friday in mind, I have my mother's disappointment to overcome. So I was wondering if you would be prepared to attend the ceremony and, once we're joined in the civil way, take us through the vows as a matter of commitment to the over-riding beliefs of the Church, and perhaps bless the wedding... unless, of course, that wouldn't be allowed by Rome to be done outside the House of God. Then, of course, you could join us for the wedding breakfast and that would cement the whole foundation to our marriage."

The priest contemplated the idea for a moment.

"Dear Peter. Yes. I think I can do all that as a semi-representative and a Holy Minister." He held out his hand. "Shall we shake on the commercial arrangement? I'll investigate my costs and let you know... oh, by the way, where do you have in mind? Palafrugell?"

Peter realised he hadn't mentioned his full plan.

"No. Sylvia lives in Barcelona. She doesn't know what I'm planning yet but I have certain contacts who I think will be able to help me arrange a marquee for the ceremony in Barcelona itself."

"This does all sound most unusual and even I'm excited by what you're planning!"

"Well, you see, since we've known each other, the Sagrada Familia has grown very close to our hearts – its architecture and our presence within that."

"Sagrada Familia?"

Peter noticed the hand had been withdrawn.

"Peter, I'm one who believes the so-called Sagrada Familia poses an interference to the Catholic faith's home in Barcelona's existing cathedral. The one you're referring to has no place in the eyes of some of us in the Faith. It's not a house of God. It's a self-opinionated monument to record the whims of an outrageously incorrect person. As a man of Catholic upbringing, I'd implore you to have nothing to do with this man Gaudi's tribute to himself. And I would dissuade your dear, devout Catholic mother not to accept any attempt at taking the vows of the Church into that.

"Peter, I cannot assist you in your confusion in any way, save, as always, to pray for you, and in particular for you not to pursue some sort of circus to cover your future wife's previous follies in life."

To say the very least, Peter was shocked. Of course it was a well-known fact that a block of very traditional Catholics had had strong opinions on the construction of the apparently unwanted cathedral. But he thought that was at the turn of the century and that two world wars and a Spanish revolution might have put such thinking into the archives, where it belonged.

Peter kept his ambassadorial cool. It was he who put his hand forward and thanked Father Ascendo for his worldly advice, and bit his tongue to withhold mention of him being a bigoted old fart.

Whenever Maria got near to religion, she seemed to reach a strangely different planet. She was a very sensible lady and had been a solid mother and surrogate father to Peter. She'd guided him in many directions and given him free rein in others. But somehow, after time spent in the presence of Father Ascendo and having in her mind been communicating with Paco, when Peter met up with her at his father's gravestone, she positively had an aura around her. She was on some sort of high and did not notice Peter's extremely irritated demeanour.

Sylvia was panic-stricken, recognising that she had never seen Peter in this mood before.

Planning their marriage had suddenly opened up wide chasms and potential gulfs, which she just had not expected to arise from such a basically happy announcement. She knew Peter was never normally one to show his anger or disappointment in the way his face was now portraying both of those emotions. He was one to always respect the other's point of view, though not one to be quickly influenced to change his own mind without hugely satisfactory evidence to encourage him to do that.

"Peter, darling. Did you have a lovely chat with Father Ascendo?"

Sylvia could see that he obviously hadn't, and that Maria's question was going to be like a red rag to a bull.

"Come on, Maria, we've had our time with Paco," Sylvia said, stepping forward and taking both Peter's hands.

On tip-toe, she lifted her lips to his left cheek, on the blindside from Maria's vision, and whispered, "Tell me about it later. Whatever's upset you has deeply upset me. We'll share it later. Say hello to your father. I've told him how much I love you and how I'll look after you for our life to come. Whatever's caused you hurt by the priest I suspect is because, in the eyes of his Church, I've sinned by my first huge and very expensive mistake in earlier times. Not Cari of course. My non-marriage.

"So I want to share your upset. Not here. Not with Maria. Not in a way that might hurt her. She's on a high for us. Please, for me. For us. Leave it till we can both share it."

All Peter could do was nod.

"Come on, you two lovebirds. We must get back to the hotel. Marco and Virginia will be waiting, and I've a surprise for you."

Peter shuddered. Surprise. He didn't want another bigoted surprise.

"You go on. I'll catch you up. As Sylvia says, I'll have a word with Papa and won't be far behind you."

Maria and Sylvia left the cemetery arm-in-arm.

Peter knelt in front of his father's gravestone.

"Father, Father, Father. Dearest Papa. I've said before how cross I was with God when he decided he needed more fishermen to trawl the seas of Heaven, but I grew to accept his ways, although I've never understood them. Now, I'm faced with a desire to satisfy Mama, to mitigate the hurt she might feel if I show through Sylvia's and my own desires, I might add, that we basically want our marriage to be sanctioned in the real world, so we can influence our lives and sentiments directly, rather than have things put upon us in God's own way.

"If we make mistakes or misjudgements, or don't live within God's architectural designs, to the standards He would want, then all the confessions of guilt and apologies won't actually rectify our actions. God must have had an inkling that man, whom He created, might fall foul of his intentions, but He created no antidote to that.

"His Son was allegedly surrounded by mistaken friends and foes, again created by God, but not with His intention that they should develop such views as they invented, of their own volition. Forgiveness via confession was therefore a difficult one for God to sanction. Yet His ministers did, because Rome interpreted that to be the right course.

"Surely that priest should by now have started to make a real contribution to the religion he preaches, which was put upon him by a group of celibate old men with no personal experience of marriage. Surely when that does go wrong, they can accept and understand people having to break their vows, perhaps rightfully shrouded with regret. The word 'forgiveness' is surely meant to be practised as well as preached." Peter knew his father would agree.

"So initially that clown showed his tainted Church colours by preening himself, expecting I was about to ask him if he would conduct my wedding service, since I'm acceptable as a widower. But my lovely Sylvia, who's had the misfortune to make a mistake in life, rocks the Catholic boat.

"I didn't want us to be married by him, or in the Catholic Church anyway. So that was upset number one. Then to say, as a commercial venture, he would read some vows to us – which incidentally, Papa, we both fully understand and will live by anyway, without his influence – and then change that simply because, at the turn of this century, a load of old diehard Catholics with no vision couldn't understand the portrayal of a 20th century family image shown in an artistic way, as opposed to the traditional and unbelievable oil images of disciples and angels and other accepted bits and pieces meant to personify the Catholic and other Christian faiths.

"Papa, I saw yesterday that God was guiding a spotlight through the outer glazed walls of the cathedral you once told me as a little boy was being built as a modern portrayal of everything God had intended, but in a very different manner. I now know that all the portrayals in the Bible of the birth of Jesus, faith and hope, charity and most particularly the images of the environment itself need a bit of modernisation. The current administrators of Catholicism need a bit of a nudge into contemporary life. Papa, you introduced all that and many, many more worldly things to me and, man to man, if I may say, to have an entrenched priest in the way of my wanting to make Mama happy disappoints me to a level of desperation.

"Papa, I love God, but in my own way, so don't worry for me in that regard. And fear not, I'll manage to diffuse the disappointment Mama may have if her God is not present at our marriage.

"Anyway Papa. You'll understand all this and, secretly, I still love you more than God, but don't, for Heaven's sake, let on. That in English is called a pun. Yes. I'm sorry that I now think and explain things in English, but you understand."

By the time he caught up with Maria and Sylvia, Peter had a skip in his step and a new challenge. If it was the last thing he did, he would now achieve his triple objective: to give Silvie a memorable wedding day; to mitigate Maria's disappointment of a wedding without God's blessing; and to show his father that he was a force to be reckoned with, as Paco always was.

Sylvia noticed the mood swing immediately. Maria was oblivious. Nothing would faze her on the day Peter announced he was marrying for a second time, especially because his choice met completely with her approval, and somehow the church in Calella was going to be involved.

The surround to the hotel pool was full to capacity. There were 60 rooms now and 100 loungers, though it was rare that every guest would be around the hotel on any one day. There were a number of trips to be made, cultural pursuits, and some guests were walkers.

Peter felt a bit out of place in a lightweight blue formal suit, which he had elected to wear for Maria's sake. He had taken his tie off, but compared with the swimmers and sun-worshippers, he was well overdressed. As they approached the pool area through the beach gate, which was a couple of hundred metres from the beach, but gave access to the road leading down to the sea, Peter took his jacket off and threw it as nonchalantly as he could over his left shoulder, supporting it on the forefinger of his left hand through the loop in the back of his jacket.

He nodded as he walked around the relaxed bodies, while Sylvia smiled a friendly greeting. Maria made a number of observations to those whose names she knew, or where she knew the circumstances of their stay and origins.

"Lovely day." "Relaxing?" "Is the water warm?" "Good to see you." At one point she stopped alongside a middle-aged English couple. She turned to Peter and Sylvia and announced, "This is Mr and Mrs Grover," then, addressing them, she said, "It's your seventh year with us, isn't it?"

"Yes, and we love it all as it's always been through all those years."

"This is my son Peter and his fiancée Sylvia, we've just popped down to church."

The husband made movements as though he was going to get up from the lounger and greet Peter formally.

"Don't move. Please stay as you are. I'll come to you." Peter bent down and took Mr Grover's sun-creamed hand. "Nice to meet you. Glad you like it. You carry on. Have a lovely day." With that the Martinez trio moved on.

They headed towards Marco and Virginia's private garden, which now had quite a large patio and a generous French canvas sunshade.

Each time Peter saw Marco these days, a lump came up into his throat. Marco showed signs of being worn down by the years of pressure of running the hotel: not so much the actual management of the food and beverage or occupancy issues, but principally the cash-flow aspects. Summer was fine, when the revenue flowed, but the season was April to mid-October at best, and after those six or seven months, they had to fund the remainder of the year. Banks were fairly accommodating but exchange rates were incredibly volatile and in some years, which they classed as having been difficult ones, they had to pay the bank back more money than they had borrowed, given exchange rate differences and greedy interest rates. Peter had tried to convert them to the American dollar or the German mark, but Marco was peseta-oriented.

Marco's diabetes wasn't helping. Peter had always thought of Virginia as being old, even 20 or 25 years previously. But she had not altered. She seemed no older to him and, in fact, it was Marco who had caught up with her in the ageing stakes.

Now Marco stood and held both arms fully outstretched. For as long as Peter could remember, way back to being the young boy who arrived with Maria, semi-orphaned, this was his invitation into the welcoming home of his uncle and aunt.

Peter was pleased to interlock with him. He now held back on the element of strength he put into the bear hug they had traditionally exchanged, which in fact was a mark of Peter's greeting to most males with whom he closely related.

"Now you come here, my potential most favourite niece-in-law."

"Marco, don't be ridiculous!" scolded Maria. "Everybody doesn't have to graduate to be related to you. Surely you can just see Sylvia as Sylvia, who we're delighted to see has deemed to give up any respectability she had to become a Martinez."

Maria was not known for her humour, but on this occasion she raised a laugh from the whole audience of three.

Marco seemed to gather renewed strength and he pulled Sylvia into a close embrace, engulfing her in his strong, well-covered arms.

"You know, my dear, we don't have many young ladies in our family."

"We do, you old fool!" Virginia now decided to make her presence felt. "We have Petra and Anne Marie, not to mention you still have me."

That met with a derisory mutter from Marco. "I think I've just been told to let you go. But it's lovely to have you join us."

Peter had noticed that the wrought iron table under the pergola was laid up for eight. José had not appeared yet, but that would still only make six for lunch. Tact being one of Peter's finer attributes, he decided not to draw the error to Maria's attention – if it was indeed a mistake, which could well have been the case because she was clearly on a bit of a high. If it wasn't and somebody else was expected, Peter would have to remain patient.

Thank God it wasn't laid up for seven, otherwise that might have meant the priest had been invited. Peter inwardly resolved that if Father Ascendo *was* invited, he would leave.

"A drink to celebrate, I think, would be a very good idea," Marco ruled.

"Not before 7pm," Maria reminded him, from the days of their pact.

"Look, this is an important moment. If everybody rules that you should all have something alcoholic, but that I should toast our happy couple's health in water, I would go along with that. Well… I'm saying I would, but I'm not bloody well going to… So, where's José?"

Maria moved away and into Marco and Virginia's bungalow.

It seemed they waited ages for the tray of ready poured champagne to appear. The young waiter carrying it had obviously forgotten the house rules and, although he was suitably white-shirted with black trousers, his demeanour displayed too much regard for informality, as he was not wearing the black tie with the hotel logo embroidered on it, and broke all house rules by wearing sunglasses. That was a prohibition rule made jointly by Marco and Maria, on the basis that if you cannot see a person's eyes, particularly if they're serving you, as a customer you would not get the right level of respect.

Peter was the first to laugh. "You really can't get the staff, you two, can you? Look at this chap's trembling arms!"

Peter reached forward and took his son's sunglasses off. "Now you might get an evening job here if they can find you a tie. Give me the tray before you drop it."

Peter placed it on the small, circular antique mosaic table, Marco's favourite piece of garden furniture, imported from Italy. He and Alex hugged until Peter pushed him away quite forcibly.

"Where's your beautiful other half?"

Absolutely on cue, Anne Marie appeared, carrying Peter Martinez Jnr.

"Look at this," Peter said, his focus really being on his namesake. He gathered them both up into his arms while Alex moved across to Sylvia.

"So, partner, not only are we an item in that regard, but now I'm apparently going to be working with my stepmother."

"No. I won't allow that," Sylvia said in a very determined manner. "We're business partners. It looks as though, according to the family tree, I will be your stepmother, but let's move on. We'll be contemporary about our relationship. You call me Sylvia, and occasionally, when I've either earned it or you need it to be a precursor to telling me I've done something you disagree with, I'm also Silvie to you. But I don't want to be seen as your stepmother. Let's agree that's accidental."

"OK. You're a lovely partner and very good too for the old man. The die is cast. You getting hitched will have a nil effect on our business relationship, but it might matter when you need time off to push the old fella down to the beach in his wheelchair."

They were all able to see the improbability of that ever happening. Peter was never going to become old, and if ever he did, he wouldn't need to be pushed anywhere… he'd have a motorised wheelchair.

Peter lifted Peter Jnr out of Anne Marie's care.

"Uncle Marco. Where the hell is this drink you organised?"

Again on cue, Tony the waiter appeared and distributed the glasses of bubbly individually. Marco, the host, came into his own. He did what he wanted to do, emphatically.

"Virginia, Maria, José," (who had joined them, somewhat confused) "Alex, Anne Marie…"

José broke into Marco's toast. "I thought you said you'd come and get me when you got back from church, Maria."

"Darling, I think I did. Anyway, there's been a lot going on and you're here at absolutely the right time. You carry on, Marco…"

"Where did I get to? Oh yes, I'll recap… Virginia, Maria, José, Anne Marie, Alex, I give you a toast."

"What about Peter?" Maria said.

"Don't be silly. The toast I'm giving is for Peter and Sylvia."

"No. You've forgotten Peter Jnr."

"If he's allowed a drink before 7pm at his age, then good luck to him! If he's brought a bottle of milk then I'll add… and Peter Jnr… Peter and Sylvia… may they have many, many years of happiness." He'd made it without further interruption.

The names Peter and Sylvia were echoed by everyone, very nearly in unison.

Peter turned to Sylvia, having joined together in responding with their glasses held high. "So who's going to be doing the talking and responding in this new arrangement we're going into?"

It was an easy audience to please. They all very well knew the answer, so they in turn, again almost as one, laughed the question off. It was Sylvia's voice that responded, at a level for all to hear. "I will, my love. Marco, Virginia, Maria, José, Alex, Anne Marie and Peter Jnr – Peter and I thank you very much for those kind wishes. We think being a part of this great family will be a huge foundation to those many, many years of happiness. On a personal note, I thank you for all of your support for me this far."

Maria set the tone. "Well done! That's right, you do the talking. Yes, well done."

Virginia followed suit. "That's right, my dear, I should have done that years ago."

Anne Marie's turn was a little more toned down. "We'll all give you all the support you need."

Marco, José, Alex, Peter Jnr and even Peter himself found the whole play being acted out amusing, spirited and acceptable. If they had each been asked if there was any real chance of it being workable, they doubtless would have proffered the view that it was unlikely.

Chapter 31

There was little doubt that food for the paying guests was always of a high standard. But every now and again, if Marco and Maria said to the chefs that they wanted a special menu for themselves, rather than panic and go to pieces the chefs made a point of really performing, and enjoyed it. So to be told on the Saturday afternoon to cater for six, and then at 10.30am that Sunday morning to raise it to eight, was a challenge to which they had risen.

Asparagus or melon with Parma ham were the starters. Poached salmon or chicken Milanese with very fresh vegetables, followed by a couple of the hotel's speciality sweets, were all very acceptable.

Peter laid down some rules right at the start of the lunch, once everybody was seated and Peter Jnr had been put into the care of the mother of a waitress who had similarly been called in at short notice. She usually provided part of the advertised in-house babysitting service. Peter asked that lunch should not be full of questions about their plans as they were only embryonic at that stage.

Maria, of course, had already been introduced to Sylvia's engagement ring before going to church. Virginia and Anne Marie loved it and both Marco and Alex inwardly wondered how much it had cost.

They had coffee after lunch and then passed an hour or so just chatting together. At four o'clock Maria organised some tea and a cake was produced, apparently from nowhere.

Peter had whispered to Sylvia that it would be nice to get away between 4.30pm and 5pm, so that they had a bit of an evening together. Just before five, Peter was able to say that they didn't want to break up the party but they ought to leave. Rarely did Peter drive in Spain. He still had his old friend the Jaguar he had taken out with him to be mothballed in Girasol when his lifestyle in the UK changed and he was chauffeur-driven in a frequently updated Bentley, to show to the business community how well BCG were doing. Usually Sylvia picked him up at the airport, though, and in Barcelona itself a car was a nuisance, and taxis seemed always to be waiting exactly where one was required. Sylvia had driven that morning from the apartment to the hotel and she had left her 450 SL Mercedes Benz convertible in the Playa car park with the hood down.

Peter sensed they would want to talk on the way back to Barcelona, so he went ahead of Sylvia to drop the roof onto the car, while she said her female-to-female adiós to first Maria, with a, "Thank you," for the super lunch and taking them to church. Then Virginia on the basis that she was pleased to have seen her in such good form; and lastly Anne Marie amidst a lot of laughter that it had not occurred to either of them that Sylvia would become her stepmother-in-law, which for no obvious reason they both found exceedingly funny.

It showed that Sylvia was naturally very fond of children as she picked Peter Jnr out of his mother's arms and gave him large kisses all over his face and cheeks and neck, making a strange noise as she blew through her lips, which created a vibration that positively made the little chap giggle.

Peter was sitting apparently patiently in the driving seat when Sylvia got to the car and automatically opened the driver's door to find Peter already there.

"Oh! You've surprised me."

"Change of responsibilities," was all that he said.

"I don't understand."

"I'm doing the driving."

"Are you sure?"

"Yup!"

"What's brought this about?"

"Well it seems you're doing the talking now, so I'd best do the chauffeuring."

"I've been waiting for you to mention that. Am I in trouble?"

"No. Not at all. Actually, it was most appropriate and made everybody laugh. It was fine. But I'm happy to drive. We've both had a bit of wine but if I get pulled over I've got Fred in the UK and you over here, just in case I lose my licence."

"Are you sure?"

"Yes. Fine. I'll drive slowly." He drove out along the drive, which he had been party to in the early re-design stages of the hotel development.

Sylvia patted his right knee. "You OK, fiancé?"

"Fine. How about you, wife-to-be?"

"I'm fine. I'm really very tired so it's good of you doing the driving. It was a truly lovely lunch. I'll write to Maria, and Marco, and thank them."

Peter knew she would.

"Can I ask you?"

"Yes."

"What happened with the priest?"

"I said you could ask me, but I didn't say I'd answer."

"I've known you a while now, but I don't think I've ever seen you so cross."

"Trust me. I was asking him to do a perfectly reasonable thing and the dear fellow found one reason after another not to be able to do that, purely because he's practising Catholicism from the dark ages."

"Is it because I've been divorced?"

"Finally… no. But that paved the way. I tell you, though, if he'd asked me if one of us was contemplating contraception and I had said yes, and he had come out with some outdated, immovable edict put upon the church by some bunch of celibates in Rome, then I think I would have punched him. He's that much of a bigot.

"So that's that. Please don't be concerned. Give me a chance to achieve what I'd like to put to you as a plan towards our perfect day."

"My darling Peter. I trust you implicitly. Don't be upset anymore. I didn't like him anyway."

They drove on in silence. Peter soon realised that, after a second exciting but emotional day, she had crashed into a sleep stimulated by the warmth and movement of the car… and a little of Marco's excellent wine.

Chapter 32

TWO MONTHS LATER

Peter was as happy as he thought he had ever been, sitting alongside Alex in the rear of the chauffeur-driven Bentley, which he had located through a VIP hire car company on the outskirts of Barcelona.

For October, it was a beautiful sunny day. The sky above was a rich blue, partly brought about by the angle at which the sun's rays were bounced back upwards to the clear atmosphere above that part of the Mediterranean.

Alex was happy too. He was so surprised when Peter rang him and explained that if he and Sylvia had been having a traditional wedding, he would have had a best man. However, as it was a civil one, Peter required a principal witness, as did Sylvia.

He had explained that when he asked Sylvia if she intended to have bridesmaids or matrons of honour, she had laughed and said it would be out of keeping, because they would look overdressed alongside her intended choice of attire. She had researched it and found out all she would require was a witness. Peter's research confirmed the same.

"So who do we invite? Should it be a couple or should we have individual choices?"

They'd eventually decided that they would each write a name on a piece of paper. They had agreed not to have to qualify the choices by gender, without actually realising that was the case with a witness anyway. What they did agree was that if either of them loathed the other's choice, both first suggestions would be scrapped and they would start again.

Peter had made a sick joke about what they should really do: write the names, as suggested, but throw the pieces of paper into a fire and see whether the smoke produced was white or black, or even grey, in the mode of finally selecting a Pope. He'd had to apologise for his wickedness but he was still smarting over the brush he'd had with Father Ascendo.

However, once Peter had networked his requirement, he realised that the so-called impossibility that confronted Maria's priest, was not common to the entire faith.

On the Monday morning after their 'engagement weekend', as they now called it, he had phoned Jorge Quinto's office. Since meeting through Professor Han, they had frequently worked together in 'making things happen', as they had become accustomed to call it. Peter got through to speak with Jorge far more easily nowadays than had at first been the case.

Jorge kept a priority list of calls he would always take and Peter had apparently climbed up that list.

He had explained to Jorge what he had in mind and his reaction had been that there was absolutely no problem.

So Peter and Alex were on their way to an event as a result of Jorge Quinto's association, as a lawyer, with the city's register office, which had enabled him to arrange the Friday afternoon's civil ceremony to be away from the city office.

Then Jorge had spoken to the chief registrar, who again was well known to him, and he explained the circumstances as Peter had put them to him. The chief had looked through the CVs of all his registrars and found one who had recorded the fact that he was of the Catholic faith, and he had accepted the slightly unusual external appointment.

That registrar had then had a chat with his own priest, who was of a more liberal persuasion than Ascendo.

The suggestion Peter had then put to Sylvia was that they could have the civil ceremony at a venue of their choice and immediately after they were declared to be husband and wife they would be able to be lead into the vows, which the Catholic Church would have obliged them to take had the ceremony been a formal one in a church of that denomination. The priest would be robed – not in the full order prescribed by Rome but sufficient to convince Maria that Peter and Sylvia were married and committed in the eyes of her God.

Sylvia was 100 per cent over the moon with that arrangement.

When they had agreed to that, they realised they had not put into place their nominee witnesses. It was a slightly tense exercise, as after each had thought through their preferences, and Max had said how much he approved of Peter's suggestion for him not to play a formal role, they decided the other should open each of their suggestions.

Peter insisted, "Ladies first," but Sylvia was more concerned about this idea than she could let on. She said if that was to be the case then he should open her choice then first.

Somewhat gingerly he unfolded it. *"My daughter Caridad,"* he announced.

Peter smiled. "I 100 per cent agree. Perfect. I'm very happy."

That put immense pressure on Sylvia, as if she didn't like Peter's choice (and having thought about it, there were some choices she would not be totally happy with), and if they had to nominate again, she would lose her choice of Cari.

With trepidation she unfolded Peter's piece of paper: *My son, Alex.* Sylvia screamed and burst into tears. They were both so very happy.

The final obstacle Sylvia had to put to Peter was about his attire. She went around and around the bush, asking Peter if he had any preferences as to what she might wear, in terms of style, colour, even skirt length, but each time she went through that procedure, he never once gave her the opportunity to ask him his intentions.

Eventually she asked point blank. "One favour, Peter."
"Just one," was his reply.
"Just one big one, please."
"OK. What is it? I'll make no promises."
"Would you and Alex wear morning suits?"
She waited for the uproar with baited breath.
"Of course. We were going to. What else befits our wedding?"

So he was on his way in the Bentley. Sylvia had a slightly more exposed mode of transport, but then it was a lovely day.

Had it been raining, Plan B would have come into play. The white Rolls Royce, courtesy of the same VIP company that had supplied Peter's car, would have been used.

Plan A, though, was the much preferred one all round.

Peter had contacted the licensing authority for the horse-drawn carriages brought into Barcelona ahead of the Olympics when, of course, they would be an enormous tourist attraction. He found out who had the best horses and compatible carriages and, after some typically Spanish negotiation, with which Peter was of course well conversant, hey presto, he produced out of his wedding programme magic topper a white horse. Well, the owner said it would be pure white on the day for the photographs, because they would dust it down with talcum powder, and they had a renovated cream carriage, which seemed to fit the bill. Sylvia had said that the colour for her day was anything naturally produced in the rose family. So Peter had organised the seats to be re-covered in a pink silk. Sylvia had given that her mark of approval at the level of 'perfect'.

Alex came down out of his dream world. Nothing could have been a greater honour in his life than accepting Peter's invitation to be his principal witness. He saw being the witness thing as a great bonding medium between him and his father.

"Papa, it really is a perfect day," he said, looking up through the retractable glass panel built into the roof of the car.

"Yes, that's another thing I got Jorge Quinto to fix for us."

"The weather?" Alex said in a serious tone. "How the hell could he fix the weather?"

"I don't know how the chap does it but look at what he's managed to do for the service. And then to get the use of the second floor pool area at the yet-to-be opened Hotel Arts really has been the greatest grand slam coup."

To be precise, his friend and acquaintance through the Olympic Association became the catalyst to organising the day. With that friendship came the ever strengthening inter-relationship with the real members of the

Olympic committee. Ramon Gaspard made up the third musketeer role in always joining Jorge and Peter in making impossible deadlines towards the Olympics come true.

Peter had never thought that the committee meeting, at which it was decided they should start putting together some preview events for the committees of some of the competing nations, would have such an important influence in his life.

Of course, tours of the stadia and Olympic village under construction were musts, and there would have to be receptions and the odd dinner to loosen those stressed nations' tongues a little, with the fresh crops of Spanish wine being prepared for the needs of the millions intending to visit the Catalan capital for the games.

Venues suggested for the receptions and so on were formal places such as City Hall or the conference centre at the zoo, museums and the like. It was Jorge who asked hadn't they got something more Olympian: "What about that monstrous building being built down by the Olympic Marina? The hugely tall one clad in steelwork."

"Oh... the hotel," said Ramon.

"Right. Hotel. Reception. Olympic Marina. What better?"

"Ideal. Yes. But it's nowhere near finished."

"It's finished enough for me."

"How?"

"Well... let's say the ground floor could be the reception venue. I've been past and the floor slabs seem to be concreted most of the way up the height of the building. So it's possible to make the ground floor area water-tight."

"But you're talking entertaining, receptions, food..."

"Yes, and electricity and all those problem areas if you intend to make them stumbling blocks. But the builders have water on site, and electrics. It's only the question then of dummying out the entire space on the basis that it's a film set... you chaps can do it, I'm sure."

Those chaps could do it. According to Ramon, though, it would need a thorough testing amongst friends, as it were.

"What the hell does that mean, Ramon? It's unlike you to put up obstacles."

"There are issues like temporary toilet accommodation to be sorted, access, health and safety. It's still a building site."

"Come on, we'll have the functions at weekends. Sites are closed by 2pm on a Friday. The chaps have earned so much money by then that they can afford speed boats and other pleasure goods, caravans, mobile homes and the like, so they're off with their families and girlfriends."

"So we could pilot the idea on a Friday afternoon as a trial?" Ramon enquired.

"That's more like you, Ramon."

Ramon turned to Peter in the meeting. "Peter, I don't suppose you and Sylvia would be prepared to be guinea pigs? What about your wedding reception? I can see that now. 'Member of IOC trials first of the entertainment facilities six months ahead of schedule...' What greater flag of confidence could be flown? Would you do that. Peter?"

"Yes, I think we would."

"Could I be invited?" Jorge enquired.

"You were going to be anyway."

"Then it's a solid yes from me."

The other members nodded it through amidst great excitement that things were really progressing.

Alex explained that he had not realised how that had come about but it was truly amazing.

"... So what about the service now? How did that get to be arranged?"

"Well, you can imagine that the Catholic Church don't do things without a Vatican-style committee paving the way for a final stance to be taken, or a Papal visit being made and finishing up with the focus on the one person. Cathedrals, when renovated, finish up in the hands of the Archbishop, but behind him there's the construction liaison link, the one that deals with Holy matters and the ultimate tone of the proceedings, and all that entails.

"The official who's going to marry us from the Registry of Births and Deaths Ministry has a surprising number of contacts in all the other religious bodies. He's the link man under the heading of 'other denominations'.

"He had the link... we've got to be careful, Alex, we're just pulling into the approach road... so I'll be quick. He linked with them here. The MD of the contracting group is a close mate of Ramon's. Again, and I don't know what, but he seemed to owe Ramon a big favour. So, in a nutshell, we're here... and look at all those bloody tourists with their cameras!

"Remember, you tip your topper forward on your head so that when you lift your head to see out under the brim, it looks level, not as though you've been out drinking all night."

The chauffeur parked and moved smoothly round to the rear of the car. He opened the offside passenger door, which allowed Peter out first. Peter's tails fell confidently behind him but were better for a little smoothing. He had instructed Alex not to sit on the tails to his jacket, for fear of creasing them.

Alex had slid across the rear bench seat and was now standing alongside his father.

"Topper, Papa?" Alex checked he'd got it right. Peter put a little weight from one finger on the brim over Alex's forehead.

"Perfect principal witness," he said, and instinctively took his son's hand and shook it.

Their official photographer asked for a couple more shots as the cameras of the queuing tourists also clicked.

A series of individual cheers went out and then a more concerted one, which blocked out the sound of the horses' hooves clattering on the cobble stones in front of the 20 steps Peter and Alex had now climbed, to form the reception committee of just two for Sylvia and Caridad.

There was a repeat photographic performance and then the ladies were released from the photo call, albeit to appear on total strangers' cameras in Tokyo, Germany, France, Great Britain…

The top level of the steps seemed a mountain for Sylvia and Cari to climb. They both wore very high-heeled shoes.

Sylvia's knees were knocking. She wasn't sure if she felt dizzy but she was now within range of Peter's eyes, which seemed to have a strange power. She fixed her focus on them and it had a sort of magnetic effect, to the point that she now felt no noticeable effort in making the climb. She was within touching distance of the man who excited her, and whom she loved so deeply.

Her legs turned to jelly, as did Cari's as both men lifted their toppers and leant forward. Peter kissed his fiancée on the lips, and Alex brushed cheeks with his stepsister-to-be.

The crowd below clapped.

"Welcome, my darling, to Sagrada Familia. Let's go and have our marriage ordained."

His way with words never ceased to impress.

Her way with clothes, and her modelling experience, never failed to make his mouth water. Who else would mix a pencil-slim pale blue skirt with a fitted, high-waisted pink jacket and what appeared to be polka dots, though they were in fact rose petal prints of a slightly darker shade of pink. The lapels of the jacket were piped in the blue of the skirt and she wore a cerise-coloured straw boater, with a band of the light blue, and high court shoes to match.

Peter manipulated Silvie to a position alongside him, he on her right. They linked arms and sauntered along, almost as though they were out for a Sunday morning stroll, to arrive in the open courtyard set out with an impressionistic Gaudi-style highly coloured desk, behind which the registrar was waiting. Alongside but slightly behind him was the priest who, as it happened, by sheer chance, colour co-ordinated with the bride's outfit and harmonised with Caridad's.

The 30 or so guests clapped. Peter caught sight of Maria and José. Marco and Virginia were alongside, standing in front of imported white wicker chair backs. Petra and the kids and Eduardo were prominent, as was Anne Marie with Peter Jnr. Ramon winked. Peter recognised Bianca from years gone by. *Thank God*, he thought. Jaimé and his wife, Michelle and Miguel… So many, it seemed, were there.

Their presence represented his life in so many ways, as now did his Silvie in this unfinished setting... which, after the ceremony, they both agreed was so symptomatic of what they needed to be able to see. They were at an uncharted beginning of the Sagrada itself, which as yet had to make its own history, as did the Arts venue. From that moment on they were to make history, not follow tradition laid rigidly before them. "We welcome you, Peter and you, Sylvia, to this... well, let me say it... unusual setting for a very usual cementing of an agreement, which I will ask you to respect in my way, and my Brother here will then also do in the way the Catholic Church and our God would wish."

He followed his set procedures and the four of them signed his register, each being the focus again of a number of cameras.

The registrar then said, "Mr and Mrs Peter Martinez, you may now kiss, but we'd ask you please do not keep your relations and friends too long. Then I'd ask you to solemnise your vows again and follow the directions of Father Jean."

The priest eventually stepped forward and addressed Peter, asking him to repeat after him:

"Yo, Pedro Martinez, te tomo a ti Sylvia Michelle Pez, como mi esposa. Prometo serte fiel en lo próspero y en lo adverso, en la salud y en la enfermedad. Amarte y respetarte todos los días de mi vida."

He then asked Sylvia to do the same. She completed the vow with, "Amarte y respetarte todos los días de mi vida."

The priest was about to say something further but she kept going.

"To love and respect every day of my life," she repeated in English...

There was barely a dry eye in the open courtyard.

A piped version of Ave Maria came gently through speakers mounted at all sorts of levels to echo off the face of Gaudi's backcloth, as all were sure he would have wanted.

Peter and Sylvia kissed.

Each of the congregation, led by one it seemed, followed suit and clapped.

About the Author

Since publication of the first two Sardana Series books, through press releases, information packs and indeed published interviews, quite a lot has been exposed about Ray, and his book writing hobby.

My earlier comments about him being coy when being unsure as to whether a storyline he had enjoyed putting together would have an appropriate appeal, has now been substantially tested.

We'd say "so far so good" with a big thank you to those from within literary circles for their reviews. The Paul Norman, of Books Monthly, review that Last Sardana is "… much, much more than a holiday read" was how we had hoped it would be.

Miriam Pereira's complimentary suggestion that it is "an emotive rites of passage …" was a surprise to Ray, because he didn't know it was!

Others who have been sufficiently attracted by Jacqueline Abromeit's cover interpretations of an author's very determined intentions and then to delve into the Martinez journey, and to comment on how they have found it, has been great.

It being "a good read" and "bursting with personalities …" and that "you don't just read this book, you watch it as well" are very satisfying comments in other reviews. It makes all those times in sunny climes when my husband and I have escaped the rigours of his "day job", to find the space in which to write, all the more worthwhile.

Thank you to those travelling with the Series, on behalf of the whole production team.

I'll let you into a secret, the next three novels stretch Ray's imagination much further.

With Blesma very much in mind as to the continuing motivation, alongside testing the results of pen put to paper, we hope we can take you forward as supportive passengers.

Hope you will enjoy!

Dean Harwood